by nancy thayer

all the days
of summer

nancy thayer

all the days of summer

A Novel

Ballantine Books
New York

6/23

All the Days of Summer is a work of fiction. Names, characters, places, and incidents are either the products of the author's imagination or are used fictitiously. Any resemblance to actual persons, living or dead, events, or locales is entirely coincidental.

Copyright © 2023 by Nancy Thayer

Published in the United States by Ballantine Books, an imprint of Random House, a division of Penguin Random House LLC, New York.

BALLANTINE is a registered trademark and the colophon is a trademark of Penguin Random House LLC.

Hardback ISBN 978-0-593-35845-0
Ebook ISBN 978-0-593-35846-7

Printed in the United States of America on acid-free paper

randomhousebooks.com

2 4 6 8 9 7 5 3 1

First Edition

Book design by Alexis Capitini

For my daughter, Sam Wilde

Acknowledgments

My daughter Sam appeared in my first novel, *Stepping,* as a toddler with chicken pox. I was writing about a woman loving her children and also wanting to have an intellectual and professional life. This year, as I wrote *All the Days of Summer,* I was inspired and cheered by Sam, a Yale-trained theologian, master yoga teacher, novelist, and mother of five children, my absolutely perfect grandchildren Ellias, Adeline, Emmett, Annie, and Arwyn. I'm grateful to her partner, Tommy Clair, for all he does for their children and his community, and I'm grateful to him for being there for Sam as she does five important things at the same time. And it's Sam, my radiant whirlwind of a daughter, who reminds me to keep the spiritual in my life, to be still, to go to the ocean and breathe. Thank you, Sam.

How fortunate I've been to have Shauna Summers as my editor. It's impossible to describe how indispensable Shauna's ideas, edits, and excellent care have been to this book.

I'm grateful to Gina Centrello, Kara Walsh, and Kim Hovey, the powerhouse beauties of PRH, and to Lexi Batsides and Mae Martinez. Thank you, Allison Schuster and Karen Fink, for your invaluable assistance with publicity. Jennifer Rodriguez, your help has been essential, and our phone conversations have made proofreading fun. (Were those last two words ever used together in a sentence before?)

My agent, Meg Ruley, her associates Jesse Errera and Christina Hogrebe, and everyone at the Jane Rotrosen Literary Agency are totally golden. I'm so glad to be with them and so grateful to them for all they do. Christina Higgins, my virtual assistant, has been dynamite, and to Chris Mason, my website manager, the best is yet to come.

Nantucket is a small island, but we've got a *huge* bookstore. Nantucket Book Partners, with Mitchell's Book Corner and Book-works, continues to champion authors and satisfy readers. Wendy Hudson, Annye Camera, Christina Machiavelli, Dick Burns, and Evelyn Hudson keep that book beehive buzzing. Tim Ehrenberg works publicity magic, bringing authors new and old to the store and whipping up excitement about their books. I think Tim might have read more books than I have.

Bookstores, book clubs, and libraries are all as necessary to a writer as breathing. I send my thanks and my love to them all. I hope to see you there, even if only virtually. Island life always depends on good weather, as we were reminded this past year when we tried to go see our grandchildren for Christmas, only to be prevented by a gale-force wind stopping all ferries and planes. (But the waves were fabulous!)

Special thanks to island historian Frances Ruley Karttunen for her remarkable research and books on Nantucket history.

My family calls me an introvert, and maybe a writer has to be an introvert, but I know I couldn't write a page if I didn't see my friends once in a while. And no, I don't get ideas from their lives. Okay, maybe a little bit. Cheers to Jill Hunter Burrill, Deborah and Mark Beale, Mary and John West, Tricia and Jimmy Patterson,

Melissa and Nat Philbrick, Gussy Manville, Dinah Fulton, Sofia Popova, Martha and Chuck Foshee, Antonia Massie, Patsy Ernst, Jane Oman, Barbara and Bob Bailey, Julie Hensler, and Curlette Anglin. A special thank-you to Katie Hemingway of Grass Roots Garden, whose knowledge and talent brighten my days.

And I love being in a writing world with Brenda Novak, Debbie Macomber, Mary Alice Monroe, Wade Rouse, Kristan Higgins, Jamie Brenner, Mary Kay Andrews, Patti Callahan Henry, Kristy Woodson Harvey, Kristin Harmel, and the phenomenal Friends and Fiction book group.

Most of all, I'm grateful for my readers. Words can't say how much it means to me to be in touch with you all through Facebook, Instagram, and newsletters. (I tried to go on TikTok, but my sixteen-year-old grandson said, "Nanny. *Don't.*")

Finally, to my husband Charley, thank you. I love you more than I love tacos.

all the days
of summer

one

It was Heather who hated Kailee first.

Well, she didn't actually *hate* Kailee. But she wasn't sure she liked her.

The first time she met her future daughter-in-law was when Heather and Wall went to a UMass Amherst football game. It was early October. The air was cool, bright, and clear, what Heather's mother had called "snapping weather." The trees were changing color, putting on a brilliant display of red, orange, and yellow, and Heather had brought a container of her famous autumn chili in a tub in the Styrofoam cooler to give to Ross, because that was his favorite food. Ross didn't play football, although he had in high school, maybe because sports seemed to be the only topic he and his father could discuss without arguing.

Heather and Wall had made plans for Ross and Kailee to meet them at the Inn on Boltwood in Amherst for drinks and dinner. It was pricey, but Heather guessed from her phone conversations with Ross that Kailee might be special. Ross was handsome, tall, wide-shouldered, with curly dark hair and a great smile. He'd had plenty of girlfriends over the years, but the way Ross spoke about Kailee . . . there was a warmth in his voice. A happiness. Heather hoped that Kailee was an easy hugger, because Heather was, and if Kailee made Ross happy, Heather wanted to hug her tight.

Heather and Wall got to the restaurant first and sat at their table reading the menu. Heather wore her light brown hair in a messy bun and her favorite blue cashmere sweater with jeans. Wall wore jeans, a button-down shirt, and his good L.L.Bean vest.

Heather looked up and saw Ross and Kailee walk in. She nudged her husband, so they were both smiling at the couple as they threaded their way between the tables. Heather noticed that everyone else in the restaurant watched the couple as they passed through, as if they were royalty, and really, Kailee looked like Kate Middleton, tall and slender, with long chestnut hair, green eyes, and the lanky, easy stride of a Thoroughbred. Ross wore chinos and a navy-blue crew-neck sweater. Kailee wore a blue-and-white striped dress, very classic, very nautical, with espadrilles. Her hair was held back with a blue headband, and small diamonds studded her ears.

She was seriously beautiful. Heather realized, as they all greeted one another, that Kailee was not in the least bit worried about whether or not her boyfriend's parents liked her. She had an air about her—an aura?—of noblesse oblige, as if she were a princess allowing her subjects to speak with her.

Heather had never known a young woman with this kind of confidence, this cool, almost icy, poise.

Heather didn't try to hug Kailee.

They all took their seats, boy, girl, boy, girl, and chatted lightly about the game—the UMass Amherst Minutemen had lost to the Eastern Michigan Eagles by one touchdown.

"I wish they would change their name," Kailee said.

"Why?" Heather asked. "The Minutemen were a trained class of militia during the American Revolution."

Kailee ducked her head to hide a smile.

"Mom." Ross widened his eyes in a *give me a break* signal.

Heather said, "Oh," and blushed. Suddenly she felt naïve in front of Ross's very sophisticated girlfriend. It was not a pleasant sensation.

She hoped that Wall would say something in her defense, or at least say something to change the subject, but Wall's attention was fixed on the menu.

Grasping for an easy subject to discuss, she smiled at Kailee. "Do you play sports?"

Kailee shrugged. "Not really. I sail and play tennis, of course." She laid a possessive hand on Ross's arm. "I'm going to teach Ross to sail next summer, if we have time."

Heather was confused. Kailee played tennis and sailed, but said she didn't play sports. Trying to find something in common with the young woman, Heather asked, "Do you play pickleball?"

"God, no," Kailee replied.

Heather coughed and picked up her menu. "I wonder what's good here." She didn't care what was good in that restaurant, she had to hide her face before she burst out laughing. What a little snot Kailee was! How in the world could her son like Kailee? True, she was beautiful, but she had all the social skills of a cobra. Heather couldn't wait to talk to Wall about her, although Wall wasn't very communicative these days. She'd call her friend Christine. She wished she could dash to the privacy of the restroom and call Christine right now. How would they get through this meal? Ross couldn't possibly be serious about this girl.

Fortunately, a waiter arrived to take drink orders.

When the conversation resumed, Ross asked his father what he thought of the Red Sox this year and they entered into a detailed discussion of each of the players and the manager.

Heather cleared her throat and smiled at Kailee. "What are you majoring in?"

"Business management," Kailee replied. "My father owns a rather large construction company on the island, and because I'm the only child, I'm going to take over the business end of things when I graduate."

"That seems like an important job," Heather said. "I can see how you and Ross have something in common. You know, Wall owns his own hardware store just outside Concord. When Ross graduates, he's going to join Wall and gradually take over the store."

Kailee aimed a kind smile at Heather, but turned to look at Wall.

"Did you see Alex Verdugo hit *two* home runs last night?" Kailee asked.

Heather sat back, wondering if Kailee had been listening to the sports talk all along. It was amazing, she thought, and a gift to humankind, that sports talk could carry people right through dinner. The other three thoroughly discussed the Red Sox, the Patriots, the Boston Bruins, Tom Brady, Patrick Mahomes, and Serena Williams.

Kailee said, "A. J. Mleczko, a Nantucket girl, won the Ice Hockey Gold Medal in the 1998 Olympics."

Of course she did, Heather thought, and only after they had moved on to the topic of golf did she remember that A. J. Mleczko now lived in Concord, where she and Wall lived, where they had raised Ross. But there was no way to toss that into the conversation, and Heather wondered what on earth had gotten into her that she wanted to be competitive with Ross's girlfriend. She hadn't always loved Ross's girlfriends at first, but she'd never felt this discomfort before.

"How's the store doing, Dad?" Ross asked.

"Great!" Wall answered. "Since all the big box stores have opened, I've had to get creative about inventory. I've added a lot of electronics. Home security systems, electronic cameras, and motion detectors. Electrical wire and cable."

As Heather listened to Wall talk, she realized she didn't know about these changes. Wall hadn't been discussing them with her, and she couldn't decide if that was a good thing or bad.

Conversation slowed as they finished their meals. No one wanted dessert, but they all asked for coffee. Wall and Heather had to drive back to Concord, which would take only an hour and a half, and Ross and Kailee were going back to their dorms.

By now, Heather realized that her son was in love with Kailee. She'd never seen him look at a woman the way he did today. She'd never seen him so happy. Heather stirred her coffee and told herself to be the grown-up.

She said, "It was wonderful meeting you, Kailee."

"Oh, Mom. Dad." Ross spoke before Heather had even finished. "I'm going to spend Thanksgiving and Christmas with Kailee on Nantucket."

Heather choked on her coffee.

For once, Wall spoke up. "Sounds nice."

"Oh, it is, it's beautiful on the island then," Kailee assured him. "The Friday night of Thanksgiving weekend, everyone gathers on Main Street and the huge Christmas tree lights are turned on, and so are all the lights on the little trees along the sidewalks. It's magical. The week after is the Stroll, which is *amazing*. And there are parties like crazy, and I want Ross to meet everyone. And," she added, giving Ross a smug look, "I want all my friends to meet my gorgeous Ross."

Her gorgeous Ross?

Ross was spending the holidays with Kailee on Nantucket?

Weakly, Heather began to speak. "Do your parents mind—"

Heather interrupted. "My parents can't *wait* to have Ross stay with us. They met him last weekend, and they like him *so much*. And our house has more than enough room for a guest or two, although my father wants Ross to stay in the apartment over our garage."

Kailee's parents met Ross last week?

Ross hadn't told Heather that. True, she'd stopped calling him once a week because, after all, he was over twenty-one, about to graduate from college, and she had to realize he was an adult. Still. It was a painful stab to Heather's heart that Ross hadn't told her he'd met Kailee's parents.

Wall signed the credit card slip. They all rose and went through the restaurant to the lobby. *Now* Kailee leaned forward to kiss Heather's cheek, and then Wall's cheek. Heather smiled vaguely. She'd fallen into a stupor, as if she'd left her mind at their table. Ross shook hands with his father and hugged Heather, and they all left the restaurant. As they walked through the parking lot, Heather noticed that Kailee drove a red soft-top Jeep.

Wall and Heather settled in his expensive black pickup truck.

Heather said, "I feel sick."

Wall said, "Well, don't do it in my truck."

"That's nice," Heather muttered, but she closed her eyes and counted to ten. She'd gotten very good at counting these days.

She wasn't sure how it happened or even when, but after twenty-three years of marriage to Wall, she didn't like him anymore. Worse, she didn't love him anymore. She was eager for Ross to graduate from college and return to Concord to work with Wall in Willette's Hardware, becoming the second Willette of the store. Wall was having a WILLETTE & WILLETTE sign made to hang above the store's door. If Ross *married* Kailee, and Heather was almost sure that was going to happen, they could move in with Wall. They wouldn't have to pay rent or a mortgage, and Wall could have some company that was not Heather's. Heather liked the idea of the three of them together, updating Wall's store, doing domestic chores together.

But Heather wouldn't be there because Heather was going to set herself free.

She was going to leave Wall.

She hadn't made this decision lightly. They'd been married for a long time, after all, and Wall hadn't been abusive or a philanderer. But then, neither had she. They'd been good parents and model citizens of their historic town. They'd been in love with each other once, when they first married. Over the years, they'd built a good life. They were settled.

But they no longer loved each other. Heather wasn't certain that Wall even *noticed* her anymore. She had become his reliable helper, no more important than his car, probably less important than his computer. She knew Wall would be bothered by a divorce, because he had his routine established and hated any change. But Heather needed change like a drowning woman needs air. She was only forty-seven. She could no longer live this metronome life, tick-tocking through the days.

Leaning her head against the window, Heather thought about her life.

Heather and Wall had started their business twenty-three years ago, when they were just married and hopeful. Heather's parents had loaned them start-up money so they could rent a large building in a small mall off Route 2. Heather had helped Wall put up and stock the shelves, organize the cash register, and a few years later, she'd been the one to train at a free Rotary course on bookkeeping. She'd organized an office in the back, and furnished it with a desk, chairs, file cabinets, and printers. She could still remember the pleasure of the day she pushed a cart through Staples, feeling like a woman preparing her nursery, a bird preparing her nest, a schoolgirl with her brand-new notebooks and pens. She bought a wall calendar and a desk calendar. Pens, pencils, yellow pads, in and out boxes. A handsome wall clock. She'd printed WALL CLOCK on a piece of paper in the largest font that would fit. She'd tacked it on the wall beneath the clock, and when her husband came into the office and saw it, he'd laughed and lifted her out of her chair and swung her around.

She'd been so optimistic then, so full of energy. Her grandmother had willed her historic Victorian house to Heather, although by the time her much-loved but senile Gram passed, the house had not been beautiful. Heather and Wall moved in, happy to have a permanent home, and for months Heather spent part of her free time working to reclaim the house's original beauty. Heather had single-handedly restored the worn-out Victorian to its former glory, while helping Wall with his store and doing the basic household work. Meals. Laundry. Cleaning. She had been young then, and she had believed that by now, her life would be different. She had a degree in English literature—a lot of good that did her—so she was glad to find she could hammer, spackle, grout, and paint like a professional.

When Ross was born, she took him to work in a laundry basket that she set on the table at the back of the room. When he was too big for the basket, she and Wall hired a bookkeeper, and Heather stayed home to raise their son. They didn't choose not to have more children. They were too busy to do anything but sleep when they lay down, and somehow another child just didn't happen. As the years passed, she had more free time, so she joined the local branch of the Safeguard Nature Society and did office work for their scientists, who counted, quite literally, the birds and the bees, and tested the water in Walden Pond, and the health of the area's trees. Heather became a star at creating pamphlets and tri-fold guide maps, and as technology became more complicated, she took classes given after five at the local schools. She became proficient on the internet and cellphones, and learned how to set up a website for their local headquarters.

When Ross was in grade and middle school, he loved to join his father at the hardware store, but when high school and football came along, he grew away from his father and the store. That was natural, Heather thought. Children grow up and rush into their own lives.

Parents could start new lives, too, couldn't they?

Heather took a deep breath and glanced at her husband, who was driving with serious concentration, as if he'd never been on this road before.

"Wall." Heather tried to sound optimistic. "Since Ross is spending the holidays with Kailee, why don't we take a trip? We could—"

"I can't take a trip," Wall grumbled. "I have to run the store."

"Okay, okay." Heather thought a moment, and then suggested, "We could go into Boston for a day. We haven't taken advantage of all that's going on there. We could visit the Museum of Science and see the new IMAX movie. Go to the art museums. Maybe the symphony. Eat at that Moroccan restaurant."

Wall said, "You go ahead. I've got work to do."

Wall's jaw was set. His hands clenched the steering wheel as if he were trying to steer through a storm. And maybe they were going through a storm, Heather thought. Maybe he had stopped loving her just as she'd stopped loving him, and he saw nothing exciting in his future. For the past few years, she had tried to involve him in her life, making him go with her to church and to lectures from the Safeguard Nature's distinguished, world-famous scientists, but it always felt to Heather as if she were dragging a heavy suitcase behind her.

"Maybe we should see a couple's therapist," she suggested softly.

Wall laughed, sounding more as if he was barking. "For God's sake, Heather, where do you get these ridiculous ideas?"

Heather closed her eyes and leaned her head against the window until they were home.

And *home* seemed so bleak when she walked in the door. This beautiful autumn day had filled her own life with shadows. Wall tossed his keys in the bowl on the front table and went right in to the den to watch television.

Heather went upstairs to the small room that had once been a nursery and now was her office for Safeguard Nature. She sank into her desk chair and woke her computer. She read through her emails, all of them about committee meetings and fundraisers. She decided to call Christine. At that very moment, her phone buzzed. Ross was calling!

"Hi, Mom," he said. "Thanks for the great meal. Kailee enjoyed meeting you and Dad."

"Oh, we enjoyed meeting Kailee," she lied, because she had to. "She's very . . . beautiful."

"Yeah. Listen, I wanted to say I'm sorry I forgot to tell you I met her parents last week. They came up for a football game and took us out to dinner. I meant to tell you, but this past week has been crazy. Between practice with my swim team and getting ready for midterms, I haven't had any free time."

"No worries," Heather said, employing the current phrase

everyone used now, and feeling kind of cool about it. "How did you like her parents?"

"They're great. Well, her dad is. Her mom is kind of stuck-up. I didn't talk much with her."

Heather smiled.

Ross went on. "I'm sorry about Thanksgiving and Christmas, too. I mean that I didn't tell you before now. We only just decided. Kailee grew up on the island and she says it's the best place in the world for the holidays. Do you think Dad's upset?"

"I don't think so. He didn't say he was," Heather said, and she was telling the truth. Wall had hardly spoken on the drive back from their dinner. "Would you like to speak with him?"

"Not now. I've got homework and I'll bet he's watching a game. Tell him I called to say thanks."

"I will."

"Love you, Mom."

"Love you, Ross."

Heather sat very still after they ended the call. It was as if the world had turned right side up, and she didn't want to move, to tilt it out of alignment. She called her friend Christine to dish about the dinner, especially about beautiful snotty Kailee and Ross's phone call saying Kailee's mother was stuck-up. Christine shared some local town gossip, and they made plans to get together to organize the church's Christmas fair.

It was odd, not having Ross with them during the holidays. Wall grumbled about joining her to buy a Christmas tree, and Heather ended up going by herself and choosing a small one, so she could carry it to the car. She put it in the holder alone, lying on the carpet to screw in the metal fasteners. The tree leaned slightly to the left, because Wall hadn't been there to help her straighten it, but for the first time in years, she thought, *oh, never mind,* and turned the tree so the crooked part was facing the wall.

Really, Christmas had become subdued since Ross went off to college. Before that, actually. When Ross was a child, and even when he was in middle school, Heather had enjoyed choosing the presents for Ross. By the time he was sixteen, Ross wanted only money. He added it to what he earned working on weekends for his father, and bought himself a computer, an Apple watch, and new tires for the truck they gave him for his sixteenth birthday.

That year, Wall told Heather to choose what she wanted and buy it. He was too busy in the store to shop for her. She knew that was true. He was selling Christmas lights almost at cost, to get people into his store. He had a shelf of small, charming replicas of Concord's most famous buildings, handmade by a local artist. He stocked decorations for the tree, lights inside and out, and yards of wires and cables to connect them to the right outlet. He came home exhausted. He told Heather he wanted nothing for Christmas but peace and quiet.

Christmas had always been Heather's favorite time of the year, and without Ross coming home, it was now as emotionally flat as a pancake, even with the little tree lit up. Still, she made it through the holiday season, baking cookies for the church Christmas party, manning the used-book table at the town fair, decorating trees in the nursing homes, and smiling as she towed Wall with her to various holiday parties.

January arrived, and people needed shovels, snowblowers, flashlights, and batteries. Wall was busy. Heather took courses in environmental issues and public policy and continued to work with Safeguard Nature. She went into Boston to see plays and hear symphonies. She ice-skated on the pond at the Boston Public Garden, with her friend Christine next to her as they wobbled along, laughing.

Christine Calloway had been Heather's best friend for years. They shared secrets, supported each other through the normal calamities of everyday life, and thoroughly discussed the British royal family. Heather had been there for Christine after her daughter's car accident and when her son dropped out of med school and joined the Peace Corps. She'd helped Christine convince her husband to move her difficult father-in-law into a pleasant assisted-living facility, where he could swear and throw dishes at the nurses instead of at Christine.

Now Christine listened to Heather's complaints about her life with Wall. Christine sympathized with Heather when Ross spent the January school break at a ski lodge with Kailee and her parents. She gave Heather a book of poetry by Khalil Gibran, which included the beautiful line, "You are the bows from which your children as living arrows are sent forth."

"That's easy for you to say, Christine," Heather responded. "Your daughter is married, living in this town, and about to make you a grandmother!"

In return, Christine asked the simple question: *What do you want?*

To her own surprise, Heather knew the answer immediately.

"I want to move to another town, a place where I feel free. I want to cook what I want to eat or not cook at all and live on popcorn and apples. I want to read all the novels I haven't read and put scented candles around my rooms without Wall yelling that they make him sneeze. I want a dog, but Wall's allergic. I want to buy a dress that makes me look sexy! God, Christine, I sound insane, don't I? I sound like I'm losing my mind!"

"No," Christine said. "You sound like you're finding yourself."

"Maybe I am," Heather agreed. "I've got to get organized. Where do I go from here? When do I leave? What do I *do?*"

Christine called Heather the next day with a plan.

"Sweetie, you're going to love this," Christine said, almost purring. "My next-door neighbor's nephew is getting divorced, and he has to sell off his Nantucket cottage, and he wants to rent it for the summer while the lawyers work out the details."

"Are you renting it?" Heather asked.

"No, *you* are!" Christine said. "I'm sending pictures. It's not a big house, and not fancy. It doesn't have a swimming pool or even a dishwasher. Two bedrooms, one bath. Very basic."

Heather scrolled through the photos. The cottage looked old and neglected. "Where is it?"

"Just off the Milestone road. Down a dirt drive. Not near anything, but there's a parking spot."

"It looks like it's in the middle of a jungle."

"I know. Bonnie said they haven't kept the garden up, or done anything, really. The couple has been fighting for years."

Heather smiled wryly. "I can imagine."

"But it's kind of perfect, right?"

Heather asked, "How much?"

"Okay, this is the hard part, but hear me out."

"How much?"

"Ten thousand dollars a month."

Heather burst out laughing. "You have lost your mind."

"Heather, listen to me. Three months on Nantucket. By yourself. Thirty thousand for three months. Do you have any idea what a bargain that is? Some island rentals go for thirty thousand a *week*. This guy just wants to rent it out quick, as is, no hassle."

"I don't know, Christine." Heather's eyes filled with tears. It sounded wonderful.

Christine pressed on. "Listen, they'll throw in the last week of May for free. Okay, some drawbacks. No air-conditioning. No television. But it does have Wi-Fi. You could watch movies on your laptop. Read books. Do some needlepoint. Not to mention lie in the sun and swim in the ocean. Plus, I'll come stay with you a lot."

Heather took a tissue from the bedside table and wiped her eyes.

"I have a secret, Christine." Heather admitted. "I have a separate bank account I've been saving all these years, money I saved on groceries or clothes. And sometimes I'd sell one of the antiques my grandparents left in the attic. Spode china, or fragile vases—things I couldn't keep around with a little boy running through the house. I liked having a little nest egg, in case of emergency."

"I'd call this an emergency," Christine said. "Sweetheart, this would change your life. And right now is the time."

"I think you're right," Heather said.

"Listen. Let's go check it out. I'll drive you down to Hyannis, we can take a ferry over, take a cab to the house, see what you think, and spend the night in the cottage. If nothing else, we'll have a free night in Nantucket."

"Okay," Heather said, terrified and happy.

On the first day of April, Heather leaned on the deck of the fast ferry, watching the mainland grow smaller and finally disappear while Nantucket bloomed on the horizon and slowly took on shape and color. She breathed in the sea air—she could smell the salt, and it was exhilarating—and felt an emotion rising up in her, a feeling she'd forgotten, a mixture of anticipation and hope.

"Nice, right?" Christine, standing next to Heather, asked.

"Nice," Heather agreed.

They took a cab to the house, although the driver, a cheery, talkative man named Eddie, had never heard of the street and had to use his GPS to find it. They bumped over potholes in the dirt, until they reached the end of the road. They gathered their bags and paid him, adding a twenty percent tip.

"Are you sure this is the correct address?" Eddie asked.

"Yes, thank you, we're sure," Heather told him.

"If you need a taxi again, give me a call." Eddie handed Heather a card with his cell number on it.

He drove away, bouncing along the rutted dirt road.

"My neighbor did say it was run-down," Christine reminded her.

Together the women trekked up the path between grass, flowers, and weeds so overgrown they almost hid the walk. Ivy covered one window. The trim and clapboard were gasping for paint. A yard woven from seedy grass and weeds was circled by a forest of oak and pine.

Heather opened the door and pushed her way in through the

swollen wood. The door opened directly onto a large living room with a fireplace at one end. An electric heater stood in the hearth. A long couch, coffee table, and two armchairs took up most of the room. At the other end were a pockmarked but sturdy dining table and six mismatched chairs. An open doorway led to a galley kitchen with a faux red-brick linoleum floor and avocado appliances.

"It's a wonder their marriage lasted as long as it did," Christine observed.

Heather clicked a wall switch, and the overhead light came on. The refrigerator was old, but clean and humming, and the electric stove worked. No dishwasher. No microwave. A coffee maker, at least. A long bookshelf, mostly bare, ran along one wall.

"Very basic," Christine said.

Heather laughed. "Let's see the bedrooms."

They went through the kitchen to a small hall with one door leading outside and one door leading to a small rectangular room. It held one twin bed, a nightstand, and a bureau.

They passed back through the kitchen to another door and a larger bedroom. Heather saw a double bed without a headboard, a chest of drawers, and a long table piled with sheets, towels, candles, and packets of toilet paper and paper towels.

"I like what they've done with the place," Heather quipped.

The curtains over the one window were a plain green, like the bedspread. Heather lay on the bed. It was softer than she liked. It wouldn't help her back, but it might help her dreams.

On the other side of the hall was a bathroom. The bathroom was basic, and the shower curtain was mildewed, but Heather and Christine turned all the faucets and flushed the toilet, and everything worked.

"One more thing," Heather said. She returned to the living room, put her laptop on the table at the far end, beneath the window darkened by ivy, turned on her computer, and logged on to the Wi-Fi with the password Bonnie had written down for them. "Send me a message," Heather said.

Christine tapped her iPhone.

"Got it!" Heather said. "The Wi-Fi works!"

Heather read Christine's message: *There's a monster under the bed.*

Heather typed back: *Good. He can keep me company.*

They both laughed, and Heather said, "Actually, let's check under the bed."

They got down on their knees and looked, and found nothing but dust balls.

"I can see why he's not asking more money for this place," Christine said.

Heather stood with her hands on her hips. "It would be fun to whip it into shape."

Together, they set about making the place habitable. Christine unpacked the groceries and wine they'd brought from home while Heather made the double bed with the sheets left on the bedroom table. She hung towels in the bathroom. They tested the lamps on either side of the couch and made a note to buy lightbulbs in town. They tossed the couch pillows around, thrilled to see no signs of nibbling or other invasion by mice.

Christine said, "It's clean and almost adorable. Now. Let's go explore the town and have dinner."

They'd kept their taxi driver's card. Eddie answered immediately when they called and soon after that, was back at the house.

"You know," Eddie said as he drove them to Main Street, "there's a bus service here. It's called the Wave. Also, you can rent bikes. Not that I don't like driving you ladies!"

"Thanks for the advice," Heather said. "Christine, stop laughing."

"The thought of you on a bike!" Christine crowed. "You haven't been on a bike in thirty years!"

"Then we're renting bikes tomorrow," Heather said determinedly. She gave Eddie his money and tip, and told him they'd call him later.

"Much later," Christine said. "We're going wild tonight."

Going wild for them meant walking around the charming town,

window-shopping, and sitting on a bench on the harbor, eating
ice cream cones. They called Eddie for a ride home, and slept a
deep, salt-air sleep.

Heather woke early the next morning. The sun was just coming
up. The morning mist was slowly vanishing. Slipping her feet into
sandals, she quietly made her way to the kitchen. The back door
opened onto a slate patio overgrown with moss, and grasses
twined with wildflowers grew to the edge of the slates and were
attempting to cover the patio. One small white plastic table and
two small white plastic chairs had been left behind, with leaves
and twigs scattered on the surfaces. Beyond the small backyard, if
it could be called a yard, was a forest, or something like it, with
deciduous trees smothered by climbing vines and more anonymous grasses and brush. It could be a house in the wilderness of
Maine or, for all Heather knew, deepest Brazil.

She carefully sank into a chair, not certain it wouldn't collapse
beneath her. It held.

The air was so pure, almost sweet. Birds were chirping busily in
the bushes, and slowly the sky brightened. The day grew warmer,
and Heather let her head fall back so her face could catch the sun.
Something rustled in the grass. A small gray rabbit nibbled on a
leaf.

Behind her, the kitchen door opened and closed. Christine sat
on the other chair and smiled at Heather.

"Good morning," she said.

"Good morning," Heather answered.

"You like this place, don't you?"

Heather nodded. "I do. Thank you, Christine. It's a kind of
miracle."

"Actually," Christine said, "it's only normal life."

"Then I very much want to have this kind of normal life for
the next three months," Heather told her.

"I'll make coffee to celebrate," Christine said, and went into the
house.

Heather remained in the silence of the wildness, happier and more relaxed than she'd been in years.

"I want this," Heather said. "Let's go back to Concord. I need to tell Wall."

"One thing," Christine said. "What if you run into Kailee on the island?"

"I won't run into her," Heather assured her friend. "She'll be living with Ross and Wall in our house while Ross works with Wall in the store."

Christine dropped Heather off at her house late Sunday afternoon. Heather carried in her duffel bag, set it near the stairs to the second floor, and went directly into the kitchen to pour herself a glass of wine. She could hear the television from the den. She summoned up her courage.

She knew she had to tell Wall now. Every other day he was at work, and in the evenings, he was irritable if Heather tried to have a conversation.

Heather walked into the den. Wall was texting on his phone.

"Hi, Wall. I'm back. The trip to the island was great!"

Wall hurriedly closed his phone. "Glad you had fun."

She stood by the doorway for a moment, studying her husband. He was still handsome, only forty-seven, with thick dark hair slightly streaked with gray, and the same long torso and wide shoulders that their son had.

When she saw that the Boston team was ahead by seven runs, she felt like fate was giving her a sign: *Do it now*. He could take a few minutes away from the game, knowing his team was ahead.

Heather entered the den and sat in a chair near the sofa. "I want to talk to you."

Wall stared at the television. "Go ahead. Talk."

She was very calm when she spoke, like a student who knew the right answer. "Wall, I'm leaving you. I want a divorce. I have a lawyer. You know her, Sarah Martin."

Wall jerked his attention away from the television. Looking at Heather, he said, "What in the hell are you talking about?"

Heather picked up the remote and shut off the television. "Wall. The Red Sox are fine. They'll win this game. You need to talk with me. You need to hear me."

"Don't be ridiculous," Wall snapped. He reached for the remote control.

Heather was already highly emotional, feeling proud and terrified that she had finally let her words into the air. When Wall grabbed for the remote, she held it behind her back. The situation was so childish, so surreal, she couldn't help but laugh, a little hysterically.

"Wall. Stop. Listen. I'm telling you I'm leaving you."

"Oh, for God's sake," he said, running his hand through his hair. "What's your problem now?"

Trembling with a mix of fear and hope, Heather said, "Wall, be realistic. You and I haven't been happy together for years."

"Life isn't about being happy all the time," Wall told her.

"But shouldn't it be about being happy *some* of the time?" Heather asked. "Wall, when was the last time we went out to dinner or to a movie?"

"We don't need to pay movie prices. We've got cable."

"All right, then, when was the last time we made love?"

Wall sighed. "We don't need to have sex. We're married. We've had more sex than I can remember."

"That means we haven't had any memorable sex." Heather laughed softly. "Wall, come on. Admit it. Whatever we once had between us has run its course. We make each other miserable. I don't want to live the rest of my life the way I have the past few years."

Wall shrugged. "Do what you have to do."

Heather said, "Wall, I'm worried about you."

"Don't bother," Wall said. "I'm fine." He crossed his arms over his chest, his mouth tightened into a thin line.

"Wall, I've rented a cottage on Nantucket. I'm going to live there this summer and take some time to decide what I want to do next. But you won't be alone. Ross will be back living here, and he'll be working for you in the store, as planned. You won't miss me at all."

"Give me the remote control," Wall said.

Heather stood up and dropped the remote on the sofa. She walked out of the room.

two

Kailee didn't hate Heather right away.

At first, she only thought Heather was a little tiresome, using her texts and phone messages to put a guilt trip on Ross because he spent Thanksgiving and Christmas with Kailee and her parents. After all, Ross was an adult and would graduate from university this spring. He should be free to do whatever he wanted.

It was the meeting in the coffee shop that decided it.

She should have been prepared. Someone who wasn't from Nantucket wouldn't appreciate who Kailee was.

And Heather certainly didn't.

Heather didn't know that Kailee Essex was descended from Bartholomew Essex, who landed on the island with a British ship in 1697. Her family was part of the aristocracy of Nantucket, along with the Coffins, Starbucks, and Folgers.

Kailee had been brought up to be a strong, confident woman. During high school she'd been one of the prettiest girls, with her

long chestnut hair, green eyes, and dimples in her cheeks. She'd
had a group of friends who giggled and gossiped and took trips
off-island to shop. During high school, her father's company,
Essex Construction, began to take on contracts to build the mega-
mansions that caused public furor and letters to the editor and
shouting at town meetings about how the trophy houses were
ruining the island. Still, her friends stayed close. Some parents
were real estate dealers who sold off historic properties to summer people who then knocked down the houses and built new
faux palaces. Some parents were interior decorators. And of
course, electricians, carpenters, and other construction workers
were in her father's employ. Kailee and her family were not alone
in getting rich and richer on the island, but she hadn't really paid
attention. She ran with her gang, danced on the beach with her
boyfriend, and even told her parents she didn't want to leave the
island for college.

They insisted she go.

She went, driving off in her red Jeep convertible with the top
down and stickers on the back bumper. One read: GUT FISH NOT
HOUSES. The other said: LOCAL SINCE FOREVER.

College had been eye-opening for Kailee, and she was the kind
of person who could learn from her mistakes and move on. She
wasn't an outstanding scholar, but she excelled at accounting and
technology, and that was what she needed for her father's company. She assumed she'd marry one of the island men, hopefully
one with a genealogy as prestigious as hers.

She hadn't counted on Ross Willette. Kailee had had a serious
boyfriend in high school, but they broke up amicably when they
started college. She dated a lot and flirted more during her first
three years at UMass, but in the fall of her senior year, she met
Ross in class.

Even with Covid masks on, it was as simple as that.

He was over six feet tall, with wide shoulders and a swimmer's
build—and it was so perfect that he was on the UMass swim
team, even though they couldn't swim because of Covid. Kailee

loved swimming. Her favorite place was at Madaket, where the Atlantic changed its mood daily, challenging Kailee, tossing her around, giving her a good game. She had a swimmer's build, too: slender torso, wide shoulders, strong arms and legs, small breasts. During the Nantucket Atheneum's annual Cold Turkey Plunge over Thanksgiving, when the water was cold, Kailee was the first one to run into the icy waves, screaming with delight.

When Kailee and Ross looked at each other in that class, they were like two heat-seeking missiles finding their target. Ross crossed the room to talk to her, and afterward they'd gone to sit on the front steps and talk. Ross had dark hair and light brown eyes that Kailee swooned over every time she looked at him. He was smart, not creepy genius level, but smart enough, and funny, and nice. His parents owned a hardware store in a historic town. Ross and Kailee realized they had a natural bond, coming from families in the construction business. Two days later, they found themselves in the same group volunteering for the local ecology center and talked more. They realized they shared the same dream: to save their planet.

Also, they were madly sexually attracted to each other. When they first kissed, it was all they could do not to make love right there on the front steps of the community building.

As the days passed, they fell more in love and knew they wanted to be together, always. Eventually, they'd marry, but first Kailee wanted Ross to get to know the Nantucket community, her friends, her father's employees, so that he felt he belonged. Her parents liked Ross a lot. He could wear a blazer and a tie and make polite conversation. Kailee's father would start Ross low, working on framing and shingling, waiting to see what kind of worker Ross was. Ross was strong. He could press Kailee over his head and hold her there forever without tiring. He didn't worry about fitting in with her island friends—Ross never worried about anything like that. He *did* worry about his mom and dad and his dad's business. The world had changed, but his dad hadn't gotten the message yet, or he'd gotten the message but didn't believe it. Ross felt closer to his mom than his dad. Kailee felt closer to her dad than her mom. Kailee believed there was a kind of karmic balance that way.

After Ross spent Christmas on Nantucket last year, he'd gone to Vermont with the Essex family to ski during January break. He'd hinted to his parents that he would work on the island this summer, but only by texts. Heather had texted, *We miss you!* And, *Bring Kailee to visit. We'd love to see you both!* Wall had texted Ross that he was needed, and expected, to work at Willette's Hardware in Concord. Ross told Kailee he really needed a face-to-face with his parents.

Today Kailee and Ross were meeting his parents in Amherst, at a coffee shop near the university, for a friendly talk. What they *hoped* would be a friendly talk. Graduation was a week away. Kailee knew Ross worried about hurting his parents by working for Essex Construction, but he needed to make it clear, and he needed Kailee with him for emotional support. Kailee planned to be sweet and adorable.

They found a parking spot on the street, slipped coins into the meter, and headed toward the coffee shop. When they went through the door, Ross took Kailee's hand.

Ross's mother waved from a table by the window. She was lovely, pretty in a soft way, wearing a flowery spring scarf around her neck. Kailee's mother was chic. She didn't dress in seasonal themes.

Heather rose to hug him. "My big boy."

"Mom," Ross said, grinning.

Kailee held back politely, letting Heather embrace her son.

"Kailee," Heather said. "We're so glad to see you again."

"You look wonderful, Mrs. Willette." Kailee tried to seem perky. She thought Mrs. Willette probably favored perky girls for her son.

"Oh, call me Heather, please. Don't you look pretty! Would you like a pastry? A cinnamon bun?"

Ross took Kailee's hand. "Mom. We just want to talk."

"Sit down," Wall said, his tone pleasant.

"I'll get our coffees," Kailee said to Ross.

Ross pulled up a chair between his parents. "How are you guys?"

Heather grinned. "You're stalling until Kailee gets back."

"Can't a kid ask how his parents are?" Ross asked. His left leg bounced the way it had when he was younger and nervous.

"Here we go," Kailee said, swooping into her chair with their coffees.

Heather and Wall looked at the other couple expectantly.

"Okay, you guys, here's the deal," Ross said. "I know we texted about this, so I'm, uh, *reminding* you that I'm going to Nantucket with Kailee. I'm going to work for Essex Construction this summer."

Ross's father's face went so red Kailee almost jumped out of her chair, wanting to catch him if he had a heart attack and fell. But Wall sat frozen except for the muscles working in his jaw.

His mother looked appalled. "But, Ross, as *we* texted *you,* that's not what we planned. Last summer, when we had our serious talk before you went off for your senior year, you were so excited about working with your father after graduation and gradually taking over the store. You've been wanting to do that since you were a little boy!"

"I'm sorry, Mom," Ross said, and he did sound sorry. "I'm older now. Things have changed. I've changed. I just don't think there's a future for me at the hardware store."

"Not much of a future for anyone, really," Kailee added gently. "This semester in our business management course, we've been studying about all the giant corporations that are displacing the small businesses, and it may be too bad, but it's what's happening."

"Not necessarily," Heather argued quietly. "For example, Willette's Hardware has many loyal customers. And people don't have to walk a mile in a parking lot to get there." She looked at Wall again, surprised he wasn't saying anything.

Wall looked as if he'd aged fifty years in one moment.

And people usually did not argue with Kailee.

"Heather," Kailee said, "Ross told me that last summer sales at Willette's Hardware were on a downward slide, and we know that's going to continue. This way, Ross will have a future, an *important* future."

Ross added, "We didn't want to tell you this too soon, but Kailee and I are going to get engaged in the fall and married in the spring. I'm going to work with Kailee's father, learning the ropes—"

Kailee cut in. "There's a lot to learn. This summer, Ross will work the different sections, to get to know the crew, hands-on experience, and the plan is that someday, eventually, Ross and I will be joint CEOs. I'll do the business stuff. Ross will focus on project management and construction."

"What does your father think about this plan?" Wall asked, stony-faced.

Ross spoke. "Dad, this is *his plan.* Bob has talked to me, and to both of us, several times. He's shown me around the sites where he's building houses, and the main office at the Madaket yard."

Wall growled, "Do you want to work for Mr. Essex for the rest of your life?"

"I do. You and Mom have always said you want the best for me. This is the best." Ross spoke urgently. "It's a very big deal, Dad. It's a huge construction company, and I want to be part of it. I'm sorry. I know you're disappointed. I didn't want to tell you before, I wanted to tell you in person."

Heather leaned forward, fixing Ross in her gaze. "You can't do this, Ross. You need to stay with your father, at least for the summer. I'm serious. You can't go to Nantucket this summer."

Ross said softly, as if speaking only to his mother, "Mom. I'm sorry. You'll be fine without me. Dad will be fine. Look, I've already been gone for four years, in college. I'm an adult. I want my own life."

"Your mother is leaving me," Wall suddenly announced, not looking at Heather.

Kailee's hand flew to her mouth in surprise.

"What?" Ross asked. "You're kidding."

"He's not kidding. I'm sorry we had to tell you now, this way." Heather sniffed back her tears. "It's true. I'm divorcing your father. I have supported you in every way all your life, Ross, and now I want to start *my* life."

Kailee held her breath. If *her* parents got divorced, it would turn her world upside down. She didn't speak. This was Ross's battle.

"But you love Dad," Ross protested. "Mom. Come on!"

"No," Wall said. "She doesn't. She's leaving me as if I'm an old dog abandoned by the side of the road."

"That's not true," Heather said sadly. She looked at Ross. "I care for your father, but we're not happy together anymore. I think we both deserve some happiness."

Ross frowned, puzzled. "Well, yeah, you deserve some happiness, but, Mom, I thought you *were* happy. *Are* happy."

Heather shook her head. Tears glimmered in her eyes. "I haven't been happy for a long time, Ross. Believe me, I've tried to talk with your father about this."

Wall interrupted, blurting, "Go ahead, blame me!"

"I'm not blaming anyone, Wall." Heather turned to face Ross. She put her hand on his wrist.

He's not yours, Kailee thought furiously, but she controlled herself and stayed quiet.

"Ross, I've been wanting to leave for years. I've seen therapists. I've asked Wall to see a marriage counselor with me, but he refuses, and it doesn't matter anyway. My mind's made up. I want to take a deep breath and start my life over. Your father and I were good parents to you. I'm asking you to do this one thing: Stay with your father this summer."

Ross was pale. He looked as if he was about to cry. "I didn't know you were unhappy. You never *seemed* unhappy. Can't you . . ."

"I've already made arrangements," Heather told him, and her voice was firm. "Your father and I have discussed this. We each have a lawyer, and we will have an amicable divorce. And your father is perfectly capable of taking care of himself."

"She's right," Wall said, lifting his chin and straightening his shoulders. "It's her decision, but I accept it. I can almost understand her leaving me. But, Ross—you're my *son*."

Ross turned to his father angrily. "I have been *your son* as long as I could help you in the store. Where were you when I had swim meets or football games in high school? Where were you when I was little and begged to go with you in your truck? You were going to the dump or the pharmacy or wherever, and you always told me I couldn't go, I was too young, and you told Mom you didn't want to have to deal with me. All I wanted was to sit in that big truck of yours and watch you drive!"

Wall was angry. He shouted, "For God's sake, Ross, don't be such a baby. I was making a living. I was supporting you and your mother. *Working* so we could afford groceries and . . . and your Legos! When you were little, you never stopped talking. How could I *think* with you pulling on my shirt and jabbering away at me?"

Looking around, Wall realized the entire room had gone silent. People were openly staring at him. Wall took a deep breath, dropping his eyes to the table, ignoring the others.

Ross's face was blotchy and crumpled as he held back tears. "Wow," he said softly.

Wall tried to make amends. "That's why I want you to work with me. I mean, now we can understand each other. And I've already had a sign made. It says, Willette and Willette." He smiled, as if the existence of the sign made everything all right.

Kailee wanted to punch Ross's father in the nose, but she said calmly, "Well, that cleared the air. I think we all know why Ross won't work for his father this summer."

To Kailee's surprise, Heather spoke up in support of Ross's father.

"Ross, sometimes men aren't good with babies and children. When you were in your teens, you loved helping Wall. Our plan for *years* was for you to take over the store. I can understand your desire to be with Kailee, but there's another way. Ross, honey, think about it. At least take a moment to think about it. Kailee's a lovely girl, but she could move to Concord as easily as you could move to Nantucket."

That was the moment Kailee began to hate Heather.

Heather continued. "You and Kailee could live in our house, with your father. You two could have the entire second floor. Kailee might like living in Concord. It's a beautiful town, and not as isolated as Nantucket is. You would be near theater and art museums in Boston. You could zip down to New York. You could have a wider group of friends. You and Dad could run the store, and I know you'd improve it. Kailee could find a job for an *important* business, an international company, not just a small island concern. Or she could work for one of the amazing historical museums in Concord, like Orchard House, where Louisa May Alcott lived. And Walden Pond. Won't you at least think about it? Maybe bring Kailee to live in Concord for a week, to see how cultured the area is? Beaches aren't as compelling in the winter months. You could always *vacation* on the island, when the weather is good."

Ross didn't speak. He sat looking down at the table, obviously conflicted and in shock. Kailee couldn't breathe. Heather had insulted her island, her world, and her father's business. She tried to gather her thoughts to reply.

But Wall spoke first, his voice like thunder. "Ross, if you don't work with me this summer, you're no son of mine."

Kailee whispered, "Please . . ."

Ross lifted his head and met his father's eyes. "I'm sorry you feel that way, Dad. But I'm going to Nantucket."

Wall shoved back his chair and strode out the door.

Heather closed her eyes and sat very still.

Kailee reached over and took her hand. "This must be upsetting for you. I'm so sorry."

Heather pulled her hand away. "Oh, I don't think you are."

"Mom, come on," Ross said.

"*You* come on," Heather responded. "Suddenly, you've lost all appreciation for your father and the business he's given his life to? Suddenly, all you care about is Kailee?"

"Mrs. Willette," Kailee said, dropping the sugar from her voice, "it's normal for people to leave their parents and make their own lives."

"Kailee," Heather said, her voice shaking, "aren't you being a bit hypocritical? *You're* not leaving *your* parents, are you? You and my son are going to make your lives with your parents and to hell with me and Wall."

Kailee blushed fiercely. Heather Willette had a point, but few people had ever spoken to her so bluntly.

Ross spoke angrily. "Mom, you know Dad has to be the one in charge of everything. He'll never take my advice. He won't let me move a nail unless he tells me to. I won't live like that. Even if I hadn't met Kailee, I wouldn't work for him."

"Ross, that's enough. I've spent too many years playing referee for you and your father. Sounds like you've already made your decision." Heather rose so quickly she almost knocked her chair over. She crossed the room, went out the door, and left the coffee shop. Kailee and Ross could tell through the plate glass window that Heather was sobbing. She stood right on the sidewalk for anyone to see, until she found a tissue in her shoulder bag.

Ross rose to go after his mother. Kailee put her hand around his wrist. Ross sat down.

Finally, Heather walked away, out of sight.

Ross dropped his head into his hands, elbows on the table. "What a mess. I feel terrible. I never meant to hurt my mother."

Kailee wanted Ross to remain on *her* side. Quietly, she said, "I can't believe your mother called me a hypocrite. I thought she'd be supportive of you."

"She does have a point," Ross said. "I'm leaving my father's store to work for your father."

Kailee's lips tightened. She was shocked at the way the conversation had gone. She knew she should be quiet and let it all settle, but she couldn't stop herself from saying, "Ross, you're an adult. You could go off to Antarctica or—or space if you wanted to."

"I know." Ross sounded sad. "But that wasn't what they expected. I did promise to work in the store, to take it over from my father. We really dropped a bomb. I thought Dad would be mad, but I never expected Mom to be this upset." He rubbed his face with his hands. "Damn, Kailee, my parents are getting divorced."

"It's so strange," Kailee said. "Maybe your mother will change her mind and stay with your father. He will need her now."

Ross's face fell. "I don't think Mom needs him."

"Would it help if you talked to your mother yourself, just the two of you?" Kailee asked.

"No," Ross replied. Turning to Kailee, he took both her hands in his. "Kailee, I love you. I want to be part of Essex Construction and build my life with you. I want to have children with you and walk on the beach with you in the winter. I'm sorry my parents reacted the way they did. I'm not surprised by my father, but my mother . . . I'll talk to her again, but not now. Not when we're so emotional."

Tears glimmered in Kailee's eyes. "I love you, Ross." She felt as if they'd been in a battle, and she and Ross had won. It probably was wrong of her to think of it this way, but it was how she felt.

"My mother's strong," Ross said. "She'll be all right. My dad will be furious, and he likes to nurse a grudge . . ."

"We'll let some time pass," Kailee said. "It will be all right."

It was the middle of May, and Kailee was so done with college. No more early morning classes, pop quizzes, professors with halitosis. She was free!

Ross helped her carry the last of her boxes to her Jeep. Kailee kissed him goodbye before he headed in his blue Chevy pickup to stop by his house in Concord, drop off some boxes, and dig out some summer clothes to take to the island.

Kailee drove down the Mass Pike and onto 495. She tuned to

her favorite station and sang with the music all the way down to the Cape. When she crossed the Bourne Bridge, her heart flooded with happiness. She was on the Cape. She was almost home.

In Hyannis, she drove onto the M/V *Eagle,* parking in the hold with SUVs, pickup trucks, a caterpillar on a flatbed, a long UPS parcel truck, five passenger cars, and a white FedEx delivery truck all crammed in four lanes from bow to stern. It was hot and noisy down in the vehicle deck, but Kailee had her to-go cup filled with ice and water and she could play sudoku on her phone during the trip.

She couldn't concentrate. She leaned her head back, closed her eyes, and thought of how her life had changed since she'd left the island for college.

Kailee had a degree in business management with a minor in technology. All her life she'd known she would eventually work for her father, and then with him, and finally take over the business on the island where her family had lived for generations. When she met Ross, she'd been awed that the universe had given her not only the man she loved, but a man who could be her companion in work as well as life.

This summer, Kailee would move back into the handsome house on Pleasant Street, a tree-lined elegant avenue with historic homes, far away from the enormous building empire where men wore hard hats and giant machines waited to waken and growl and shake the earth like sci-fi special effects come to life. She would work at the company's on-site office learning about Essex Construction's financials from George March, the company's financial officer. One day a week, she would help her mother with her various town committees and charity and fundraising work. It would be years before Kailee and Ross headed the firm, but her grandfather had started the business, and since Kailee was an only child, she knew her place in the family dynasty.

Ross would start working for the company at the basic, dusty, lumber-toting, nail-hammering level. His home would be the small apartment over her house's garage, and Kailee's parents had told Ross he was welcome to join them for dinner whenever he wanted. Kailee and Ross knew she would be in his apartment often.

Kailee hadn't spoken with Ross's parents since the disastrous meeting in early May. She pitied them, especially Heather, who had been so rude. Kailee didn't want Heather to be unhappy. Actually, she didn't give a hoot about Heather's happiness. Ross belonged to Kailee now, and together they were going forward into the future.

The ferry slowed and turned. It rumbled at turtle speed into the slip, slamming up against the dock. Machinery squealed as the ramp was lowered and the mooring lines connected. All around her, motors started, and slowly the exodus began.

She steered her car off the boat and onto dry land with tears in her eyes. Nantucket. Her home. She was born here, raised here, and she had no desire to go anywhere else. She was totally an island girl.

It would be different now, she knew. Some of her high school friends had gone to college and on to a big city for work. Some had stayed home after high school, married, and had babies. Plus, of course, new, younger princesses had been crowned homecoming queen or starred in plays and musicals. Now Kailee would work full-time. She would make it through the busy season, and so would Ross, and in November, when island life really slowed down, she and Ross could make plans for the future, for their wedding, for the spot on the island where they would build a house of their own.

Kailee drove down Water Street past the Dreamland Theater, the library garden, Lilly Pulitzer and other boutiques, and turned right on Main Street. She smiled. This picturesque cobblestone avenue, wide enough for angle parking on both sides, with buildings of brick put together in the 1800s, this was her red-carpet road home. Murray's Beverage was the first place she legally purchased a bottle of champagne. Half the clothes she owned came from Vis-a-Vis. Over the years, she'd bought medicine, lipstick, sunglasses, and ice cream from Nantucket Pharmacy, and books from Mitchell's Book Corner. Upper Main was one of the prettiest streets in the world, with towering trees and flowering bushes sheltering proud brick mansions and Greek Revival homes with columns.

She turned onto Pleasant Street at the corner where the Hadwen House stood. She passed the Nantucket Garden Club's garden, and Moor's End with its high brick wall hiding its rose garden maze, and at last, near Jefferson Lane, her home stood waiting. The house itself was close to the sidewalk and street, and a brick driveway ran beside it to the garage and garden in back.

It was almost six o'clock, and her father's truck wasn't in the drive. During the long summer nights, he and his crew took advantage of the light and worked late. They were always under deadline.

Kailee lifted her duffel bag onto her shoulder and hurried up the drive. She opened the front door.

"I'm home!" she yelled exuberantly.

Her mother's voice floated from the back of the house. "I'm working."

Kailee dropped her duffel bag in the large front hall and went through the house to her mother's office.

Evelyn had had her husband build a conservatory, with a glass roof and walls and wicker furniture with green-and-white striped cushions and a pale green carpet on the floor. It was almost impossible to see through the ferns and other greenery to Evelyn's antique French provincial desk with intricately carved legs. Kailee thought that only her mother could turn an office into an Eden.

Kailee studied her mother. Evelyn was nearly fifty, and always beautifully dressed. Long ago, Kailee had asked her mother why she always wore jewelry or elegant dresses even when going on errands.

"I'm representing Essex Construction," Evelyn had said. "I must look groomed."

"Groomed," Kailee had scoffed. "Sounds like you're a dog."

"If I am," Evelyn had said, "I'm a French poodle with a diamond collar."

Kailee had laughed. "I see you more as a Jack Russell terrier. Always going, never stopping."

Kailee repeated, "I'm home!"

Evelyn continued tapping away on her computer. "Just a minute, sweetie." She finished something, then turned to Kailee.

"Good trip?" Evelyn asked.

When she turned to Kailee, Kailee saw that her mother's face seemed older. She had gray pouches under her eyes. "You look tired, Mom."

"I'm extremely busy with the Essex Nature Foundation. We've had the paperwork checked out by legal, and we're having a gala at the end of the summer, just before Labor Day. The only day we could get, actually. My first task is to build a website for the foundation. I'm perusing the websites of other organizations on the island. I don't want to imitate or irritate the other groups. I've made a list of the key people who will be, I hope, founding members. So if I look tired, it's for a good cause." Evelyn changed the subject. "When does Ross arrive?"

"He'll take the eight o'clock slow boat and be here around ten-fifteen. You guys don't have to wait up. I'll watch for him and show him up to his apartment."

"Good. He can carry your boxes in. I assume you can start working with George in the office tomorrow."

"Yes. I can't wait."

Evelyn smiled. "I remember when we bought you your own small desk with a toy computer and a real calculator and folders and paper and pens."

"It was so much fun!" Kailee closed her eyes and for a moment she was back there. "It was like going to paradise."

"It's changed, I'm afraid. Back then, your father's business was so small I could do all the bookkeeping. Now we've got a full-time accountant and a complicated financial system."

"You and Dad could sell everything," Kailee suggested on the spur of the moment. "The land, this house, his business, and you'd be multi-millionaires."

"We'd never do that. We belong to the island and these days it needs our help."

"I'm glad you're doing this, Mom, but it's kind of weird."

"Sweetie," Evelyn said, "think of it as payback. This island has given us so much. We want to love it back."

"Got it." At times like this, Kailee wished she had a more normal mom, one who would hug her and welcome her home, maybe even bake her a cake with a silly heart shaped from icing. But her mother was on a mission, and when Evelyn started on a project, she finished it.

"I'll unpack the Jeep," Kailee said.

"Mmm." Evelyn was already back at work, reading glasses on her nose, documents in her hands.

Kailee returned to her Jeep, took out her luggage, and brought everything into the front hall. She took her wheelie suitcases up carpeted stairs to her room.

"Oh, groan," she said when she entered her bedroom.

She had a canopy bed with teen pink curtains. Swimming trophies lined her shelves, along with often-read classic paperbacks. Pooh, her childhood teddy bear, sat on her vanity table next to her fingernail polish.

"OMG," Kailee cried in dismay. "This is such a *teenager's* room."

She jumped up and began yanking down the ruffly pink curtains of the canopy over her bed. She was an adult now, almost engaged to be married, ready to take on the serious work of her father's business. She needed to get all the pink out of her room.

She took down and folded the canopy curtains, detached the wooden finials and posts, and set them by her door to take to the attic later. Ross was stopping by his house in Concord to pick up his stuff. He would come over in his truck on the eight o'clock ferry and arrive at ten-fifteen. Kailee was going to walk down to the terminal so she could see him when he arrived.

And then their real life would begin!

three

S ummer had been calling her all her life.

On this sunny, bright May morning, Heather arrived, after driving her old Volvo station wagon down Route 3, into Hyannis, and onto a car ferry. She left her car and walked up to the upper deck to watch the boat make its way into the wide waters of Nantucket Sound. She allowed herself one more time to replay her last conversation with her son. Had she done everything possible to make him comfortable with her divorce?

She hoped she had.

Several days ago, Ross had driven to their house in Concord to pick up boxes he'd been packing up over the previous two weekends. Wall had been at his store when Ross was there—Heather guessed that Ross came during the day when he knew his father wouldn't be at the house.

She had tried to talk things over with her son. Once, she'd brought him a glass of iced tea and lingered in the door as he tossed his board shorts and T-shirts into a duffel bag.

"Ross," Heather had said in a mild, friendly tone, "would you like to sit down for a moment and talk? I don't mean about you and the store. I wonder if you have questions or concerns about your father and me getting a divorce."

Ross shrugged. "I'm not surprised. He can be a real dick."

Angered, Heather snapped, "Are you thirteen years old? Is that all you can say about your father? About our marriage? Do you think you're going to live your entire life with Kailee and never once be a 'real dick'?"

Ross sighed. "I'm sorry, Mom. I shouldn't have called him that. What I meant was that he can be really difficult to deal with. And frankly, he's never been Mr. Warm."

Heather went into the room and sat on the armchair in the corner, even though it was covered with clothes Ross had tossed from his drawers.

"Sit down with me a moment, Ross. Please. I don't want you to feel sad or lost because of this divorce."

Ross lowered himself onto the side of his bed. "I don't feel sad or lost. I'm totally amped about my future. I love Kailee and I love Nantucket. I love my father, too, and I understand, because believe me, I've spent some time working through this, I understand that he based himself on the fifties' role model of strong silent guy because *his* father was that way. *I* can't be that way. I don't expect you to have to live with him. I completely get it that you want to break away and start your own life."

"Good," Heather said quietly. "Ross, there's something else . . ."

"Okay."

"I want to tell you something that's kind of odd. I mean, *you* might think it's odd. It didn't start that way—it was Christine's suggestion—"

"Mom," Ross said, "just tell me."

Heather took a deep breath. "I've rented a cottage on Nantucket for three months. Well, the last week of May through August. I wanted to get away from here, to be alone and think about my future, and Christine, you know Christine, she's been my friend forever, she knew someone who wanted to rent out a cottage on Nantucket for the summer. So we went there in April, and I've rented it for the summer." She paused, waiting for Ross's reaction. She worried that he would be angry, feeling shadowed.

Ross said, "Cool."

Heather almost laughed with relief. "It's small. Isolated. I'm going to do a lot of walking on the beach and I'll read a lot of books and think about my future. But I want you to understand that when I rented the cottage, I thought you and Kailee were going to live in Concord, in our house, and you were going to work for your father."

Ross shrugged. "Okay. That's nice. So maybe I'll see you out there now and then."

"That's the thing," Heather said. "I don't want you, or especially Kailee, to think I moved there to follow you. Because, truthfully, I'm not going there to check on you. This time, as they say, it's all about me."

"No problem. I think you're making a bigger deal of this than it is."

"I hope so," Heather said. "But I think maybe, if you could just not tell Kailee right away, it would be better for all three of us. Give us all some time to settle into our lives there. What do you think?"

"Fine, Mom." Ross stood up again. "I've got to load up and get going. I don't want to miss the boat."

Heather watched Ross fold his good dress shirts the way she'd shown him four years ago when he headed off to college. She could remember how eager *she'd* been to leave her parents, to be an independent adult, how she'd considered her parents safe and stable and last year's news.

Ross turned from his suitcase to face Heather.

"Mom," he said.

"Yes?" She couldn't help the hopeful expression that came to her face. Was he going to say something loving?

Ross said, "Sorry, but I need to get the clothes you're sitting on. In that chair."

Heather's heart broke a little, but she smiled. "Of course." She moved to his bedroom door. "I've got packing to do myself."

She went to her bedroom, shut the door, and smiled and cried at the same time. She and Wall had raised a good, healthy son. She would always love him more than he loved her. She would always care for Ross, always worry about him, but he had cut the last tie that bound, and his adult life would begin, and hers would, too.

Now an announcement over a loudspeaker broke into her thoughts. They were arriving in Nantucket. Drivers needed to go to the car deck and get into their vehicles.

Heather joined the group filing down the stairs onto the wide car deck. She found her old Volvo, settled in, and waited as the ferry docked and the ramp was dropped, like a drawbridge to a castle in a fairy tale.

But this was no fairy tale, this was her real life.

Heather drove off the car ferry, down lower Orange to the rotary, and along Milestone Road to an anonymous dirt road she'd marked on an earlier trip by tying a blue ribbon to a tree branch. She parked her car near the entrance between the unkempt hedges, took her key from her shoulder bag, walked up the slate path, and stood for a moment at the front door.

Her front door.

After the humming and honking of travel, it seemed remarkably quiet in this small space on the island. She turned the key, and there the cottage was, plain and simple.

"Hello, new life," Heather said.

She brought in boxes of groceries and filled the refrigerator with anything perishable. She'd opened all the windows to let fresh air in, glad to see all the window screens were intact.

And now she was standing outside the house she would live in for the next three months.

What could she do to make it her own?

She went inside to unpack. Summer clothes, a snuggly terry-cloth robe, bathroom essentials, scented candles, and books, only a few, because of their weight. She set framed photos of herself with Ross, and one of Ross in his graduation robe on top of the bureau.

But she didn't want to think about Ross. She wanted to dive right into the glorious new world of her new life. She didn't have to set her time schedule to anyone else's. She could have breakfast at noon and read a good book until late into the night. When had she ever had such freedom? Returning to the living room, she tossed a multicolored light blanket from Johnny Was over the sofa. She set scented, colorful, fat candles on the mantel. She piled a stack of books on the side table. She wheeled the electric radiator from the fireplace out of the room and hid it behind the refrigerator. She swept out the hearth and dusted all the flat surfaces of the room.

But it remained dim at the far end of the living room because much of the window was darkened by ivy. Well, she'd fix that now! Years ago, she'd bought her own tool kit from a catalog. It contained everything she needed—hammer, pliers, screwdrivers, wrench—and no workman coming to the house to repair a window or doorframe ever took her tools, because the handles were all pink. Wall had been furious with her. He had a fully furnished tool kit in the garage. He ran a hardware store, for God's sake. So, Heather hid it under a bureau and used it secretly when necessary. It was light, simple, essential. No lugging fifty pounds of Wall's tools around.

Her kit included scissors, and she went out the front door with them to set to work.

It was the ivy, the persistent ivy growing from the ground up to the roof, that darkened the window. She considered pulling up the roots, but hesitated. What if the owner liked the ivy? Everyone had to have light. He'd probably be grateful. She attacked the relentless plant.

It was difficult. She cut just below the window and tried to yank the vines that hung down away from the wood and glass. But the ivy was tough. Her scissors weren't up to the task. She needed some garden shears.

And some lunch. And a library card. And a long spell of sitting by the ocean.

She was on no one else's time clock here, for the first time in years.

She quickly showered, pulled on a sundress and sandals, found the woven straw bag she'd used for endless summers, and set out to drive into town. It was almost three o'clock in the afternoon. She felt giddy with the strangeness of it all. She'd made lists, but right now she didn't care about efficiency, although she did stop at Marine Home Center to buy a pair of clippers and some gardening gloves.

On Main Street, she lucked out and found a two-hour parking spot in front of Murray's Beverage. The library was in the next block. She walked over, went up the steps, into the building, and felt at home at once. Books and people reading books everywhere. She got a visitor's library card and browsed the fiction section, as happy as a child in a candy store. She stopped in at Murray's and bought some wine. She went to the Harborside Stop & Shop and bought cheese, smoked salmon, crackers.

After gazing at the busy harbor, she drove back to her house. Now she was getting used to the route she took, and she realized how on the island, compared to the real world, nothing was very far from anywhere else. But all the roads were busy, with UPS trucks, convertibles, dump trucks, and SUVs. When she turned off onto her narrow dirt road and parked in front of her small house, she sat for a moment, appreciating the silence.

She kicked her sandals off at the front door and in bare feet carried in her bundles of wine and books. The living room was pleasantly dim and cool after the bright heat of the day. She filled a large glass with water and ice cubes—the water on Nantucket was the best she'd ever tasted—and settled in on the couch to assess her books to find the perfect one for right now.

She was happy.

———

She woke in the morning to find that she'd fallen asleep on the couch. Her book was on top of her chest, and she'd pulled the quilt down around her with only her feet showing. She studied them. She needed nail polish.

She was a morning person, surprised to find it was almost nine o'clock. She made coffee and drank it while she showered and dressed. She'd heard of the delicious morning bun made at the Wicked Island Bakery, so she shouldered her woven summer bag and headed out to the car. She found the bakery easily, just off Orange Street in a small mall. She waited in a queue of mostly young men wearing carpenter's belts and scalloper's caps embossed with the names of various beers. They wore heavy work boots, and the sight of these young men with their rumbling voices, dusty jeans, made Heather think of Ross.

Her boy. She remembered the time he'd first held a small wooden mallet, pounding colored pegs into a wooden bench. Wall had been on the floor with him, praising his skill. In school, Ross had hated English and reading and made bad grades, but was a whiz with math. He attained his height early, shooting up to six one at thirteen, and he'd entered puberty that year, too. Gravelly voice, hairy legs, the swim team, girlfriends. Wall had given him The Talk soon after, while Ross rolled his eyes, because he already knew all that. Heather had bought several packets of condoms when he was fifteen. She'd put them in his top bureau drawer without mentioning them to him. He never asked her about them. But a year later, they were gone.

He was a man now. She missed him. He was working for another man and living in that man's house. With a sudden surge of curiosity, Heather started the car and drove toward Pleasant Street. Ross had given her the address of Kailee's home, where he would be sleeping in the apartment over the garage. She added the address into her GPS and followed the directions. It wasn't a long drive to Pleasant Street. This was such a small island.

When Heather saw 66 Pleasant Street, she almost ran into a tree. She knew the Essexes were wealthy, but this? This house was a beautiful old mansion, where a governor or senator would live. Brick walls, shining white trim, gables on the third floor, a widow's walk on the roof, and the entire backyard hidden by well-established arborvitae hedges. In the double drive, a Mercedes SUV sat next to a Jeep soft-top. Ross's pickup truck wasn't there. Of course not, he was at work.

A car passed by.

She didn't want to be caught parking in front of the Essexes' house. She drove away, making wrong turns onto one-way streets that led her into a maze of avenues. The houses were so different from the magnificent gingerbread Victorian she'd lived in in Concord. Here, the gray-shingled houses looked the same, although window boxes filled with flowers and gates into secret gardens suggested interesting lives within.

She entered "Milestone Road" into her GPS. Once she got there, she could find her rutted dirt path and her rented house.

Back in her own tiny home, she made a large pitcher of iced tea. She poured herself a glass, pulled her new (cute!) flowered gardening gloves over her hands, and set out with her clippers to remove the ivy that darkened the window. It was hard work. The ivy was tough, clinging to the wood of the house so that she had to pull with all her might once she'd cut the vine. She stopped after an hour to drink a glass of iced tea while she sought advice about ivy on her iPhone. Ivy grew up from the ground, and the final step in eradicating it was to spray it with herbicide. There had to be another way. She was aware that the waters in and around Nantucket were affected by the toxins in weed killers. She read more and discovered that vinegar would work. Maybe tomorrow she'd go buy vinegar. For now, she was heartened by the light shining through the window. The very dusty, dirty window. She went back outdoors.

Walking to the front of the chaotic front yard, she put her hands on her hips and surveyed her work. Runners from the vine still rambled sideways above the window, too high for her to reach without a ladder. But the window was clear. She found a bucket under the kitchen sink, filled it with soapy hot water, and returned outside. She scrubbed and rinsed over and over again, until her body ached.

She tossed the rinse water out of the bucket and over a patch of what could be flowers. She stepped into the house.

And laughed.

The living room was bright, so welcoming! The early summer light filled the room, highlighting the quilt over the couch with its patchwork of colors. Six fat scented candles, each a different color, brought a sense of energy to the room, and the piles of books she had on the side table tempted her to the couch.

Now this looked like a place where someone interesting lived. Maybe someone slightly . . . bohemian? Artsy? At the least, unusual.

She wanted a rug on the hardwood floor. She wanted pictures on the wall, and a mirror to reflect back the light from the window. A coffee table covered with art books. Maybe a dog.

A dog? What was she thinking? Her husband was allergic to dogs. She'd always wanted one, but she couldn't have one here, because she'd be leaving in three months.

For now, she made herself a bowl of popcorn and settled on the sofa with a mystery novel.

That night, in her unfamiliar soft bed, she had trouble sleeping. She took two Tylenol but her body still ached all over from her determined attack on the ivy. Her mind flashed with images of Wall, their bedroom, their life together. She heard rustling in the bushes. Deer, she told herself. Rabbits. When something skittered against the outside wall, she sat up in bed, her heart pounding.

All right. Enough. She would not start her new life being afraid of the dark.

Heather put her feet on the floor, slid them into her flip-flops, and went through the cottage without turning on the lights. She opened the kitchen door and stepped out onto the patio.

It was quiet. Clouds floated over the moon, casting light and shadows. She sat in a patio chair and watched and listened. A breeze whispered through the leaves in the forest. It was very late, she was very tired, and now she felt safe. At home.

She returned to bed and fell asleep at once.

She woke at six in the morning. She sat on her petite patio with a cup of coffee and watched the sun burn away the mist. What was she doing here when she could be at a beach? She filled her tote with sunscreen, water bottle, and beach towel, and headed for Surfside.

Some people were already there, having health swims or playing with toddlers in the waves. Heather dropped her tote and walked to the east, where the land eventually curved. The air was pure and sweet, and blue streamed into purple into turquoise as the ocean slowly rose and fell to the sand. Gulls flew overhead. In the distance, tiny, funny birds with long orange beaks pecked at the edge of the waves. She felt that she was at the beginning of the world.

Certainly, she was at the beginning of her new life. She walked along the beach, stepping in and out of the cold waves, bending to gather shells and pebbles, loving the sun on her shoulders. She returned to her cottage, knowing she'd done the right thing.

She made herself another cup of coffee and forced herself to think practically. Then she phoned her husband.

"I want to sell the house," she said.

Wall replied immediately. "Fine."

"I'll call Jim Cooper," she said. Jim had a real estate agency and he was a good man.

"Fine," Wall said. "Take care of it. I'm busy."

For almost a week, Heather kept solitude and silence within her. Sometimes she woke at six. One night she read a book until one in the morning and slept until nine. One day, she made her own bread and ate a lot of it hot from the oven, slathered with butter, accompanying it with a slightly expensive Chardonnay. Every morning she drove to a beach and walked along the water's edge. Sometimes she walked around town, viewing the amazing gardens. For three days in a row, she ate all her meals out. Nothing expensive, mostly enormous breakfasts from the Downyflake and sandwiches from food trucks eaten on the beach, but when she got home, no dishes!

One day, Christine called her to ask how she liked it in the cottage. They talked for an hour, sometimes laughing so hard Heather's stomach hurt. When they said goodbye, Heather realized she didn't have to be a complete hermit. She wanted to have friends on the island, friends to laugh with. She'd never been one to hang out in bars. She'd research events at the library and attend some of those. She'd find a way.

Sunday morning, she showered and dressed and went to St. Paul's Church. She liked the medieval feeling of the stone building and especially the Tiffany windows. She enjoyed the choir and the minister's sermon, and the special quiet when people prayed together. She stayed for coffee hour where she met several amiable women who invited her to join their bridge club or their birding group. She accepted the bridge invitation. The birders gathered before dawn, and Heather wasn't ready for that quite yet. A tall, red-haired woman Heather's age, Miribelle Hunter, invited her to help sort book donations for the church fair. Heather accepted quickly.

When she arrived home after church, she saw how weedy and overgrown the lawn looked. She really had to do something about it. She could rent a lawn mower, if there was a place here that rented lawn mowers, and do it herself, but she decided it was time to let Ross know she was on the island. She texted him and asked him if he could come help her with her small lawn.

four

Kailee's father had an office in their Pleasant Street house, a large room with a massive mahogany desk, leather chairs, and a long work table covered with files and rolled-up architectural plans. When she was a child, her father let her play quietly in the corner of the room while he worked. She had felt so special then, allowed in his inner sanctum. In the past few years, she seldom went into the room. Her father wasn't often there, always busy on a site.

Tuesday morning, the first workday for Kailee and Ross, they entered Bob Essex's study, trying not to look at each other with coded joy: *Our real lives are beginning.*

Bob Essex was already behind his desk. "Sit down. We won't be here long. Ross, you'll follow me in your truck out to our work site in Tom Nevers. Kailee, you're going to work with George most of the time, but I want you to give a day to your mother. Help her with her new organization. And don't think what she does is not important. We're getting a lot of flak from environmentalists and we're not the only ones."

"But my place is in the business office," Kailee insisted.

"Absolutely. George is waiting for you. Now, Ross. At the moment, we've got two new houses in progress and we're renovating an older house over on Orange Street. You shadow me today, Ross. I want you to see why we prefer building new to restoring old. Some houses were built two hundred years ago, and their plumbing is ancient. The last old house we worked on, we took away the clapboard to find brick, and behind brick, clapboard. With historic houses, we've got the owners wringing their hands and stressing that we'll destroy the integrity of the house, and meanwhile, the walls are crumbling around them. Anyway"—Bob slapped his hands on his desk and stood up—"let's get going."

Kailee watched her father and the man she loved leaving the house. Ross looked over his shoulder as he went out the door and winked at Kailee. She winked back.

Kailee went into her mother's conservatory. "Good morning, Mom. I'm going over to work with George now."

Evelyn was writing a note by hand. She didn't look up when she said, "Good morning, darling. How's Ross settling in?"

"Really well, I think. He likes the apartment, even though it's so small. He's shadowing Dad today."

"Remind him he's invited to join us for dinner every night," Evelyn said. "Also, he can help himself to anything from the kitchen. Especially any fruits or veggies. Men think a cheeseburger is a vegetable if it has ketchup on it."

They laughed together.

"I told Ross he shouldn't feel like we're living together. When he comes home from work, he might want to kick back with a pizza and a beer. And I want to see my old friends."

"Sensible arrangement," Evelyn said.

Yes, Kailee thought, *and some nights I can slip out of the house and pay him a visit.*

"I'm leaving for work now," Kailee said happily.

Her mother, focused on her own work, waved in answer.

It didn't take long to drive to the office. George March's sleek black BMW convertible was parked in the drive. George and his husband, Gary, loved life's luxuries. Their home had been decorated by Marina White, in a symphony of blue and white. Gary was a bartender at Horizon, a high-end bar famous for its cocktails. George was only forty, but already going bald, which made him feel tragic even though Gary, with his thick blond hair, said he didn't care. Kailee had always loved George. She'd known him since childhood. Years ago, he gave her candy when she visited him. She wondered how he'd feel about her working with him now.

Kailee went up the steps, opened the door, and entered the office, which looked like a real workplace, not like her mother's frilly green sanctuary.

"Darling!" George rose from his desk and came around to hug Kailee. "Quel happiness! You're working with me! How are you? Tell me *everything*."

He was so dear, so familiar and kind, that Kailee *wanted* to tell him *everything,* but she held back.

"I'm so excited to be working with you," Kailee said. "I don't want to bother you, though, or get in your way."

"Oh, please, God, get in my way," George said. "Here." He ushered Kailee into a brand-new executive chair just like his own.

Kailee sank into the comfortable cushioned leather. "How do you get any work done?" she said.

"Darling, because I'm like you. I love playing with numbers. Remember when you were a little girl and I gave you a ledger with math problems and you worked on them for hours?"

"How could I forget?" Her computer waited on a mahogany desk, which was next to a set of metal file cabinets. "What shall I do first?"

George's voice was affectionate when he said, "Let's look at the specifics. Go on, wake up the computer. The password is Kailee."

"Really?" Kailee's voice squeaked a bit with emotion.

George said, "Kailee, I've been waiting for you for years."

For the next few hours, George led Kailee through the labyrinth of the company's financial workings. Crew salaries, pensions, sick leave, vacation leave. Health insurance for the staff. Invoices for materials. Payments for goods. Jobs under way. Jobs finished. George showed her the safe where they kept cash and the three credit cards they used for ordering small goods. The combination of the safe was in the numbers of Kailee's birth date. Kailee had never felt so at home.

Sunday, Kailee and Ross took a picnic lunch to 'Sconset beach, walking far down to the east to get away from other people. They swam, ate lunch, and slathered each other with sunscreen, then lay down side by side on their extra-large striped towels.

"How's it going for you?" Kailee asked.

"Good. It's good. I like construction. Dean's a great foreman. I think he's happy with my work."

"Mmm, I'm glad." Kailee turned onto her front and lay with her face away from his, her big floppy hat over her face. "How many times has your mom called you?"

"None, actually." Ross sounded like he was about to fall asleep.

"She must have texted."

"Once. Only once."

Kailee lifted her head. "You're kidding! I thought the two of you were close. When we met, I got the definite feeling that she thought I was taking you away from her."

"Hey, look who's working for and living with her parents, and planning to work for them all her entire life. Live with them, too, probably."

Kailee took a deep breath. Why had she even mentioned his mother? She was in an odd mood. She'd missed a period; that was probably why she was edgy. She'd missed her period several times before, like when she left the island for college. She didn't want to fight during their time at the beach. "That's different," she said calmly.

"Different how?" Ross asked.

"Okay, well, first of all, you and I will have our own house, eventually. And Essex Construction is a large, successful business. Someday we will be in charge of it. So, you're already in our family, too."

"I guess." Ross turned on his front, looking away from Kailee. "But I still want to be in touch with my parents."

"I never said I didn't want you to be in touch with them! I wish I hadn't brought it up. I only asked if you've heard from her."

"Well, no, I haven't."

They were quiet for a while, calming down.

Kailee asked, "But do you worry about your mom?"

Ross laughed and turned on his side to face Kailee. "Shut up."

"You shut up," Kailee said, turning to face him.

They moved toward each other, kissing.

"Ever done it in the ocean?" Ross asked.

"Oooh, you naughty boy," Kailee teased.

They got up and ran toward the water.

How things had changed. Seeing old friends was like being hit with a water balloon. Here were the girls Kailee had gone through high school with, giggling about boys, weeping over a breakup, complaining about parents, teachers, dreaming of going to Paris, Hawaii, Rome. The memories they'd made! The intensity of their conversations! The stripes in their hair!

Some of her friends hadn't left the island to go to college. Maggie had married her high school boyfriend, and they already had two children. Their house was a small rental cottage far out at Madaket. Caleb, her husband, was an electrician, and making a pile of money wiring new houses for the mega-millionaires, so soon they'd be able to buy a real house. Until then, they made do in a one-bedroom summer place with electric heaters in the winter. It helped that both parents invited the family to stay for a week during the coldest part of winter and babysat every chance they could get.

Kailee had been to Maggie's home once, to see the new baby. This time, she tripped on a toy before she could manage to hug Maggie, who had another baby in her arms and smelled of milk and baby poop and unwashed hair. There was no coffee table because her oldest was learning to walk, and could be injured on the edge. Maggie dragged out a metal folding chair from behind the thrift-shop sofa and handed it to Kailee.

"Someday, all this could be yours!" Maggie joked, collapsing on the sofa. Her baby was gnawing on her shoulder, grunting and whimpering and filling her diaper.

"She's teething," Maggie told Kailee. "I've got various baby liquids on all my clothes."

Eric, her son, was sitting on the floor with cardboard boxes, hitting them with a toy hammer.

"Almost ready for Essex Construction," Kailee said, and they both laughed.

"I know how this looks to you, Kailee," Maggie said, "but I've never been happier. It would be different if our parents weren't such troupers about helping out. But these babies—sometimes Caleb and I are raving lunatics and sometimes we stare at our babies as if we were in church. Caleb wants to start Eric on baseball and I'm dreaming of Wendy taking ballet."

"They're beautiful," Kailee said.

"How are *you?*" Maggie asked. "I've heard you're back on the island to stay."

"Yes, I'm back working for my father, and Ross is, too. He's living with us, in the apartment over our garage."

"That sounds convenient." Maggie lifted her T-shirt and lowered the baby to her bosom. "I've got nipples of steel," she said, wincing as the baby latched on.

Kailee gazed at the pink fat baby. "I want one of those."

"I can tell you how to get one," Maggie joked.

They both laughed. So many of their high school years had been filled with discussions about how to *not* get pregnant.

Kailee reached into the backpack she'd lugged in with her, and brought out two bottles of cranberry-lime-infused sparkling water. She opened one and handed it to Maggie.

"Damn, girl, you know what to do! Are you pregnant already?" Maggie tilted her head back as she chugged.

"No," Kailee said. "I don't want kids yet. Ross and I have talked about getting married, and we will, but he's got to spend time getting to know the island, deciding if he can live all his life here."

At the other end of the sofa, Eric had stopped banging with the hammer and lay on the rug, rubbing his cheek with a piece of quilt. His eyes were closing. Wendy detached from Maggie's nipple. Her head fell back on Maggie's arm, and she slept, snoring.

Kailee rose. "Nap time for you all, I think."

Maggie was heavy-lidded with exhaustion. She slid down onto the sofa with the baby cradled against the back. "I'll let the butler show you out."

"Love you," Kailee said, and very quietly went out of the house, pulling the door shut.

One night Kailee met Dan Porter at Charlie Noble for a drink. Dan had been Kailee's close friend since sixth grade. He was impossibly handsome and screamingly funny. Kailee had stood by him when he came out, and she'd assured him he was smart when he didn't get high scores on his SATs. She'd attended his wedding to Donnie and they'd texted at least once a week when she was in college. He was the host and co-owner of Donnie and Dan's bar and restaurant.

"I saw Maggie and her babies the other day," Kailee said.

"God help them," Dan said, and tossed back a shot of tequila.

Kailee slugged his shoulder. "Stop it! She's happy!"

"I know she is, and I'm glad. We get together now and then, especially in the summer, if her parents will take the kids for a few hours. Maybe you can join us someday."

"Sure. How are you?"

"Honey, I'm smokin'. Donnie, love of my life, is a genius in the kitchen and I'm good with everything else."

"You're smart. The love of my life comes with relatives," Kailee said. "Ross's mom can't let him go."

"But he's here, on-island, working for your dad, right?"

"Right."

"Don't look for trouble," Dan said. "Stay cool."

"I'll never be as cool as you are," Kailee said.

"That's true." Dan laughed wickedly. "Let's get the gang together sometime, go to the beach, drink too much, and get an Uber home."

"Sounds great," Kailee said.

Kailee convinced Ross they needed a date night. They went to Cru, where an outdoor patio was next to the wooden pier where small yachts were docked. Everyone around them was laughing and tanned. It was a perfect June evening.

Beneath wide beach umbrellas, they ordered martinis and oysters, and gazed out toward the harbor, where larger yachts from distant places were in their slips.

"So," Kailee teased Ross, "you get to spend all day out in the fresh air and I get to spend all day bending over a computer screen. How did that happen?"

"We're out in the fresh air now," Ross told her. "We're drinking martinis and slurping oysters at a waterfront bar. How did *that* happen?"

Kailee smiled and leaned back in her chair. "Maggie's invited us to dinner Saturday night," Kailee said. "You'll like her husband, Caleb. Well, you'll like Maggie, too."

Ross leaned forward. "You know how you said you have your mom's summer calendar?"

"Yeah . . ."

"I'm thinking, you could check to see when your parents are out to dinner, and you and I could invite friends for dinner at your place. The apartment over the garage doesn't have room for four people."

"That is such a good idea, Ross!"

As they ate their entrées, they idly talked about their day, did a lot of excellent people-watching, and let the sweet Nantucket air caress them into a state of careless pleasure. The sun floated lower in the sky. Kailee took off her sunglasses. She slipped her foot out of her flip-flop and ran it up Ross's leg.

"Hey," he said. "Be good."

"Oh, I will be," Kailee promised.

When they left, Ross put down his credit card. The bill was over two hundred dollars.

"Ross, let me put that on our work card," Kailee said.

Ross shook his head. "I'm eating some of my meals at your house. I'm living in your parents' apartment. I don't want to be a complete sponge."

"You're not!" Kailee objected, but let him pay.

Holding hands, they strolled up Straight Wharf and Main Street. It was early summer, and the air was gentle with a sense of freshness, almost celebration. Shop doors were flung open, window boxes were colorful with spring flowers. The windows were luscious with intricate gold watches, swirling dresses, diamond necklaces, and the latest enticing books.

Kailee paused by a jewelry shop.

"You're looking at engagement rings," Ross said.

"You caught me," Kailee joked, leaning against him.

Ross frowned. "We need to make a plan. Not just drift."

"Baby." Kailee took both of Ross's hands in hers and faced him. "We have a plan."

"I know." Ross put his arm around her and they ambled along toward the bookstore. "I guess I just get freaked out at taking so much from your family. Living there—"

"In the garage apartment!"

"Eating there, and working there. I don't want to take advantage. I don't want to be seen as taking advantage."

Kailee nodded. "I promise I'll tell Mom you paid for our dinner tonight."

"That's good, except it's also kind of all twisted, right? Like you and your family and the business come as a set."

"Are you feeling guilty because you're not living in Concord, working for your dad?"

Ross nodded. "Probably I am. Part of it is that I know you would never consider leaving Nantucket to live with my parents while I work in my dad's store."

Kailee nudged him playfully. "Honey, Nantucket is Nantucket, right? Different from anywhere else."

"It's wonderful here, yeah."

"That's why you can make a zillion times more money here than at your dad's shop."

"But I have to spend a zillion times more money to live here. Like, tonight, dinner for two costs over two hundred dollars? That's just insane."

Kailee took a deep breath. They had been down this road before, and she had not made any kind of ultimatum that Ross work here, live here. He'd been excited when they first talked about it, last winter when they were falling more deeply in love.

"Do you miss your parents, honey?"

"What? No. I like working construction better than being in the store with my dad all day."

"I'll bet you miss your mother."

"Actually, I don't." Ross paused, as if he had something else to say. "I mean, I love her, but I left home when I started college. I should call her or text her."

"Let's take a selfie to send her!" Kailee pulled her phone from her pocket.

"Good idea. Let me use my phone." Ross bent down so his face would be level with Kailee's.

He snapped a few shots. They decided which was the best, and Ross texted, *Hello from Nantucket!* and sent it off.

"We should go home," Ross said. "I've got to get up early for work tomorrow."

They headed down Broad Street, holding hands. It was twilight, a gentle darkness falling around them. Lights winked on in shop windows and restaurants. They were together, Kailee thought. This was the way love went. Work, arguments . . . pleasure.

Across the street at Bookworks, a woman stood gazing in the window. It was so weird—the woman looked just like Ross's mother. Kailee started to tell Ross, but stopped herself. It couldn't possibly be Ross's mother. Heather would have called if she was on the island. Plus, it would be too weird if Ross's mother came to the island, as if she missed him too much. As if she was sneakily checking up on her baby boy.

"Ross?" She tugged his arm, forcing him to stop walking.

"Why are you whispering?" he asked.

"I think that's your mother over there." She nodded her head in the woman's direction.

Ross swallowed. "Yeah, it kind of looks like her."

Kailee went cold all over. "Ross. *Is* it your mother?"

Ross sighed. "Probably."

"Probably? Do you know something I don't know? Did your mother come to the island to see you?"

Ross stalled. "Well, no."

"Well, *what?*"

Ross took her arm and steered her back down toward Federal Street and across to the town building where there were benches. They sat down. Across the street, there was a long line of people waiting to get ice cream at the Juice Bar.

"Kailee, I was waiting for the right time to tell you. Mom rented a cottage here on Nantucket."

"Oh my God! I don't believe this!" Kailee reared back from Ross as if he'd suddenly grown two heads.

"Kailee, wait. Let me explain. She rented the cottage before she knew I was going to be here all summer. It has nothing to do with us and everything to do with her divorce from Dad."

Kailee was furious. "And you're only telling me this *now?* Is this some kind of *secret* between the two of you? How long has she been here? Since the first of the month, right? That's when rentals start. Damn it, Ross, why didn't you tell me before now? Did you think you could hide it from me?"

"I was going to tell you, Kailee. I was just waiting for the right time. I'm sorry."

"God, Ross, don't you see how this makes it seem like you're closer to her than to me?" Kailee burst into tears.

Ross stammered, searching for words. "That's not how it is, Kailee. *I love you.* I want you to . . . like Mom, as much as I like your parents."

"But why didn't you tell me?"

Ross sat back, folded his arms over his chest, and stared up at the sky. "Because I thought you would freak out."

Kailee stared at Ross. She wanted to stomp off in righteous indignation, but more than that, she wanted to be with him. She'd seen her parents argue before, then make up and laugh, all within one hour. How did people learn to do that?

She had to learn how to do that.

She looked down at her hands, taking those supposedly helpful deep breaths, and thought. So, Heather had rented a cottage on the island before she knew her son was going to live here. So, okay. But Ross hadn't told her. He'd kept a secret from her. But he was afraid of upsetting her.

And here she was, upset.

She loved Ross so much. She wanted to be with him all their lives.

She put her hand gently on Ross's arm. "Ross, you were right. I did freak out. I'm sorry I'm so jealous. I hope I didn't ruin our evening."

Ross turned to Kailee. "I'm sorry I didn't tell you before now. I've only known for about a week, and we've been so busy. Look, I'm not going to spend time with my mother, I mean not a lot of time. I'm here with you. And she's here to think about her future. She didn't come here because of us."

Kailee nodded. "And there is an *us.*"

"Don't you ever doubt it," Ross said. Leaning down, he kissed her softly on the mouth.

"Let's go home," Kailee said.

five

"Look at all this!" Miribelle cried. "Can you believe it?"

Heather was with Miribelle Hunter in the basement of Gardner Hall next to St. Paul's Church on Fair Street. In the middle of the room, piled on long tables, were overflowing bags and boxes. At the far end, behind a long table, stood a dress rack, and at the other end, masses of books were piled. Another table ran down the side of the room, loaded with boxes marked MISCELLANEOUS.

"Where do you want me to start?" Heather asked.

"Sonia Ryder's coming in later to deal with the miscellaneous. You can sort the books. Hardback fiction, paperback fiction, hardback nonfiction, soft cover nonfiction. Put them spineside up and fill a box as full as you can. I'll start the clothes."

For a while, the two women worked in silence, concentrating on their sorting. Then Miribelle held up a lacy red bra and matching thong with the store tag still attached.

"Could you wear these?" she asked Heather.

"Not even when I was fifteen," Heather answered.

They both laughed, and began chatting in a sporadic, friendly way. Miribelle was a few years older than Heather, and had a retired husband who was addicted to golf, two daughters, and three grandchildren. Miribelle wore her red hair in a pixie cut, and her green eyes sparkled when she spoke about tennis. She was quick and athletic, with a wiry build, a cross between a hummingbird and a kingfisher. *I've been looking at too many bird books,* Heather thought, smiling to herself.

A loud thump broke their concentration.

"Honestly," Miribelle said. She hurried to open the door. In came a man with an upright vintage steamer trunk in his arms. "Oh, my gosh," Miribelle cried, "Mrs. Hewson finally gave in!"

She directed the man to a corner where the trunk was out of the way. "Look, Heather, it still has its stickers on it, *Wagon-Lit,* the *Venice Simplon-Orient-Express,* the SS *France.*" She opened the doors to find a tidy set of drawers and a small rod for hanging shirts.

Heather peered over Miribelle's back. "That's from a completely different age."

"You're right," the man said. "It's totally useless, and Miribelle's been coveting it for ages. I'll bet you fifty dollars she's going to buy it and not even put it in the fair."

"Stop it," Miribelle said. Turning to Heather, she said, "This is my brother, Miles. He lives like a monk."

"Not exactly a monk," Miles corrected her, grinning.

"Oh, stop. Miles, be nice. This is Heather Willette. She's on the island for the summer. She's helping me with the fair. Heather, don't believe a word he says."

"Hello, Heather." Miles shook her hand. "Are you a new summer person?"

"I am, yes." Was that really true? Heather imagined that her cottage didn't really fit in with the real *summer person* house.

"I hope you have a great summer," Miles said.

Heather froze. Was that a twinkle in his eye? It was a twinkle in his eye. Was he flirting? Or was Heather delusional?

"Stop that, Miles," Miribelle said. "Is that everything?"

"I've got a garden bench in my truck," Miles said. "Miribelle, come help me carry it in."

The Hunter siblings went off, leaving Heather alone in the room. She stood at the table of books, pretending she was concentrating on them. Really, she was trying to stabilize herself, like someone who just parachuted from a plane. When Miles Hunter had walked into the room, the sight of him had made Heather's heart thump, and when he spoke, his voice had made her weak at the knees. He looked like his sister, red-haired, wiry, energetic, and tall, wide-shouldered, with a kind of playful charm, like a red setter always ready to jump a fence and run.

"All right," Heather whispered to herself. "Calm down. You're still married. Try a bit of self-control."

When Miribelle and her brother returned, Heather was using a felt marker to write MYSTERIES on the side of a box.

"Let me carry that for you," Miles offered. "We always stack books in the corner."

"Oh, thanks." Heather moved down to another box and wrote COOKBOOKS on all sides while Miles closed the box, swiftly tucking the flaps beneath one another. For a moment, as his arm brushed her, she forgot how to spell COOKBOOKS.

She forced herself to concentrate. She began to cull through the books and separate out the travel books.

"Can I help?" Miles asked, and without waiting for her to answer, he taped the bottom of a box firmly, turned it over, and took the books Heather handed him.

Honestly, Heather thought, *this man gives off some kind of animal aroma, like the spoor of a horse.* Did horses give off spoors? She thought "spoor" applied only to wild animals. Was Miles a wild animal?

She needed to sit down.

"What's this pile of books over here?" Miles asked.

Heather blushed. "Oh, Miribelle said I could take books home to read and bring them back in time for the fair. We've got six weeks."

Miles lifted each book carefully, studying the cover. "You like mysteries," Miles said. "Wow, and science, too. I read *Underland*. Robert Macfarlane is a brilliant writer."

"Good to know," Heather said, glad she could even speak. "What do you like to read?" She didn't look at him as she spoke, but continued sorting the books.

"Thrillers. Jack Reacher. Well, he's the character in Lee Child's books—"

"Oh, I know! Isn't Alan Ritchson perfect for the television role? He's so big and muscular—" Heather stopped. Trying to be always politically correct was such an effort these days. What if Miles had said that Scarlett Johansson had the perfect figure for the skin-tight suit in *Black Widow?*

"I agree completely. Tom Cruise wasn't right for the part," Miles said.

"Okay!" Miribelle came to the book table, dusting her hands as she walked. "Time for lunch. You've accomplished a lot, Heather. Thanks."

"It was fun." Heather picked up her stash of five books. "I hope it rains tomorrow."

"Want to join us for lunch?" Miles asked.

Before Heather could respond, Miribelle slugged his arm. "Not today, Miles. We're meeting the Eastons at the club." She turned to Heather. "Another time."

"Sure." Heather smiled as she slid her tote over her shoulder and walked to the door. "Bye." She waved and left the room, wondering if she was more relieved or disappointed not to be able to join Miribelle and Miles for lunch.

"I think it's really odd," Kailee said. She was trying to keep her voice down even though they were in the apartment over the garage and she didn't want to fight. Although, they were fighting. Now, Heather had texted Ross and asked him to mow her lawn.

"Odd?" Ross shook his head. "What's odd about it? Mom asked me to bring out a mower and mow her yard." Ross had taken off his work boots and was putting on his sneakers.

"*Her* yard?" Kailee threw her hands up in the air. "How do you not see that your mother followed you here? She's living here so she can be near her baby boy."

Ross sighed. "Don't be crazy. I told you she rented her place before she knew I was going to be here. She's been here for over a week and she hasn't called until now, and it's perfectly reasonable for her to call me. Who else could she call?"

"Exactly!" Kailee said. "She doesn't have friends here. She's only here because of you."

Ross tied his laces and stood up. "Kailee, please. You and I are living in your parents' home. We see them every day. Mom just wants some help with her yard. It will take an hour or so."

"She should call her landlord."

"She did. He's not picking up." Ross put his hands on Kailee's waist and pulled her to him. "Come with me."

"I'm not going to yank weeds for your mother." Kailee pulled away.

"I didn't mean that. Just come. Say hello. Be nice."

"Be nice." Kailee folded her arms over her chest. "You don't think I'm nice?"

Ross shook his head and walked away. "I'm out of here. I won't be back in time for dinner."

Kailee followed Ross as he clomped down the stairs to the driveway. He got into his truck, waved at Kailee. She forced a smile and waved back. She knew her *you don't think I'm nice* remark had been irrational. There had been times in their relationship when Ross would have responded with a grin and said, "I think you're very nice," and kissed her. But they'd moved on from the sweet passion of early love to the more difficult bog of a long-term relationship with reality.

What was she afraid of? Maybe, that with the divorce, Heather expected Ross to be his mother's emotional-support person.

Still, Ross was right. She should go out there and be nice. After all, Heather was going to be her mother-in-law and Kailee would have to deal with her all of her life. Heather's life.

If she went out and said hello, Ross would be so happy.

Kailee brushed her hair, redid her lipstick, found her car keys, and drove out to the rutted dirt road off Milestone Road.

Ross had driven his blue Chevy pickup. It was parked in front of his mother's yard. He'd taken the mower out and was standing in the door of the house, talking with his mom.

Heather was pretty, Kailee had to admit that. Not beautiful or chic like Kailee's mother, but attractive. The house Heather had rented was definitely *not* pretty. And really, the yard was a jungle.

"Kailee!" Heather waved from the door.

Ross turned and saw Kailee, and his smile was more than enough reward for her presence.

"This place is so cute!" Kailee lied.

"Come in and have some iced tea," Heather said. "We'll let Ross get to work."

Kailee's heart thumped. *You're not the boss of Ross,* she secretly argued, and immediately gave herself a mental slap for the childish thought.

"Let me give you a tour," Heather said, laughing. "It's safe to say this is not the typical Nantucket summer cottage."

"It *is* small," Kailee said, "but cozy. I love the quilt on the couch." And the scented candles on the mantel, she thought, and the vase of real flowers, probably from Stop & Shop, but still colorful. Far from posh, but not pathetic.

In the kitchen, Heather took out a pitcher and poured them each a glass of iced tea. Outside, the lawn mower roared as Ross worked.

"I think the living room will be the quietest place," Heather said, leading the way.

"Wow! You have a lot of books." Kailee sorted through them. "You have a wide range here, serious books and mysteries."

"I'm an addicted reader," Heather said, settling into an armchair. "What do you like to read?"

Kailee shrugged. "Really, I don't know. Mostly stuff for college, you know. Plus, I'm not really a reader. Unless it's spreadsheets, invoices, payroll. I work in my father's headquarters. Also, I'm helping my mother start her foundation. I'm building the website for her."

"How wonderful. Tell me about the foundation."

Kailee leaned forward. "It's the Essex Nature Foundation and it's an offshoot of our construction company to show we care about the island. It will have three parts: fundraising, volunteer fieldwork, and education." Kailee took a sip of iced tea. It was comfortable here, with windows open all over the house and fresh air filling the rooms. She slipped off her sandals and curled up on the sofa. "Do you mind?" she asked.

Heather laughed. "Of course not. That's how I often sit."

"I'm helping Mom prepare a letter to send out to about a dozen key people she wants on the board. You know, they say for people on benevolent boards, the three *W*'s are important: wealth, wisdom, and work. But really, wealth is what we need with the organization just starting out."

"I understand. I'm on the board of the Safeguard Nature Society," Heather said. "If there's anything I can do to help, let me know."

Kailee's heart stopped a moment. She forced a smile. "Thanks, I will. But you're only here for the summer, right?"

"Right. Although, it's so wonderful here." She gazed at Kailee. "Have you ever dreamed of doing anything else?"

Well, that's insulting, Kailee thought.

Heather sensed Kailee's reaction. "I mean when you were a child. Ross always wanted to drive big trucks. From the time he was three, he was obsessed with them. Then he joined the middle school swim team and practiced like a maniac and his father and I knew Ross was hoping to go to the Olympics. He was brokenhearted when his school team lost in the state competition."

"Aw, poor Ross." Kailee smiled, thinking about her lost dream. "I wanted to be a ballet dancer when I was really young. In middle school, I wanted to be an actress or a model. So did half of my friends."

"You would be a fabulous model," Heather said.

"Thanks. But somewhere along the way, I realized I wanted to stay on Nantucket. I really love it here."

"I get that. In the few days I've lived on the island, my perspective on the world has completely changed."

Kailee's heart sank. "You mean you want to live here permanently?"

"Oh, I'd never be able to afford it. But I'd like to be near the ocean, nearer to nature."

"Maybe on the Cape?"

"Maybe."

"Mom." Ross came into the house. "Come see what I've done." His face was red and his T-shirt damp with sweat.

"Wow, you're fast," Heather said. "Want an iced tea, darling?"

"I'd rather have a beer, but not yet. Come out."

Both women went into the yard. Ross had used a lawn mower with a bagger. He'd dumped several loads of shorn grass and weeds inside the surrounding forest.

"It looks wonderful!" Heather said.

"I'm going to install an outdoor light that comes on when anyone walks into the yard," Ross said.

"Is that really necessary?" Kailee asked.

"It is. The owner should have done it. I don't like the idea of Mom out here alone. In fact," Ross continued, "I think I'll stay in the second bedroom every couple of nights. It would be a good thing for my pickup to be parked in front of this place."

I hate you, Kailee thought. *I hate both of you.*

"That's so kind, Ross," Heather replied. "I'll go get you a beer."

Ross put his arm around Kailee's waist and pulled her close. "Thanks for coming out. I'm glad you're here."

"Anything for you, kid," Kailee said.

Heather returned with a bottle in her hand. "It's Heineken. Is that okay?"

"Great. Thanks." Ross tipped the bottle back and took a long drink.

"Let me show you my plans," Heather said. "I think I'll plant some hydrangeas next to the house. Already full grown and ready to bloom. I can buy them here on the island. I'll pick up some grass seed and sprinkle it around the yard and pray for rain. Lots of petunias around the border of the yard—"

Kailee interrupted. "You're renting this place, you know. Why would you spend your money improving another man's property?"

Heather laughed. "Because I love flowers. I love color and I'll have three months of color. And most of what I'll plant will be annuals, so they won't be here next summer. They're only for me."

"You know," Ross said, fondly teasing, "we've got these things called beaches. People lie in the sun there. They go swimming. They do things like collect shells—"

"Sweetie, I do know that. I drive out to Surfside or 'Sconset every morning and walk on the beach for an hour or so."

"Cool," Kailee said. Her phone vibrated in her pocket. "Ross, we've got to get home. Dad's grilling steaks tonight."

"Great! Want to join us, Mom?"

"No, thanks," Heather said. "My new mystery is calling my name." She smiled at Kailee. "It was lovely getting to know you better. We'll have dinner out here sometime. And, Ross"— she turned to hug her son—"thanks so much for the yard work. I won't have to have tick inspection every time I walk from the car."

Kailee followed Ross's truck back to her house. She was relieved Heather hadn't jumped at the chance to join them for dinner. In fact, Heather seemed to be comfortable with her life in the cottage. Maybe she *hadn't* come to the island to shadow her son.

Maybe Kailee had gotten Heather all wrong. Or partly wrong. Kailee was *not* happy about Ross spending the night at his mom's house. It was as if Kailee and Heather were choosing sides in a game, and Ross was the prize.

Well, Ross belonged to her. Kailee decided to push for an early wedding date.

six

One afternoon, Heather joined a tour with the Nantucket Conservation Foundation. They walked from Sanford Farm down to the Ocean Walk and up through Ram Pasture. It was a six-mile walk, with a variety of landscapes, and several other people were on the tour. Heather returned to her cottage happy, full of new information, suntanned, and exhausted. She showered, slipped into a caftan, and poured herself a glass of wine.

"Aaaah," she said, settling onto the sofa. Her legs ached pleasantly from all the walking.

A knock came at the door, and before she could open it, Ross came in.

"Hi, Mom!" Ross carried two brown paper bags. "I brought us fish and chips from Sayle's for dinner."

"Oh, wow!"

Ross set the bags on the coffee table. "I thought I'd stay out here with you tonight. I don't want you to feel ignored."

"Darling, I'm fine alone. I came to the island knowing I'd be mostly alone."

"Yeah," Ross replied, his voice muffled from the refrigerator door as he reached in for a bottle of beer. "Still."

He took a sip of beer, then found silverware and napkins for them.

Heather reached out to stop him from opening the bags of food. "Ross, wait. I want you to know you don't need to worry about me."

"I'm not worried. Just . . . concerned."

Heather smiled. "Well, don't be. But I do love Sayle's fish and chips."

For a few minutes, Heather and Ross tore open the bags, allowing the steamy delicious smell of batter-fried cod to drift into the room. There was clam chowder, and a small tub of coleslaw, and the most delicious French fries she'd ever eaten.

"This fish tastes amazing," Heather said.

"Probably caught today," Ross told her.

Heather rose, poured herself another glass of wine, and brought Ross another beer. When they were through eating, they licked their fingers, satisfied.

"We ate like a pair of starving dogs," Heather said. "Let's sit out on the patio. It's nice at this time of evening."

"Sure." Ross rose and followed her out.

Heather closed her eyes for a moment, listening to the evening songs of the birds, inhaling the sweet scents carried on a sea breeze.

Her son interrupted her reverie. "Mom, you're so alone out here."

Heather opened her eyes and smiled. "Well, Ross, I'm learning that alone is not a bad way to be. I *like* being alone, making my own schedule, going where I choose, reading or walking on the beach."

"But—"

Heather interrupted. "I also see people. I have friends, or possible friends. I've joined a bridge club that meets Wednesday nights. I go to church, and I've been helping Miribelle Hunter sort items for the church fair. I went on a long tour with the Nature Conservation Foundation today. We walked over six miles. I'm exhausted, but it was amazing, all that I saw and learned." The sky was a deep shining blue. *Sometimes,* Heather wanted to say to Ross, *sometimes this moment is enough.*

Instead, she asked her son, "How about you? How do you like it here?"

"I'm great! I like working for Essex Construction, and well, being with Kailee."

"This might be early to ask, but are you sure you want to live your entire life on this island? It's beautiful, at least in the summer, but everything here is so expensive. How will you ever afford to buy a house? And are you sure you want to work all your life for your father-in-law? I get it that gradually you'll move up the ladder from pounding nails to management but are you sure you want to make that your life's work? You have a degree in business management. You could go anywhere."

Ross put his hands on top of his head, a habit he had when he was troubled. He blurted, "Kailee thinks you don't like her."

Heather took a moment to consider her words. "I don't know Kailee, really. Actually, I haven't spent enough time with her to know whether I like her or not, but the important thing is, you love Kailee and she makes you happy and that makes me happy."

"Mom. I do love Kailee. I do want to live my entire life on the island. I'm learning a lot by working for Mr. Essex, and I like him. The only thing that's difficult is I feel funny living in his apartment over the garage. I mean, I'm not paying rent, he won't take it, but I don't want to be a leech. Plus, a lot of evenings, they want me to join them for dinner, to have a real meal, and it's nice, but kind of formal. I want to be with Kailee but not her parents."

Heather smiled. "I have an engagement in town tomorrow evening. Why don't you ask Kailee to pick up some nachos or whatever and come over here. You could do whatever you want. I'm sure I won't be home until after ten."

Ross's face lit up. "Really?"

"Really."

Ross took his phone from his pocket. "I'll call her now."

Heather checked her phone to find out what movie was playing at the Dreamland tomorrow night.

Heather had never gone to a bar by herself in her life, and she wasn't going to start now. She spent the hour before the movie strolling around the town, admiring the windows of all the stores and fantasizing about working in one of them and living on the island. She bought a large bag of popcorn and a Diet Coke for the movie, and sat in the back, with no other person around her, and enjoyed munching away while she watched *Spider-Man: No Way Home*. It was exhilarating. Why had she never seen a Spider-Man movie before? Probably because Wall thought they were mind-trash. But she wasn't with Wall now.

It was dark when she left the theater, but the streets were full of light and life. Couples holding hands, families with babies in baby carriers, friends patiently waiting by a bush as their dogs "read the newspaper."

She bought an ice cream cone at Jack and Charlie's and sat on a bench at the harbor, people-watching, and feeling slightly foolish because she'd had popcorn and ice cream for dinner. The benches were set on a walkway between two wharves, and along the wooden wharves, clever boutiques were humming with business. For a moment, she was self-conscious, a woman sitting without a husband or friend, but many single people hurried past, as well as couples and families, and a few women smiled at her, rolling their eyes toward the unruly group of children and dogs, clearly envious of her chance to sit by herself enjoying the evening.

And then someone she knew came along.

Miles Hunter walked down the walkway, a beautiful young woman at his side. Her hand clutched his arm possessively.

Oh, dear heaven, Heather thought. These men and their young women! She was all at once furious, and she didn't want to be caught noticing the couple, so she dug around in her shoulder bag, as if she'd lost something.

"Heather!"

Miles stopped in front of her. He was wearing a navy blazer and tie, so obviously he'd just taken his girlfriend out to dinner. Heather wanted to throw her ice cream at him, just because.

Smiling, she said, "Hello, Miles. Lovely evening, isn't it?"

"It is." Miles put his arm around the young woman's shoulders, and Heather realized that even though she was tall, the girl was only around sixteen. "Heather, I'd like you to meet my daughter, Emma Hunter. Emma, this is Heather Willette, a new friend who's been helping us with the book sorting for the church."

"Emma, how nice to meet you," Heather said, thinking: *You have no idea how much I mean that.*

"Hi," Emma said. "I love your name. It's like a little song. Heatherwillette!"

Miles smiled fondly at his daughter. "Emma is a musician. She plays guitar. She's got a voice like an angel. She's in her first year at the Berklee School of Music in Boston."

"Dad," Emma said, teasing, "why don't you tell her my height and weight, too?"

Miles squeezed his daughter's shoulder. "I'll save that for later," he said, grinning back. "Emma's going to sing a solo tomorrow morning in church. You should come hear her."

"I'll be there," Heather promised.

"What are you doing for the Fourth?" Miles asked.

Puzzled, and slightly overwhelmed, Heather asked, "The Fourth?"

"The Fourth of July," Miles answered. "We take the boat out into the harbor to watch the fireworks. Drinks and picnic dinner are provided."

"That sounds exciting," Heather said. "I hadn't realized the Fourth was so near."

"Join us," Miles said.

"Yes, please!" Emma begged. "It's the best!"

"All right," Heather agreed. "It sounds wonderful. Where shall I meet you?"

They discussed times and what launch to take and Heather's ice cream melted all down her hand.

Miles and his daughter strolled away. Heather sat smiling, watching the lights blink on in the shops as the sky slowly changed from blue to indigo. She wrapped what was left of her cone, dropped it in a wooden trash barrel, and cleaned her sticky hands with a Handi Wipe she'd stashed in her bag. She remembered all the days she'd carried wipes and tissues when Ross was little. It had become a habit to have a small packet in her shoulder bag, along with her keys and phone.

When Ross was a child, Heather had no doubts about who she was and what she was for in the world. She was Wall's wife and Ross's mother. Over the years, she'd volunteered at several local organizations, and then for Safeguard Nature. But in the past few years, she had chafed at the cocoon of her life. She had only one life, and she knew she was meant to be more, do more. She'd tried to discuss this with Wall, but it made him impatient and angry. She had everything a woman could want, her husband had argued. What more did she want?

She walked up and down the wharves, stopping to study the T-shirts, bright scarves, and wooden boats while letting her mind roam. She remembered a post she'd read online, a clever appendage to a common adage: *When one door closes, another door opens.* Someone had added: *True, but it's scary waiting in the hall.*

That was where she was, Heather decided. She was living in that in-between space, waiting for a door to open.

Maybe, she thought, she'd have to build a door herself. She could do that. She had a tool kit.

Such frivolous thinking! It was odd where her mind took her when she let it roam free. She checked her watch. It was almost eleven. She could go home.

The night was dark and the headlights of passing cars flashed like comets whizzing by as she made the now-familiar drive back to her cottage. Ross had left on the outdoor light.

As she went up the slate path, she had a sense of being in her own little kingdom, with the forest around her friendly now, like guardians.

The living room and kitchen were tidy.

Ross had left a note: *Thanks, Mom. Hope you had fun in town.*

She spotted a plate of oatmeal-raisin cookies holding down a note.

Thanks, Mrs. Willette. I thought you might like these cookies I made today. XO K

Heather smiled. What a nice gesture! She'd eat them for breakfast tomorrow, before she went to church.

When she woke the next morning, the sky was cloudy. She filled her water bottle and headed out to Surfside for a beach walk, certain that as she walked, the sun would slant through the clouds until the sky was blue, as it usually did in the early mornings. No one else was on the beach, and for a moment, Heather gazed out at the water, feeling like the only human on the planet, which was actually a bit unsettling. She strolled along the edge of the waves, smiling when another woman came to the beach with her dog. They didn't know each other, and they didn't try to talk. They went in different directions. Still, Heather was glad for just this much company.

Back home, she showered, dressed, and drove into town, parking on Pine Street and walking to St. Paul's Church. The small stone building was crowded with summer visitors like her, but she found a place in a pew at the back. The Tiffany stained-glass windows in the apse shone like jewels, and the familiar rituals of standing, kneeling, singing, reading, her voice joined with others, satisfied some need deep in her heart. Emma sang "Morning Has Broken" in a clear, sweet voice that brought tears to Heather's eyes.

Afterward, Heather went to coffee hour, which was held on the

lawn on this brilliant sunny day. She chatted with the others gathered around the table of finger foods. Someone had brought
lemon cookies, and Heather was munching happily when Miles
Hunter approached.

"Did you enjoy the service?" he asked.

"I did. Emma has a beautiful voice."

"I'm glad you heard her, seated so far at the back."

A warm blush spread through Heather as she realized Miles
had noticed where she sat. "I heard every note, clear as a bell."

"I'm glad. Listen, Heather, I have a question. I hope it's okay to
ask . . . Would you be interested in a part-time job?"

Heather was curious and interested. "What kind of job?"

"A kind of receptionist, secretary, typist, proofreader job. I'm
an estate lawyer. I retired when I was divorced, came to the island,
and began a small practice. Mostly wills. My office hours are every
morning, five days a week, but sometimes, in an emergency, I'll
come in the afternoon. My secretary, Abby, left for a three-month
bike trip around Europe with her friends. She'll be back in September. I thought I could trim my schedule, but this summer I'm
busier than ever. Miribelle told me you're on the board of Safeguard Nature, so I'm sure you know how to handle a computer."

"This would be just for the summer?" Heather asked. A job!
She was surprised at how much she wanted it. Her heart flipped
up and down, as if it had joined a marching band. *You're never too
old to learn something new about yourself,* she thought.

"Yes. Unless you stay longer, of course." He cleared his throat.
"I paid Abby forty dollars an hour."

Heather realized he was trying to talk about a delicate subject—
money—but the amount he mentioned was shocking. "Forty dollars an hour? That seems extreme."

Miles laughed. "Welcome to Nantucket. Our cleaner gets thirty-
five an hour. And Heather . . . I'd like to, um, see you socially, too.
I'd like to get to know you. But I don't want you to be uncomfortable working for me. I mean, I'm not trying to hit on you."

Heather flushed. "That's fine, Miles. I understand."

"I mean, I *do* want to hit on you," Miles continued, with a slow smile. "But that's separate from honestly needing some secretarial help."

Miles wanted to hit on *her? She* wanted to hit on *him.* Heather met his gaze and held it. A job would be a good way to get to know him, and she did want to know him *well.* "I'd like to work for you, and I'm certain I won't feel compromised. Could I have a little time to think about it before I answer?"

"Sure. And, Heather . . . if you want to stop in and see the office, it's above Nantucket Pharmacy, which is too bad, because the stairs are steep and most of my clients are older. Thanks for considering it."

Miribelle crossed the grass to join them. They spoke about the service, Emma's voice, and the church fair. When the crowd thinned out, Heather slipped away to walk to her car. The June morning was almost too beautiful to believe, and she couldn't stop smiling as she drove to her cottage.

At home, she slipped off her shoes and padded barefoot out to the patio where she sat, mentally listing the pros and cons of taking the job. The pro was, of course, money, which she could use until the Concord house sold and the divorce was final. Also, she'd enjoy working. She liked seeing people. She liked having a purpose.

She liked Miles.

The cons were that she wouldn't have a free schedule and she'd lose her carefree mornings.

The pros outweighed the cons. A lot. When she started looking for a regular job, she'd have a good reference from Miles. She smiled. It would be very nice to work with Miles. She would earn her good reference.

seven

Kailee spun in front of her bedroom mirror. *Yes!* This dress was perfection. Very grown-up, almost prim, but not. Navy-blue gauze swirled over a navy-blue slip dress. Her hair was swept up into a sophisticated chignon, and she wore drop pearl earrings, which were boring, but it was her mother's party, and her mother's friends wore pearls. And liked boring. She wore four-inch beige stilettos, because she thought it gave her more gravitas.

She wanted to show that she was capable of handling authority. Growing up, Kailee was a complete girlie girl. She did shadow her father often, and when she was a young child, he taught her how to use a hammer and a Phillips head screwdriver, but she was really interested in sparkly things. She wanted frilly dresses and dolls with frilly dresses. She owned five Barbie dolls and the entire house, car, and salon.

When she was in high school, her parents sat her down and had a serious talk with her about their hopes for her life. They hoped she would eventually take over Essex Construction from her father, which would mean knowing the basics of owning a business. Kailee was already aware of the basics. Her father had taken her around the building sites and into the office all her life. When she was little, her father and his secretary or crew boss would talk while she sat quietly, playing a video game. As she grew older, she listened to the discussions, and afterward, in the truck, she'd ask her father questions about the business. She knew a lot.

But in high school, her parents told her she needed to decide what her major would be in college, and if she wanted to eventually run the company. Kailee had known this question was coming, and she felt honored and terrified. But she never thought she couldn't do it, and the more she learned, the more she liked it. She enrolled in business management at UMass Amherst, and in the summer, she shadowed George March, the CFO.

It had seemed like magic, like a gift of Fate, when Kailee met Ross in a tax law class.

Ross, whose father owned a hardware store. Ross, big, brawny, easygoing, kindhearted, and strong. Ross, who had the experience to understand and admire her father's company.

And Ross loved her. That last year in college, they were inseparable. Kailee had never known such happiness.

The only shadow in her life was a tinge of worry about her mother. Evelyn had always been energetic and passionate. But in the past few years, she'd gone into a kind of hyperdrive, donating time and money to organizations like A Safe Place and Nantucket Food, Fuel, and Rental Assistance. She hired landscapers to help keep her large garden weed-free and watered, and a cleaning crew swept through the house twice a week. A housekeeper named Gravity cooked the evening meal, but Evelyn had started baking cookies to take to the construction crews, which she'd never done before.

Kailee suspected that her mother was trying to show the town that the Essexes were not all bad, even though some of the Essex houses were discordant with nature and with the island's standards. Kailee made a mental note to talk to her mother about this.

The doorbell rang, bringing her back to the present. Kailee tore herself away from the mirror and ran down the stairs. Ross was coming to the party. Kailee's mother had invited Heather, too, in a gesture of friendship, even though Heather was not from the island. Kailee worried that Heather would feel out of place or, worse, that Ross would feel obligated to stick to his mother's side all evening so Heather wouldn't be alone.

Heather couldn't find a place to park on Pleasant Street. So many cars were already parked near the Essexes' house, that magnificent, historic mansion, that Heather almost decided to go home. People were strolling up the slate sidewalk and through the doors. It would be a crush. No one would miss her.

Well, someone would miss her, Ross. Her son would be there with his girlfriend and Kailee's parents, and Evelyn Essex had called to invite her to the party, and Heather had promised to come, only because she couldn't think quickly enough to give her regrets.

She'd brought only one nice dress to the island, thinking she'd only need it for church. Last week Rosie, who worked at Marine Home Center, told Heather about the Hospital Thrift Shop on India Street, where clothes had been donated by such wealthy women that they still had tags on them. Heather had paid a quick visit, found a black crepe dress that fit her perfectly, and she'd been so pleased with herself for wearing it—she looked really good in it—but now that she was here, she terrified herself with the thought that inside she'd meet the woman who had donated the dress.

But that might not happen, Heather told herself. And it would be lovely to see Ross, even for a moment, and Miribelle Hunter had said she'd be there, so she'd have a friend to talk to.

She finally found a parking place on a side street, double-checked her makeup in the visor mirror, and walked to the house, smiling as if she were looking forward to a pleasant evening.

A housekeeper greeted her and directed her to the conservatory in the back. Sounds of laughter lifted her spirits, and the large room with all its greenery was dazzling.

"You must be Ross's mother." A tall and very handsome man in a blazer, his white shirt open at the neck, approached Heather. "I'm Bob. Kailee's father."

"Oh! Yes, I'm Ross's mother. Heather. Please call me Heather. What a beautiful house you have."

"Thank you. Come, let's get you a drink."

Bob Essex put a gentle hand on her shoulder to guide her to the bar where two men poured wine, sparkling seltzer, bourbon, and Scotch. She was happy that she'd worn the black dress. She felt its silky skirt swishing against her legs as she walked.

Heather asked for a white wine and turned to survey the room. "What a crowd," she observed. "You have many friends."

Bob laughed. "I don't think they're all friends. Nantucket is an innocent Eden for summer people, but the town politics are fierce and complicated."

Heather said, "Ross—"

"Ross will be just fine. Kailee belongs to the town, and people love her, and once everyone gets to know Ross, they'll love him, too." He nodded hello and winked at a couple walking past. "I hear you're here for the summer. Is your husband coming, too?"

"My husband and I are divorcing," Heather said. "Don't worry, we're both fine with it. It's an amicable parting that's long overdue. As Ross probably told you, Wall has a hardware store just outside Concord. He's got scores of friends and customers."

"Will you return to Concord?"

"I don't know," Heather answered honestly. "Somehow, I don't think I will. I have friends there, too, but I think I'll move. Our house is a handsome Victorian, but too big for two people and I've listed it with a realtor."

"Where will you go?"

"I'm not sure. A friend found me a small rental cottage here on the island, and I'll be there for three months while all the paperwork of the divorce and the sale of the house take place. After that, I don't really know. I was on the board of Concord's branch of the Safeguard Nature Society, so I spent a lot of time in Boston. And I have friends in every suburb, it seems." Was she talking too much? Why was it so easy to talk to this man? Usually, handsome men intimidated her.

"How do you like living on the island?" Bob asked.

Before she could reply, Ross approached her. "Hey, Mom. Hi, Mr. Essex. Cool party."

Kailee was with Ross, stunning in a navy-blue frock and pearl earrings. "Hello, Mrs. Willette."

"Call me Heather, please." Heather gave her son and Kailee each a quick peck on the cheek. "I've just met your employer," she said, with a smile.

A gorgeous woman wearing a sleeveless white dress with a slender gold belt joined them.

"You must be Heather. I'm Evelyn. I'm so glad you came."

Heather started to reply, but Evelyn looked at her husband. "Darling, Corky Moss is over by the camellias, looking lonely. Why don't you say hello?" Without pausing, she asked Heather, "How do you like our little island so far?"

"I haven't seen all of it, but it's beautiful," Heather said. "And this house is stunning."

Evelyn sparkled at the compliment. "Thank you. It's been in Bob's family for generations."

"Our house in Concord is a family home, too. It's a Victorian gingerbread—"

"How nice," Evelyn said. "Excuse me . . ." She hurried across the room to greet an elderly woman wearing an antique pearl and diamond choker.

Kailee said, "Sorry she flitted off like that. She's always that way at parties."

"She's always that way, period," Ross added.

"Ross!" Kailee looked hurt.

"That's not an insult, babe. I just mean she's a high-energy person. A hummingbird kind of person."

"Your mother is lovely," Heather said. "I'm so pleased to be invited to this party."

"Heather!" Miribelle Hunter swept up. "You're here! I'm so glad to see you." She kissed Heather on her cheek.

"Miribelle, how nice. And we don't have to work," Heather joked.

Kailee almost dropped her drink. How in the big wide world did Miribelle Hunter, one of the island's most powerful and wealthy women, know Ross's mother?

"I'm getting another drink, honey," Kailee said to Ross. She slipped into the scrum waiting for the bartenders.

"I'll be outside," Ross told her, and headed for the French doors opening to the garden.

"More tonic and ice than vodka, thanks." Kailee smiled at the bartender while listening to the conversation of the two women near the bar.

"I have to tell you," Miribelle was saying to Heather, "my brother thinks you're an extremely interesting woman. Only 'interesting' wasn't the word he used."

Kailee blinked. What? Miles Hunter liked Ross's mother? How did they even know each other?

"I think your brother is extremely 'interesting' himself," Heather said, and Kailee, watching, realized that Ross's mother was actually kind of a babe.

A sunburned man in his forties appeared at the bar, wedging himself between Kailee and the two women.

"How're ya doing, honey?" he said to Kailee.

Kailee smiled at Gene Sharpe. "I'm doing fine, thank you, Mr. Sharpe. How are you?"

She wanted to step on his foot with her stiletto heel for calling her "honey," but he was one of the new super-rich on the island who wanted to belittle everyone else. Her father's company had built his sprawling mansion. Her mother wanted to ask him to join the board of the Essex Nature Foundation.

"The wife and I just got back from a cruise in the Caribbean," Mr. Sharpe said.

Kailee smiled and listened, furtively watching Ross, who was across the room, talking with a very young woman.

"I do believe I've lost your attention," Mr. Sharpe said, good-naturedly.

"Oh, I'm so sorry. I was just— My boyfriend is over there, in the navy blazer. By the garden doors. Talking with a beautiful woman."

Mr. Sharpe laughed. "Tall guy? Brown hair?"

"That's right. His name is Ross Willette. He's working for my father this summer."

"And he's talking with my daughter, Ann," Mr. Sharpe said, and let out a long belly laugh. "You are right, she is beautiful."

I hate this party, Kailee thought.

But she remembered her manners. "Where did she grow up?"

"Greenwich," Mr. Sharpe informed her. He shook his head, amazed. "Ann went to Stanford. She starts medical school this fall. *Harvard* Medical School. My wife and I are astonished, frankly. We had no idea she was *that* smart."

"You must be so, so proud of her," Kailee said. She liked Ann now that she knew Ann would be in med school, not around to charm Ross.

"We are," Mr. Sharpe agreed.

"How long will you and your family be on Nantucket?"

"Now that the house is finished, on and off. We love it here. We come to the island as often as we can. It's not a long trip for us. We fly private."

"Have you seen all of the island?" Kailee asked. "So many of the most magical places are off the beaten path."

"I'm not much for hiking," Mr. Sharpe said, and asked the bartender for another drink.

Kailee smiled. "The places I'm talking about don't require boots." *Take the plunge,* she told herself. *Mention ENF. Go on!* Her heart pounded in her throat. "My mother is starting a new foundation, the Essex Nature Foundation. Nantucket's beaches are beautiful, but so are its ponds and moors and hidden forests."

"What's a moor?" Mr. Sharpe demanded, looking oddly offended. "Like in Scotland?"

"Well, sort of," Kailee said, floundering. "Maybe I could take you and your wife—and Ann, if she'd like, to see some of the less well-known parts of the island."

"Hmm," Mr. Sharpe replied.

Miribelle Hunter interrupted them, saying hello and doing the air-kiss. "Kailee, you look lovely tonight. Gene, guess what. I've found someone who plays bridge. Heather Willette, over there talking to the minister. She's joining our bridge club for the summer."

"Excuse me," Kailee murmured. "I see someone I . . ." She didn't bother to finish her sentence.

Ross was still listening to Ann Sharpe, so Kailee headed for her high school boyfriend, standing across the room.

"Hey, Tris!"

Tris Greenwood looked down in surprise. He looked older, more adult. He looked really good.

"Kailee. I was hoping you'd be here." Tris leaned down and kissed her cheek. "How are you?"

"I am *so* glad to be home," Kailee said. "I really missed the island. And my family, of course. How are you?"

"I've already got boats in the water," Tris told her. "I'm renting them, servicing them, sometimes taking customers around the island and over to Tuckernuck." He changed the subject. "I hear you've brought a, um, friend here for the summer."

"I have! That's Ross over there. He's working for my dad this summer."

Tris grinned down at her. "Let me know if you two want to go over to Tuckernuck."

"Will do," Kailee told him with her brightest smile. The thought of island friends welcoming Ross gladdened her heart.

After the party ended, Kailee's parents, Kailee, and Ross sat in the den doing an instant replay. Kailee and her mother had kicked off their high heels, and the men had removed their blazers. Several of the guests had expressed interest in the ENF, and both Kailee's parents talked about how glad they were to see some of Kailee's old high school friends.

"And your mother," Evelyn said to Ross. "I had no idea she knew the Hunters!"

Ross shrugged. "I think she met them at church. She helped Miribelle Hunter sort through the books for the church fair."

Bob stretched. "Maybe you should invite Ross's mother to join the ENF."

Evelyn shifted in her chair. "Maybe."

Ross stood up. "I don't know about the rest of you, but I've got to work in the morning. I think I'll head out."

"Oh, wait," Evelyn said. "Ross, did you get enough to eat? I know there were lots of little goodies, but why don't I make you a sandwich—"

Kailee stood up, too. "Mom, that's sweet, but we've both had enough to eat. I'm tired, too, and you need to go to bed."

Evelyn blinked. "Kailee, I think you're right. I'm tired."

After the house was quiet, Kailee slipped out the kitchen door, crossed the drive, and went up the stairs to Ross's apartment. She knocked lightly on the door.

Ross was in a white T-shirt and tighty-whities, his normal sleep-wear. "Hey, babe, nice surprise."

They kissed sweetly and then urgently. Ross took her hand and led her to his bed. When they slipped under the covers, Kailee scooted next to him, running her hand over his chest.

Ross turned onto his side and pulled Kailee closer to him. "Nice everything."

"It looked like you especially enjoyed the party tonight." *What* was she doing? She wanted to tape her mouth shut. "When you were getting to know Ann Sharpe."

Ross reared back sharply, shaking his head. "I wasn't flirting."

"*Good.* Oh, Ross, I'm sorry. I know I get jealous," Kailee said. "It's a good thing you work with men all day."

Ross pulled her even closer. "Kailee, you know you never need to be jealous. You're the most beautiful woman in the world to me."

She wrapped her arms around him and sighed with contentment.

The next afternoon, Heather drove up the narrow, bumpy, cobblestone lane to Lincoln Street. She found the right house—how could she miss it? It was a Cape Cod on steroids. A huge white clapboard building with lots of dormers and roses growing over everything. The long brick driveway was wide enough for two cars abreast, so she parked behind a large white Range Rover.

For a moment she sat, reassuring herself. She'd met Stephanie Collins at coffee hour after church. Stephanie was probably fifty, a lean, weather-skinned woman with an athletic frame. She had a short, no-nonsense bob, piercing blue eyes, and a nose like a beak. She'd unashamedly grilled Heather, asking where she came from, why she was here, who she knew, chirping "I see," after everything Heather said. When Heather mentioned she played bridge, Stephanie Collins finally smiled.

"You're just what I need," she said, not bothering to ask Heather if she'd like to join her bridge club. That was assumed.

Clearly, Stephanie was wealthy and active, born, she'd laughed, with a tennis racket in her hand. When Heather admitted she didn't play tennis, she could see the disappointment in Stephanie's eyes. Still, Heather could play bridge.

She had agreed to come this afternoon, but now she felt uncomfortable. Heather had never gone to the Bahamas or skiing in the Alps, and stickers on the back of two other vehicles in the driveway indicated private boarding schools. Miribelle Hunter would be there, she remembered, so that made her more comfortable. And she *had* promised, and she didn't want to leave Stephanie's group without a fourth.

She opened the car door and stepped out into the hot, humid day. The air was sweet with flowers, and the view from the cliff was a stunning, seemingly endless blue. And this was Stephanie's *summer* home.

Bracing herself, Heather marched to the front door and rang the doorbell.

A young woman wearing a beige dress opened the door and ushered her into the large front hall. "This way, please," she said.

Heather followed her down a long hall to a screened-in porch at the back of the house. Two card tables were set up, and another table held lemonade, iced tea, and cookies. A cluster of women of varying ages were chattering away as they poured their drinks.

"You're here. Thank heavens!" Stephanie swooped down, wrapped a comradely arm around Heather's shoulders, and announced, "Everyone! Introduce yourself to Heather Willette. She's saving our bridge club!"

"Don't be so sure," Heather joked.

Laughing, the ladies came toward Heather, barely saying hello before Stephanie summoned them to their places. Miribelle remained at her table. She waved at Heather and gave an encouraging wink.

"You're my partner today," Stephanie told Heather.

"Good luck," a younger woman with glasses told Heather. "Stephanie's a beast."

Heather smiled nervously. She hadn't played bridge in a while, but she did have a good head for numbers. And she had luck with her first hand, which she thanked heaven for because the women played with a deadly intensity. The room was quiet except for bidding and passes. At the far end of the porch, a standing fan blew the air around, its low hum the only friendly noise in the room.

Stephanie and Heather took the first rubber.

For the next set, everyone relaxed. They brought lemonade and cookies to the table on little flowered plates, and chatted as they sorted their cards.

The conversation got interesting when Heather admitted that yes, she was the mother of Ross Willette, who was working for Essex Construction.

"I've heard that he's Kailee's boyfriend," Donna, a sharp-eyed blonde, said. "My son used to date Kailee in high school. She's such a nice girl."

"That may be true," Stephanie said, acid sharpening her tone, "but the Essexes aren't as nice as they used to be. They're selling out Nantucket."

"Replace paradise with a parking lot," Peggy, to Heather's right, said.

Heather sorted through her cards intently, wondering how to respond. "I don't think the Essexes own *all* of Nantucket," she said mildly.

Patrice, who sat on Heather's left, agreed. "It's not fair to blame the Essexes. They've been building houses on this island for decades. I know the homes are getting larger—"

"They're becoming *castles*," Stephanie said.

From the other table, a woman said, "Yes, and the owners live here for only a few weeks, and they have their own cooks, housekeepers, landscapers, chauffeurs. They're putting nothing into the economy."

"Two hearts," Stephanie said.

Heather coughed. How could she concentrate on cards when her future daughter-in-law was being criticized? *Just listen,* she told herself.

But the others didn't want her to be silent. They wanted to mine for gold.

"Do you know anything about this new house?" Donna asked Heather. "On the top of a hill overlooking the harbor? From the ferry, it looks like a hotel."

"No," Heather told them. "I know nothing about the new house."

"But your son is working for Bob Essex, right?" a petite woman from the other table asked.

"Yes, he is, but we don't talk about business." Anger heated Heather's belly. Her hands were trembling, and that was embarrassing.

"What's Evelyn Essex really like?" inquired a thin older woman with a gleam in her eye. "Is she as difficult as we've heard?"

Donna lowered her voice, as if in a conspiracy. "Evelyn looks so young," she cooed. "Has she had any work done? Botox or plastic surgery?"

Heather sat up straight and looked at Donna. "I'm sorry. I can't say. I've only met her once. But her daughter, Kailee, is very nice and very smart."

"That family," another woman at the other table said spitefully. "They're a problem."

"Now, now," Stephanie cooed, "let's focus on our cards, shall we?"

The tension in the room dissolved. Heather concentrated, but the other team won. She was exhausted when the party broke up, but she smiled and promised to return next week, even though she knew the others wanted to peck at her for all the information on the Essexes they could get.

eight

The rain was a quiet, steady rain, forecast to keep up into the evening. Heather had spent time in town, visiting the Whaling Museum, shopping for groceries, treating herself to a long luxurious browse through the library, deciding which mystery would be perfect for a day like this.

She'd been here for three weeks now, and it surprised her how much she felt at home. Her lawyer back in Concord was preparing her divorce papers, and a friend of hers who was a realtor was handling the sale of the house.

Sarah Martin, Heather's lawyer, reported that Wall was fine with signing papers for a no-fault divorce, citing "irretrievable breakdown of the marriage," which was legal in Massachusetts. Both Heather and Wall had to go before a judge to get approval of the separation agreement. After that, they had to wait thirty days for the "judgment nisi" to be issued, and wait ninety days for the judgment to become final. Then they would be legally divorced.

Wall hadn't called. Nor emailed. Heather wasn't surprised. She was certain Wall knew in his heart that he and Heather had run out of love, as if they'd bought a package that was only half full. He was a handsome and intelligent man. She was sure he'd have women bringing him casseroles soon.

She'd called Miles and told him she'd like to take the job.

When she arrived home, she found Ross's truck was parked in front of her cottage. She ran through the rain and into the house. Ross was lounging on the sofa, playing a game on his laptop.

"Hey, Mom!"

"Hi, darling." Heather hung her raincoat on a hook and crossed the room to kiss the top of his head. "What's up?"

Ross clicked off his laptop, stood up, cleared his throat, and sat down again.

"Oh, dear," Heather said. "Is everything okay?"

Ross said, all in a rush, "I want to ask Kailee to marry me."

"That's wonderful, Ross. But I thought that was already decided."

"Yeah, but it wasn't official, and I want to make it official. I want to set a date for the wedding, and I want to give Kailee a ring, and I was hoping . . ."

Heather looked down at the small diamond on her hand. "Of course, you could have my engagement ring, but I think Kailee deserves better. And because of, um, my divorce, I'm afraid it would seem like a vague kind of bad luck. But I have your grandmother's ring in a safe in our bank at home. I don't know if you've seen it. It's old-fashioned, but splendid. A ruby surrounded by diamonds."

"That sounds perfect, Mom. How soon can we get it?"

Heather cocked her head. "Is there a rush? Is Kailee pregnant?"

"No, Mom, God. It's just that it's hard, living apart from her. Besides, I'm ready for my life to start. I like the work. I like Kailee's parents. And I want to make Kailee happy." He blushed.

"Sweetheart." Heather fought back tears. She knew Ross would hate for her to go what he called *all gooey*. "Let's make a plan to go up to Concord on Saturday, if you can get the day off. We can pick up some summer clothes and I'll go to the bank. Kailee can come with us if she wants."

"Thanks, Mom! You're a champion." He started for the door and turned back. "I'll ask Kailee to join us, but don't tell her about the ring, okay? I want it to be a surprise."

Kailee wore a silk dress and gold lightship basket earrings and her long hair held back by a slender headband. It was the first ever meeting of her mother's Essex Nature Foundation, and so far, eight people had joined, some, Kailee knew, because they cared about the environment, and some because they wanted to see Evelyn's home and garden and were willing to donate good money to do so.

The meeting was held in the conservatory, around a round wicker table where the Essexes often ate dinner in the summer. Evelyn had chaired the meeting and would continue to until the board decided on a president. Today, Kailee took notes.

"One last item," Evelyn said. "I think we should consider inviting Heather Willette to join."

Stephanie Collins said, "I like her. But she doesn't live here year-round."

"No," Evelyn agreed. "Her winter home is in Concord, Massachusetts. She serves on the Concord branch of the Safeguard Nature Society."

"Well, then, she'd be perfect for us," Roy Sanders said.

The others around the table agreed.

When the meeting ended, Evelyn invited the group to tour her garden. Gravity, with a starched apron over her flowery summer dress, carried around a tray, offering iced tea or iced white wine. Evelyn walked through the low wintergreen boxwood hedges dividing the gardens, naming the flowers, explaining how her vision had shaped the garden.

———

After the board members had left, Kailee was surprised to see Heather arrive.

"Hi, Kailee. Your mother invited me to stop by to see her gardens."

"Oh. Right. She's still outside." Kailee led Heather through the house to the open French doors to the garden.

Heather paused. "I'm driving up to Concord to sort through some clothes and belongings at the house. I'd like Ross to join me—it would be only a day trip—to choose whatever *he* wants to keep, and I thought you might want to choose a few keepsakes, too." Heather added, smiling, "Since you're going to be part of the family, you might want Ross's grandmother's quilts, that sort of thing."

"That's so nice," Kailee said. "Um, when are you going?"

"This Saturday." Heather rolled her eyes. "I know, everything is happening so fast. My lawyer said it's a seller's market these days, people are paying over the asking price for a house in the suburbs of Boston."

"It's the same way here," Kailee said, stalling. "I, um, I haven't talked with Ross about all this, but I'm sure we won't need crystal or china . . . no one uses them anymore."

"But you might like our silver," Heather suggested. "It's sterling, with the letter 'W' engraved in the handle. It belonged to Wall's parents."

"Wow." Kailee rocked back on her heels. "I haven't even thought about all that. I mean, whether I'll take Ross's last name. I mean, Essex is an important name on this island. Historical."

"But if you have a child someday, and I hope you do, will you name him or her Essex-Willette?" Heather was still smiling.

Kailee's spine stiffened. "I think that's something Ross and I will decide."

"Of course." Heather frowned. "Anyway, think about joining Ross and me for the quick trip." She slung her own laptop case over her shoulder. "I'm going out to enjoy your mother's gardens."

"Thanks!" Kailee chirped, forcing a smile. As Heather walked away, Kailee picked up her laptop and purse and quickly made her way into the house and up the stairs to her room. She sat on her bed and stared at the wall.

She knew she was being irrational. Wasn't she? She and Ross hadn't discussed the last-name thing yet, and as much as she wanted to be his wife, she also hated the thought of losing the name Essex. It had been Bartholomew Essex who arrived with a group of British to settle Nantucket Island. The town's history was woven into her heritage.

And it was true, things had changed. *She* was changing, but she hadn't foreseen all the decisions she'd have to make.

If only Heather hadn't come here for the summer, casting her ownership of Ross like a shadow that would never fade.

But! Kailee had such a brilliant idea she jumped up and raised her arms in a victory sign.

What if Heather met a summer man, some nice divorced old guy who had a home in California or Texas. What if they fell in love—Heather was still attractive—and they married and lived in California or Texas. Wouldn't that be wonderful for Heather?

Kailee scurried back down the stairs, down the long hall leading to the conservatory, and out the French doors to the garden. She stood, smiling, gazing at the flowers, wondering if any men on the board were widowed.

Saturday, Kailee sat in the backseat for the drive from Hyannis to Concord in Heather's old Volvo station wagon. Ross had offered to sit in the back, but Kailee had protested.

"Your legs are too long!" she'd said. "I'll sit in the backseat."

And she had. Her tote, filled with cosmetics, money, a sweater in case it cooled off, and her phone, was on the floor near her feet. She considered checking her phone but didn't want to seem rude, plus Ross was right here with her.

Still, she'd felt grumpy and left out during the entire hour and a half drive. Was this her fate? To always make a stupid decision when it came to her and Ross and his mom? Kailee had never been so moody before. She felt cranky and uncomfortable and achy. Maybe she had a flu. She closed her eyes for a while, but that only made her feel carsick. Was she totally *allergic* to Ross's mom?

"Here we are," Heather announced as she pulled into the driveway.

Ross opened her door and helped her out, and Kailee stood there, amazed. The house was a three-story Victorian, with pristine white gingerbread woodwork adorning its wraparound porch. Two arched stained-glass windows ran down the sides of the massive beveled oak front door, and another more elaborate stained-glass window decorated one side of the house.

"You grew up here?" Kailee asked.

"He did," Heather answered when Ross stayed quiet. "My grandmother left the house to me when she passed. It needed a lot of work, because she lived to ninety-nine and spent the last five years living on the first floor, and she couldn't see how it was literally falling apart around her. Wall and I actually camped out in the library on the first floor while we renovated and repaired the other two floors. It was a labor of love. Come see."

Kailee kept a tight hold on Ross's hand as they entered the house he grew up in. She thought her own home was so fabulous but this, this was breathtaking. The entrance hall was enormous, with an elegant staircase curving up to the second floor, and the entrances to the living room, library, and dining room were through wide, arched doorways. The mantels over the fireplaces were supported by elaborate, carved corbels, and in one room hung a huge oil portrait of a soldier in a blue wool army uniform with ruffled shirt front and cuffs, topped with a white wig.

"Is that an ancestor?" Kailee asked breathlessly.

"No, Kailee," Heather admitted, chuckling. "I found it at an estate sale."

"We call him Percy," Ross said.

"I bought it for the frame, really," Heather said, admiring the extravagantly carved and gilded wood.

Kailee floated through the magical house, a home built from fairy tales, and when she saw the garden, she gasped. Beds of flowers bloomed everywhere and grass paths led between them to a small pond with a bridge arching over it. Nearby stood a wicker bench beneath the pale slender branches of a tall willow tree cascading down, swaying gently, their movement causing the water to shimmer.

"My mother would love this garden," Kailee said.

"I'm going up to pack more clothes," Ross said, turning away.

"Yes, let's go with him," Heather suggested. "I want to show you the quilts."

The beautiful house made Kailee feel sad, and she didn't know why. It seemed alive, a person, waiting there in its beauty to shelter its people. Kailee had always been proud of her ancestry, the history of the Essexes dating far back into the record books of England, and the first written records of Nantucket. She'd lived elsewhere, of course, mostly recently in Amherst, Massachusetts, whose history and buildings were even older than Nantucket's. She'd stayed with friends in Colorado, in California, in Quebec, and she felt deeply responsive to all those histories. But she'd never considered living anywhere but Nantucket. It held her, heart and soul.

Heather pointed out the linen cupboard that held the quilts. She went into her bedroom, to pack more clothes into her suitcase.

Heather saw Kailee watching her from the doorway. She smiled. "Happily, I've discovered I'll need some of my nicer things for the parties I've been invited to," she told Kailee.

"How long will you be staying on Nantucket?" Kailee sweetly inquired.

"My lease runs through Labor Day," Heather said, kneeling down and reaching into the back of her closet. "But I might see if I can stay on through September. I've heard it's beautiful then." She stuck her head into Ross's room. "I've got to drive to the bank to pick up some things. I'll be back in fifteen minutes."

"Cool," Ross said.

Heather felt odd as she drove to the parking lot in the center of the beautiful town of Concord. She experienced the sense of being both at home and a stranger here. She'd lived here so long she thought every brick in the buildings was engraved in her memory. She'd bought cold medicine at the pharmacy, browsed the Barrow Bookstore, met her friends for lunch at the Colonial Inn. She prepared herself emotionally in case she ran into an old acquaintance who would ask her about the divorce, but she made it into the bank without seeing anyone she knew.

A sweet-faced young woman took Heather into the vault containing the locked safes. She opened the lockbox and took out the red satin box holding her grandmother's gorgeous diamond and ruby ring. The deed to the house was there, so she took that, too, and tucked it into her purse. A velvet box held a miscellany of bracelets, necklaces, and cameos—no one wore cameos anymore—and as she slid the box into her tote, Heather paused to wonder why. With a small gasp, she realized that when she took everything that was hers, the lockbox was empty.

Well, Heather thought, *there's a metaphor for our marriage.*

"Don't be silly," she said aloud. "We had some wonderful years."

Moving briskly, she slotted the box back in its row, returned the vault key to the clerk, and left the bank. Everything she did seemed to lift weights off her shoulders.

She returned to the beautiful old Victorian house. How she had loved it, how tenderly she had repaired and painted it. Odd to realize she wouldn't miss it. She walked up the curving staircase and down the hall to her bedroom. Once, *their* bedroom. Her suitcase was on the bed, filled with summer clothes. She zipped it up and carried it out to the hall.

"I'm finished!" Ross called, coming out of his room with two full duffel bags. Kailee followed, with another bag in her arms.

"I'm ready, too," Heather said. "Kailee, would you like any of the quilts?"

"Yes, I'd like two if that's all right. The hearts and the linked circles."

Eight quilts were in the wide closet, all carefully folded and protected inside cloth bags with drawstrings. Heather helped Kailee lift the quilts out, and as they went down the staircase with their belongings, Heather sighed with pleasure and regret. She hoped that this visit to their house helped Kailee realize that Ross was leaving a home as beautiful as hers.

They were all in the driveway, packing bags into the hatchback, when a sleek black Porsche pulled up to the curb. *Oh, no,* Heather thought. She had asked her lawyer to notify Wall that she'd be in the house during the weekend to get some of her possessions. She'd thought that would make Wall stay away.

But here he was. He looked better than he had in years, with his dark hair styled so that it surged up like much younger men were wearing it these days. He wore a white button-down shirt, jeans, and—cowboy boots? That was a new fashion choice for Wall, but it did give him a kind of swagger as he walked over to hug Ross.

"Hello, kid. I heard you all were in town."

Confused, Ross sputtered, "Gosh, Dad, um, hi!"

"Hello, Wall," Heather said, not moving from her spot on the driveway. The sight of her soon-to-be-ex-husband in cowboy boots wrenched her heart with pity and amusement at the same time. "How are you?"

"Better than ever," Wall said. "I'm seeing a nice woman, Nova. She's a great cook."

"*Nova?*" Heather had to ask. "That's an unusual name."

Wall smiled smugly. "She's twenty-seven."

"Wait. What? Dad, how long have you known her?" Ross asked.

"Long enough," Wall said, looking very pleased with himself.

Heather asked, "Is that your car, Wall?"

"It's Nova's," Wall answered. "I'm keeping some stuff here and living with Nova until this house sells. Then Nova and I are moving into her place."

Heather glanced over at Kailee. Kailee stood there frozen. Obviously, her training in manners hadn't prepared her for this.

There was an uncomfortable silence.

Heather waited for Wall to ask her how she was, but he didn't, no surprise there. She said, "Sorry, Wall, but we've got to hit the road."

"Fine with me." Wall waved as he went up the walk to their house.

Heather sank into the comfortable seat of her Volvo. This time Ross insisted that Kailee sit in the passenger seat, and he sat behind.

"Have we got everything?" Heather asked, reverting to her mother role.

"We have," Ross told her. "All packed away and ready to go."

Heather steered the car out of the driveway and headed for the Mass Pike.

Kailee struggled with her words. "Ross, did you know . . . Your father looked . . . Mr. Willette seemed different."

At last Heather could let out her laughter. "Dear Lord in heaven," she gasped as she tried to get herself in control. "Cowboy boots!"

"Mom?" Ross said. "Are you okay?"

"I am," Heather told him. She looked over her shoulder at her son. "Really, truly, I am. I'm glad for Wall. He looked good, didn't he? And he's got a girlfriend named Nova!"

Heather wanted to burst into song. Totally irreverent show tunes from *Cats* played in her mind, with a hallelujah chorus mixed in.

"I would be so sad if my parents got divorced," Kailee said mournfully.

Probably it was too soon in their relationship for Heather to snort dismissively. She forced herself to take a deep breath.

"Obviously, sweetheart," Heather said, "your parents have a different and better relationship than Wall and I had." She added, "I hope so much that this divorce doesn't make Ross sad."

Ross yawned and said, "I'm not sad, Mom."

In the rearview mirror, Heather saw that Ross was twisting the safety strap so that he could sit sideways, with his feet up on the seat.

"I have some news, too," Heather said.

"You do?" Ross yelped.

"You've met a man!" Kailee guessed, clapping her hands.

Heather chuckled. "I've got a job. Starting on Monday. Only mornings, five days a week. As a receptionist and secretary for Miles Hunter's law office."

"Wait, Mom, do you need money?" Ross asked.

"No, darling. I think this will be fun. It's just for the summer."

"That's nice," Kailee said.

"If that's what you want to do," Ross mumbled.

"It's what I want to do." She glanced over at Kailee. "I think I'll put on some music. Is eighties rock okay?"

"Absolutely," Kailee said.

During the ride back down 495 and over the Bourne Bridge to Route 6, Ross slept, his head against the window. Heather put the radio on 92.9, volume low enough not to wake Ross and just loud enough that Kailee didn't feel responsible for a conversation.

Kailee closed her eyes and daydreamed. She liked Heather much more after this trip. She'd expected Heather to be maudlin, needing Ross to console her, but Heather had been just fine.

And Ross's house! A fairy-tale home. Why would Heather leave it? So sad.

They arrived in Hyannis, boarded the slow boat, and went up the metal stairs to the main deck. Heather bought a container of clam chowder and went out to sit on a bench, watching the water as they passed through. Kailee and Ross had kale and sausage soup and played video games. Riding the slow ferry was like time suspended, lulling and relaxing. When the boat nudged against the pier, Kailee smiled. *Home.*

It was ten-thirty when Kailee and Ross entered the Pleasant

Street house. They were surprised to see Kailee's parents waiting up for them in the living room.

"Come talk for a moment?" Evelyn asked, patting the sofa beside her. "How was the trip?"

Ross settled in a wing chair across from Kailee's father. "It was good," he said. "I'd forgotten how much stuff I've saved from when I was a kid."

Bob Essex leaned forward. "Here's some advice, for what it's worth. Don't try to keep everything. Keep just one thing, something that doesn't take up much space, that you can always keep with you. I have the baseball Big Papi signed after a Red Sox game."

Ross said, "That's a good idea. Although I would like to keep my swimming trophies."

"Yeah, I get it," Bob said. "But let me warn you, they'll end up in the basement."

Evelyn interrupted, "Don't worry, Ross. Your mother will keep all the photo albums of your young years. And depending on where she lands after the divorce, she'll probably save a lot of your trophies and important things."

Kailee cocked her head. "How do you know, Mom?"

"Because I've saved boxes of your childhood drawings and prizes," Evelyn answered cheerily.

Kailee was amazed. Her mother had never been sentimental. "Mom, Dad, you should see their house. It's gorgeous! A huge old Victorian—"

"We've seen it," Bob said. "On Google Maps."

"Did you see the back garden?" Kailee asked.

"Not close up, of course," Evelyn replied.

"It's a spectacular Victorian," Kailee's father announced. "I've looked at the real estate ads. It's going to sell for a very nice sum."

Ross forced a yawn—Kailee could tell—and stood up. "I'm tired. I think I'll go on over to the apartment. Good night."

He left the room.

"Were we being insensitive?" Evelyn asked Kailee.

Kailee shrugged. "I don't think he's upset about the house."

"But his parents' divorce," Evelyn said. "Selling his childhood home, breaking up the family possessions, all that can be heart-breaking."

Bob rose. "Also, it could simply be that he had a long day—you all got up at five-thirty to make the six-thirty boat. Anyway, I'm going to bed now. I'll leave you ladies to pick over his emotions."

Evelyn looked at her watch. "It's eleven. I'm going up, too."

Kailee stood by the kitchen door as her parents went through the house, checking locks and turning off lights. The quilts from Ross's home were in the front hall, leaning against the table like orphans, next to the tote Kailee had brought. She decided to carry up her tote and come back down for the quilts. But once she was upstairs, her bed looked so inviting, she stripped off her clothes, got into bed, and fell asleep without brushing her teeth.

nine

Monday morning, Heather parked her car in the town parking lot across from the harbor and walked to Main Street. It wasn't quite nine o'clock, but the shop doors were open, and people were sitting on benches, drinking coffee and chatting. She crossed the street, wondering if she should stop in at the Hub for a coffee, but she'd had two cups already this morning. She was very much awake.

She passed Nantucket Pharmacy and found the narrow, dark green door with MILES HUNTER, ATTORNEY AT LAW written on it in gold letters.

The door was unlocked. She opened it and found a set of steep stairs. She went up, pleased that she wasn't breathless at the top, and stood in front of another door, this one with a glass inset and Miles's title again, in more gold lettering. She tried the doorknob.

She walked into the room. It was pleasant, cozy but bright. Two long windows faced Main Street, an antique chandelier hung from the ceiling, and lamps stood near the leather sofa and the leather chair. Two of the walls were lined with bookcases filled with serious-looking legal volumes, the kind Heather would never want to read. Two chairs faced the desk, and the desk—*her* desk!— was obviously old, dark burled mahogany, with chips and scratches here and there but still a serious, dignified piece of furniture. A large blotter covered the center of the desk. A large laptop waited beneath a banker's lamp of brass with a green shade.

Heather walked around the desk and sat in the nicely padded executive chair. It was very comfortable. She liked the mix of old and new here, the solid antique desk holding the metal and glass laptop. Opening the middle drawer of the desk, she found a long narrow box filled with pens and pencils, a small container of paper clips, a ruler, rubber bands, several thumb drives, and Scotch tape. The drawer on the right held small pads of yellow lined paper. Next to the computer was a large cellphone. On the other side was a pile of folders with colored tabs. Miles's secretary was organized.

She opened the bottom drawer and tucked her purse inside, as she had done decades ago in her cramped little office at Wall's store. She clicked on the laptop and opened the calendar. It was neatly filled in with Miles's appointments.

A sense of satisfaction flowed through her. She had never wanted to be extraordinary. She'd never longed to sing opera, run the Boston Marathon, win the Kentucky Derby, or be governor of the Commonwealth of Massachusetts. She'd always thought that a normal person, an average person, possessed treasures that the luminaries had lost. Privacy, for one. And time, time to day-dream or simply to enjoy the slant of the sun and the taste of a fresh, warm tomato, without rushing, without having to hurry on to the next thing.

In elementary school, when her teachers asked her what she hoped to be when she grew up, she'd answered, "Me." The teach-ers had laughed.

But here she was, quietly relishing the cushions of her chair, the friendly, eager blinking of the computer screen, the sounds of laughter coming from the street.

Miles was orderly, too. Maybe lawyers had to be that way by profession. Heather scanned the list of tasks needing done. The top folder contained the scribbles of an older man who wanted an addendum to his will; would Heather please translate those sentences into a legible document? Heather opened the folder and skimmed it. The handwriting was almost impossible to read.

This was going to be fun.

The door opened and Miles came in, dressed for business in a suit and tie. He brightened when he saw Heather.

"Oh, good! I'm glad you're here. What do you think?"

Heather smiled, trying to tone down her pleasure at seeing him. "I like it a lot. The reception area is professional but welcoming."

"Good. Our first appointment today is with Mr. and Mrs. Warren. They're in their eighties, and they have three children and a complicated will that they've already changed twice. They're wealthy, slightly eccentric, not senile. Many of my clients are older, and they need to have a sense of control, now that their lives are . . . changing."

"Of course."

Miles nodded and went through into his office.

Heather opened a file on the computer and began working on the addendum.

A few minutes later, the door opened again, and two apple-cheeked octogenarians entered.

Heather said a simple "Good morning," and Mrs. Warren nearly levitated.

"Oh, Miles told me he was going to have a new secretary and I'm glad, because he works hard and his work is very important. You know, we keep having second thoughts about our wills, well, third and fourth thoughts, I should say—"

"Muriel," said Mr. Warren.

Heather used the momentary silence to introduce herself. Muriel Warren was enraptured to meet Heather. Heather gently interrupted the other woman to show the couple into Miles's office. He rose to greet them.

Heather shut the door and sat at the computer, wondering whether all Miles's clients were equally talkative.

Three more people came in that morning. They weren't all talkative, but they were certainly at the eccentric end of the spectrum.

When the final client left, Miles came out and plopped down in one of the chairs facing Heather's desk.

"What do you think?"

"I think you're an extremely kind man," Heather told him. "I've seen your billing hours and you always give them more time than you bill for, which seems odd to me, because they all have more than sufficient funds."

"That's true. But I've known these people since I was a kid learning to swim. They knew my parents. I played with their children. I didn't leave a Boston money-making machine to be just as stressed and miserable here on Nantucket. I like these people. I love some of them. It's difficult, getting old, getting sick, being ignored. I like taking my time, talking to them."

"In that case, I think you're wonderful," Heather said.

Miles grinned. "In that case, let me take you to lunch."

"Sounds great," Heather said, smiling back.

Heather entered her cottage feeling exhausted and beyond happy. Could any day be more satisfying? She'd worked for Miles in the morning. She'd had lunch with him. Miles was divorced. He had one daughter, Emma, whom she'd already met. He'd lived in Boston for the past twenty years, part of a legal firm dealing with complicated estates. He, his wife, and their daughter had summered on the island. When Miles was divorced, he'd moved to Nantucket permanently. Here he worked with estates and wills.

They'd talked and laughed easily about town politics, celebrity yachts, baseball teams. Afterward, she'd gone to the church to help Miribelle sort more books for the church sale. She'd worked, flirted, and talked with a friend while surrounded by books. What a day!

She poured herself a glass of cold Chardonnay and went out to her mini-patio. A small pot of pansies sat in the middle of the table. Spots of color from petunias and double-edged begonias brightened the border of her yard. She'd bought already blooming plants from Bartlett's Farm, wanting the color right away, and now she wondered if she should buy more.

She should buy more, definitely.

Something moved at the far corner of the yard. Porcupine? They didn't have those on Nantucket. A squirrel would be up a tree, so it had to be a rabbit. She watched carefully to see if the rabbit was eating her flowers, and then a small brown creature with long curly ears stuck its head out from between the flowers.

"Hi, little one," Heather called softly. "Who are you?"

She rose and slowly, quietly, walked toward the animal. When she was a foot or so away, she squatted down and held out her hand.

"Hello. I won't hurt you."

The dog warily emerged, trembling all over. Its coat was matted with weeds, and it was painfully thin. But its eyes were hopeful.

"Oh, sweetie, are you lost? You've been lost for a long time, I think. Are you hungry? Maybe thirsty?"

Slowly, step by step, it came closer, its fluffy tail daring to wag carefully. Finally, it came near enough for Heather to touch it. She stroked its head, murmuring softly, and it allowed her to pick it up and bring it to the patio. She took a cushion off one of the patio chairs and put it on the slates, then gently set the dog on the cushion.

"Wait here," she said.

Heather hurried into the house, filled a small bowl with water and another bowl with bits of chicken she'd cooked the night before. She carried both bowls outside and set them in front of the dog.

"Maybe you'd like this," she told him. Her?

The dog cautiously approached the chicken, sniffed, and took a dainty bite. After chewing it with a doubtful look in its eye, it dove nose-deep into the bowl, almost inhaling the rest of the meat. It lapped some water, and its tail begin to wag.

While the dog ate, Heather took several photos on her phone and posted them on Nantucket Year-Round Community on Facebook with the comment: *Missing a Dog?*

Now what? Heather wondered. The dog had no identifying collar.

"What's your name?" she asked her—him? "Of course, you can't tell me. I know that. I'll try to find your family. First thing tomorrow I'll call Nantucket Island Safe Harbor for Animals. Maybe you have a chip in your skin. I posted your photo on Facebook. Maybe someone will claim you. Until then . . . I'll bring out a towel for you to sleep on. Or, if you want, you can go wandering off. Maybe that's the kind of animal you are. Don't fence me in, I love to wander, and so on."

When she stopped speaking and took a sip of wine, the dog carefully shuffled a few inches closer to her, tail moving slowly, carefully.

"Oh, no, you want to sit on my lap, don't you? You want to be cuddled. Actually, I'd love to cuddle you, but you're awfully dirty."

As if the dog understood her, she took a few brave steps and sat at Heather's feet, carefully laying her chin on Heather's shoe.

"I'm not going to have dinner, if that's what you're thinking. Well, I'm going to have a salad, but I had a huge lunch today with a very nice man."

The dog's tail swayed faster. Her eyes were fixed on Heather's face.

"I'm an idiot, aren't I, talking to a dog." Heather glanced at her phone. No response to her Facebook post.

The dog scooted a few more inches, until she was able to lean her head against Heather's ankle. It was a very nice feeling. Heather sat quietly for a few minutes, enjoying the gentle warmth.

"All right," she said finally. "Here's what we're going to do. I'm going to bring the large plastic bucket out here filled with warm water and soap. If you let me give you a bath, I'll consider letting you sleep in the house tonight."

The dog watched with big eyes as Heather went into the house and came back with the bucket in one hand and a pitcher of warm water in the other. Over her shoulder, she carried a towel belonging to the owner, so Heather made a vow to replace it.

She got down on her knees next to the pan.

"Want a little bathy?" she asked the dog, and groaned. "No baby talk, Heather," she ordered herself.

But the dog seemed to understand. She came to the pan and looked questioningly at Heather.

"I hope you know that if I try to bathe you, I'm risking getting bit by you, and you might have rabies and I might die. Okay? This will be harder on me than on you."

Very slowly and gently, she put her hands on the little dog and lifted it into the suds. She barely fit. Heather rubbed soapy water into the dog's fur, and the dog sat very still. She could feel its tiny heart beating fast, and tears came to her eyes.

"What a brave girl you are," she said. "And look at all the yuck in the water. You're going to feel so much better when we're through."

She massaged soap and water on the dog's ears and muzzle, and the dog stared trustingly at Heather the entire time. Finally, she slowly poured the pitcher of warm water over the little dog, lifted her out of the water, set her on the patio, and began drying her with the towel.

"Look at you," she said. "You're really lovely, aren't you? How could someone let you go?" She dried the dog's furry chest and tummy and the dog, with a sigh of pleasure, fell onto its back with its midsection exposed, letting Heather dry it everywhere. And Heather was right. She was a girl.

"You know," Heather said, "someone let me go, too. Sometimes when that happens, you don't have to be sad. Sometimes it's wonderful."

The dog wagged her tail.

Heather energetically scrubbed the dog dry, talking to her all the time, telling her who she was and how much she'd always wanted a dog, but they would have to be sure the dog didn't belong to anyone else. She emptied the water into the wood, rinsed the pitcher with the hose, and left it outside to dry.

Later, when darkness fell, Heather moved inside to read a book. It didn't seem right to leave the dog outside, so she invited her in, showing her where a dry towel was, in the kitchen by the door.

"You can sleep here tonight," she said.

The dog followed her happily into the living room and sat by the sofa as Heather turned on the reading lamp, put her feet up on the sofa, laid her head against a pillow, and began to read. The dog sat quietly, staring at her.

"Fine," she said. "But you'll have to leave when your owner contacts me."

She picked the dog up and settled it on her lap.

The dog curled itself into a ball, gave out a long sigh, and fell asleep.

Heather closed her eyes. What a comfort it was to have a warm little body next to hers. And what a relief it was to have someone to talk to, even if it was only a dog.

This little cottage was feeling more like a home.

She had a feeling no one would text or call to claim the dog.

And she was right. The next morning, she woke with the dog curled next to her hip, snoring. Heather checked her phone. And smiled.

Bob Essex had informed his crew that if they could work on Sundays, that was great. If they needed a day off, that was fine, too.

Ross told Kailee on Saturday night that he was taking Sunday off. They spent Saturday night together in his garage apartment.

In the morning, he made her coffee and toast in his galley kitchen.

Ross leaned against the kitchen counter. "I want to do something special with you today."

"You did something special to me last night," Kailee teased. "Besides, we have that luncheon with Mom's group at the yacht club."

"Would it be so bad if we skipped it?" Ross asked. "We've spent a lot of time with ENF. I'd like to have you alone today."

"We spent last Saturday with your mother," Kailee reminded him. She didn't want to argue, and Ross was wearing his board shorts, his chest bare, so the muscles he'd been building up hauling and hammering looked totally cut, and he hadn't shaved yet, and she loved that day-old bristly beard, and somehow an afternoon spent with her mother's very pleasant but much older and less enticing environmental friends did not seem like the best choice.

She stood up and went to him. "Babe, you know I'll do whatever you want to do." To prove it, she slipped a strap of her silk nightgown off her shoulder and pressed against him.

Ross gently put his hands on her shoulder and pushed her away. "Not that. Not now. Something else."

"Well, what?" Kailee felt insulted by his lack of desire.

"I'm going to buy us lunch at Something Natural. We're going out to Surfside and sit on a blanket and watch the ocean. And some other stuff."

Now she was curious. "Some other stuff?"

"Put on your bathing suit and meet me out front in fifteen if you want to find out." His eyes were twinkling and he was trying to hold back a smile.

"See you in fifteen," Kailee said, and stood on tiptoe to kiss his cheek.

She went down the steps behind the apartment and hurried behind the spruce hedge to the back door of her house. Like many old houses, it had narrow stairs from the kitchen, which the maids had used when the house was built in the early 1900s. She hurried up the stairs in her bare feet, trying not to make any noise, and ran across the carpeted hall to her room. She took the quickest shower of all time, pulled on her red bikini, found her straw beach tote always filled with a bottle of water, a tube of sunblock, and a beach towel, and plopped her big floppy sun hat on her head.

She quietly stepped out into the hall.

"Good morning, Kailee," her mother said. Evelyn wore a silk caftan swirling with flowers. "Why are you wearing your bathing suit? We've got lunch at the club in a couple of hours."

"I'm sorry, Mom, but Ross and I decided to skip it. We haven't had a day at the beach together in a long time."

"It would only be lunch," Evelyn said. "You could have the afternoon to swim."

"I'm sorry, Mom," Kailee said again, and hurried down the back stairs.

Ross was already in his pickup truck, sitting behind the steering wheel. When Kailee scooted inside the cab, just the sight of him, the reality of him, overwhelmed her with desire and happiness.

"I want to kiss you," she told Ross. "I want to sit on your lap."

Ross laughed. "I think I can arrange that, but we're going to the beach first. Besides, I don't think your parents would approve of you sitting on my lap in my truck in their driveway."

"Oh, parents!" Kailee said. "Let's not even think about them today."

Ross had called in sandwiches and drinks to pick up at Something Natural. After that, it was a short drive to Surfside, but a line of cars was headed in front of them, going the same way. The parking lot was almost full. The beach was spotted with umbrellas, towels, families building sand castles, teenagers screaming as they threw themselves into the waves. Ross and Kailee walked west, away from the crowds, and found a quiet spot to make their own for the day.

The wind was lazy, the waves languid, the sun shaded by clouds. Together they spread out beach towels and anchored them with a cooler of water and lemonade packed in ice, Kailee's beach bag, and the food from Something Natural. They swam for a while before returning to enjoy their sandwiches and chips.

"Let's walk," Ross said.

They ambled along quietly, letting the waves drift in and wash over their feet.

"This air," Kailee said. "It's nectar. So pure, so sweet."

"I smell salt," Ross said.

They rounded a long corner where the beach narrowed. No other people were near. The sea and the sky and the world were all theirs.

Ross stopped walking. "Kailee."

Kailee turned to face him. She looked up at him, trying to figure out his mood. Was he going to break up with her? Tell her he couldn't keep up with the business, or he didn't like being trapped on an island? She hated herself when she got like this, with all her worries and fears surging in her mind and heart.

Ross knelt in the sand before her.

"Oh," Kailee said, and she broke out in goosebumps.

With the eternal blue of the sea and sky behind him, Ross asked, "Kailee Essex, will you marry me?"

She'd known this would happen someday. They'd discussed it, and they'd made commitments to each other, but she thought Ross would need a full summer on the island before he could decide.

"Oh, Ross, yes." She knelt in front of him and started to embrace him.

"Wait." Ross reached into the pocket of his board shorts and took out a red satin box. He opened it and held it out to Kailee.

The ring was amazing. A red ruby surrounded by diamonds. It sparkled in the sunlight.

"It was my great-grandmother's," Ross said.

"It's beautiful." Kailee held out her hand.

Ross slid it onto her ring finger. The stone slipped around to the underside of her finger. "It's too big. We'll need to get it sized." He started to take it off, but Kailee stopped him.

"Let me wear it now. I need to look at it. Oh, Ross, we're engaged!"

She threw herself at him and they lay on the beach kissing and laughing, with the waves nibbling at their toes. Kailee lay on her back and held her hand up so she could see the beautiful ring.

"When should we tell my parents?" Kailee asked. "And your parents? Well, your mother. And our friends? Want to make a post on Insta? And I want to facetime people so I can flash the ring."

"When should we get married?" Ross asked. "Do you want to wait until next spring so we can have your dream wedding?"

"I can't wait that long!" Kailee hugged Ross hard. "Christmas wedding! Let's do a Christmas wedding!"

"That would make sense," Ross said. "Then in January we could go to the Caribbean for a honeymoon."

"What a genius idea! Oh, Ross! We have so much to talk about. Who will I choose for my maid of honor? Who will you ask to be your best man? What about flowers? A reception on Nantucket in December will be difficult. Most restaurants close for the winter."

"Let's focus on the present." Ross stood up and brushed sand off his arms and legs. "We should go back. The tide's coming in." He reached out a hand and pulled Kailee up.

Kailee danced into the shallow surf and rinsed most of the sand off, all the time holding her hand up so she could watch the ring sparkle.

She returned to the stretch of beach that was becoming slimmer second by second. She stood on her tiptoes and threw her arms around his neck and kissed him long and hard, curling her fingers in his thick dark hair. "I've never been so happy in my life!"

Ross put his hands on her waist and looked deep into her eyes. "Me, too. Let's go home and seal the deal."

"Oh, yes!"

Kailee packed up the cooler, shook sand out of the beach blanket, and stuffed sunscreen in her beach tote. "I think I've got it all. Let's go."

"Where's the ring?" Ross asked.

"What?" Kailee looked at her left hand. No ring. Her heart flushed with fear. "It fell off!"

They both stared down at the sand around them. Where they stood, the sand was dry and loose. A few inches away, the incoming tide made the sand wet and thick.

She dropped to her knees and ran her hand over the cool, dry sand. "It must have fallen off right here. When I shook out the beach blanket . . ." She glanced up at Ross. "Help me look. It has to be here!"

Ross knelt and joined her, gently brushing sand away from the prints their feet had made.

"The sand is dry here, the ring could have sunk . . ." Kailee dug frantically, a terrier searching desperately.

Ross took one of her hands. "Kailee. Stop. Stop a minute. Let's think when we last saw it."

"When I was in the ocean," Kailee told him. "You saw me. I kept holding my hand out to watch it sparkle in the sun. I was holding it on my finger with my thumb pressed against it, and when I walked out of the water, the ring was still on my hand. Then I reached up to kiss you, and it might have been here, when we were kissing, that it slipped off. It has to be right around here."

Kailee returned to her digging. She couldn't bear to look at Ross's face.

"Go slower, Kailee," Ross said. "In this kind of sand, any movement could cause it to sink lower."

"Right," Kailee said. "Right." With her palms, she smoothed layers of sand into piles. Separate grains slid down from the top, and other grains joined it, and half of what she brushed aside she had to brush aside again.

They widened the circle of search. Ross didn't speak, and Kailee began to cry silently, gulping back sobs. How could this happen? How could she have, in one instant, lost that beautiful ring?

"It *has* to be here. It must have fallen off when we were talking," Kailee said, extending her search to the side of their footprints.

Ross reached into the cooler. "Drink some water. You're hyperventilating."

Kailee drank, but choked as she sobbed. Tears fell as she continued to sift the sand. This could not be happening. It was too awful, too much like an omen of bad luck for their marriage. And wouldn't Heather hate Kailee for her carelessness with a family heirloom? She dug again, in a kind of frenzy, she had to find it, she *had* to.

Before her, the sea carelessly continued to come closer. Behind her, a long trench of sand lay empty.

Kailee drank thirstily from the water bottle. She was exhausted and her skin burned from the sun. She felt defeated. "I shouldn't have worn it when it was too big," Kailee said. "I'm so sorry. This is terrible."

"I should have given it to you on dry land," Ross responded, his voice a monotone. "It's no one's fault, Kailee. It just happened."

"But I want it so much!" Kailee wailed. She put her arms around her knees and lowered her head.

"Let's go home," Ross said. "We're getting sunburned. It's okay, Kailee. It's not the worst thing in the world."

Kailee took his hand and stood up, hiccupping and sniffing. "We can come back and look, can't we? We'll post it on social in case someone finds it."

Ross shrugged. He looked as if he wanted to weep. "Let's go home."

"Just one more try." Kailee bent over and scooped sand up with her hands, tossing it to the side. "Where could it have gone?"

"It's okay." Ross reached down to pull her up against him, comforting her. "It's only a ring. It's not a person. It's not a tragedy."

She sobbed against his chest. "It's beautiful. One of a kind."

"You're beautiful," Ross said. "You're one of a kind. You're what I care about."

Kailee sniffed back her tears and gave him a wavery smile. "I've never felt so lucky and unlucky at the same time."

Regretfully, she took his hand and they walked away from the spot where the ring had fallen. The sand had been churned into small volcanoes. The tides slowly rose, licking at their footprints.

Ross didn't say a word on their drive home.

ten

Heather skipped church on Sunday to sit on her patio, trying to read but actually checking her phone constantly to see if anyone was missing a dog. By early afternoon, when no one had texted, she made a list of items she'd need to take care of a dog. Bags of dried food. A collar. A leash. A proper water bowl. Some treats. A chew toy. A dog bed.

The dog lay on her feet, asleep again.

She scooted her feet away. The dog looked up at her.

"I have to go into town to buy things for you. Okay? I don't want to shut you in the house, and I don't have a leash or collar. If you want to leave, you're perfectly free to do so. Why do I sound like a parent when I talk to you?" She picked up the dog, cuddled her for a while, and finally looked into her deep brown eyes.

"I have to go. You can't go with me. Please stay in the yard. I've set out your water bowl and a comfy towel and I'll buy you a nice doggie bed and a chew toy. See you later!"

Heather put the dog down and went into her house, gathering her purse and car keys and putting on lipstick. Before she left, she looked out at the patio. The dog sat there, staring hopefully into the house.

In town, Heather hurried through her shopping. At Marine Home Center, she bought two fans, one for her bedroom and one for the living room. She rushed because of the dog, but she did stop to buy herself a pint of ice cream, because the day was warm. When she returned to her cottage, she dumped the brown paper bags on the kitchen counter and went to the sliding glass door.

The little animal was curled into a ball, nose tucked under her tail, next to Heather's chair.

Happiness filled Heather like bubbles. When she stepped outside, the dog jumped up, swishing her tail so hard she nearly fell over. Heather knelt, hugged the dog, and put a collar on her, talking to her all the time. She refilled the water bowl, poured some dry crunchies into the food bowl, and watched the dog eat. She set up the fans, and changed into shorts, T-shirt, and flip-flops. Finally, she sat on the patio, eating ice cream, reading, and thinking of names for the dog.

"Cleopatra. No. Angela. No. Sugar?" The dog stared at her with hopeful eyes. "All right. Sugar it is."

Her phone trilled. It was Jim Cooper, her real estate agent.

"Heather. How are you?"

"I'm fine," Heather told him. "Better than fine. What's up?"

"I've got amazing news and depressing news," he announced.

"Tell me," Heather said.

"Good news first. You've had an offer on your house that is over the top, even these days when it's a seller's market." He quoted a seven-figure sum.

For a moment, Heather's heart stopped beating. That Victorian house was where she'd spent countless hours listening to books on tape as she scraped faded paint and scrubbed bleach onto mildewed skirting boards and the elaborate gingerbread on the porch. She'd painted and outfitted the nursery where Ross slept when he was a newborn. Over the years, she'd papered his room according to his age. Bunnies, spaceships, cartoon characters—when he was fourteen, he'd painted over all that and hung posters of rock bands and movie posters with sexy girls. She and Wall had made love in the bedroom, eaten countless meals in the kitchen, served extravagant Thanksgiving and Christmas dinners. She kept the cupboards filled with snacks and the fruit bowls filled with apples, bananas, grapes, pears, and oranges for the times Ross brought friends home from college.

"That's wonderful, Jim," Heather said. "What's the bad news?"

"Wall wants half the proceeds."

"Oh!" Heather hadn't even thought of this. "But the house is in my name only. My grandmother left it to me."

"Wall's lawyer argues that Wall paid for the utilities and upkeep, insurance, and real estate taxes."

Heather tried to remember it all. "It's true, some years. On the other hand, I worked for him for several years without a salary. So that should be figured in, although I can see Wall's point. He should have something from the sale of the house. But not half the proceeds. What do you think?"

"Keep in mind that after sales commission is deducted, that amount will be smaller. You have to buy yourself a new house, and you ought to look at the real estate prices in Concord. I'm not sure you'll be able to find another house in this area. It's very pricey now. Any suburb of Boston is expensive."

"Wow. You're right. I haven't been thinking of next steps. Can you give me a couple of days? I want to talk with my lawyer. Wall should have something, but I need to think about this."

"Of course. My advice, stay away from those gorgeous beaches while you're cogitating on numbers."

"I will. Thank you."

Heather sat staring at the bowl of roses she'd put on the kitchen table.

She was almost free, really beginning her new life. She knew she needed to get a job, and not the part-time easy-peasy job she had at Miles's law office. Working for Miles was never boring. True, she did do a lot of typing of tedious contracts, but she also got to meet and chat with wonderfully interesting people, and she found it oddly satisfying to enter appointments on the computer's calendar. It felt like she was keeping at least some of the world in order.

Sometimes Miles would leave early or call her to tell her not to come in because his client wanted to take his appointment on the golf course or on a boat. Often, she was invited to lunch with Miles. She looked forward to those times immensely but tried not to encourage herself to think they were anything romantic. And she knew the job would last only for the summer.

She had to find a new house just for herself, but where? Did she want to remain in Concord? She had friends there. She volunteered there. But houses in Concord were outrageously expensive—obviously, given what the offer for the Victorian was. Could she move to Nantucket? Did she want to? It was gorgeous now, in the summer, but how would she feel when winter came and the wind stopped the arrivals of ferries and planes?

Plus, would Kailee absolutely *hate* her if Heather moved here? How would it look to everyone, that she had to follow her son from place to place, as if she couldn't bear not being near him. There must be some kind of fairy tale about mothers like that.

She should move to New York. Denver. Charleston. Houston. Seattle. Chicago.

She didn't know anyone there. She loved her solitude, but she couldn't live the rest of her life reading books in a rented cottage.

What had she done, coming to Nantucket? What should she do?

Kailee sat on her mother's slipper chair, watching Evelyn dress for dinner out with friends. She'd been in exactly this place a million times over the years, always fascinated by the careful attention her mother gave to choosing her makeup and her jewelry.

But she had never been this miserable, here or anyplace else.

"What should I do?" she begged her mother.

Evelyn met her daughter's eyes in the mirror as she fastened her earrings. "What you need to *do*, Kailee, is grow up and take responsibility for losing that ring. If you can't manage a personal crisis, how will you ever learn to make business decisions, where people's livelihoods rest on your word?"

"Well, that's harsh," Kailee said.

"Life is harsh," Evelyn told her. "Kailee, you are smart and clever. You can figure this out for yourself. Talk it over with Ross. His mother's not going to hate you for this. She will be disappointed, maybe heartbroken. Maybe insulted. Prepare yourself for that. You can handle it."

"I'm afraid, Mom. I have a terrible feeling . . ."

"Stop it, Kailee!" Evelyn stood up, and she was trembling. "I can't handle any more. I can't solve your problems. I'm so tired of you always needing something from me!"

The sight of her mother, her perfect cool-as-ice mother, yelling at her, shocked Kailee to the core. She couldn't remember when her mother had ever spoken to her like this.

"I'm sorry, Mom." Kailee sank back into the chair and tears filled her eyes.

"Oh, and now you're going to cry. Well, it's not going to work anymore. You're an adult. Take care of yourself and stop leeching off me."

Kailee shot to her feet, angry. "I don't leech off you!" Lowering her voice, she asked, "Mom, are you okay?"

"I'm fine. You just ask for too much." Evelyn turned her head to check her reflection in the mirror. She slipped into her heels, tossed a silk scarf over her shoulder, and went out the bedroom door.

Kailee stood in her mother's bedroom, her arms wrapped around herself, shivering. Her mother had raised her voice many times when Kailee was a teenager, but for most of her life and especially the past four years, Evelyn and Kailee had been, if not close, at least civil. Her mother's outburst was frightening. Kailee hurried to the hallway, hating her mother, worried for her mother, and feeling lost and alone. Ross was having a night out with the friends he'd made on the site crew. Her mother and father were going to dinner with friends, Maggie was certainly dealing with her children, and Dan was probably working. What could Kailee do? Where could she go? She knew she had to face Heather and apologize for losing the ring, but right at this moment she wanted someone to comfort her.

She called her friend Dan, her gorgeous, witty, childhood friend. "I need advice," she told him.

"Come here, my darling," Dan urged. "Let me ply you with sympathetic words and spirits."

Donnie and Dan's Seafood Pub was tucked into Old South Wharf, along with art galleries and posh clothing boutiques and jewelry stores. It was small inside, but they'd created an outdoor space with a colorful awning and jewel-hued tables and chairs.

Dan wore board shorts and a red tee that accentuated his washboard abs and his dark coloring. His black hair shone like obsidian, and his brown eyes were thickly lashed. He was beautiful, kind, and funny.

He was waiting for Kailee at a table outside, in a corner, and when he saw her, he stood and hugged her.

Kailee wanted to stay in his arms and cry all her tears out.

Dan pulled her chair out and they both sat, leaning on the table toward each other to speak without others hearing. "Cece is playing hostess tonight, so I can devote myself to you. I ordered you a Cosmopolitan. Tell me everything."

"Oh, Dan, I'm so glad you're here. You're exactly what I need right now. I did the most terrible thing and now Ross's mother will hate me."

"No one will ever hate you," Dan said. "Here's your drink. Take a sip and start from the beginning."

The sweet, strong liquid slid down Kailee's throat like elixir. Being here with her old friend was like being enclosed in a safe, transparent bubble. She and Dan, over the years, had cried and raged and talked each other into solutions for all sorts of problems.

"You haven't met Ross yet, but he's wonderful, Dan. He's *so* wonderful."

"As wonderful as I am?" Dan asked.

That made her smile. "No one is as wonderful as you are."

She continued to tell him how Ross had proposed yesterday, on the beach west of Surfside, and he'd given her his great-grandmother's heirloom ring, and Kailee had lost it in the sand and she had to tell Heather, who would think she was careless and would be nice but secretly angry, or maybe burst into tears or be furious, and how gorgeous the ring was and how she and Ross had looked and looked and hadn't found it . . .

She slugged back the rest of her drink. Dan motioned for the waiter to bring them another. Kailee took a tissue from her beach tote and wiped her tears.

"How does Ross feel about all this?" Dan asked.

"He says it's okay, not to get so upset, but how can I not, when it's his great-grandmother's engagement ring, and I lost it forever."

The tears came in a storm that shook her body. Dan put his arms around her and hugged her to him as she sobbed against his shoulder.

Finally, she calmed, and sat back in her chair. "Your shirt is wet," she said, with a rueful smile.

"Never mind the shirt," Dan said. "I have an idea."

"You do?"

Dan smiled his sweet smile. "One word. Or maybe it's two, connected by a hyphen—"

Kailee slugged his arm. "Stop it. Tell me!"

"Metal detector."

Kailee nodded. "Oooh. That's a good idea. But where would I get one?"

"You can rent them at the Sunken Ship." Dan held her arm. "If we go now, before the sun sets, I'll go with you."

"You're a genius, Dan!" Kailee said. "I couldn't live without you!" She hugged him hard, wrapping her arms around his neck and kissing his cheek.

"This is ridiculous," Heather said aloud.

She was not going to sit here brooding, worried about her future. She was on Nantucket, it was a beautiful early evening, she had a sweet dog. She needed to be out among people, and Sugar might enjoy it, too.

When she worked in the law office, she always dressed sensibly, what her mother would have called *decently*. No sundresses even on the hottest day.

But she wasn't working now, and she had a pretty, candy-striped sundress that made her smile just to look at it. She slipped it on, put on new mascara, lipstick, and blush, and checked herself out in the mirror. Good. She looked really good.

"Sugar," she said, "we're going to have an adventure. I'm taking you into town!"

She clicked the leash onto Sugar's collar, slid her striped tote over her shoulder, and went out the door. She turned on the radio as she drove to town and sang with Beyoncé. On Main Street, she found a parking place in front of Erica Wilson, which was a miracle on a busy summer evening. She lifted Sugar out onto the cobblestoned street, urged her over a curb and onto the brick sidewalks, and allowed her a moment to sniff a tree. Sugar's tail waved so fast, Heather was surprised she didn't achieve liftoff.

Finally, she tugged the leash and the two of them strolled down the beautiful street. Trees rose above them, lush with summer leaves. Store windows glowed with gold rings, silk dresses, shell necklaces, silver candleholders. She stopped in front of Mitchell's bookstore, checking out the books in Mitchell's windows. The store was busy. She'd go in later, when she didn't have a wiggly pup with her.

Out of the corner of her eye, she saw a tall, handsome man come out of the store, a book in his hand.

"Hi, Heather," he said.

"Oh!" She was so surprised and delighted to see him, she had a hot flash. Next to her, Sugar swished her tail furiously. "Hi, Miles. This is my new dog, Sugar. How are you? Did you get a book?" She wanted to kick herself. He had come out of a bookstore. Of course, he bought a book.

"I did. The new Nathaniel Philbrick." Miles squatted down and held out his hand for Sugar to sniff. "Hello there, Sugar. You seem like a happy dog."

"We're just strolling," Heather said. "She's never been in town before."

"I wish I could join you," Miles said. He stood up and stepped closer to Heather.

Heather's breath caught in her throat. He was staring at her as if he was going to kiss her, and suddenly she wanted that more than anything in the world.

"I wish you could join us, too," she whispered.

"Hey, Miles," a man said, clapping Miles's shoulder as he walked into the bookstore.

Miles stepped back. "I really have to go to a family thing. But listen, you look beautiful in that dress."

Heather couldn't look away from him. She managed to say, "Thank you."

Miles turned to go, stopped, and put his hand on Heather's wrist. "Really. Beautiful."

Heather felt as if she were glowing so brightly, she lit up the street. What *was* that? Had she diverted back to high school sensations? She could have kissed him, right there on the street.

People were going in and out of the stores, strolling down the streets, as if nothing amazing had just happened. Maybe this was just summer on Nantucket, where magic happened when you least expected it.

Sugar yipped and pulled on the leash. Heather crossed the street. Friends sat on benches gossiping, laughing, and families came out of Nantucket Pharmacy carrying ice cream cones and board games. Heading toward the wharf, she stopped to study the windows in Vineyard Vines and Jewel in the Sea. Sugar stopped to sniff a wooden bench, a streetlamp, a blob from someone's ice cream cone. She licked up the blob, but retained her dignity and didn't water the passing trash barrels and fire hydrants.

Heather stopped for a moment to gaze at the small craft tied up to Old South Wharf, and followed the white shell lane between the small boutiques—once fishing shacks—on the wharf. Peter England's clothing tempted her, but she didn't want to take Sugar into such a beautiful shop, so she continued to walk past artists' studios until she came to the wooden dock extension at the end of the shell lane. Delicious aromas drifted from a restaurant with an awning-covered patio. Laughter made her pause to take in the evening, the bright blue sky above, the salty warm air, the restaurant packed with people in ice-cream-colored clothes, and a couple cuddling at a table at the end. The man was handsome, dark-skinned, dark hair, and a gold bracelet on his wrist as he held a lovely young woman . . . who was Kailee.

Heather stood frozen, grateful that Sugar was determinedly investigating the shells. Was that Kailee? How could it be Kailee? It couldn't be Kailee—

The girl lifted her head, and her long chestnut hair fell down her back, and the man was smiling a lover's smile, his arm still around Kailee.

Heather couldn't see Kailee's face, which was a good thing, because then Kailee would see Heather standing there with her mouth hanging open.

"Come, Sugar," she said, pulling the dog away from her smells, and walking quickly to the wooden wharf, where she turned the corner and leaned up against a wall.

Her heart was racing. She felt unaccountably *guilty*, which made no sense, because she wasn't the one betraying Ross. What to do—should she tell Ross? That would seem too sneaky, too malign. Should she ask Kailee for a private talk? Kailee would think Heather had been spying on her. There had to be a good reason Kailee was with the man. Maybe she was saying goodbye to an old boyfriend. Maybe the man had a relative who had died.

Maybe Ross would offer Kailee the ring and she would refuse it, not wanting to marry Ross because her old lover had returned.

Maybe Heather should get a grip.

She walked down the wooden planks of the wharf, scarcely noticing the various sailboats tied up in their slips. Above her, diners at the Anglers' Club sat on the deck talking and laughing as if all was well with the world.

Heather walked to a spot on Commercial Wharf where Sugar discovered a pile of discarded shells to investigate and she could gaze out at the Boston Whalers and small sailboats tied up to the dock. She took out her phone, called Christine, and explained what she'd just seen.

"What should I do?" Heather asked.

"What *can* you do?" Christine countered.

"Okay, I've got three choices. I could tell Ross, and then Kailee would hate me forever. I could ask Kailee to meet me and I could tell her what I saw, and she'd hate me forever and suspect me of being a spy. Or I could say nothing to anyone."

"Say nothing, definitely. Your summer goal is not to make Kailee hate you."

Heather laughed. "You always do know how to cut to the core."

"Other than that, how is the island?"

Heather walked to the sea wall and sat on the edge. "It's magic. So beautiful, it's almost unearthly. I actually love my cottage, and did I tell you? I have a dog! She's a beautiful little mutt. Sugar's always excited to see me when I come home."

"And the divorce?"

"A few hiccups, but it's almost done. It's going more smoothly now that Wall has Nova."

"I've asked about her," Christine said. "She teaches yoga. Her father is P. Z. Drake, who invented something electronic."

"*P.Z.* sounds like someone who *would* invent something electronic," Heather said.

"Whatever, he has a lot of money, and he gave Nova money to buy a farm outside of Concord where she's building a covered riding ring for her horses."

"Wow. I think Wall is serious about her. I think he might live with her."

"Honey, he lives with her now. Sometimes he shows up to work in tight-fitting jodhpurs and riding boots."

"You're kidding!" Heather laughed at the thought.

"Are you jealous?" Christine asked.

"Not at all. I'm glad for Wall. He's gotten his second wind."

"He *is* handsome," Christine said.

"I know he is. I'm sure he's more handsome now that he's happy." Heather snorted. "Hey, maybe I'm prettier because I'm happy!"

"You're always pretty, Heather. And how are things going with what's-his-name? Miles."

"Christine, Miles and I don't have *things*. I work for him five mornings a week, and he's very professional. Although . . . he did invite me to go out on his boat on the Fourth of July, to watch the fireworks from the water."

"That sounds romantic," Christine said.

Heather nodded. "We'll see. Thanks for talking me through this problem. I won't do anything for now."

"I'm always here for you," Christine said.

While she'd been talking, the sun had slipped toward the horizon, softening the bright blue of the sky. The wind was quiet, the waves sliding gently up onto the sand.

She wandered back toward Main Street to her car. Sugar cheerfully hopped into the passenger seat and curled up to lick her bum. Heather started the car, pulled on her seatbelt, and cried all the way home.

The Sunken Ship was across from the Whaling Museum, and it had everything. Surfboards. Watches. Mermaid crowns. Fishing poles. Board games. Scuba gear. Straw fedoras.

And they rented metal detectors. Kailee and Dan carried them to her Jeep. They didn't weigh much, and she thought they looked easy to work. It wasn't the best they sold, but she thought it would do the job. It was basically like a long black stick with a waterproof coil attached to a digital display and a band for the lower arm.

Dan snapped on his seatbelt. "How cool is this? We're going beachcombing."

"Serious beachcombing."

"We'll find it," Dan said. "I'm sure we will."

Surfside beach in the early evening glowed. The sun was low in the sky, and a few puffy clouds drifted over the ocean, turning the water shades of blue, turquoise, and peach. Kailee and Dan walked down the steep path to the beach to see several parties gathered, some finishing a picnic meal on a blanket, others wading in the shallow waves.

"We're past here," Kailee said. "Way to the west."

"Right behind you," Dan said.

They each carried flashlights in addition to their phones with flashlights. They walked several hundred yards, playing the lights on the sand, even though they hadn't reached the spot where Kailee had lost the ring.

"I think it was here." Kailee clicked off her light and surveyed the position of the dune and the pattern of the waves. "I can't be sure. The water changes the beach constantly."

"We will be brave of heart," Dan said, putting on the low booming voice of a warrior king. He knelt on the sand and began to sweep the top away with both hands.

Kailee turned on the metal detector and slowly waved it over the beach. Dan rose and followed, kicking away sand closer to the dunes.

Nothing.

They kept walking. One moment they both gasped as the detector beeped, but when they dug down into the sand, all they found was the tab from a soda can.

They kept at it until the sun had set and the sky turned indigo, small stars winking on one by one.

Kailee sank onto the sand. "I'll never find it, will I?"

Dan said, "Truthfully? I doubt it. But, Kailee, Ross loves you.

He won't drop you because you lost a ring. You're going to marry him. You've got to start trusting him now. Someday he'll do something as careless, too."

"I don't know if that makes me feel better or worse," Kailee said.

The friends laughed ruefully and turned back to slog through the deep sand to the path up to the parking lot.

Heather drove home, full of emotions. Sugar was asleep on the passenger seat. She snored, with a small, endearing squeak each time.

Pulling into her drive, she was surprised to see Ross's truck parked there. It was ten o'clock, late for working people. Was something wrong? She checked her phone. He hadn't called. She'd left a light on in the living room, and it glowed golden through the bushes.

"Come on, Sugar," she said, and the dog obligingly jumped out of the car and trotted up the walk to the cottage. Ross was sitting on the top step.

"Ross, hi, darling. I should give you a key to the front door. I'll have one made tomorrow at Marine."

Her son rose. "Hi, Mom."

She kissed his cheek. "You smell like beer."

"I had a few with the crew. Who is this guy?" He held out his hand and Sugar warily sniffed it, then licked it. Ross laughed.

"This *girl* is Sugar," Heather informed Ross. "She found me, and we're very good companions."

"Good for you," Ross said.

Heather unlocked the door and her son followed her inside. She unclipped Sugar's leash. The little dog sauntered into the kitchen, half asleep but still present in case food showed up.

"Would you like some coffee?" Heather asked.

"No, Mom. Listen, I have to tell you something."

Heather went pale. "Are you sick? Are you hurt? Are you—"

"I'm fine, Mom. Let's sit down." He sat on a chair in the kitchen.

Heather sat across from him. "I'm all ears." A memory flashed up: when Ross was three and home from his first day at preschool, she'd asked him how he'd liked it and said, *I'm all ears.* Ross had wrinkled his nose and cocked his head. *No, you're not!* he'd yelled. But that was long ago.

"Okay, Mom, here it is. I asked Kailee to marry me."

"That's wonderful! How did she like the ring?"

"She loved it, Mom. But it was too big for her—"

"We can have it sized."

"Mom," Ross snapped impatiently. "Mom, she lost it."

"What?" The news came like a punch in Heather's stomach. She didn't care that much about material things, but the ring was an heirloom, a link to her mother and grandmother. "How?"

Ross wiped his hands on his thighs. "It wasn't her fault, that's what I want to tell you. I proposed on the beach and put it on her finger, and she hugged me and we went for a walk, and I guess it slipped off into the sand."

Heather put her hand to her heart. "Oh. Oh, Ross."

"I know. We looked for it like crazy, we sifted the sand and dug around where we'd been standing, and we couldn't find it. It's my fault, Mom, for proposing on the beach. I thought it would be romantic, and it was, but I didn't think we could lose the ring. I mean, all that sand . . ."

Heather covered her face with her hands. She didn't want Ross to see how much this shattered her.

What a loss, she thought. *What a terrible, heartbreaking loss.* The ring that her grandmother had worn, and her mother, and Heather . . . Did Kailee do it on purpose? Could she not even let that much of Heather's family into their marriage? Was Heather meant to lose everything from her past? Clearly, "losing" the ring in the sand was a direct message to Heather that Kailee didn't want anything of Heather's around, not even a beautiful, expensive heirloom ring.

Tears streamed down her face. Ross stood up, paced a few laps around the kitchen, and sat down again.

I shouldn't be here, Heather thought. *I have to leave, and I have no-where to go.*

She rose and went to the kitchen sink, rinsing her face with cold water. She filled a glass with water and drank it down. She took deep breaths and calmed down.

Sugar sat in her bed, looking anxiously up at Heather. Heather knelt next to the dog and stroked her soft, silky head. Then she returned to the table and faced Ross.

"God, Mom, I had no idea it meant so much to you," Ross said. "I'm so sorry. I feel terrible about this, and Kailee does, too."

Heather said, "It did mean a lot to me. It was my grandmoth-er's, passed on to my mother, and then to me. I'm sure Kailee didn't mean to lose it."

"It's not *her* fault," Ross protested. "Don't say *she* lost it. I was there, too."

Heather's sadness was morphing into anger. "Well, then, you *both* lost a meaningful connection to your family. And it doesn't matter, but that ring was worth a lot of money. I know Kailee doesn't need to worry about money, doesn't want *my* money—"

"Mom, stop it!" Ross pushed away from the table and stood up. "Kailee didn't mean to lose the ring! *I* didn't mean to lose the ring! Kailee *wouldn't* lose that ring on purpose! Mom, I'm sorry. *We're* sorry. And I know this makes you sad, but I don't know how to fix it."

"I don't think you can fix it," Heather said sadly. "Not everything in the world can be fixed."

Ross pulled a chair close to his mother. "Mom. Come on, Mom. This isn't like you, to be so . . ." He stopped, as if he couldn't think of the right word.

"Pitiful?" Heather suggested. Something ignited in her heart. She was furious, not pitiful!

"No, I *don't* mean pitiful," Ross said. "You've never been pitiful and you never will be. I guess the word I want is 'negative.' You're acting like, like someone has died. It's only a piece of jewelry, Mom. I can pay you back, eventually, if you're worried about money. But you need to understand that Kailee did not lose the ring on purpose."

Heather trembled as she tried to tamp down her anger. "That ring has been in the family for three generations. I gave it to you. You gave it to Kailee. Now it's gone. That's all I need to know."

Ross shouted, "Come on, Mom! Don't be this way!"

Heather didn't respond.

After a long moment of silence, Ross asked, "What can I do?"

"There's nothing to be done. I'm tired. I need to go to bed."

"Mom, don't be so sad. I'm really sorry. Kailee's really sorry."

"I love you, Ross." Heather was exhausted. "Go home."

"Okay. Good night." Ross rose from the table, waited for her to say something, and when Heather didn't speak or even look at him, he left.

Heather followed him to the door and waited as he walked to his truck. Anger remained burning inside her, and bitterness, and a righteous curiosity that made her take up her phone and call Kailee, now, while Ross was in his car.

"Hi, Heather." Kailee's voice was wary. "Did Ross tell you about the ring? I'm so sorry."

"Hi, Kailee," Heather said, and her voice was shaking. "Yes, he told me about the ring, but I *didn't* tell him about the man I saw you embracing earlier this evening. Is he the reason you 'lost' the ring?"

Kailee gasped. "Oh. My. God! Have you been following me?"

Heather's voice shook. "Tell me about the man you were with tonight."

"You are such a crazy woman." Kailee was laughing in great breathy sobs. "That *man* I was with was my friend Dan. He's gay. He's married. He helped me rent metal detectors and we went out on the beach and tried to find the ring!"

Heather sank down onto the sofa, closing her eyes and allowing the knowledge of her mistake to sink in. "I didn't know that. I didn't know anything about Dan. Oh, God, Kailee, I am so very sorry. I shouldn't have jumped to conclusions. I wish I could take it all back. Please forgive me."

"What you mean is please don't tell Ross that you called me. That you've been spying on me."

"I wasn't following you, Kailee. I was just wandering around town. I apologize. And for what it's worth, I didn't mention this to Ross."

"Am I supposed to thank you for that? Well, I won't mention it to Ross, either. He'd feel terrible. Unless you have any other news flashes, I'm going to hang up."

"Again, I'm sorry, Kailee."

When the conversation ended, Heather simply sat, staring at the empty fireplace. For the first time, she wished she had a television. It was so easy to take a break from problems by watching nature or game shows. She knew she could turn on her computer and watch something there, but she didn't have the energy.

She shouldn't have come to Nantucket. She'd known Kailee lived here. Early on, she'd sensed that Kailee was uncomfortable around her. If Heather had rented a place on the Vineyard or in Maine, she wouldn't have accidentally seen Kailee in another man's arms. Had she been right or wrong to call Kailee? She really didn't know.

She wondered if life was a matter of saying goodbye, over and over again. She remembered when she watched five-year-old Ross walk into his kindergarten room, she'd waved bravely at him, and then sat in her car for ten minutes, sobbing because he was no longer a baby. When Ross started dating, she had secretly judged each girl: Was she good enough for Ross? Would she break his heart? And when he packed his car and drove off to college at UMass Amherst, she'd waved goodbye from the front door, and then sat down on the floor, leaning against the door, crying again. Ross was now a man.

Still, when he was in college, he'd come home for holidays and the summer. His home, his bedroom, was in the Willette house.

Until he met Kailee. Then he'd been with her. Now he was with her.

But that was good, Heather thought. Ross truly loved Kailee

and in the face of true love, the loss of a ring could not be worth such heartbreak.

Heather rose and went through her nightly routine. Letting Sugar out for one last pee. Locking the doors. Turning off the lights. Connecting her phone to its charger on her bedside table. Putting on her nightgown. Brushing her teeth, smoothing Pond's Cold Cream into her face and Jergens Lotion into her hands.

She lay in bed, relaxing in the comfort and promise of rest. But her mind still churned.

When had she started saying goodbye to Wall? They had loved each other when they were first married, although the excitement of opening the store and moving into the Victorian had been part of that love. It might even have been the cause of their love.

When Ross was in high school, Heather had been asked to serve as a volunteer for the Safeguard Nature Society. She'd always volunteered for local organizations, and she enjoyed it all. The world opened up to her. Her life wasn't only about her beautiful house, her carefully prepared meals, her quiet evenings watching television with Wall. Safeguard Nature was on a different scale. It was an important national group, and when she attended the meetings, she was amazed at the size of the problem and at all that could be done to help. When she was asked to join the board of the Concord SNS, she was thrilled, honored, proud.

Five years ago, a fundraising gala was held on a late September evening at the Museum of Fine Arts. Heather was told the dress was formal. She bought a beautiful floor-length dress. She ordered a tux for Wall.

But Wall refused to go. Those society affairs were nothing but an excuse for the rich to show off, he'd said. Heather had pleaded with him. She couldn't go without him. But he'd been adamant. She'd spent that evening weeping in the bedroom. Wall had not tried to comfort her, not once. Heather had finally gone into the guest bedroom, locked the door, and fallen asleep alone.

Now she knew that that moment, that locked door, was when she started leaving Wall.

Over the next few years, Heather had been brave enough to go to the gala evenings with two other women, one divorced, one widowed. She loved the beautiful clothes, the sparkling champagne, the celebrities who spoke, and the many guests who wrote substantial checks. So what if they were only showing off clothes? Somehow, these galas made a kind of magic, a belief in fairy tales, a sense that life could change for the good, that they could help nature. For the next gala, she had the diamonds in one of her grandmother's rings reset as earrings. They were gloriously beautiful, but when she showed them to Wall, he'd said, "Why bother? You're not the diamond type of woman."

And there was another significant moment of farewell. Heather had stared at Wall, shaking, wanting to slap his face, wanting to plead with him to be kinder.

"Wall," she'd said softly, "we've lost each other."

Wall had said, "Oh, for God's sake." He'd left the room.

Heather had stood there, alone.

She'd been alone for so long.

"Okay," she said aloud in her lonely bedroom. "No more self-pity." She turned on her bedside light and picked up a book. It was a novel by Elin Hilderbrand so she knew it would be a compelling read. And *her* characters would wear diamond earrings.

A moment later, her cellphone buzzed. It was Miles. Maybe he needed to cancel work tomorrow?

"Hey, is it too late to call?" he asked.

"No, of course not."

"Good. So, Heather, I'd like to take you out to dinner. Maybe Wednesday night? There's a restaurant in 'Sconset, the Chanticleer, have you been there?"

"No," Heather quickly answered. "I mean yes, I'd like to go out to dinner with you, and no, I haven't been to the Chanticleer."

"Good. I think you'll like it. I'll pick you up at seven if that works for you."

"Seven is fine." *Is this actually happening?* Heather wondered. *Is this entire evening a dream?*

"Good. Well. I'll see you then."

"And tomorrow morning, at work, right?" Heather asked.

"Yes, of course, right. So, um, good night."

"Good night."

Heather sat staring at her phone. She was miserable and happy at the same time, like the yin-yang symbol, and that made her envision a Magic 8 Ball, like they had in her childhood. Ask a question, turn the ball, and the answer is positive. Turn it again and get a definite *no*. Or ask a question and the ball simply says: *Ask again later.*

This evening she'd been on a roller coaster of emotion. Seeing Kailee with another man, Ross telling her they'd lost the engagement ring, her disaster of a phone conversation with Kailee, and now Miles had asked her out to dinner.

She was suddenly extremely sleepy.

She put the phone on the bedside table, turned off the light, scooched down into her bed, pulled the covers up over her shoulder, and closed her eyes. A moment later, she felt Sugar jump onto the bed and curl up next to her back.

"Sugar, I have a date with Miles," she whispered.

Sugar's tail thumped several times, almost as quickly as her beating heart.

eleven

Kailee had felt much better after her time with Dan. She returned home and saw that Ross's truck wasn't in the driveway. He was out having a few beers with the guys he knew from the building site. She went up the steps to his apartment and let herself in. She wanted to tell Ross that she and Dan had looked and looked for the ring. She wanted to stay here with Ross tonight, to remind him how much they belonged together.

She had to cleanse herself of her anger at Heather and the bizarre phone call. She hated Heather for interfering in her life, for suspecting that Kailee would be with another guy, and she wanted to fly into a giant tantrum when Ross arrived home.

But she couldn't do that. She didn't want to be responsible for a break between Ross and his mother. She leaned her head against the sofa, and closed her eyes, resting.

She heard his steps on the stairs and sat up, feeling just a little bit nervous.

"Hey," he said, hanging his keys on the hook by the door.

Kailee said quietly, "Ross, we need to talk."

Ross sat down on the other end of the sofa. "I know. I was just with my mom. I told her about the ring, and she's not mad."

Kailee sat up straight. "You told your mother about how *I* lost the ring? You didn't think to take me with you?"

"I thought you'd be glad. It was a hard thing to do. I didn't know how she'd react."

Kailee tried to keep from screaming. "I'll tell you how she reacted. She called me. She's angry and paranoid and she's been spying on me. She saw me with Dan and thought I was being unfaithful to you. I told her Dan is gay and married and she apologized, but damn it, Ross, she has it in for me. She hates me."

Ross looked miserable. "She doesn't hate you, Kailee. It's just . . . she's having a hard time. Getting divorced. Selling her house. I guess that ring was symbolic, kind of."

Kailee glared at Ross. He looked trapped and miserable. Kailee was overcome by a surge of love and sympathy. She moved closer to him on the sofa and put her hand gently on his thigh.

"Okay, well, *my* mother has been super-mean to me lately. I guess it's hard for parents when everything changes. I really feel guilty and sorry and helpless about losing the ring. I can't fix that, but I'll try harder to be nice to your mother. I don't want her to be unhappy because I don't want *you* to be unhappy."

Ross turned to Kailee. "I don't think I've ever loved you more. Somehow what you said makes me feel closer to you."

Kailee went into his arms and held him tight. It was as if they'd been caught in the rain, and now the sun had come out.

The next morning, the sound of voices woke her. The bedside clock read six forty-five, so Ross was getting ready to leave for work, but from the sound of his voice, he wasn't talking about business. She slipped into the bathroom, dressed, brushed her teeth, and went down the hall to see him standing in the living room, his cellphone in his hand, looking puzzled.

"Good morning, cutie pie," Kailee said. "Is everything okay?" Maybe, she thought, someone found the ring and turned it in to the police.

"That was my father."

"Is he okay?"

"Yeah. He's coming to the island today and wants to take you and me out to lunch. He's bringing Nova with him. He wants us to meet her."

"That's good, right?"

"I don't know. I don't know what to tell my mother."

"Ross, listen to me. You don't have to tell your mother anything. Your mother left your father. Now your father wants to see us, and wants us to meet the new woman in his life. Your father is happy. He wants you in his life. This is a good thing, Ross. Don't complicate it by telling your mom."

He sighed. "I guess. Anyway, I told him we'd meet them for lunch in town. At the Rose and Crown. At twelve-thirty, more or less. Can you make it?"

"Absolutely!"

Kailee showered and dressed and went over to the house to check in with her mother. She'd promised Evelyn she'd help her in her office this morning. The work was easy. Organizing files into folders on the computer. Sending emails about the Essex Nature Foundation. Kailee kept checking the time. She was itching to go to the company's office and join George with the real business, but her mother clearly was stressed and needed Kailee's help.

Still, she was glad when Ross arrived to take her to lunch.

The Rose and Crown restaurant was near the Whaling Museum, just a short walk from the library, post office, and Main Street. It was a casual, friendly place, with a bar at one side and booths and tables at another side. Kailee wore a pale green sundress and tied her low ponytail with a matching ribbon. She held Ross's hand as they entered the restaurant, wondering why she felt nervous. Mr. Willette and Nova should be the nervous ones.

The happy couple were sitting at a table in the back. Mr. Willette wore a white button-down shirt with jeans. Nova wore a loose-fitting paisley swirl of a dress. She was very pretty, with her blond hair in a layered pixie cut that looked razored and expensive.

As they walked up to the table, Mr. Willette stood and held out his hand. They all shared polite greetings, then sat, son facing father, Kailee facing Nova.

"How was your trip over?" Kailee asked. It was the fail-safe conversation starter.

"Smooth as glass," Wall replied.

"Have you been to Nantucket before?" Kailee asked Nova.

"Oh, yes. When I was at boarding school, my best friend Jennifer Hughes invited me to stay for the summer. It was so much fun, but by the time I turned eighteen, I found it a little . . . boring . . . it's such a small town. I went backpacking for a few years in Europe and Scandinavia."

"What's your favorite city?" Kailee liked Nova, who was as sharp as the edges of her hair. She made Heather seem old and out-of-date.

"Paris, of course," Nova said.

Kailee overheard Wall and Ross, talking easily. Ross was saying how much he liked his work and the island. Kailee listened with satisfaction.

". . . Montreal?" Nova was asking.

"No, I've never been there," Kailee told her.

"The shopping is marvelous!" Nova said. "Shoes from Italy, clothes from Paris . . . we should go sometime. It's only a short flight."

"That sounds like fun . . ." Kailee wasn't sure what to do. It *would* be fun to shop in Montreal, but would Ross be upset because it would hurt his mother's feelings if Kailee went traveling with Ross's father's girlfriend?

Nova was still talking. "I always stay at the Ritz, right near the shopping district. I need to go there soon, for maternity clothes."

Just at that moment, the waitress appeared to hand out menus and ask for drink orders. Kailee had never been so happy to have a conversation interrupted in her life. As the four discussed what to choose, Kailee subtly pressed her knee against Ross's, trying to get his attention. He assumed she was flirting, and leaned back against his chair, laying his arm over her chair and fiddling with her ponytail.

The waitress went away.

Kailee took advantage of the moment of silence. "Ross, did you know that Nova is going to have a baby?"

Ross stared at Kailee, so puzzled it seemed she'd spoken in Klingon.

Wall smiled and puffed up his chest. "It's true. We'll be giving you a special little Christmas present, Ross."

Nova beamed. "We're going to have a baby."

Ross looked dumbfounded.

Kailee was counting nine months on her fingers.

"That's why I wanted to meet with you today, Ross," Wall said. "Nova and I are going to get married and I'm hoping you'll be my best man."

"Wow," Ross said. "This is all so fast. A *baby,* Dad?"

Nova leaned forward. "A baby." She looked at Ross. "A little half sibling for you." She laughed and clapped her hands.

"I don't think so," Ross said.

"Look, son," Wall began.

Ross interrupted. "Sorry, Dad. It's just a surprise. Give me a minute to take it all in."

"Do you need to phone your mother to tell her?" Wall said.

Ross reared back as if he'd been slapped. "What? Why? No! I'm not taking sides if that's what you're implying." His jaw tightened and he huffed a breath out of his nose like a dragon. "But come on, Dad, if Nova's having a baby in December, that means she got pregnant in April. This divorce isn't all on Mom and it's kind of shitty that you've been letting her take the blame."

Again, with perfect timing, the waitress appeared to take their orders. It gave everyone a chance to sit back and take a breath.

Wall surprised them by asking, pleasantly, "How's Heather?"

"She's fine," Ross answered briefly.

"Glad to hear it," Wall said. "Back to the main subject. Son, I want you to be my best man at our wedding."

"Dad," Ross said patiently, "are you and Mom even divorced yet?"

"We've started the process. We've made arrangements. Everything will go smoothly. We'll be divorced in three months."

"What that means," Ross said, tapping his fingers on the table-top, "is that it will be four months before you and Nova can get married."

Nova laughed and stroked Wall's arm. "True. We're going to slide right under the wire for the baby."

Fortunately, the waiter appeared with their lunches. Conversation lapsed, but Kailee knew that Ross's mind was racing. Hers certainly was.

Kailee broke the silence. "Where will you get married?"

Nova clapped her hands together like a girl. "We're going to have a Christmas baby, so we're renting the ballroom at the Copley Plaza in Boston. We'll have a quick private ceremony with family, and then go into the ballroom for a fabulous reception with lots of guests. My father and mother will be at the ceremony, and, Ross, you'll be Wall's best man. You must understand what it's like to have no siblings." Nova turned beseeching eyes at Kailee. "*You* understand, don't you? What it's like to have no siblings."

A shiver passed through Kailee. Was this a little creepy? That Nova seemed to know so much about her? Nova exuded the air of a sweet young thing and hid the silky strength of Batwoman.

"Do you have a date?" Kailee asked.

"Christmas Day, of course! I'll be lucky if I don't have the baby at the altar." Nova leaned against Wall, staring up at him with adoring eyes. "It will be perfect if you're best man, Ross, and of course we'd like you there, too, Kailee."

Ross said, "I'm not sure I want to leave Mom alone on Christmas Day."

Wall looked at his son. "You left your mother and me alone last Christmas when you came here with Kailee's family."

"That was different," Ross said.

Kailee spoke up, "I can't be away from my parents at Christmas. I never have before."

Nova actually seemed to emit light as she said, so sweetly, "We'll invite your parents to the ceremony, too."

Ross looked as if someone had hit him in the head with a hammer.

Kailee said, "Wow, you guys, this is a lot to take in."

"Oh, I know!" Nova pouted sympathetically. "And we have a favor to ask, too. We found some of Ross's baby clothes in a box in the storage room, and we'd love to have the clothes for our baby." Triumph gleamed in her eyes as she claimed what had been Ross's.

Ross looked like he was being strangled. His face turned red. He was speechless.

"Let's maybe wait on that," Kailee said. She put her hand on Ross's knee to comfort him. "I think that's a very delicate subject. I mean, Ross and I will be having children, and we should have his baby things for his child."

"Oh, we can give them to you when our child grows out of them," Nova said.

"No." Ross almost growled. Ignoring his food, he put his two fists on the table.

"Son," Wall started to calm him.

Ross turned on his father. "No, I will not be your best man. No, I won't let you have my baby clothes. Both my grandmothers and Mom made most of those clothes for me. They are heirlooms. They are mine. And no, Kailee and I will not be there for your Christmas fantasy wedding."

Wall spoke up again. "Ross—"

"No, Dad. Obviously, you and Nova were together before Mom asked you for a divorce. I've always tried to do what you wanted me to do, but not anymore. Kailee is my family now. We have our own plans to make."

"Ross, I think you're overreacting," Nova said.

Ross ignored her. "I can't eat and think about all your plans at the same time." He put his hand on Kailee's shoulder. "Let's go."

Kailee rose and took Ross's hand.

"I've got to get back to work," Ross said. "I'll drop you at your house on my way to the site."

"That's good." Kailee gave Ross a few moments of quiet while they rode down Main toward Pleasant. When they arrived at her house, she opened the truck door, then turned back to look at him. "Are you okay?"

"I'm fine."

Kailee reached over and touched his arm. "Ross, are you going to tell your mother about your father, and the wedding, and the baby clothes?"

"Yes. I'll probably stop by there after work tonight. She's going up to Boston tomorrow for the first divorce meeting before a judge. I don't want her blindsided by this information."

Kailee pasted a sympathetic smile on her face. "If you need me, call. And I'll wait up for you."

"Thanks, Kailee."

"I want to help, you know."

"I know you do. And you are helping." Ross shifted impatiently. "I've got to get back to work."

"Take care, sweetie," Kailee said. She hopped down from the truck and went up the walk to her house. Ross drove away.

Kailee gave herself a moment to breathe in the afternoon air. It was warm, but not hot, and beds of blue hydrangea lined the front of their house, with pink-and-white petunias winking from the soil. How could her mother do it all, Kailee wondered. Evelyn did have a gardener and a housekeeper, but Kailee was certain she'd never be able to accomplish this network of perfection. Her mother's plans for the Essex Nature Foundation were complicated. Kailee doubted that she could work for her mother and learn about her father's business, too. She knew her mother needed help, but Kailee hadn't studied in order to plan parties. She'd studied to learn how to run Essex Construction, and she was eager to start.

She didn't bother going into the house. Her mother would undoubtedly ask her to do *just one more thing*. Kailee jumped into her red Jeep. She'd already put the top down. A breeze blew against her neck, cooling her as she drove, and she didn't have far to go to get to the business office.

She was working on a spreadsheet when her cell rang. At the same time, George's cell rang. And the office's cell buzzed.

Kailee hated being interrupted, but she answered.

Their housekeeper, Gravity, said, "Kailee, your mother has had a heart attack. She's at the hospital. Your father's on his way there."

Kailee drove to the hospital, parked in the emergency lot, and ran through the electric sliding doors into the waiting area. She checked at the desk and hurried down to a room at the end of a corridor.

Her parents were there, arguing. Her mother was sitting up in a hospital bed. She wore a hospital gown and a furious glare. Kailee's father looked like a man who'd hiked thirty miles through a desert, dehydrated and wan, every wrinkle on his face suddenly exaggerated.

"I'm fine!" Evelyn snapped at Kailee the moment she walked into the room. "This is ridiculous. I want to go home."

"She's *not* fine," Kailee's father argued. "She's had a mild heart attack and needs more tests run. She needs to be in the hospital for at least one night."

Kailee went to the high hospital bed and kissed her mother. "Mom, I'm so sorry."

Naomi Landers, a physician and the mother of one of Kailee's friends, came into the room, chatting away as she performed a thousand mysterious tasks with electronic gadgets. She was tall, thin as an IV pole, with long dark hair clamped up behind her head, and a stethoscope hanging over her white coat.

Dr. Landers said, "Bob, Kailee, you should be glad. She's had a warning signal and now she can get her life calmed down."

"My life is exactly the way it's always been!" Evelyn snapped.

"Yes, my dear," Naomi replied. "But *you* have changed. Your body has changed. You can't do what you did five years ago."

Evelyn wrenched her face away from the doctor. "But I want to! I can't sit around knitting!"

"No one says you have to knit," Naomi said. "But you're going to have to change your life. Your schedule. If you keep on like you've been going on, a serious heart attack is waiting for you."

Kailee sat on the side of the bed, took her mother's hand, and said, "I'll look at your calendar and see how I can help."

"I don't think you understand," Evelyn said. "I have some very important things to accomplish. If I don't, our island will suffer and people will . . . will hate me." She lay back against her pillows and squeezed her eyes shut.

Naomi left the room, quickly returning. "Okay, I'm going to give you a little IV Valium. It's an anti-anxiety agent."

"I'm not anxious!" Evelyn snapped. "I just want to go home."

Naomi continued her work, moving slowly, speaking calmly. "You need to relax, Evelyn. We'll take care of you here. Your husband and daughter can take care of things out there." Naomi shot piercing looks at Kailee and Bob. "They're going to leave now, and you're going to sleep."

Kailee tried to kiss her mother, but Evelyn angrily turned away. Kailee walked out into the hall to find Ross waiting there. She told him what she'd learned, and Ross pulled her into his arms. While they were standing in the hallway, Kailee's father joined them.

Bob said, obviously trying to be the boss of something, "Let's go home. Evelyn's resting and there's nothing more we can do."

Dr. Landers agreed. "Your father's right, Kailee. And you must be Ross."

"Yes, Doctor, I am." Ross took his arms from around Kailee but held her hand.

"She's going to be rested and spitting mad by tomorrow, so you all need to get *your* rest, too. When you come back tomorrow, we'll have instructions printed out for you."

"Thank you."

In their own cars, the three drove back to the house on Pleasant Street. They went in the back door and found Gravity waiting for them in the kitchen. It was three-thirty.

"How is she?" the housekeeper asked.

"Cranky," Bob said.

Gravity let out a sigh of relief. "Sit down a moment, you three. Have a nice glass of iced tea."

Kailee watched her father for a cue. She was relieved that he sat. He seldom showed emotion, and she knew he must be aching with worry for her mother. They told Gravity about the doctor's diagnosis and instructions and agreed they were too shaken to do any real work. Gravity left, reminding them to call her anytime. Kailee's father went upstairs to take a nap.

Ross put his hand on Kailee's. "She'll be okay. She was her normal self when we left."

"I know," Kailee said. "And you can go back to work, but I—"

Ross was indignant. "I'm not going to work now!"

"I didn't mean it the way it sounded. I mean, I want to go work on Mom's stuff. Emails, organizing, anything. It will help me pass the time. It will make me feel that I'm helping her become less stressed."

"That's a good idea, Kailee. I guess I'll go back to the site and do some heavy lifting. We've got a lot of daylight left. Call me when you hear anything. On the way home I'll stop by Mom's and see how she is."

Kailee bristled. "You don't have to worry about *your* mom. *She's* not in the hospital."

Ross leaned back in his chair and closed his eyes. Kailee thought he was probably counting to ten.

"She's still my mom," Ross said quietly. "She's still going to be your mother-in-law."

Kailee burst into tears. "Oh, God, I'm so mean and jealous, aren't I? I'm sorry, Ross. I'm so worried about my mother."

Ross stood up, pulled Kailee up against him, and hugged her. "It's okay. Your mother will be fine. And you've had way too much family for the day. My dad. That Nova woman. Now your mother. I'll stay here with you if you want."

Kailee clung to him, grateful for his strong arms and his sturdy heart. "I don't want to let you go," she said.

"Then I'll stay right here," Ross assured her.

"You're mine," Kailee said to him.

Ross chuckled. "Yes. I'm yours."

"I have to blow my nose," Kailee said.

Ross pulled away. "On my shirt?"

Kailee laughed and stepped away from him. She took a tissue from the box on the counter and blew her nose heartily. "I love you, Ross. I'm okay. Let's both get to work."

After Ross left, Kailee went into her mother's office and sat at her computer. Evelyn's desk was piled with folders. Evelyn had downloaded dozens of pages from environmental groups. Her computer screen was framed by reminders stuck on Post-it notes.

One of the notes, in Evelyn's handwriting, read: *Ask Heather to join ENF?*

NO! The word rose automatically in Kailee's mind. She wanted to reach out and rip off the note, crumple it, and toss it in the wastepaper basket.

Stop it, Kailee told herself. *Stop being so bitchy.* She needed to be nicer to Heather, nicer to everyone. It might be the karmic move that would keep her mother safe.

Kailee worked on the computer until she heard her father come downstairs. She met him in the hall. He had bags under his eyes, and she knew he hadn't slept.

"Let's have a drink," Kailee suggested. "It's after six."

"Brilliant idea," her father said.

Kailee poured Glenfiddich over ice for him and made a vodka tonic created mostly from tonic for herself. She sat in the den with him. He'd turned on the television and was watching BBC news.

After a while, Kailee said, "Dad? Could we watch something else?"

At that moment, Ross came in. He'd just showered, so his hair was damp, and his clothes were clean, not covered with sawdust.

"Bob, we're ahead of schedule out at the site. I texted my mom. She's out, so I left her a message."

Bob said, "I called Evelyn. She's bored but calm."

"She's calm?" Kailee grinned. "I think that calls for a deluxe pizza."

Her father did a thumbs-up. "Genius. Let's order two."

They ordered the pizzas and ate them while watching *The Mark of Zorro* on an old movie channel. They phoned the hospital and were told that Evelyn was in good shape, and asleep.

They said good night and went to bed. Kailee didn't want to leave her father in the house alone, and she didn't want Ross to leave her alone, so while her father was in his bedroom, alone without his wife, Kailee was in her bedroom, with Ross sleeping next to her, and she felt safe.

twelve

Heather arrived home after grocery shopping and let Sugar out for a run around the yard. She was yipping and jumping with excitement, trying to sniff new smells and water new spots. Heather sat on the front step and watched her, smiling. Sugar had learned not to go beyond the walls of trees. She was in her territory, and proud of it.

"Come, Sugar. Dinner!"

Sugar was a smart dog and knew exactly what Heather was saying. She scurried up to her, her tail wagging her entire body, and followed her through the house and out the kitchen door, where Heather set her bowl of food. She returned to the kitchen, poured herself a glass of wine, and took it out to the patio. She'd put large pots here and there on the patio, not minding that the pots only looked like terra-cotta but were made from some new miracle material that was lightweight and made it easy for her to lift. Candy-cane geraniums grew happily in the pots, and around the edge of the yard, her petunias were multiplying daily, creating waves of purple, white, and pink. She sighed, relaxing.

This morning, Miles had been so busy with clients that Heather didn't have time to be embarrassed or even flirtatious, which was a good thing. She'd worked on the computer, answered the phone, adjusted Miles's work calendar, and chatted with the clients who were waiting to see the lawyer. Most of them told her they'd known Miles when he was just a boy. He was such a great fellow, they said. They would trust him with their lives.

When the last client left, Miles remained in his office. Noon came, and no one was waiting, so Heather stuck her head around the door.

"Is there anything else I can do?" she asked.

Miles looked up from a long document. "No, Heather, thanks."

"All right. I think I emailed you, but I won't be here tomorrow. I have to go off-island."

Miles grinned. "Just be sure to return."

"I will." She tore herself away from his gaze and left the office.

As she drove home, she thought about tomorrow. She was driving off the boat and off the Cape, up to the western part of the state to the Concord District Court where she would stand before the judge and ask for a divorce. Her lawyer told her it wouldn't take long. Since Wall and she had both signed legal papers declaring the irretrievable breakdown of their marriage, it would take only a few moments for the judge to accept the separation agreement. Heather would be able to drive down to Hyannis and catch the five-thirty ferry. She'd be home by eight-fifteen. Ross had promised to come feed and walk Sugar, so she wouldn't be alone all day.

It was quiet in her yard. She had space to consider her choice one more time. She'd thought about divorcing Wall for so long, but she'd never dreamed she'd be sitting here, on Nantucket, drinking wine, with only a dog for companionship. She loved the moment in movies when two lovers finally came together for that long, romantic kiss. As a girl, she'd always wondered what happened to Cinderella and the prince after they married. During her teenage years, she realized that married life was not all sugar and violins. Her parents had not divorced, but they'd allowed their marriage to grow stale. They'd stayed together, rather like two legs holding up a table, and at night Heather had heard them arguing in their bedroom. And yet, when her father died at seventy, her mother died three months later. They definitely had been a matching set.

Heather thought of the friends she had in Concord who were older. Both men and women, all clever, educated, witty. Marjorie Smith, a grand dame who'd been head of a private school, had told Heather one day when they were having tea that this death thing had been arranged incorrectly. Everyone feared getting older, Marjorie had said, because of weakening bodies and eventual death. Wouldn't it be better if, at eighty, suddenly you were twenty again but you could eat all you wanted without getting fat and have all the sex you wanted without getting pregnant? That way, people would look forward to getting older, and death could nab you when you were cheerfully eating cake.

Heather smiled, remembering. She missed Marjorie, who'd passed away two years ago. She'd miss so many people in the town, and the beauty and history of Concord itself, but she knew she needed to leave it. To live somewhere else.

She wished she could live here, on Nantucket. Could she afford it? The sale of the Victorian house in Concord might give her enough money for a small place, like this cottage, but she'd have to work, and she'd have no health plan or pension. Miles wouldn't need her full-time, but maybe he could recommend her to another law office. She needed a serious job.

Sugar raced over to her, carrying a stick in her mouth, demanding she stop brooding and play with her. Heather laughed and rose and threw the stick. This was a game Sugar could play endlessly, and it was almost twilight when Heather and her dog went inside.

Heather had bought herself a sandwich from Sophie T's. She found her current mystery novel, leaned it against the salt and pepper shakers, and sat down at the table to eat. Not until she got ready for bed did she listen to her messages on her phone.

Her son said, "Mom, I'm at the hospital with the Essexes. Evelyn had a slight heart attack. I won't be able to get over to see you tonight. Don't worry, Evelyn's sitting up in bed and talking, but Kailee and her father and I are hanging with her until the nurses chase us out. Love you."

Was there anything she could do? Heather wondered. It would be odd to send flowers to the hospital if Evelyn would be going home tomorrow morning. She could call Evelyn, but not while Evelyn was surrounded by nurses, doctors, and beeping machinery. She decided she could do nothing, maybe make a casserole when she returned from Concord and take it to the Essexes, although with all their friends, they would be smothered with casseroles.

Heather prepared herself for bed, set her alarm, and fell asleep at once, thanks to the pure ocean air.

In the morning, Heather drove her car onto a car ferry, and waited until they were well under way before calling Ross. She got sent to voicemail, so she simply said, "Hi, Ross. I hope Evelyn is doing well. I'm going to Concord for the day. Will you still be able to stop by the house and let Sugar out for a pit stop and a run? Love you."

When they arrived in Hyannis, Heather set the car radio to classic rock and drove steadily west and north to Concord and the courthouse. She parked the car, slid back her seat, and changed from her comfortable sneakers into her more appropriate low heels. She checked her phone for messages—none—and gave a quick review of her hair in the mirror. She didn't want to appear windblown, peculiar, unable to answer a judge's questions truthfully and sanely. But she did feel nervous. What if the judge refused to approve the separation agreement? What if she forced them to go to a marriage counselor? Her hands were sweaty and her heart was thumping. Finally, she left the shelter of her car for the judgment of the court.

Her purse took a trip through the conveyer belt as she stepped into the security metal detector. She knew she had no metal on her. She'd removed her wedding ring long ago, and used her phone to tell the time. She was waved on. After studying the list of names near the elevator, she went up to the second floor, looking for the family and probate court.

"It's this way." Sarah Martin hurried up to Heather. "I'll sit with you but this is basically pro forma. It will be over in a flash."

"That's good," Heather said, but her attention was attracted by Wall sitting on a bench outside the courtroom. A very pretty young woman sat next to him. Heather thought, *That must be his girlfriend.* She was happy for him, and relieved for herself. The seriousness of being inside a court of law seemed daunting, as if the judge would say, *No! You cannot have a divorce! You are going to jail for twenty years. Guard, take her away!*

She'd clearly been reading too many mysteries. It amazed her, how much she wanted this divorce. She smoothed her dark blue linen dress and wished linen didn't wrinkle so easily.

Wall stood up and walked toward her. "I'm glad you made it. We'll be called any moment."

Heather smiled. "Hello, Wall. I see you've brought a friend."

Wall was calm, almost triumphant. "This is Nova." The young woman rose and linked her arm through Wall's. "My fiancée."

Good grief! Heather thought. *She's younger than Ross!* But she didn't flinch. "Hello, Nova," she said politely. Nova wore a loose summer dress printed with pink flowers and a pink headband in her hair. Heather wanted to wish the girl good luck, but she simply smiled.

"I'm so happy to meet you," Nova said, in a high-pitched, breathless voice. "I loved meeting Ross and Kailee yesterday."

Surprised, Heather echoed, "You met Ross and Kailee yesterday."

"Yes," Wall said. "We had lunch together. Didn't he tell you?" His eyebrow was arched and his eyes were wide in gleeful surprise.

Heather almost rolled her own eyes.

Nova bent toward Heather, smelling like vanilla ice cream and speaking in sugary tones. "We were asking if he would mind if we used some of his baby clothes for our baby." Nova gave a loving look at her belly and put her hand over it.

"You're pregnant?" Heather asked.

"Yes! We're having our baby in December, and we're getting married that month, too." Nova glowed with happiness. "And Ross will be Wall's best man!"

"He will?" Heather asked.

"Yes, on Christmas Day."

Heather did the math in her head. Her eyes met Wall's. Why hadn't he told her about Nova? Why had he let Heather carry the guilt?

And why in the world hadn't Ross called to tell her all this?

"I'm surprised Ross didn't tell you," Wall said.

Heather could hear the smugness in his voice. "He did call last night," Heather told him. "He said that Evelyn, Kailee's mother, had had a heart attack and they were with her in the hospital."

Nova's eyes went wide. "Is Kailee's mother very old?"

"Not at all," Heather responded pleasantly. "She's younger than Wall. But these things happen."

"Willette!" the court clerk called.

They filed into the small courtroom. Nova slipped into a seat in the second row. Heather and Sarah sat at opposite tables from Wall, both before the judge.

Heather forced herself to concentrate. The judge was a young Black woman who seemed extremely solemn and also slightly bored, as if she'd seen it all before. Heather couldn't understand why, but she was struggling to contain a fit of nervous laughter. How long had Wall been with Nova? Nova was pregnant? She knew Evelyn had been hospitalized, but couldn't Ross have left Heather a message about his lunch with his father? And was Evelyn okay? Heather should have called this morning to see how she was. Her mind flipped back and forth like curtains in a breeze.

The judge asked Heather if their marriage was irretrievably broken. Heather nodded and said, "Yes."

A moment later, Wall answered yes to the same question.

A few moments later, the judge said the divorce would be final in four months. Heather and the others rose and walked out of the courtroom.

Sarah spoke quickly to Heather and hurried off. Wall approached Heather, while Nova went to the bathroom.

"So," he said, "we're divorced." He wore a striped button-down shirt and a tie, but no jacket. He stood with his hands in the pockets of his trousers, as if wanting her to notice that he'd lost weight. He was still handsome, much like an older Ross. Heather would always think he was handsome.

But before today, she'd thought that no matter what, he wouldn't lie to her. Now here they were, and Nova was pregnant, living proof that Wall had emotionally and romantically left Heather before Heather had left their marriage.

"So," Heather answered, "how long have you been seeing Nova?"

Wall blushed. "I didn't think it would last. I thought . . . but I really like Nova. I mean, she's smart and kind and she really loves me."

"You didn't answer my question, Wall."

Wall sighed heavily. "Look. Do we really have to do this here? We're divorced. You asked for it. I'm moving on."

"I'm glad. Now, I've got to get back to the island."

Heather was turning to go when Wall put his hand on her shoulder. She froze.

"We had some good times, didn't we?" he asked.

Heather took a deep, calming breath. "Yes, Wall, we did. Good luck. I mean it."

As she left the courthouse, Heather considered driving by their house, but she wanted to get going, to get *home*.

And why did she think of Nantucket as home? Her small cottage was only rented for three months. From there, she could live anywhere. In a stucco house in New Mexico, or a condo in Miami, or out in western Massachusetts, in the beautiful Berkshire Mountains where the bears roamed. But she felt so content in Nantucket, so attuned to the island, so pleased every day to walk by the ocean, and she was making good friends. It was true that she had no idea what it was like to live on an island in the winter. It was true that she probably could find a house on Nantucket that she could afford from the sale of her Concord house, but it would have to be the tiniest house on the island. How would she pass the winter?

Books, she thought, puzzles. Church. She'd buy a television. She'd walk on the beach during storms, watching nature in all its moods. She belonged to a bridge club. She'd join a book club. And work. She'd have to work. She wanted to work.

She steered her car away from the congested racecourse of Route 128. The traffic thinned slightly and driving was less challenging. Her senses had been on high alert all day, and as the road headed south, she relaxed. All would be well. The divorce would take place, and Wall would not suffer, because he had Nova.

Suddenly, shaking with emotion, clutching the steering wheel tightly, keeping alert, eyes fastened on the road, Heather wept. She wept because what kind of woman was she not to realize that her husband was sleeping with another woman? What kind of a mother was she when her son had lunch with his father and didn't tell her, when he agreed to be the best man at his father's wedding on Christmas Day? What kind of mother was she to be silently but deeply angry because her son's girlfriend had lost Heather's grandmother's ring? What kind of a mother was she when she accused his girlfriend of cuddling in public with another man?

No wonder she wanted to live alone. Obviously, she had no resources to recognize anything beyond herself.

She arrived in Hyannis and drove to the Steamship Authority terminal. She gave the attendant her ticket and waited in line for the car ferry. She drove up the ramp, leaving solid land for the boat. One of the crew directed her toward an aisle of cars. She pulled into place, turned off her engine, and took a deep breath. She'd made it just in time to go on the five forty-five boat, which meant she'd arrive at eight-fifteen, just as twilight was falling. She realized she was hungry, so she dried her face and put on fresh lipstick, left her car, and went up the steps to the deck with the concession counter. She bought a glass of wine and an egg salad sandwich and took it outside. On the bow of the ferry, people were celebrating some occasion with much noise and laughter. She went to the long deck along the starboard side, where benches were placed. She sat, ate, drank, and let herself be rocked by the steady motion of the waves. The waters they were passing through changed colors as the sun sank toward the horizon. Birds sat placidly in the sea, not bothering to notice the huge ferry passing them. Stars came out in the pale sky, and the moon was a curl of light.

Heather remembered how content she'd been when she met Wall, stable, reliable, calm, Wall. Working with him as they started the hardware store had given her such hope. What they sold had been real. Weighty hammers, acid paint thinner, bristly paintbrushes, clattering nails. By that time, Heather's parents were retired and traveling. When Ross was born, her parents were happy for her, but they were never around.

The ferry slowed and rumbled as it made a full turn to enter its slip at the wharf. Heather joined the line of people going down to their cars. She sat patiently waiting while the boat docked and the ramp was lowered and fixed. She felt weary and yet oddly elated. The two and a half hours of the ferry's crossing had been a kind of time capsule in which she could recall what she'd had with Wall and Ross and work and friends. It had been a good life, until it wasn't.

And now? She'd come to Nantucket because Christine had suggested it, had found the cottage for her to live in for the summer. Her husband was marrying a young woman who would take care of him, and her son was marrying an ambitious woman who came with an entire construction company attached.

Now Heather had no one to care for.

Now Heather could be completely herself.

She had only to discover who that was.

As Heather was waiting to drive off the ferry, her phone pinged. She had a text from Ross.

Working late. Stopping by your place at nine. OK?

Heather couldn't help it. She smiled, replied *Okay,* and her day brightened.

At home, Heather changed into shorts and a T-shirt, put Sugar on a leash, and went for a walk down the dirt lane to Milestone Road, allowing Sugar to stop and sniff three hundred places along the way. When Sugar saw the roaring traffic going to and from 'Sconset, she cowered and began to bark savagely, so Heather turned back toward her cottage and threw a ball for Sugar to catch. She found a stick at the far end of the backyard to chew on. Heather went inside and poured herself a glass of rosé. She called the Essexes' number to see how Evelyn was. Her call went to an answering machine. Heather left a brief message of good wishes. She let Sugar inside and curled up on her couch and read.

Sugar barked when she heard Ross's truck on the lane. Heather walked around the house to greet her son. Ross's clothes were stained with sweat and coated with wood dust, and he looked tired.

"Ross, have you come straight from work?" Heather asked.

"What was the first clue?" Ross joked.

She was glad for his easy manner. "Would you like a beer?"

"Please."

She led him out to the patio, brought him a cold beer, and settled in a chair across from him.

"Man, this tastes good," Ross said. He downed three-fourths of the bottle in one swallow.

"How's Evelyn?" Heather asked.

"She's okay. Still in the hospital. They're doing tests. She might have high blood pressure."

Heather nodded. "I wouldn't be surprised. It's been a big day. I drove to Concord today. Your father and I are now officially divorced." Before Ross could respond, she said, "Also, I met Nova. I learned that Wall and Nova were here on the island, having lunch with you and Kailee." She tried to keep her voice from shaking, but she was hurt . . . and angry.

"Mom, I'm sorry. I wanted to tell you, but I didn't have time with Kailee's mom and all that. Everything was crazy. I should have told you. I'll tell you now. Dad called to say he and Nova would be on the island, and would Kailee and I meet them for lunch. We did. He asked me to be best man at his wedding, and I absolutely *refused.* Kailee and I left and didn't even eat lunch. I was furious when I realized that he was, um, seeing Nova before you left him. But Nova is having a baby in December, and I do want to at least *see* the baby because he or she will be my half sibling."

"Your half sibling," Heather echoed.

"Mom, I'm up to my ears in work, plus Kailee and her mom's heart attack. For some reason Bob has skipped me up to shadowing Riley Sweet, who's the site manager on the house at Pocomo. I think Bob has to concentrate on helping his wife get better, and Kailee has to help deal with all her mother's correspondence, and everything's a mess right now."

Heather nodded. "Okay. I get it. I'm glad we're talking. I know your life is with Kailee now, and you seem happy to work with Bob Essex, so that's all good. I don't have to know every single thing you do, but I'm grateful to be in your life. Just not too far in to interfere." She took a deep breath. "Actually, I've been thinking . . . I might want to buy this cottage and live here year-round." She quickly added, "I don't know that I'll do that. I don't even know where I'll be at Christmas, or after the summer. Don't tell Kailee yet, not until I have plans in place. This is a difficult time for that family. And, Ross, I know they're lucky to have you."

Ross stared at his mother as if she'd turned into a genie. "You could afford to buy a house on this island?"

"Yes. The house sold for much more than we thought, and

because my grandmother left it to me, we have no mortgage to pay off." Heather rose. "I'll get you another beer."

She returned with a beer for Ross and a glass of sparkling water for herself. "Listen, Ross, there's something about this island that makes me feel alive. Maybe it's the ocean, the walks on the beach, the openness. I've also made friends, some good friends—"

"Wait a minute, Mom." Ross looked even more amazed. "Do you have . . . like, a boyfriend?"

Heather smiled. "I have many friends. You know I attend church. I've been helping with their summer sale. I've joined a bridge club. We play every Thursday night. I enjoy being here. People know me as *me*, so it's like a new start in life. What I'm trying to say is, you don't have to worry about entertaining me or taking care of me. I'm only beginning to understand how young I am, how much fun I can have, how much freedom I've got to explore my opportunities."

"You sound like you're on drugs."

Heather laughed. "Do I? I am on a high, in a place I never expected to be." She looked down at her hands. *My grandmother's ring,* Heather thought. *My discomfort with Kailee. I have to let these things go. I can't change anything. I've got my own life to make my own mistakes in.* Looking up, she said, "Tell me more about Evelyn."

Ross relaxed. "She wants to come home tomorrow, and she's driving Kailee mad. The doctor wants her to stay in the hospital, and Kailee's trying to organize her paperwork without making her mother freak out."

Heather nodded. "We mothers can be a problem."

Ross tipped back his beer, finishing the last drop. He sat for a moment, staring at the bottle. Finally, he looked up at Heather. "Mom, I'm sorry Kailee and I lost that ring. I know she's worried that you will, I don't know, always kind of hold it against her."

"I'm sorry the ring was lost, too," Heather answered honestly. "It meant a lot to me. But your happiness is the most important thing in my life . . ." She stopped herself. "No, I won't say that, because I don't want you to feel that my happiness depends on yours. I simply mean, it's too bad about the ring, but we won't dwell on it."

"Thanks, Mom." Ross yawned and stood up. "I'd better go home."

Heather walked him through the cottage to the front door. "How do you like your garage apartment?"

"It's great. A total man cave. I can shower and eat junk food and watch baseball." He smiled. "Bob has a cool den in the basement, with leather sofas and a huge TV and a bar. Sometimes I go over there. Sometimes I eat dinner with them all in the dining room, and that's kind of boring, because Evelyn is such a perfectionist."

Heather smiled. "You mean you have to eat with utensils instead of your hands and take part in polite conversation?"

Ross smiled, too. "Yeah. What you said." He hugged Heather. "I love you, Mom."

"I love you, too."

thirteen

Wednesday morning, Kailee woke in a state of alarm. She sat in her bed, taking deep breaths, saying aloud to herself, "It's okay. It's okay. She's okay."

It was six-thirty, so she showered, dressed, and went down to the kitchen. The house was oddly quiet and she saw that her father's truck wasn't in the driveway. Nor was Ross's. Ross had probably gone to work. Her father was probably at the hospital with her mother.

Kailee made herself a cup of coffee and took it out to the garden. In the early morning, the day was fresh, sweet, renewed. The flower beds had been neatly edged by her mother's gardener, and green shoots carried swelling buds. The new dawn rose climbed the trellis, pale pink petals swelling within their green shells.

"She'll be back soon," Kailee told the garden. She spoke aloud, as if the garden were capable of hearing, and maybe it was. In any case, she thought it was what her mother would want her to do. She'd overheard her mother talking to her plants often.

"It was only a mild heart attack," Kailee continued. "Evelyn had pains in her chest, and she couldn't get her breath, and she was nauseous. Dad drove her to the hospital. They gave her an EKG, and some blood thinners and anti-inflammatories. When I got to her, she was sitting up in bed with wires attached to her chest, covered by a hospital gown and sheets. She was indignant about having to wear the gown."

A catbird flashed across the yard, perching on a holly tree near the house. Kailee's mother believed the catbird knew her and chatted with her when she sat on the patio or worked in the garden.

"I'm supposed to check Mom's calendar and take care of whatever she'd planned for today."

The catbird twittered.

Kailee looked at it. "I know I can't replace Evelyn. I'm not intending to do that. I can't replace my mother."

The catbird flew away. Kailee bent over, covered her face with her hands, and cried.

It had been frightening to see her uber-capable mother shrunk down into a slender body in a room full of machines and instruments. Evelyn's lipstick and other makeup had faded, and her hair was disheveled.

"Evelyn's hair was a bird's nest." Trying to be cheerful, Kailee called out to the birds in the garden. "That's cool with you guys, right?"

And now, here Kailee was, with an empty coffee cup, abandoned by the catbird.

In the conservatory, Kailee approached her mother's desk with trepidation. Her mother would hate anyone messing with her correspondence, but Kailee had to do it, and she realized with a shiver down her back that her mother might not be able to work full force again this summer. She sat in her mother's executive chair, opened her computer, and began making notes in her phone about what she had to do.

Evelyn was president of the Essex Nature Foundation, secretary of a conservation foundation, treasurer of a historic organization, and vice president of Save the Water committee. She was on the board of A Safe Place, Nantucket Food, Fuel, and Rental Assistance, the Nantucket Atheneum, and the Nantucket Historical Association. Kailee brought up her mother's calendar for the entire summer. Not one day was clear and free of commitments.

"Mom, this is crazy," Kailee said aloud.

She spent an hour studying her mother's messages and emails. She made another cup of coffee and drank it with one hand while moving the mouse with the other.

"Look at me," Kailee said aloud to herself. "Multitasking."

At noon, she called her father.

"Do you have a moment, Dad?" she asked.

"I answered the phone," he replied.

"Okay, listen. Mom has too many things going on. She'd have to be mainlining Red Bull to get them all accomplished. Even with me helping, she can't possibly do them all. I think she has to resign from some of her boards or give up the idea of the Essex Nature Foundation for this year."

"Dr. Landers is meeting us at two this afternoon, in Evelyn's room," her father said. "Let's run this past her with the doctor present."

"Okay," Kailee said. "I'll be there."

"One thing, Kailee," her father said. He paused. "Look. Your mother is very sensitive about the criticism our company is getting from everyone about the kind of construction we're doing. See if there are other things she could drop. She has to keep ENF."

"But if we drop the other committees—" Kailee began.

"I know, I know. It's a problem. But we've got to take care of your mother. Let's see what Landers says this afternoon."

At five minutes until two o'clock, Kailee entered her mother's hospital room. Her father was already there, arms folded, leaning against the wall rather than sitting next to his wife, holding her hand. Kailee knew at once they'd been arguing.

"Hi, Mom! I brought you some flowers!" Kailee held out a vase filled with pink peonies in lush full bloom.

"Did you pick those from my garden?" Evelyn asked.

"I did. And there are plenty left, I promise." Oh, dear, Kailee thought, her mother was already in a bad mood. "I'll just put the vase over here where you can see it, okay?"

"Nothing is okay today," Evelyn said.

Kailee studied her mother. She was still in her hospital gown, with two IVs dripping into her arm. She had brushed her hair and dabbed on lipstick, but she was pale and seemed incredibly thin in that big bed.

"Hello, everyone." Sylvia Hall swept into the room. "Dr. Landers is on her way."

Kailee went over to stand near her father. Sylvia checked the IVs and pulled a rolling table with a computer on it to the side of Evelyn's bed.

"A little constipation going on?" Sylvia asked.

Evelyn flushed. "Do we really have to discuss this now?"

Before Sylvia could answer, Dr. Landers entered the room.

"Good afternoon, Evelyn. Hello, Bob. Hello, Kailee." She turned the computer toward her. "So, Evelyn, the EKG and ultrasound show that you had had a mild heart attack on Monday. That means the damage to your heart was minimal and not permanent. You've been given nitroglycerin and a blood thinner and an anti-inflammatory. Your pulse is steady and has been for two nights, but I'm not happy about your blood pressure. I see on your chart and from talking with your PCP that you do not take any blood pressure medication. Correct?"

"Right." Evelyn stared at the doctor, listening carefully.

"On your chart, it indicates that you often have high blood pressure."

"I'm a busy person," Evelyn said haughtily. "I often need to work under stress."

"Yes, well, you're going to have to stop doing that for a while."

"Oh, I don't think that's—"

Dr. Landers interrupted as if Evelyn hadn't spoken. "Do you smoke?"

"No. You should know that. I filled out a questionnaire."

"Do you exercise regularly?"

"I don't work out, but I'm not lying around eating chocolates." Evelyn almost spat out the words.

"You need to add aerobic exercise to your daily life, even if it means cutting out other activities."

"*Activities?*" Evelyn was incensed. "I don't have *activities*. I—"

"You need to take a thirty-minute walk at least three times a week. Or get an exercise bike or a treadmill." Dr. Landers held up her hand in a *stop* signal. "I get it about your work, Evelyn. I know who you are. I'm aware of how many boards you're on. And I'm telling you, you need to cut back. Hire an assistant. Block out some time in each day for exercise. You have to change your life."

"I'll help her." Kailee stepped forward. "My mother has asked me to help her with her committees this summer."

"That's nice," Dr. Landers said. "Maybe, for a few months, you can be completely in charge of the committees. Your mother needs to reduce her level of stress. Live a more balanced life."

Evelyn was breathing heavily. Kailee moved closer to her mother and held her hand. It was frightening to see her mother in such an emotional state. Evelyn didn't take orders. She gave them.

"Is that all?" Evelyn answered through gritted teeth.

Dr. Landers studied Kailee's mother for a long silent moment. "Evelyn, I don't think you understand that you're at risk. I think—"

"I'm *fine*." Evelyn shoved back her covers and swung her legs over the side of the bed. "I just need to get home."

Dr. Landers said, "Evelyn, look at the screen. Your blood pressure just rocketed up." She moved closer. "Please calm yourself. Please get back in bed. Make yourself comfortable. I'm keeping you here for one more night."

To Kailee's dismay, her mother raised her voice, nearly shouting, "This is not who I am! I do not stay in hospital beds!"

Dr. Landers leaned toward Kailee's mother. Kailee thought she
was going to hug her, reassure her, tell her that everything would
be all right.

Instead, Dr. Landers picked up Evelyn's hand and felt her pulse.

A nurse entered the room. She conversed softly and quickly
with Dr. Landers, left the room, and returned with a white paper
cup in her hand.

"Evelyn," Dr. Landers said, "I want you to take these two pills.
They are low doses of a beta-blocker, Tenormin, and a diuretic.
I'm also giving you an anti-anxiety shot. You're in danger of giving yourself another heart attack. It's important that you calm
yourself. You are safe, your husband and daughter are here with
you. All you have to do is rest."

"Mommy," Kailee said, "please get back in bed."

Evelyn grudgingly accepted the pills and drank them down
with a sip of water. She slipped her legs back under the sheets and
lay against the pillows. The nurse gave her a shot in her forearm
and left the room.

Evelyn began to cry, slowly, silently. "Bob," she said to her husband, "I can't stay here. It is very difficult for me to be in a strange
bed, with other people telling me what to do." She covered her
face with her hands and whispered, "I'm afraid."

Bob bent over his wife, holding her hand and smiling at her.
"You can do this for one more night, Evelyn. You're a strong
woman. Kailee can keep things on schedule. Think of it as, maybe,
you're a Rolls-Royce in the garage having your tires rotated. You'll
be back on the road soon."

Evelyn laughed and touched her husband's face. "You're such a
smooth talker. I feel better already."

Kailee slipped out of the room, deeply moved by her parents'
connection. She missed Ross. She hoped they could have a marriage as loving as her parents'.

———

One of the pleasures of having a dog, Heather decided, was having someone to talk to, someone who didn't judge or get bored.

"Can you believe this, Sugar?" Heather stepped out of the shower and took a towel from the rack. "I have a date tonight! Isn't that weird and wonderful?"

Sugar wagged her tail.

"Miles is very handsome, Sugar. Quite posh. I wonder where we'll go to dinner."

She picked up her hair dryer. Sugar ran from the room. She hated the noise.

She dressed slowly, taking pains with her mascara, blush, and lipstick. She slipped into a lavender silk dress she'd bought online. Online shopping was becoming one of her bad habits. But the dress fit perfectly, with a cute wrap tie at the waist. She twisted her hair up in a chignon, pulled a few strands of hair free to soften the effect, and added colorful earrings shaped like daisies. She wore nude espadrilles, keeping in mind Nantucket's uneven brick sidewalks.

She was ready, and it was only six-thirty.

"Let's go for a walk, Sugar," Heather said. This would give her some outdoor time and help Heather calm her racing heart. She hadn't been on a date since before she married Wall. Surely, whatever a *date* meant had changed in the past twenty-five years. She felt like a newly hatched chick, clumsy and wet-feathered, going on a date with a rooster.

When she heard a car coming up the drive, she kept a firm hand on Sugar's leash. The dog was almost as excited as she was to see the silver Triumph convertible stop outside her cottage. Miles stepped out, looking like someone from a Hallmark movie in his blazer and white flannels. His thick red hair had been ruffled by the wind, and his nose and cheeks were sunburned.

"Don't judge," Miles said before he even said hello. "The car is my father's. I'm obligated to drive it every so often to keep it in shape. I know I look ridiculous, the clichéd old guy with a fast car."

Heather was so startled she laughed. "All you need is a cute young chick in the passenger seat."

"You'll do very nicely," Miles said.

Before Heather could point out that she was hardly young, Miles came right up and kissed her cheek. "I'm so glad to see you."

Sugar jumped and barked, demanding equal attention. Miles immediately knelt to pet the dog until Sugar's tail whirled like a pinwheel.

"Are you ready to go?" Miles asked as he rose. "Would you like me to put up the top? Will the wind mess your hair?"

"Oh, please keep the top down," Heather said. "I'll just put Sugar in the house." Miles exuded good cheer like a nerve gas, and her heart tripled its beat and she couldn't stop smiling.

Miles helped her into the car. "Let's not try any serious conversation in the car, because we won't be able to hear each other."

"Good idea," Heather said. "Maybe no serious conversation all evening."

"I like the way you think," Miles said, as he turned the key and the engine hummed to life.

No serious conversation all evening? Where in the world had that thought come from? Heather felt young and carefree as she sat back in the leather seat. It was the island magic, she thought. She'd heard people speak about the island magic, and here it was. She didn't feel old, and she didn't worry that Miles might be, as her mother would say, *simply out for what he could get,* which meant sex, of course. Maybe Heather was out for what she could get, too. She laughed out loud at the thought. She'd had no alcohol, but she was already inebriated.

Miles drove into the small village of 'Sconset on the east end of the island and parked in front of the Chanticleer. They were seated at a table next to the window, and they ordered drinks, a vodka and tonic for Heather, and sparkling water for Miles, because he was driving.

"How are you liking Nantucket?" Miles asked.

"Truthfully?" Heather shook her hair, running her hands over it to smooth it. "I love it. Everything about it."

"How did you find your hidden cottage?"

"Where to start?" Heather said. "Luckily, a friend, Christine Calloway, who lives in Concord, had a friend who wanted to rent it, and I was at a divide in my life, leaving my husband, and this was my hideaway and summer vacation all rolled into one."

It was easy to talk with Miles. He was kind and funny and he seemed interested in Heather. They talked comfortably as they ate their oysters and sea bass.

Miles told Heather he'd made enough money when he was in Boston to take care of him for the rest of his life but he realized he didn't like the life he'd been living. He often thought with envy of his grandfather who had been a lawyer in a small town but never worked on the weekends and always went fishing on Saturday and to church on Sunday. On Sunday afternoon, he and his wife would sit on the porch and read and talk and just enjoy the day. Miles wanted to do that. He wanted to watch the shadows fall over the grass and sit outside with a glass of iced tea.

Heather loved listening to him talk. He didn't speak with animosity or bitterness about his ex-wife who was still in Boston with most of his money, enjoying the ballet, theater, opera, cocktail parties, and fabulous new clothes. The way he spoke made Heather feel free to talk about her own marriage. Her unhappiness, which made her leave Wall. How she'd just found out that for months he'd been involved with a young woman. That woman was in her twenties, and pregnant with Wall's baby. She felt no bitterness about that. Actually, she didn't care. She loved being free. And she was getting to love Nantucket.

After dinner, they walked through the small town of 'Sconset, passing tennis courts and the small rotary and down the hill to the beach and the sleeping ocean. Other people were around, sitting in the sand watching the waves roll in, or strolling down the avenue, looking at the summer houses. The rugosa roses were in full bloom, perfuming the salty ocean air with sweetness.

Walking back up the hill, they held hands.

Miles took the Polpis road back, winding smoothly around the curves, past Sesachacha Pond and the Nantucket Shipwreck and Lifesaving Museum, past the entrance to the UMass field station and Moors End Farm. At Milestone Road, he turned left and drove back to the entrance to Heather's hidden cottage.

The moment he turned off the engine, Sugar barked from the house.

"You have a reliable watchdog," Miles said. "But I still want to walk you to your door."

When she unlocked her door, Sugar exploded out of the house, barking and rushing to use the nearest bush. She provided the perfect touch of humor, which Heather needed because she couldn't decide whether or not to ask Miles in for coffee. He was right there, standing next to her, tall and warm and handsome.

"I had a good time tonight," she told Miles.

He smiled down at her. "So did I. Let's do it again. Remember, the Fourth of July celebration is on Monday. I hope you'll join us. We always find a spot in the harbor right under the fireworks. Spectacular view."

"I'll be there," Heather said. And without even thinking about it, completely on impulse, she put her hands on his shoulders, stood on her tiptoes, and kissed his lips.

She intended to make it a quick, sweet kiss, but Miles put his arms around her and kissed her back, pressing her body against his, prolonging the kiss so that it flushed Heather's body with heat and a desire she'd forgotten she could have.

Sugar hurried up to them and barked like crazy, tail spinning like a windmill in a storm.

They both laughed, drawing apart and smiling at each other.

"Next time we go out," Miles said, his voice husky, "I'll bring a nice big steak bone for Sugar."

Miles left. Heather called Sugar to her side and walked around the house, letting the dog have some outside time. Letting her body simmer down. Letting her happiness fill and surround her.

fourteen

Kailee set her alarm for six o'clock. Thursday morning, she slipped into a sundress, pulled her hair in a low ponytail, and went down to make a cup of coffee.

She took her coffee into the conservatory, settled in her mother's comfortable executive chair, woke her mother's computer. She opened her mother's email. Evelyn had twenty-four more unanswered emails since yesterday morning. Dinner parties, cocktail parties, board meetings, volunteer events, phone numbers, reminders, notes, and lists of names that meant nothing to Kailee. Kailee couldn't attend all the parties. She couldn't even answer all the emails.

"Good morning." Kailee's father entered the room, freshly shaved and showered. "Is there any coffee?"

"Oh, I used the Keurig," Kailee said. "Dad, we need to talk. Mom has so many—"

"Let me drink my coffee first," Bob said. "I think better after coffee. And maybe eggs?"

"Eggs?" Kailee asked. While she was in college, she'd forgotten that her father had a routine set in granite. Gravity didn't arrive until ten. This meant her mother waited on her father in the mornings. That should change.

"Soft-boiled on toast is what your mother usually does. Helps me cut down on sugar. Protein energy."

"Right." Now was not the time to argue about breakfast. Kailee left the desk, went through the conservatory and hallway and into the kitchen. She filled the Keurig with water and a recyclable pod.

"That smells good," Bob said, taking his place at the kitchen table. "Did you bring in the newspapers? They should be at the front door." He had *The New York Times* and *The Wall Street Journal* delivered to his door every day.

Kailee didn't answer for a moment, concentrating on boiling water in the egg-poaching pan, putting whole wheat bread in the toaster. She made an egg and toast for herself, too, and another cup of coffee, set coffee and the eggs on toast in front of her father. She went down the hall to get the newspapers from the front steps. She returned, slapped the papers on the table, and sat down at the table across from her father.

"Have you heard from the hospital? How's Mom?"

"I haven't heard from the hospital, which I take as a good sign." Bob sprinkled salt and pepper on his eggs. He held the paper with one hand and ate with the other.

Kailee ate her own breakfast quickly. When her father left, Kailee rinsed the dishes and put them in the dishwasher. She wanted to return to the construction office, but she knew she should make notes to take to her mother when she saw her later in the morning.

First, she called Ross.

"Good morning, sweetie," she cooed. "Where are you?"

"I'm at work, babe. Your father wants me to go around with the building inspector today, to learn how all that works."

"He's moved you up," Kailee said.

"I'm sure I'll be back pounding nails tomorrow," Ross told her. "But I'm getting an overview of how things get done on this island. Hey, how's your mother?"

"I'm going in at ten to check on her," Kailee said. "I'll let you know."

Her father had never had Kailee shadow the building inspector. Kailee was glad for Ross, but also jealous and slightly paranoid. Grudgingly, she returned to her mother's desk and sorted through the emails and paperwork, classifying by organization and date. She studied her mother's various symbols, finding which group they referred to, but she knew she'd have to ask Evelyn to translate for her. She printed off a few documents for her mother and put them in a folder to take to her mother to sign. Finally, it was almost ten o'clock.

Kailee arrived at the hospital to find that her father was already in the room, and so was Dr. Landers. Her mother was sitting on the side of the bed, fully dressed. It was obvious that the physician and Evelyn had been arguing for a while.

"Evelyn, let me repeat. This is not a good idea. I'm still not happy with your blood pressure," Dr. Landers said.

"Well, *I'm* not happy with *you!*" Kailee's mother snapped. "Oh, good, Kailee, there you are. You can drive me home. Bob, you can go on to work now."

Dr. Landers and Evelyn glared at each other. Dr. Landers sighed.

"Very well," Dr. Landers said. "Sign this release form." When Evelyn had signed, she said, "I'll see you again, soon. In the meantime, stop by the pharmacy and buy a home blood pressure measuring kit. Use it several times a day. And rest. We don't want you to have another heart attack, Evelyn. Take this seriously."

Evelyn seized Kailee's arm and ushered her out of the room.

Over her shoulder, Kailee said, "Thank you, Dr. Landers."

"Have you had breakfast, Mom?" Kailee asked, as her mother hurried them both down the hall.

"I haven't had coffee," Evelyn said. "They won't give me coffee and you know I'm not going to be pleasant until I've had coffee."

They left the hospital and crossed the parking lot, arriving at Kailee's Jeep. Kailee held the door open for her mother, who snapped, "For God's sake, I can open my own door!"

Kailee got into the driver's seat, took a deep breath, and turned to her mother. "Mom, I know this is hard for you, but you've got to calm down. You've got to rest. When we get home, you should relax. If you sit on the living room sofa, I can go over these accounts with you. You can sign the checks and I'll get them in the mail today. Then we can talk about your bizarre secret codes."

To Kailee's surprise, her mother smiled.

"My darling daughter, you've taken to this like a duck to water."

Kailee was so pleased, tears came to her eyes. "We'll see what you think by the end of the day. And I *am* going to make you rest."

When they returned to the house, Evelyn immediately went up to take a shower and put on clean clothes. Kailee searched the cupboards for a caffeine-free pod, found one, and put the coffee on her mother's bureau, saying, "Here's your coffee." She hoped her mother wouldn't guess it was caffeine-free.

Evelyn came down in one of her gorgeous flowing caftans, a concession to Dr. Landers while still looking fabulous. Kailee sat in the living room with the folders on the coffee table. Evelyn sat on the sofa, signed the checks, and studied the calendar with Kailee.

"I will skip this meeting today," Evelyn said. "Send them my regrets—but don't mention my little heart blip."

Kailee laughed. "I'm sure everyone in town knows you've been in the hospital."

"You're right. Mention my hospital visit for a *minor* event. Tell them I'm home now."

By noon, they'd taken care of necessary tasks, and Kailee thought it was time for her mother to rest.

"Want me to fix some lunch for us?" she asked her mother.

"No, thanks, sweetie. I think I'll go up and take a nap. Spending two nights in a hospital is no way to get any sleep."

Evelyn left the room.

Kailee sat stunned. Her mother never took naps in the middle of the day. Was it possible that her mother felt weak? Just *slightly* weak. Maybe her mother would agree to resign from some of her boards. She'd talk to her about it when Evelyn got up.

In the kitchen, Kailee took a pint of ice cream from the freezer and a spoon from the drawer.

Gravity was putting clean dish towels into their drawer. "How is your mother?"

"Cranky," Kailee grumbled.

"We all like to be in control of our lives," Gravity told her. Gravity had been with them forever, and she knew the family well.

Kailee admitted, "I suppose I'm cranky, too."

"That seems reasonable right now," Gravity remarked. She winked at Kailee and went down the hall with a dust cloth.

Evelyn didn't come down that afternoon. Kailee kept checking on her, and she was always asleep with the door closed. *Is this a good thing?* Kailee wondered. *Should I wake her or let her sleep?* How was she going to be in charge of a company when she couldn't decide about what action to take with her mother?

Today, she chose the easy option and let her mother sleep. She called George to let him know how her mother was and to find out if she'd missed anything important in the office.

"Everything's tickety-boo," George said. "Don't worry about a thing."

But I want *to worry about the company's finances!* Kailee thought. She said, "Thanks, George. I hope I see you tomorrow."

She was working on her mother's emails when, suddenly, her mother said, "Oh, good. I'm glad you're keeping me up-to-date."

"Jeez, Mom," Kailee said, turning around to find her mother at the door to her office. "You almost gave *me* a heart attack."

Evelyn smiled. "We wouldn't want that."

"How do you feel?"

"Truthfully? I'm tired of people asking me how I feel."

Kailee shut her computer, rose, and went to hug her mother. "You look good. Let's go watch girlie TV until Dad comes home."

"Only if you'll fix me a drink," Evelyn said.

"Is it safe with the meds you're taking?"

"I've been checking that on my phone. I can have a small glass of red wine."

Kailee laughed as she walked with her mother into the den. "*Of course.* You were on your phone. I thought you were sleeping."

Evelyn smiled smugly as she settled onto the sofa. She looked pale but glamorous in her caftan. Kailee fixed them each a drink—a small one for both of them to keep her mother happy. Evelyn wanted to catch up on the world news but Kailee suggested they watch a Hallmark movie instead. Later, they heard the door open and Bob came into the room. When he saw that Evelyn was up, a smile lit his face. He went directly to his wife and kissed her.

"You must have gotten some sleep. You look good."

"I'd feel better if Kailee would let me have another pitiful ounce of wine." Evelyn spoke with a hint of laughter in her voice. "God, I'm glad to be out of the hospital. That was ridiculous."

"Gravity made her special stew," Kailee said. "I'll go set the table." She left, knowing her parents would be glad for some time alone together.

The three ate in the dining room, with proper cloth napkins. Kailee knew her mother would appreciate that. They spoke of trivial matters, and when Evelyn mentioned wanting to answer a few more emails before she went back to bed, her husband reminded her she had promised to watch an old movie with him tonight.

"It's *His Girl Friday,* starring Cary Grant and Rosalind Russell," Bob told Kailee.

"Watch it with us," Evelyn said. "You'll like it, I promise. It's very clever."

"How can I resist?" Kailee asked.

She hurriedly cleared the table and tidied the kitchen. She found some Neapolitan ice cream in the freezer, scooped up three bowls, and carried them into the den.

"An old type of ice cream for an old type of movie," she joked.

"Not *old*, dear," her mother said from the sofa. "*Classic.*"

A glow of warmth filled Kailee's heart. Her mother was back to herself, making the world accurate, one word at a time.

The next morning, Kailee was in the kitchen, fixing her father's breakfast and lots of coffee for them both, when her father came down. She heard the front door open and close.

"Good morning, Dad," Kailee said, sliding his eggs and toast onto his place at the table. "How are you?"

"I'm okay, but I'm worried about your mother." Bob sat down, thumped the papers onto the table, sipped some coffee. "I bought a home blood pressure kit, and I took her blood pressure just now. She had gotten up while I was in the shower and was planning to come down and, as she said, 'do a few little bits and pieces of work.' I told her she had to rest. She argued. I made her let me take her blood pressure, and it was high, too high, and she said it was my fault because I'd bossed her around and now she's angry and I'm worried."

"Did she go back to bed?" Kailee asked.

"Yes, but you know she'll get up when she hears my truck leave the driveway."

"I'll take some breakfast up to her. I've got eggs and toast ready."

"No coffee. You know that, right? Nothing with caffeine."

Kailee slid into a chair across from her father. "You're really worried about Mom, aren't you?"

"I am. You should be, too. She had a heart attack, heart event, whatever they call it, and her blood pressure is far too high. I had to bully her into taking her medications this morning."

Kailee laughed, trying to ease her father's tension. "Dad, Mom isn't going to snap to it like your employees do."

"Well, she damn well better!" Her father sat with his hands clenched into fists on the table. "Kailee, your mother is stubborn and she thinks she's invincible. In the hospital, her heart was all over the place, she was arrhythmic, but she couldn't feel it, so she doesn't accept what the doctor told her." He tossed his napkin onto the table. "I've got to get to the site. I'm relying on you to keep your mother quiet."

"I was planning on going to the office," Kailee began.

"Let George handle it today. You stay home with your mother."

Her father rose from the table, kissed her cheek, and left.

Kailee warmed the plate in the microwave, poured a small glass of orange juice, and carried a tray up to her mother's bedroom.

Evelyn was slipping on a loose caftan.

"Get back in bed, lady," Kailee ordered. "I've brought you breakfast."

Evelyn's face looked like thunder. "You should be working on my committees, not waiting on me. Take those things away and bring me some coffee."

To her surprise, Kailee burst into tears. "Mom! Stop it! Get back in bed! Don't you get it? We don't want you to die. Dad's worried and I'm worried and you're being a royal pain about it!"

"I don't like people telling me what to do," Evelyn said, folding her arms over her chest.

"You have to do what Dr. Landers said, Mom. You have to rest." The tray was heavy in her arms, and the eggs were getting cold, and Kailee hated having to worry about her mother, her super goddess, invincible mother.

"All right. All right." Evelyn plopped down on top of the covers.

Kailee set the tray carefully on the bed.

Evelyn drank the juice. "How's your father?"

"Worried about you. You know, Mom, the best thing you can do for us and for you is to rest."

"Fine, I'll die of boredom," Evelyn huffed.

"Why not watch television?"

"*That* suggestion makes my blood pressure rise, I assure you."

"Here's an idea. I'll bring up our laptops and you can tell me what I need to do."

"I like that idea, Kailee. Thank you."

"Great!" Kailee went down to the conservatory, worried with each step. Was this the wrong thing to do? Should she keep her mother away from all business matters? She was literally keeping her mother in bed, and that seemed the best she could do.

Kailee hefted her mother's laptop on top of her own and set two paper calendars and a pile of file folders on top. She carried it all upstairs.

Her mother was sitting in one of the small upholstered chairs by the window.

Kailee sighed. "Mom, you're supposed to be in bed."

"I can't think in bed," Evelyn retorted. "I can work better sitting up."

"Fine." Kailee set her laptop and file folders on the bed. She took Evelyn her laptop and sat on the end of the bed facing her.

At first, they worked in sync, checking off events in the calendar that could be dropped, events that should be kept, and those that absolutely must be kept.

"Mom, you've got to cut this list in half. You can't possibly take care of yourself and do all this."

Evelyn leaned forward with a piercing gaze. "You think you know so much because you're young. Tell me this, then. If your father doesn't build these homes, another company will. Your father tries his best to destroy as little wild land as possible. An off-island company wouldn't care. This is the world you live in now, Kailee. Nothing is easy. Nothing is pure. Nothing is unrelated."

Evelyn stopped talking. She put her hands to her chest.

Kailee jumped up. "Mom. Are you okay?"

Evelyn took a deep breath. "I'm fine."

"Should I call—"

"Don't call anyone. I only need to rest."

Kailee stood, reaching out a hand to help her mother move from the chair to her bed. Evelyn ignored it, so Kailee swept all the business materials off the bed and into one pile.

"Mom, let's take your blood pressure now," she suggested.

"I'm fine." Evelyn slipped between the sheets and lay on her side, facing away from her daughter. "I need to sleep."

"What can I do?" Kailee asked.

"Just leave me."

Kailee left the room, but waited in the hall in case her mother called out for her. Finally, she heard the soft snuffling noises her mother made when she slept, so she went downstairs, stepping quietly.

She walked into the conservatory and set down the laptops and file folders. She sat at her desk and burst into tears.

It was an impossible situation. Should she call her father? Dr. Landers? Or wait, and check in half an hour to see how her mother was? But could she get close enough to assess her mother without waking her?

And *this* was not what she was supposed to be doing! She was supposed to be with George March, learning how to handle the company's accounting. Instead, Ross was with her father, and Kailee was home playing nursemaid to her mother. Evelyn's email and messages were piling up with questions from friends and acquaintances: How was she? Was it true she had a heart attack? Was she at the hospital? Could they send flowers? Would she be able to make the July meeting of the various committees she was on?

She blew her nose, wiped her eyes, and forced herself to breathe deeply. She called her friend Maggie and got voicemail: *Can't talk. At pediatrician's. Don't worry. Scheduled checkup.*

She called Dan. Another voicemail: *Leave a message.*

Kailee opened the French doors and walked out into her mother's garden. The landscapers had already been here, weeding, watering, and mowing the lawn, and the air carried the unmistakable fragrance of newly cut grass. Kailee strolled around the garden, admiring the flowers and envying the landscapers' job. It was hard work, she knew, but it didn't involve making half the town angry at you.

The more she thought about it, the more she thought her mother's idea was a good one. Nothing could stop development, but something could be done to protect the island's wild lands.

She returned to her desk and opened her computer. She would reread the mission statement for ENF and email her own friends, inviting them to join.

She could do this. She *had* to do it, for her mother's sake.

fifteen

During the first few days of July, clouds spread over the island, and a brisk wind skipped over the waves, sending the beaches into flying sand particles that pocked the skin and stung the eyes. Shops, restaurants, and the Dreamland Theater had a record number of visitors, most of them grumbling about the weather.

"This is the summer of our discontent," Evelyn said, rephrasing Shakespeare. She had been out of the hospital for four days and was dressed and down in her conservatory, helping Kailee with email.

"Mom," Kailee chided, "how can you be discontent when you've received so many cards, emails, even flowers from your friends?"

"Because many of those so-called friends are delirious with joy to see me grounded."

"That's not true," Kailee insisted. It had been difficult these past few days, trying to get even a small amount of work done while at the same time assuring her paranoid mother that every committee she was on was not rushing to pass bylaws that Evelyn would have strongly opposed. "And look, Grace Mooney has agreed to join ENF. She's sent in a very nice donation to get the organization off the ground. Maybe you should call her and thank her and ask for her ideas."

"Oh, that woman would give me a heart attack," Evelyn said. "She's incredibly bossy and uses her money as a bribe to get her own way."

"But, Mom, you don't know that her goals aren't the same as yours," Kailee protested.

"You're right," Evelyn said. She put her hand on her heart and took a deep breath. "You can deal with her. I think I need to go rest."

Kailee jumped up. "Maybe we should use the home blood pressure ma—"

"I'm fine, Kailee. I just need to lie down." Evelyn slowly walked from the conservatory into the living room and settled on a sofa.

Kailee's own heart thrummed with worry.

When her phone rang, she answered it without looking to see the identification.

"Hi, Kailee." Ross's mother's voice came over the phone. "I know you're in a rush, and Evelyn's not back to her best self yet, so I thought I'd make dinner and bring it over for us all to have together tonight."

"Oh." Kailee's mind crashed. Would her mother like this?

Heather continued, "Ross told me you're overwhelmed with your mother's health and all the work you're trying to keep up with. I could bring over my meatloaf, which actually is especially good, and some mashed garlic potatoes, and some asparagus and maybe even a blueberry pie from the Bake Shop. Around seven? When the men get home? If I stay to join you all for dinner, I'll clean the kitchen and leave you a little time to spend with Ross."

Kailee thought a moment before answering. She wouldn't be

thrilled to spend the evening with Heather. But Gravity would appreciate a night off, and Ross would be pleased. And Kailee would score some points with Ross by including his mother.

"I don't have to stay, if it's easier for you . . ."

"No!" Kailee said. "I mean, yes, it would be wonderful to see you and to have a home-cooked meal. Thank you so much, Heather."

"Good," Heather said. "I'll be there at seven."

"What was that all about?" Evelyn asked, when Kailee put down her phone.

"Heather offered to bring us dinner tonight. Meatloaf, garlic mashed potatoes, maybe a pie."

"Oh, good," Evelyn said. "Now we can concentrate on ENF."

"I'll concentrate on the work," Kailee said decisively. "*You* go back to bed."

To Kailee's surprise, her mother nodded and went upstairs.

Kailee tidied the kitchen, then headed into the conservatory to deal with her mother's folders.

Evelyn came down for lunch. She sat with Kailee at the patio table, shaded by a wide striped umbrella, overlooking the lush garden.

"You're not eating much," Evelyn noticed.

Kailee shrugged. "I guess I'm not hungry." She jiggled her iced tea so that the ice tinkled against the glass.

"How is Ross's mother?" Evelyn asked, finishing the last bite of her crab salad.

"Heather? Good, I think. You'll see her tonight, when she brings dinner over."

"Oh, right, dinner." Evelyn smiled. "I've heard that people love her. She's terrific at bridge and the Hunters especially have taken her under their wing."

Kailee pushed her crab salad away. She'd bought it last night, so it should be fresh, but the smell made her nauseous. "Too bad for the Hunters, then. Her cottage is rented only for three months."

Evelyn slid her plate to one side and leaned both arms on the table, fixing Kailee with a hawk's gaze. "Why don't you like Heather?"

Kailee shrugged. "It's not that I don't like her, Mom. I just think it's weird that she followed Ross here and then made friends, as if she thinks she belongs here."

Evelyn cocked her head. "My lovely only child. You're going to have to get used to sharing Ross. Not just with his mother, but with the guys he works with, with Essex Construction and its demands. You already have your family here, and your best friends. If you're lucky, sooner or later, you'll have children, and you will find yourself spending much more time, energy, and love on them than you do on Ross."

Kailee ducked her head, staring down at her hands.

"I'm not scolding you, Kailee," Evelyn said, her voice softer. "But you're an adult now, and adults have desires and needs different from romantic love. You and Ross need to make a living, to support yourself financially. Right now, you're both living in a kind of childish bubble. You've got to start paying income tax and buying your own groceries and cooking your own meals and doing your own laundry. You won't have help paying for a mortgage on a house when you're married. Even though we had a house, with all the utilities, insurance, taxes—well, the first few years were hard. Your father and I argued more back then than during any other time of our lives. And we always had Gravity to help with the housework and prepare dinner."

Kailee tried to rein in her emotions. "Well, Mom, I've always thought you and Dad would give me a house when I got married."

"*Give you a house*. Listen to yourself. Have you even looked at how real estate prices have rocketed? In the past few years, partly because of Covid, wealthy people have bought land and houses to escape to. Normal people can't afford a house on the island."

"But we're not normal people," Kailee said stubbornly.

"But Ross is." Evelyn held up her hands to stop Kailee's response. "I don't mean we don't like Ross. We do, very much. But I suppose we always thought you'd marry a wealthy man. We weren't sure you would even want to live on Nantucket, after having a glimpse of the rest of the world. New York, when you went down with your dormmates on January break, to see plays and museums. Or California, when you visited your friend out in Santa Barbara. And, Kailee, you still might want to travel some more before you settle down with Ross."

Tears welled in Kailee's eyes. How could her mother get her so wrong? "I've *always* said I want to live here, on the island. I *always* planned to work for Dad and someday run the company. Ross understands. He loves Nantucket, and working for Dad, and he loves *me!* You're my *mother!* Don't you want me to live on the island?"

With her last words, Kailee burst into tears.

To her dismay, instead of comforting her, her mother said, "I'm going to lie down in my bedroom with a cold cloth on my forehead."

Evelyn rose and left the table, not even bothering to take her plate into the kitchen.

Kailee sat stunned. Of course, she'd argued with her mother before. But every time, they'd made up and hugged. Plus, her mother always came around to Kailee's view of the topic in question.

But now!

Get a grip, she told herself. Her mother was right. Kailee *was* living in a bubble. When she and Ross married, she'd have to buy groceries, cook meals, do the laundry, clean the house. At university, her life had been almost carefree. She'd had to study and take classes, but she liked that. She partied a lot in her first two years, and settled down during her junior and senior years, working hard to make good grades. But she'd never had to prepare a meal. There was always the school dining hall and pizza or takeaway. Some nights she'd eaten day-old sandwiches, using her towels as napkins. It was one kind of no-fault eating.

But now she was a college graduate, an adult. Her mother was right. She had to grow up.

Heather had never been hesitant about cooking for a crowd. When Ross was a teenager, his friends would roam the house like starving musk oxen, eating everything in sight. She'd never made so much lasagna and cake. The past four years, with Ross at university, she'd tried making gourmet meals for herself and Wall. She watched cooking shows, bought cookbooks, and spent time choosing a wine to go with the meal, although she didn't know how to judge wine except from the price.

Wall had not enjoyed her gourmet attempts. He'd eaten them all as if it was a kind of ordeal to get through, and gone off to the den to watch television. Heather continued to prepare feasts for the holidays and the summers when Ross was home, but for the past year she had stopped trying. Wall was perfectly happy with a sandwich, chips, and a beer while he watched football. For that matter, she was glad for the time to read.

But now she was ridiculously nervous. How could anyone go wrong with a meatloaf? She made two loaves in one large pan, assuming the leftovers would make good sandwiches for the next day. She peeled potatoes, a chore she'd hoped never to do again in her life, but the garlic mashed potatoes were delicious. She sauteed the asparagus in butter, made a tossed salad with almonds and cranberries mixed in with the lettuces, and put the dressing in a small Tupperware container.

She showered and dressed casually in white pants and a loose blue shirt. She took Sugar for a brisk walk, promising her a longer one later. She loaded her meal into two canvas totes and put them in the back of her car.

As she neared the Essexes' home on Pleasant Street, her palms were wet, and her heart was pounding.

"For heaven's sake!" she said aloud in the car. "You'd think I was auditioning for a position as a cook!" She hadn't been nervous when she'd gone to the Essexes' house for a party, but then she'd not been responsible for anything.

The car smelled deliciously of meatloaf, spices, and garlic.

It was fine. She knew the food was tasty.

At the Essexes' house, she noticed, with a twinge of anxiety, that Ross's truck wasn't in the driveway. She'd been hoping he'd be there to greet her.

She parked on the curb, did a quick check in the visor mirror to be sure she didn't have lipstick on her teeth, and got out of the car. It was a beautiful evening. People in shorts zipped past on their bicycles and a young mother pushed a dozing baby in a stroller along the brick sidewalk.

Heather took the food from the back and carried it to the front door. She knocked. She waited.

The door opened. Kailee was there, wearing shorts and a striped T-shirt. Her smile was forced, but Heather could tell she was making an effort.

"Hi, Heather! Come in! Thank you so much for doing this! The guys aren't home yet, but they'll be here any moment. Give me a bag and we'll put everything in the kitchen."

Heather followed Kailee down the hall and into the gleaming, modern kitchen. Heather set the bags on the table.

"Let's keep the meatloaf warm until everyone's here," Heather suggested, lifting the meatloaf from the tote.

Kailee looked wide-eyed, shocked, as if Heather were present-ing her with a python. "Heather," she began. Kailee doubled over and vomited onto the floor.

Heather almost dropped the meatloaf. Instead, she set it on top of the stove and knelt next to Kailee. She pulled Kailee's hair back from her face. Kailee was shuddering and gulping and crying. Heather rose, and ran cold water over a kitchen towel. She handed the towel to Kailee and put her arm around her.

"Can you stand up?" Heather asked.

Kailee nodded. Heather helped Kailee into a chair, pressed a wet paper towel against Kailee's face, and put Kailee's hands up to hold it. She hurriedly cleaned up the vomit—it smelled bad enough to make Heather want to vomit, too—and sprayed the floor with a disinfectant. She ran cool water into a glass and handed it to Kailee.

"Usually, people wait to eat my food before they vomit," Heather joked.

"I'm so sorry." Kailee's voice was little more than a whisper. "I don't know what happened. I didn't really eat lunch . . ."

"How do you feel now?" Heather asked.

"Kind of shaky." Kailee raised her head and met Heather's eyes. "I must have a stomach flu."

"You might," Heather agreed.

"I hope you don't catch it," Kailee said.

"Me, too!" Heather said, smiling.

The door into the kitchen flew open. Bob Essex and Ross stormed the room, huge men bringing in the enticing aromas of sunshine, wood chips, and sweat.

"Hello, guys," Heather said.

Kailee jumped up. "You're here! We just have to heat up the food and set the table. Have a drink while you wait. Heather has brought us the most delicious dinner. No pizza tonight!"

"Hi, Mom." Ross's eyes lit up. "Meatloaf?"

Heather smiled as her son crossed the room and kissed her cheek.

Kailee waited for him to kiss *her,* and she smiled at Ross as sweetly as she could. He winked, but did not leave his mother to come kiss *her* cheek. She couldn't help it. She felt like Ross was choosing his mother over her.

"Bob," Ross said, "I think you've met my mother, Heather."

"I have, and I'm delighted to see her now." He crossed the room and shook Heather's hand. "How can we help?"

"We're good," Kailee said. "We're almost ready."

Bob turned to Kailee. "How's your mother?"

"Better, I think. She's coming down for dinner."

"Want a beer?" Bob took two from the refrigerator and handed one to Ross. "I'll go up and check on her."

"No need. I'm here." Evelyn entered the kitchen, dressed in a loose caftan, her hair brushed, light makeup brightening her face.

"How wonderful!" Evelyn cried, when she saw the food. "Heather, thank you!"

"Yes, thank you," Kailee echoed. All signs of stomach flu had disappeared.

Heather said, "You're welcome," and she nodded at Kailee, telegraphing with her eyes that she would not mention Kailee's surprise moment in the kitchen.

But Heather was fairly certain she knew what had happened. She could be wrong, but she didn't think she was.

Kailee had set the dining room table with her favorite placemats and napkins, white linen with blue stripes. She'd taken the bowl of hydrangea flowers from the living room and set it in the middle of the table. She'd considered lighting candles, but that would make the evening seem too formal. Her father and Ross brought their beers to the table in the bottle. Heather offered to open a bottle of Pinot Noir, but Kailee's mother politely refused wine, so Heather said she'd be happy with water, and Kailee agreed.

To Kailee's relief, conversation flowed. Her father asked her mother how she felt, and her mother asked the two men how the day had gone, allowing Bob and Ross to deliver a two-man account of how they finished a project early because Ross had suggested a certain modification that actually made the back wall stronger, and everyone complimented Heather on the delicious food.

"I'd love to have your recipe," Evelyn told Heather. "My meatloaf is either dry or soggy."

Kailee relaxed. Occasionally she'd feel Ross's eyes on her. She'd glance at him and find him smiling right at her, and she'd go warm all over. The meatloaf was tasty and the garlic mashed potatoes were so light and warm that she had two heaping helpings of them, and would have had a third if the men hadn't eaten them all. She ate one spear of asparagus, but it tasted funny, and she had to force herself to swallow it. That whole vomiting episode in the kitchen had been ridiculous and surprising. She hoped she wasn't coming down with a flu. That was all her mother needed, Kailee giving her the flu.

When dinner ended, her father helped her mother return to the bedroom. Ross helped Kailee and his mother carry dishes in from the dining room.

"I'll tidy the kitchen, start the dishwasher, and see myself out," Heather said.

"Mom, thanks! That was a fantastic meal. I've been missing your meatloaf." Ross rinsed the beer bottles and tossed them into the glass recycling.

Heather was at the kitchen sink, rinsing dishes before putting them in the dishwasher. "I'm glad you all enjoyed it. I don't have a chance to cook for more than one these days, and this was fun."

Ross kissed the back of his mother's head.

"See you." He opened the back door on the way to his apartment. "Want to watch some baseball, Kailee?" he asked, shooting her a look that indicated baseball wasn't the first thing on his agenda.

"Sure," Kailee said, folding a dish towel and hanging it on the rack.

"Kailee, could you wait a moment?" Heather asked. "I'd like to ask you about one of your committees."

"Okay." Kailee paused by the door, suddenly feeling very much like the deer in the headlights.

"I'll go on up," Ross said, and left.

Heather cleared her throat nervously. "Kailee, is there a chance you're pregnant?"

"Are you kidding?" Kailee asked. "No, I'm not pregnant. Ross and I will have children, of course, but we want to wait until we're settled, maybe in five years or so. Just because I barfed doesn't mean I'm pregnant. Something must have been off with the crabs I had at lunch." She knew her face was red with indignation.

"I'm sorry I asked, Kailee." Heather spoke in a low voice, not quite a whisper. "I was worried because when I was pregnant with Ross, I had terrible morning sickness. Actually, all-day sickness. Many women do."

Kailee thought, *This is my life, and Ross's.* She said sweetly, "No worries. And thank you so much for tonight's dinner."

"You're welcome," Heather said. She dried her hands, filled her totes with pans she'd already washed clean, and said, "I'll go out with you."

Kailee opened the kitchen door, waved for Heather to leave first, and followed her out. Heather walked down to her car. Kailee waited until Heather had driven away to go up to Ross's apartment.

sixteen

The evening of the Fourth of July on Nantucket was dazzling, and not at all what Heather had envisioned. As she was whisked by launch from the pier to the Hunters's magnificent sloop, she met other guests who were all easy to chat with.

Miles greeted them, helping them onto his boat. The location in the harbor was perfect for viewing the fireworks, drinks and finger food were set out in the cabin, and Heather had more fun than she'd had in a long time. Miribelle sat next to Heather for a while, talking as if they were old friends. Miles's daughter, Emma, sang patriotic songs while her friend Angel played the fiddle. Emma introduced her to Angel, also at the Berklee School of Music. The fireworks were magical.

Miles spent very little time with Heather. He was always surrounded by friends, although he did take a moment to say hello and to tell her how glad he was she'd come. The rest of the evening he was elsewhere, laughing, talking with other people. Often women. Often gorgeous young women in their thirties with glorious abundant hair swinging down their bare backs in their teeny-tiny sundresses.

"They're exquisite, aren't they?"

Heather looked up to see a woman in her sixties taking a seat next to her.

"I'm Julia English, grandmother of that adolescent creature wearing little more than mascara."

Heather laughed. Julia's hair was silver and she wore a caftan over what could be called, kindly, a voluptuous body, and long, clanging metal earrings.

"I'm Heather Willette. Mother of Ross Willette—"

"Who is Kailee Essex's current boyfriend and an employee of Essex Construction."

Heather smiled. "You must know Kailee and her parents."

"I live on this island. I know everyone and their parents. I will not go so far as to say they are my friends."

Heather took a breath. "What do you mean?"

"Surely, you've heard. Essex Construction has built several outrageously enormous houses that spoil the pristine view of the island and ruin the natural landscape, and he's building more."

"I'm new here," Heather admitted. "Isn't there an ordinance or reviewing committee that limits the size of buildings on the island?"

"There is. But we have no way of enforcing it. Lawsuits would bankrupt the town. These new billionaires want to slap us in the face with their money. If they could outline their new homes in neon lights, they would. Talk about shock and awe."

"I don't know what to say." Heather paused, gathering her thoughts. "I don't know Bob and Evelyn well, but I'm sure Essex Construction isn't the only company on the island building luxury homes."

Julia smiled. "I like you. You're not afraid of a discussion."

Heather laughed. "That's because I'm only here for the summer. I'm simply enjoying this island, and this holiday night."

Miles approached the two of them, a bottle of champagne in his hand. "Let me top you up. The fireworks will start momentarily. Heather, I'm glad you've met Julia. She secretly runs the town."

"If only," Julia replied.

Miles laughed. "Heather, I'd love to show you the very best view of the fireworks." He held out his hand.

He led her through the crowd, past the cabin, and up to the bow of the boat.

"Now," he said, "we lie down and look up at the stars."

Heather paused. "If I fall off, I'll land in the water."

"If you fall off, I'll jump in and rescue you," Miles promised.

"Wouldn't that be interesting," Heather joked.

Awkwardly she scooted toward the middle of the boat and lay back, head to foot touching the bow.

"Wow," she said. Like this, she sensed the water beneath them, a gentle rocking motion, making the sea seem alive. The world seemed bigger to her because of the darkness. It was slightly scary, but more exciting. She wore dark blue deck shoes, white capris, and a red tank top, all of them perfect for a national summer celebration.

Miles lay next to her. He wore board shorts, a rugby shirt, and he was barefoot.

Heather wished she were barefoot. She would slowly touch her toes to Miles's. The sexual chemistry between them trembled like a storm cloud wanting to split open and release its wildness, but with a dozen other people on board, this was definitely not the time or the place.

The air was hot and humid, so thick that earlier in the day people worried that fog would roll in, covering the sky, postponing the fireworks display as it had in previous years. But the sky remained clear.

Above them, the fireworks exploded in multicolored spirals and whorls, drawing applause and screams of delight from the crowd on Jetties Beach. Other small boats were in the harbor, too, tied to buoys, some full of people drinking champagne right out of the bottle, some blasting American anthems from their speak-ers. "The Star-Spangled Banner" rang into the air just as an Amer-ican flag in fireworks lit up the sky.

The grand finale was a multitude of pinwheels, spirals, and screaming rockets that silvered the sky and slowly faded. All around them, boats sounded their horns, and on the shore, the crowd yelled with appreciation. The fireworks were over. The crowds began to disperse. Most boats motored back to their slips. The launch arrived to ferry guests back to land.

Heather and Miles made their way back to the others.

Julia approached, cocking her head, studying Heather. "Are you Miles's girlfriend?"

Heather grinned. "You should ask him."

Julia laughed, her hoop earrings swinging. "I'll take you to lunch at the yacht club. Wednesday at noon. My treat."

"That sounds delightful," Heather said.

When the other guests were on the launch, Miles helped Heather on, and kept hold of her hand as they were sped over the water.

"Want to sail away with me and spend the night?" Miles whis-pered.

Heather smiled up at him. "Maybe next time."

Miles took her hand and helped her step up onto the wharf. "Don't make me wait until the next Fourth of July."

They stood so close that she could feel his warm breath. "I want to kiss you," Heather whispered. "But not here. Not now."

"Sometime soon," Miles said, his voice low.

Heather found her car, waved goodbye to the others, and set-tled in for her drive home. Who was she? she wondered. Who had she become? This woman who spoke her mind without hesitation to the sharp-tongued Julia? This woman who had held Miles's hand and almost kissed him only a few moments ago?

"It's true that I've become braver," Heather said, quite aware that she was talking to herself out loud in her car. "That doesn't mean I was weaker when I was with Wall, or if I was, it wasn't his fault." She considered calling Christine, but it was almost ten o'clock at night, and Christine was probably at a party. Heather could call her tomorrow. Out loud, she said, "I *really* want to kiss Miles." An imaginary firework went off in her body.

At home, she let Sugar out to run around the yard while she sat on the patio drinking ice water. The air was slightly less humid than it had been on the water, slightly cooler. The fragrance of the geraniums she'd potted and put on the corners of the patio drifted through the air. She wondered whether Kailee was pregnant. If she was, what then? Well, that was for Kailee and Ross to decide. For now, Heather was taking things day by day.

When she woke that morning, Kailee was nauseous, but she lay very still until it settled. She would not be sick today. She would be strong. She would make her father's coffee, and she would prepare breakfast for her father and her mother and herself.

She had just made the coffee when her father entered the kitchen.

"Good morning, Dad," she said, setting his coffee before him at the kitchen table.

"Good morning, Kailee," her father said. He had pouches beneath his eyes that hadn't been there before her mother went to the hospital.

"Did you check on Mom?" Kailee asked as she buttered the toast.

"I did. She's awake, but resting."

"Here's your breakfast." She set his plate in front of him and sat down to her own breakfast.

"Kailee, it would help if you stayed here today. You could work on your mother's emails—and before you say anything, I know you should be working with George, and you will be, but let's get your mother back on her feet first."

Impatience rippled through her, but she knew her father was right. "That's fine. I'll stay here today."

Her father put his hand over hers. "I know you want to be in the Essex office. I want you to be there. But until the doctor gives your mother the all-clear on her health, we need you to help her."

It crushed her to see her father so worried. "Of course, Dad. I understand. I'll keep watch on her, and when Gravity's here, I'll spend some time in Mom's office."

Her father nodded and patted her hand. "Thank you."

Kailee stood up. "I'll take Mom's breakfast up to her."

She set a plate and an orange juice on the tray for her mother. She went up the stairs and knocked lightly before entering the room.

She spoke quietly. "Good morning, Mom. I have your breakfast."

"Thank you, dear." Evelyn was still snuggled down in her bed, and when she saw her breakfast, she didn't sit up. "Just leave it here. I think I'll sleep a little more."

Well, that was alarming. Her mother was never one to sleep late. Kailee set the tray on the other side of the king-size bed, smoothing out the duvet. She knew her father was sleeping in the guest room until Evelyn had recovered, but she worried about her mother being alone all night.

"Can I bring you anything? Would you like me to open your curtains?"

Evelyn laughed lightly. "You sound like a housemaid from *Masterpiece Theatre*. No, I'm fine, dear."

Kailee wanted to *do* something *helpful*. "Have you taken your pills?"

"Yes. Your father helped me take them this morning."

"Oh, good. Well, call if you need anything. Your cell is right there on the bedside table."

"Mmm." Her mother closed her eyes.

"I'll be downstairs," Kailee reminded her. "I'm going to work on your emails and stuff."

Her mother opened her eyes. "Kailee, don't think that work is less important just because it is done in the house."

"I understand."

As she went back down the stairs, she heard her father's truck starting and the automatic garage door settling with a clunk. She heard the sounds of a ladder clinking and workers chatting as they prepared to paint the house across the street. In the summers, it seemed that every home on the island was being worked on. The people who lived here for the summer wanted every window shining, every picket fence freshly painted white, every rose blooming whether it was the plant's blooming season or not. They wanted a dream, and Nantucket often was a dream, but only because people helped to make it that way.

She went into her mother's conservatory and began checking emails. The major charity events didn't take place until late July and August, so that was a relief. Some emails were simply inquiring about her mother's health, and Kailee answered as she'd been told to, saying that Evelyn was fine, and resting.

She settled in and studied the trustees and staff of various foundations. To her surprise, several of her high school friends' parents were on the list, and even one high school friend, who'd gotten a degree from Boston University in biology with a specialization in ecology and conservation, worked for the Linda Loring Nature Foundation. Gwen Parsons. Kailee had never been close friends with Gwen, who seemed to be a grind and an overachiever. Gwen's parents lived in Madaket, and on weekends, Gwen was always out there, the east end of the island, helping her mother work in her bird sanctuary.

Kailee sat back in her chair and thought. After a moment, she emailed Gwen and asked if they could meet for lunch someday next week.

At noon, Kailee went quietly up the stairs to check on her mother. Evelyn was still sleeping, curled on her side, her breakfast untouched. Kailee texted her father to let him know Evelyn was still sleeping, and she went into her room to get her laundry basket.

And then she lay down on her bed and fell asleep instantly.

Two hours later, Kailee woke, feeling hot, sweaty, nauseous, and shaky. Maybe she did have the flu. She had to get NyQuil or DayQuil or aspirin. It wasn't like her to sleep in the day, and she'd never felt this bad except once in her freshman year, when she'd gotten way too drunk and had a daylong pukefest of a hangover.

She brushed her hair, made a face at herself in her private bathroom mirror, and started to turn away, but nausea overtook her. She leaned toward the toilet and vomited. Afterward, she rinsed her mouth and stood holding on to the sink, panting slightly. A few minutes passed, and she became steadier, easier within herself, the kind of normal she felt after vomiting.

But she had to get some medicine. She must have caught something. There was always a flu going around.

She brushed her teeth, put on lip balm, and went down the hall to check on her mother. Evelyn was still sleeping, but she'd changed position and kicked off her duvet. Should she really still be sleeping? Kailee had no experience with heart problems, except those involving men and love.

She whispered, "Mom, are you okay?"

Evelyn stirred slightly. "Mmmm. Just tired."

"Would you like some sparkling water? Some toast?"

"No, thank you, dear."

Evelyn didn't move as Kailee went around the bed and lifted the tray of uneaten breakfast food off the bed.

When Kailee went down to the kitchen, Gravity was there, scouring the sink.

"Good morning, Kailee," Gravity said. "How are you? You've been looking peaked."

Kailee set the tray on the counter. "I'm fine. And Mom is still sleeping. How are you?"

"I'm good, sweetheart." Gravity concentrated on scouring a tough spot.

"I've got to run an errand," Kailee said.

"Take your time. I'll call you if we need you." Gravity assured her.

Kailee kissed Gravity's cheek and went out to her Jeep and

drove to Dan's Pharmacy, only a few blocks away. She walked past the mascara and lipstick aisle—one of her favorite places on the island—and headed down the aisle for medicine. She stood studying all the possible choices for all the amazing problems a human being could possibly have, and decided to try the Pepto Bismol, even though the startling pink color made her want to hurl.

"Hi, Kailee."

Kailee jumped a little, surprised to have someone speak to her when she was so deep in her own world.

It was Heather. *Of course* it was Heather. Heather had nothing to do except appear magically wherever Kailee was. Heather looked bronzed by the sun, and her shorts and sleeveless top were the turquoise that Kailee considered *her* color.

"Oh, hi, Heather. How are you?"

"I'm fine, thanks. How's your mother?"

"She's okay, I think." Kailee paused. "Actually, she's been sleeping all day."

"And is her stomach upset?" Heather asked.

Kailee looked down at the pink bottle in her hand. A bolt of lightning pierced her from scalp, straight down her body, to her toes.

Oh. No.

"No," Kailee answered quietly. "It's for me. I think I have a stomach bug."

"I'm so sorry. That's a miserable feeling." Heather looked away. "I need more sunblock."

"Heather."

"Yes?" Heather smiled.

Kailee looked up and down the aisle. No one else around. She whispered, "Heather, would you do me a favor? Would you, um, buy a pregnancy test? Maybe two different kinds? If I buy one, everyone in town will know about it. But they don't know you."

Heather reached out and steadied Kailee with a warm hand on her arm.

"Of course. Buy your Pepto Bismol, go out to your car, and I'll meet you there in a few minutes."

"Thank you."

"Thank *you*. It's a compliment to think that I could be pregnant at forty-seven."

Kailee made her purchase and went out to her car. The sun was beating down, and the intense heat pressed against her. She took the bottle from its white bag, cracked open the lid, and drank some straight from the bottle.

She gagged. The medicine oozed down her throat like a melted crayon. She had a water bottle in her car, thank heaven, so she gulped it, not caring that it was warm.

Heather approached the Jeep. "Are you okay?"

"I'm not sure." Kailee was at the point of tears. "Heather, could I come to your house now? I mean, to do these tests? I mean, our housekeeper or someone would spot anything I put in the trash. I don't want my family to know . . . not yet. Not while my mother's still weak."

"Of course you can, Kailee. And you can trust me. I'm good at keeping secrets."

Heather handed Kailee the white paper bag holding the tests. She went to her car, exited the parking lot, and headed toward the rotary. Kailee followed.

What had she done? What was she doing? She wasn't pregnant. She couldn't be. She should forget the whole thing and go home. She could text Heather that she didn't need to take the tests.

But, really, she should take the tests. She'd tried to remember when she and Ross had made love. She was on the pill, so they never worried, but it was possible that in the past six weeks or so, with all the hassle and emotions about leaving the university and her friends, with Heather popping up in Nantucket and Kailee losing that amazing engagement ring, and then Ross's father and his girlfriend, Nova, wanting Ross to be in their wedding at Christmas, with all that, Kailee probably had forgotten to take her pills for a night. Or two.

She parked behind Heather's car on the dirt road and walked between the bushes onto the slate path. *Follow the yellow brick road.* The terrible Munchkins with their screechy voices sang in her head. She'd always hated that movie. And now here she was, about to find out what was behind the curtain.

Oh, man, she was going nuts.

Heather was in the kitchen.

"Would you like some sparkling water?" Heather asked, as she poured herself a glass.

"No, thank you," Kailee said, standing in the living room with her purse in one hand and the white pharmacy bag in the other. "I'll just . . ."

"Is there any way I can help?"

Kailee flashed on a time at university when one of her dorm friends had taken a pregnancy test and Kailee and Madison had waited with her. The agonizing wait. Then the beautiful blue NO, and they all yelled and jumped up and down.

"No, thank you. I know where the bathroom is. I'll just . . ."

"Go right ahead. I've got some things I need to do in the kitchen."

Kailee was weak with gratitude for Heather's understanding of Kailee's need for privacy. She went down the short hall and into the bathroom. Horrible little place, with no bathtub, just a shower, and when she sat down on the toilet, she faced the full-length mirror hanging on the back of the door.

She prayed while she peed, at the same time wondering if it was sacrilegious to pray while peeing. Her hands were shaking so hard she could scarcely hold the sticks. Finally, she put them on the counter and washed her hands and waited.

In the kitchen, Heather's own stomach was flip-flopping with an unexpected excitement. Was she soon to become a grandmother? The thought made her oddly delirious. Little babies were adorable. Several of her friends had grandchildren. But it wasn't Heather's choice. It was up to Kailee and Ross to decide.

But if Kailee and Ross had a baby . . . So many questions danced in Heather's head. Where would they live? The Essexes' Pleasant Street house was big enough for Ross, Kailee, and a baby, but would Evelyn have fully recovered from her heart problems by then? Could Kailee work as hard and efficiently for her mother as she did now?

Maybe Heather could take care of the baby several days a week, for a few hours.

The thought was enchanting, and Heather was surprised at herself.

Fifteen minutes had passed. Surely Kailee had done the tests by now.

Heather went to stand outside the bathroom, listening.

Kailee was sobbing, wretched, tearing noises.

Heather tapped on the door. "Kailee? May I come in?"

Kailee made a noise that sounded like *yes*. Heather opened the door.

Kailee was sitting on the toilet lid, her face scarlet and wet with tears. On the bathroom sink, two different sticks lay. Heather didn't touch them.

She went to Kailee, knelt on the fluffy bath mat on the floor next to her, and put her arm around the weeping girl.

"And the answer is?" Heather asked, trying to sound absolutely neutral.

"I'm pregnant," Kailee cried. "Oh, I can't be, I don't want to be, it's not the right time!"

Heather studied Kailee's face and wondered what to say. Should she say anything? Heather remembered when she first realized she was pregnant with Ross, she felt profoundly connected to a force beyond her comprehension while also being proud of the capabilities of her own body. Heather and Wall had adored Ross. They had wanted more children. They never could find out why Heather never got pregnant again.

Should she share any of this with Kailee? She didn't want to be critical or disapproving of whatever choice Kailee and Ross made.

Heather said, "I want you to know that whatever you and Ross decide, I support you."

Alarmed, Kailee said, "Oh, please don't tell Ross yet. Don't tell my parents."

"I won't, Kailee. Really, don't worry. This is totally your information to share."

"Ross and I have a plan. We want to work a few years, build a house on the island, with Dad's help, of course, and maybe when we're about thirty, start a family. We think three or four children."

Heather said softly, "You know, life doesn't always go according to plan."

"You don't have to tell *me* that. I certainly didn't plan that I'd spend so much time working for my mother." Kailee paused. "That sounded mean. I love my mother. I didn't want her to have a heart attack!"

"Neither did she," Heather gently reminded Kailee. "Would you like me to leave you alone for a while? Want to lie down in the guest room? You look tired. And you don't have to decide anything right this minute."

Kailee stood up. She caught her reflection in the mirror. Her face was puffy from crying.

"I should go home," Kailee said. "Gravity's there with Mom and she was sleeping when I left. Still, I think I should be there."

"You're right." Heather rose, too.

The women left the bathroom and walked down the hall to the living room.

Heather held the front door open. "Let me know if I can help."

"I will." Kailee walked down the path, then stopped. She turned to face Heather. "Thank you. Really, thank you."

Heather wanted to hug Kailee, but wasn't sure she should. She said only, "You are more than welcome."

seventeen

The next morning, Heather was in the law office, trying to make sense of a scribbled memo. Miles was gone for the morning, meeting clients at home. Her cell rang.

"Heather? It's Evelyn. Do you have a moment to talk?"

Surprised, Heather answered, "Of course, Evelyn. How are you?"

"Oh, I'm absolutely fine. Much ado about nothing, although that's why I'm calling. You're going to think this is an odd request, and it is, but you're the only person I can talk to because you're so new to the island and yet part of our inner circle."

Inner circle? Sounds like a cult. "I'll help in any way I can. Ask away." *Just don't ask me if Kailee's pregnant,* Heather thought.

"That's nice of you." Evelyn cleared her throat. "This is not meant to be a criticism of my daughter, but the truth is, she doesn't seem to be getting on with my ENF work. Her father and I have talked, and we know that Kailee wants to work for her father and not for me, and this ridiculous heart business is slowing me down, but it's imperative that we get this gala organized before the end of summer, because that's when so many moneyed people leave. I guess what I'm saying is, Heather, would you work for me?"

Heather was speechless.

"We'd pay you," Evelyn hurried to stress. "You could do much of the work in your home, on your laptop. We can be in touch all the time, texting, emailing, whatever. I can email you the ENF mission statement right away, so you can see what an important cause it is. Kailee hasn't accomplished much. She spends so much time in her room, sulking."

"Evelyn, thank you for asking, but I don't think I can help. I don't know many people here."

"That's exactly why you'd be perfect. You're the only person on the island that no one is angry with." Evelyn laughed lightly as she spoke. "Also, much of the paperwork is filling out forms. We need to get nonprofit status from the state, that sort of thing. Kailee told me you're on the board of the Safeguard Nature Society, so you must have a basic understanding of how a nonprofit is run."

"So, it's mostly secretarial."

"Um, actually, it's also social. That's where you're perfect! You've already met so many of the people . . . and you're someone I can trust, because you're almost part of our family. Please say you'll consider this."

Heather was hesitant. "I'm working weekday mornings for Miles Hunter, until his secretary returns from Europe."

"Then you'll have afternoons free to help me," Evelyn said. "And of course, attend some events in the evening. You'll be paid for those hours."

"I'll think about it, but I'm not sure I'm the right person for the job."

"You know, Bob really likes Ross. And Ross is a genius working with the men. If we told Kailee she could return to working in our main office, Kailee would be so much happier. That's what she's always wanted."

Heather said, "I see." She thought that Kailee *really* needed to speak with her mother. But it was not her place to speak for Kailee. "You know I'm renting my cottage only until after Labor Day. I couldn't work for you permanently."

"Maybe, maybe not," Evelyn said playfully. "You might fall in love with Nantucket and decide to move here."

"Nantucket *is* beautiful," Heather agreed. "Let me think about this, and I'll call you back soon."

"Bless you, Heather. Just talking to you makes my blood pressure fall."

Just talking to you makes my blood pressure rise, Heather thought. She didn't want to be responsible for Evelyn's state of health.

The two women said goodbye. Heather sat gazing at the computer screen. Should she discuss this with Ross? Would he have some insights into the Essex family?

No. She should wait until Kailee told Ross she was pregnant. After that, any number of things might change.

Kailee lay in bed, chewing on the saltines she'd bought and hidden in the drawer of her bedside table. Last night, when Ross asked her to sleep over with him, she'd refused, saying she wanted to wake early and get ready for work. Ross was tanned from working outdoors, and his nose and cheeks were red. He looked good, and she loved being naked with him, running her hands from his sun-darkened arms down to the pale skin of his belly. But even that was not seductive enough to keep her from sleeping in her own bed. She really did want to wake early for work.

Also, she did not want to throw up around him.

The crackers seemed to be working. She sat up, waited to let her body adjust, and moved carefully, tenderly, trying not to jolt herself. Simone de Beauvoir had pronounced that biology was destiny, and Kailee got that. She knew men couldn't get pregnant, but they *could* share half of the nurturing the baby once it was born.

If it was born. She'd had friends at university who'd had abortions and friends who'd had miscarriages at six weeks. That might happen to her. Until then, she would continue fulfilling *her* destiny, the one she'd been born and raised for.

Kailee slipped on a sleeveless navy-blue dress and sandals. She put on a headband and small gold earrings. She made several pieces of dry toast to take with her, and filled her water bottle with nothing but water. Coffee gave her indigestion.

Her father had already left, so Kailee went upstairs to check on her mother. Evelyn was curled in her covers, sleeping deeply. The sight both soothed and worried Kailee. Her mother was doing the right thing to recover from her heart attack, but seeing the powerful Evelyn Essex sleeping in daylight hours was freaky. *Just wrong.*

Kailee quietly shut the bedroom door and hurried down the stairs. She would call her mother later in the day to see how she felt and if she needed anything.

The day was hot and humid, but Kailee kept the top down on her Jeep. A breeze blew against her neck, cooling her, and she didn't have far to go to get to her father's business office on South Beach Street. George was delighted to see her. After they talked about Evelyn's health, Kailee booted up her computer and got to work.

That evening, Kailee's mother came downstairs, dressed and seeming back to her normal self again. Kailee was sprawled on the sofa, reading her friends' Instagram posts.

"Mom, you look so well!"

"Thanks, darling. I'm feeling much better. And I'm hungry."

"Gravity made chicken Parmesan."

"Good. Could you steam some broccoli? I'd like to walk around my garden."

"I'm on the job," Kailee said. "Enjoy."

Evelyn strolled out the French doors into the early evening warmth.

Kailee watched her mother and said a quiet prayer of thanks.

Her mother was young, really, and if she would manage her stress and workload better, she'd stay healthy.

Maybe, Kailee thought, it would give her mother joy to have a grandchild to love. But she had to talk with Ross before she told her parents, and before she talked to Ross, she needed to decide how she felt, and what she would choose to do.

Kailee set the dining table with blue and white placemats and napkins then steamed the broccoli. She found the Bartlett's heirloom tomatoes and sliced them, lightly adding salt and pepper over them.

"Your mother's up!" were the first words her father said when he entered the house. He went right out to the garden, put his arms around his wife, and kissed her forehead. Kailee watched her parents with happiness. Would she and Ross be this affectionate when they were nearly fifty? She knew they both wanted more than one child, and they didn't want children until they were thirty and comfortably established, so maybe she should deal with her problem herself. But what if Ross and her parents found out somehow? They'd be furious with her.

A spitting noise alerted her to the broccoli pan steaming over. She hurried to turn off the stove, put the broccoli in a bowl, and add some butter. She was just turning to call her parents when they both came in from the garden.

The three sat at the table, eating and discussing the latest scandals and community battles. Kailee was happy to have her mother eating with them, but her mind kept drifting back to her own particular problem.

"Earth to Kailee," her father said.

Kailee pulled her mind back to the present. "Oh, sorry, Dad. What did you say?"

"Your mother might have found a helper for ENF," Bob said, beaming at his wife. "Now your crazy mother can fit some downtime into her schedule."

"That's great, Mom!" Kailee wanted to cheer. "Who is it?"

"Heather," Evelyn said.

Kailee was astounded. "What?"

Evelyn leaned back in her chair and relaxed. "I spoke with her today. Heather seems to me the perfect choice. She's done committee work for years, so she has experience. She's going to be part of our family, but she's new to the island, so no one is angry with her."

"Yet." Kailee's father laughed.

"Did Heather call you?" Kailee demanded.

"No, I called her," Evelyn replied calmly. "I was lying in bed going crazy, and I wished I knew someone who was intelligent and computer-friendly, and I thought of Heather."

"What did she say?" Kailee held her hands clasped under the table, digging her nails into the soft part of her palm. She would be furious at Heather if Heather had told her mother Kailee was pregnant.

"She said she'd think about it," Evelyn said.

"She'd think about what?" Kailee demanded.

Her mother leaned forward. "Darling, are you okay? I said that Heather said to give her a day to think about it, but she thought it might be perfect for all of us."

Kailee's stomach was churning with anxiety. She swallowed water, hoping to settle it. "She should just move in here and we can all live together."

"I don't understand your objections," Kailee's father said.

Kailee took a deep breath. It killed her that Heather knew one of the most important secrets of her life and Kailee had not yet told Evelyn.

Kailee reached over and took her mother's hand. "I'm sorry. Mom. Heather is *fine*. I'm just emotional, with all the things we need to settle. I mean, planning our wedding, and where we will live, and until a few weeks ago, my mind was totally on school. And I was anxious, of course, when you had your heart attack."

"Heart event," Evelyn corrected.

"Heart event. And really, truly, *seriously,* I hope Heather works with you. She's nice, and she's smart. I'm glad you'll have someone to help you."

"Good," Evelyn said.

"*Women.*" Bob huffed. "Don't tell me they don't get more emotional than men."

Evelyn said teasingly to her husband, "I'll bet you'll get emotional if we don't have any dessert."

Kailee jumped up from the table. "I'll go see what we have."

She hurried into the kitchen and opened the refrigerator. Someone had given them a Boston cream pie. Kailee had the sudden urge to sit down on the floor and eat the entire thing. Instead, she carried the pie into the dining room, acting carefree and thinking she had to make a decision. Soon.

It was hot and humid the night Heather went to dinner with Miles. She wore her sleeveless blue dress and pearls, because Miles was taking her to the yacht club.

"We eat here often in the summer," Miles said. "There's a big parking lot and a beautiful view."

They were seated on the screened porch, looking out over the lawn and the harbor. Sunlight slanted across the water where sailboats and motorboats crisscrossed in their trails.

After the waiter took their drink orders, Heather leaned across the table and said, "I think you and I are providing an interesting view for the others."

"Oh, yes," Miles said. "You're the first woman I've brought to the club since my wife and I divorced."

"That seems . . . unusual. Not to have a woman, even just a friend, in your life."

Miles unrolled the napkin wrapped around his silverware, slowly, as if studying it. "When I moved here, I wanted a major life change. I *needed* it." He cleared his throat. "About six years ago, my best friend OD'd. He was a criminal lawyer, the best, a genius in the courtroom. He had an almost terrifying instinct. I'd known him in college, where he was always a leader, football quarterback, fraternity president, and good grades, *and* he was a good guy."

Miles was silent while the waiter set their drinks before them.

Then Miles took a big sip of Scotch, and said, "That kind of law requires stamina, and good instincts, but also a pit bull mentality. It can be a game you don't want to lose. But when you get older . . . well, it's hard work. Your worldview is pretty bleak. Paul resorted to drugs. I think he probably OD'd on purpose. I think he was just tired."

"I'm sorry," Heather said.

Miles nodded. "The thing is, I knew then I had to get out. I wanted the intangible sense of, well, I guess I could call it freedom. As I've said, I got divorced. I moved to my family's Nantucket house, and liked it so much I stayed as a year-rounder."

"That's quite a change," Heather remarked.

"True. I can't describe the feeling of relief once I'd made the decision and moved here. It helped that Miribelle and her family live here full-time. She made me go to church with her, and forced me to buy a sailboat, and insisted I play tennis with her." Miles was smiling now.

"You poor thing, with such a bossy sister," Heather teased.

The waiter came to take their dinner order. After he went away, Miles asked Heather if she played tennis.

"I don't. My sport is walking. I walk on one of the beaches every morning," Heather told him. "Around six o'clock. The sun has already risen, but it's low in the sky. I love watching the water change."

"I walk in the off-seasons," Miles said thoughtfully. "Have you been to Squam Swamp?"

"No. Tell me about it."

They talked easily all evening, mostly about the island, and the book by Peter Brace called *Walking Nantucket,* which led them into Heather telling Miles that Evelyn Essex had asked Heather to help with the ENF so that Kailee could work in the office.

"I think it's a great idea," Miles said. "Miribelle agreed to be on the board, and she's no dummy."

"I'm not sure I know enough about the island to work on ENF," Heather said.

"I'd be glad to be your guide," Miles offered, with a teasing grin. "I could show you some places that few people know about."

Heather knew she was blushing. "I'd like that," she said, even as she tried to rid her mind of the picture of being alone with Miles in a hidden glade.

After dinner, they strolled around town. In summer, the shops were open late, and the bars and restaurants were crowded. Laughter and perfume drifted into the air. They walked down South Wharf and far out on the long pier to look at the enormous yachts docked there. The evening was cooling down and stars were appearing in the sky.

Miles drove Heather back to her cottage, and when he turned off the ignition, he said, "Wait."

She thought he was going to lean over and kiss her, but to her surprise, Miles got out of the car. He came around, opened her door, helped her out, and walked her to the door. The light Ross had put up illuminated the front of the house and the path, and all around them and above them, a velvet darkness lay in silence.

Then, standing on the doorstep, Miles put his hand on her chin, tilted her face toward his, and kissed her softly.

Heather sighed. She put her hands on his shoulders and looked up at him. "This makes me remember being a teenager with my boyfriend kissing me on my parents' doorstep."

"Really? Well, next time, believe me, you won't feel like a teenager." Miles put his arms around her, pulled her close, and kissed her so thoroughly she didn't want him to stop.

He pulled away, keeping his arms around her. "I'll plot out some hidden gems on the island. We can go to one of them on our next date."

"Oh, good," Heather said. "I'd like that."

She forced herself to put the key in the lock and open her door. Sugar shot out between their legs and raced for her favorite spot.

"Do you want to come in?" she asked, thinking, *Please come in. Come in and ravish me!* And then she thought that she didn't even know what being ravished felt like.

"Not tonight," Miles said. "I'll call you."

Sugar, finished with her bodily function, raced over to Miles and gazed up as longingly as Heather felt.

Miles gave Sugar a fond pat on the head. "Good night," he said, and walked back to his car.

Heather called Sugar inside, shut the front door, and leaned against it, touching her mouth lightly with her fingers, remembering the magic of Miles's kiss.

eighteen

Kailee tidied the kitchen after dinner and scavenged more saltines for her bedside table, before going up to her room. Her parents were in the den, watching some British detective series, and when Kailee saw lights on in the garage apartment, she brushed her teeth and hurried over to be with Ross.

She knocked on the door.

Ross yelled, "Come in!"

She found him on his sofa, watching an American detective series.

"What is it with detectives?" Kailee asked, plopping down next to Ross.

"I'll tell you in fifteen minutes," Ross said. "This show is almost over."

That gave her fifteen minutes to worry about her problem, but she was sure that Heather hadn't talked to Ross about the pregnancy. He would want to talk to her immediately about that.

Finally, Ross clicked off the television, turned to her, and kissed the end of her nose.

"Good day?" he asked.

"Kind of . . ." Kailee said, and now that she had his full attention, she wasn't sure what to do. "My mom seems better."

"That's good."

Kailee stood up. "I need a glass of water. Want one?"

"No, thanks. I ate with the guys at the Brotherhood tonight. I don't have an ounce of space left in my digestive system."

"Well, thanks for that image," Kailee teased, returning to the sofa. "Have you talked to your mom today?"

"Nope. Have you?" Ross lifted Kailee's feet and put them in his lap.

Kailee took a long drink of water. "My mother told me she's asked your mother to work on ENF."

"Really? That's weird. My mom isn't, like, someone who's spent a lot of time on the island." Ross took the glass from her hand and put it on the coffee table. He pulled her legs closer, until she was almost on his lap.

Kailee tried to focus on her news. "I know. That's why my mother thinks your mother is perfect. Heather is a neutral person. And it's kind of cool that our mothers like each other."

"It's kind of cool that you and I like each other," Ross said, and scooted closer, putting his arms around her.

"Ross, wait. We need to discuss something else."

Ross kissed her mouth while she was still talking.

"Ross . . ." Her intelligence faded as his touch, his kiss, his warm body, woke her senses.

Ross nuzzled her cheek. "Come on, babe, let's not get all serious. The guys were moaning tonight about how exhausted they were with weary wives and crying babies. Let's enjoy our summer, we're still young."

Kailee knew she had to tell him sometime, but not after that crying-babies remark. She wrapped her arms around him and kissed him back.

It was Sunday morning, which meant no work. Ross lay on his side, deeply asleep. Kailee slid out of bed, dressed, and tiptoed down the steps from the apartment. She ran across the drive to the back door and made it just in time to grab a garbage bag from the back hall. She vomited profusely, feeling sweaty and hot and shivery and cold all at the same time. She leaned against the wall, catching her breath.

After a while, she tied up the garbage bag and buried it in the plastic bin outside. She went into the kitchen, drank some water, and ate some saltines. Her parents weren't downstairs yet. They usually slept late, thank heavens.

But she couldn't keep on like this, vomiting in private. Every day mattered. She knew this.

She would decide today.

She needed to grow up. Whether she had the baby or not, she needed to be an adult. She tiptoed up to her room and showered quickly. She tossed her pajamas into the laundry basket and pulled on a floaty sundress.

Quietly, she returned to Ross's apartment. He wasn't up yet, and she knew he craved his long Sunday sleep-ins. She set her laptop on the counter and scanned recipes, matching them up with what was already in the freezer. *Meatloaf!* Everyone had thought Heather's meatloaf was so delicious. But Kailee could cook a meatloaf. She had cooked before, mostly spaghetti or macaroni and cheese, but today she'd make a meatloaf and steamed vegetables, and mashed potatoes with gravy! Ross would love this menu. He'd be so impressed!

Once again, she hurried into her parents' house. She found her mother's apron on its hook inside the pantry and tied it on. She checked in the hall mirror to be sure she'd tied it tight enough to show off her slender waist. It didn't say KISS THE COOK, which was too bad, but she looked cute in it anyway. She took a pound of frozen hamburger from the freezer and set it aside to thaw. She could always use the microwave to thaw it fast if she needed to. She found a package of frozen vegetables in the freezer, and they could be microwaved in seven minutes! She dug out a box of macaroni and a bag of grated cheese. She carried them all back to Ross's apartment.

Quickly, she googled recipes for meatloaf. Ross didn't have all the ingredients in his galley kitchen, and she couldn't face running up and down the stairs to the house one more time. She basically stuffed the meat with bread crumbs and lots of ketchup. She put it in a pie pan because that was all she could find. She set it in the oven, pleased with herself. Ross would wake to the aroma of a cooked meal. They could have it for lunch and in sandwiches tomorrow.

But she was exhausted.

She fell onto the sofa and slept.

"Hey, sleeping beauty."

Kailee had trouble coming out of her dream. Ross was there, leaning over her, so handsome. She sat up, yawned, and stretched her arms.

"I guess I took a nap," she told him. Then, before he could answer, she sniffed the air and cried, "The *meatloaf!*"

Surging to her feet, she raced into the kitchen, put on her oven mitts, and opened the oven door. A rush of heat nearly knocked her over. She bent over and brought out the meatloaf. It was black. Incinerated.

"Oh, no!" she said, bursting into tears. If she couldn't even cook a meatloaf, how could she be a wife and . . . mother?

"You made a meatloaf?" Ross grabbed a hot pad and took the ruined meatloaf away from her. He set it in the sink. "That's so sweet of you, honey. Let's have PB and J sandwiches for lunch and order a pizza tonight. I'm in the mood for one, anyway."

Kailee fought back tears. "We can't eat pizza every night of our lives!"

Ross shrugged. "No, but we'll eat it tonight." Reaching around her, he pulled a seltzer from the refrigerator, popped the cap, and took a long drink.

"Let's go to the beach," he said to Kailee.

"I've got to go to the bathroom," Kailee said, and raced away.

Early Monday morning, Heather and Sugar took a long walk along Surfside Beach. The sun was slipping up past the horizon, and the air was soft and golden. Frothy waves skimmed the sand, carrying secrets and signs from far across the ocean, past cruise ships and over sea creatures, its sparkling ions rich with information about the world.

She returned to the cottage, showered and dressed, and kissed Sugar goodbye. As she drove to Miles's office, she reflected on what a strange summer this had become. Spending time with Evelyn on ENF was the last thing she'd expected—no, the last thing she'd expected was knowing that Kailee was pregnant before her son knew. She hoped Kailee had told him this weekend.

No. The *last* thing she'd expected was to meet someone like Miles, and feel massively attracted to him in a way she hadn't felt since high school. Or ever. Sometime this summer, she was sure, she would go to bed with him. The thought terrified her.

She climbed the steep steps to the law office, sat at her desk, and was relieved to find that Miles had all his morning appointments scheduled for out-of-the-office meetings. She had several files to transcribe, which would require her to focus. Good thing, because after lunch she was going to Evelyn Essex's house.

She had been hesitant about working for ENF, but when Evelyn named the salary accompanying the position, she had readily agreed. At noon, after quickly munching a sandwich in her car, she drove to the house on Pleasant Street.

When she pulled into the driveway, her cell rang.

"Heather, it's Evelyn. Would you mind coming up to my room? I had a little turn and I think I'll stay in bed awhile more."

"Evelyn, you shouldn't be working at all today. Did you notify your doctor?"

"Nonsense. It's not that serious. And I promise you I *will* have a heart attack if I don't get some work done on ENF."

"All right. I'm in your driveway now. I'll come right up."

"You can come through the front door. I told Kailee to leave it unlocked. The stairs are on the right—"

Heather laughed. "Evelyn, if I can't find you, I'll call you."

Heather entered the Essexes' house. The air was cool and dry, a pleasure after the humidity and heat. She set her laptop on the front hall table and went up the stairs and entered Evelyn's lusciously appointed bedroom. A window seat with a rose-and-lily-covered cushion looked over the garden. Two doors led into what had to be walk-in closets, and another door was slightly open to the en suite bathroom. A thick Aubusson carpet and silk curtains, both in shades of pink, lavender, and cream, turned the room into a romance novel fantasy that had nothing to do with the outside world. Evelyn was sitting up in the king-size bed, leaning against the velvet headboard, her sheets and snowy plump quilt pulled over her legs.

"Good afternoon," Heather said, and then, "Is this what you wear to sleep in? Really?"

Evelyn wore a pink silk gown and a pink silk wrapper. She looked ready to drape herself across a piano and sing.

"Yes, this is what I wear!" Evelyn was indignant. "What do *you* wear to bed?"

"A T-shirt and a pair of Wall's old boxers," Heather admitted. She studied the room, but before she could ask, Evelyn spoke.

"Okay, then. I cleared off my bedside table and moved it so you can sit in that side chair and use the table for your laptop. I have my bed table—isn't it clever?—so if you'll bring up my laptop and yours, and the folders on the ENF, we can get to work."

"Evelyn, why did you move your bedside table yourself?" Heather asked.

"It wasn't that hard. Don't make a fuss. Let's get some work done."

"Just saying . . . maybe moving that table and setting that heavy

lamp on the floor was what caused you to have your 'little turn.'"
Heather spoke lightly, teasingly, not wanting to make Evelyn
upset.

Evelyn barked, "I'm fine! Now are you going to help me or
not?"

Heather paused, uncertain. She knew nothing about heart attacks, but she could see with her own eyes that Evelyn's face was
tense and her hands were clenched on the covers.

"I'll get them right now," Heather said, and turned to leave the
room.

"I hate this!" Evelyn yelled.

Heather looked at Evelyn, who was suddenly crying, her hands
over her face, her shoulders heaving. Heather realized that she
and Evelyn were nearly the same age. She could understand why
Evelyn hated being grounded.

"Oh, Evelyn." Heather went to the bed and sat on the side. She
put her hand on Evelyn's duvet-covered knee. She said reassur-
ingly, "Evelyn, it's okay."

"No, it's *not* okay," Evelyn wept. "I hate being like this. This is
not who I am. I don't get heart attacks. *I* don't stay in bed. I'm not
even fifty years old. I'm doing important work!"

Heather tried to come up with something light and wise to say
that wouldn't embarrass Evelyn further. Then she glanced at the
rug, where Evelyn had set her bedside lamp, and saw the orange
pill bottles scattered across the rug.

"This is just a guess," Heather said, "but is it possible you didn't
take your medications today?"

Evelyn looked up, tears streaming from her face. "They make
me feel so *dull.* Lethargic. *Lazy.*"

"So you didn't take them."

Evelyn reached for the box of tissues sitting next to her on the
bed. "Now *you're* going to tell me what to do."

"I'm going to get you a glass of water, and if you don't take
them, I'll call your husband or your daughter."

For a long moment, the two women glared at each other.

Evelyn gave in. "Fine. I'll take the damn pills. On one condition. You'll make me a cup of coffee."

Give me patience, Heather thought, immediately laughing at her pun. "Evelyn, guess what I just thought. *Give me patience.* Patients, get it?"

"I'm not your patient," Evelyn snapped. She dried her eyes and blew her nose. "But yes, I can see how that's funny. I need some patience, too."

Heather went into the bathroom, taking a moment to admire the shining marvel of chrome, tile, and glass, and ran water into a cup. She brought it and the pills to Evelyn and watched her swallow them.

"I'll get the laptops," she told Evelyn.

"And the ENF folders," Evelyn reminded her.

Heather hurried from the room before Evelyn could ask for coffee again. She went down the carpeted stairs, her heart full of sympathy for Evelyn. Some people would love nothing more than forced bed rest, but obviously Evelyn was not one of those people. Clearly, she needed to be busy, to be in charge, in control. Heather gathered the folders and laptops and returned to Evelyn's bedroom.

Evelyn had dried her face and managed a weak smile. "I'm sorry I blew up at you, Heather."

"I understand. This reminds me of when I was in labor with Ross. It was a long labor but all I could do was breathe and sit on that hospital bed, unable to escape the pain. It made me feel, maybe this is wrong, but it made me feel *trapped.* I couldn't get up and walk down to the bookstore or the coffee shop. I couldn't chat on the phone with friends. I had no control, and it was frightening."

"Well, I had an epidural with Kailee, so I didn't experience that particular fear," Evelyn said, her voice taking on its natural superior one. She tried to soften it by adding, "But I damn well know what you mean."

Heather helped set up the bed table over Evelyn's legs, set the laptop there, and handed Evelyn the folders. Evelyn gave Heather her ENF username and password, and they worked together for almost an hour, until an email arrived for Evelyn that made both women blink.

Evelyn, I won't call you dear because at this moment in time you are certainly not dear to me with your scheme to make the islanders forget about the devastation your husband is wreaking with his construction company. Will I give your fake organization some money to damage this fragile island? I think not.

Most sincerely, Donna Skatel

"Wow," Evelyn said. Color was draining from her face and her hands shook.

"Deep breath," Heather instructed. She slipped from her chair, went to Evelyn's side, and held Evelyn's hand. "Don't let her hurt you. There's always someone like this in any group. Some sour grapes, cranky old witch who enjoys being angry."

"Donna Skatel isn't old," Evelyn said. "She's my age, and smart, and active in the community."

Heather sank down onto the side of the bed. "Evelyn, I think this is the Donna in my bridge group."

"I see. Well, Donna and I have never got along, but this is over the top. Of course, you couldn't know that." She clicked her perfectly manicured fingernail against her laptop. "I think I have an idea."

"I'll stop going to the group," Heather offered.

"No, don't do that. Keep going. You can be my spy."

Heather laughed. "Evelyn, I don't think I'll learn anything interesting." She suddenly flashed on the time one of the women had asked if Evelyn had used Botox. "And I don't think I'd be a good advocate for you because I've only been on the island a month or so. I've certainly heard about the island's problems and read about them in the *Inquirer and Mirror,* but I'm in no place to judge."

Color was returning to Evelyn's face. "I *am* hoping that ENF will help improve our construction company's image, but that's not the only reason I'm doing it. I grew up here. So did Bob. Our parents grew up here, and everyone in our family back to the sixteen hundreds. What people like Donna don't understand is that if Essex Construction doesn't build houses, the billionaires will simply hire another company. Maybe even an off-island corporation. This way people have jobs, and Bob can keep an eye on what the owner is planning for his land."

"It is a difficult situation," Heather agreed. "But you know what, it's lunchtime, so we can't focus on this any longer. I'm going to make you something delicious for lunch. And you can read this book." She lifted a novel by Debbie Macomber out of her purse.

"I don't read novels," Evelyn objected.

"That's probably why you had a heart attack," Heather told her. "Read this and you'll be happy."

Heather hurried down the stairs and into the kitchen. *What do you serve to a heart attack patient?* She was sure fats were out. According to the health experts, it seemed fats were never *in*. Chicken noodle soup? Was that too salty?

Why was she even here, making Evelyn's lunch?

She settled on an avocado toast, the toast multi-grained, and a glass of V8 juice.

Back in Evelyn's room, she set the tray on Evelyn's bed table. Evelyn slipped a bookmark into the novel and laid it next to her.

"Where's your lunch?" Evelyn asked.

"I ate earlier," Heather said. "And now, I have to do some errands. Maybe this is a good time for me to—"

"No. Stay." Evelyn saw Heather's face. "I mean, please stay. We've got so much to do. First of all, I don't want you to feel that you're waiting on me hand and foot. Also, Heather, oh, please sit down again. Let's talk about our children."

"Okay," Heather said reluctantly. She sat down facing the bedside table with her computer.

Evelyn took a small bite of her lunch, chewed carefully, and wiped her mouth with the linen napkin Heather had put on the tray.

"Heather, you and I are soon to be family," Evelyn said. "I want to tell you how very much Bob and I like Ross. Bob is over the moon, actually, because Ross is a remarkable worker, liked by the guys, grasping the overall plan and the details. Ross is a tremendous asset."

Heather wished she'd made herself lunch so she could be chewing away busily, giving her time to think about how to answer. She really didn't want to hear any more secrets.

"I like Kailee very much," Heather began. "And I understand how she wants to work for the family company. She's smart. I know she'll do a good job." Heather paused. "You know, I didn't intend to spend the summer here until April. My husband and I are getting divorced. We're selling our big house in Concord—"

"Concord is beautiful," Evelyn said.

"Yes, well, so is our house, but it's too big for two people. My friend Christine suggested I rent the little cottage off Milestone Road. The entire place would fit in your living room, but it's just what I need for the summer. And honestly? I'm amazed at how much I like Nantucket. I feel so at home here."

"I imagine Miles Hunter is part of the island's charm." Evelyn cocked her head knowingly. "You'll soon find out you can't keep a secret on the island."

Heather thought: *And you'll soon find out that I can.*

"What I want you, and everyone, to know, is that I rented the cottage before I knew that Ross was coming here to work. I don't want anyone to think I'm stalking my own son."

"Oh, we never thought that," Evelyn replied. "And it's so good that you're here. You and I can conspire about the wedding. Kailee's thinking of sometime next spring, with a reception at the yacht club. We'll take you to dinner there some evening. Kailee and I can't decide whether to go off-island for her wedding dress or to have one specially made."

Kailee might up the date for the wedding, Heather thought.

"It's good that we're working together, you and I," Evelyn said. "It's sort of karma."

It's sort of weird, Heather thought, but didn't say.

"You know, I'm tired now. I think I'll take a nap."

Heather dutifully lifted the tray off Evelyn's lap. "I've got some errands to run, but I'll have my cell with me. Call if you need anything."

"I will. And thank you so much, Heather."

nineteen

Kailee was sitting in George's office—the company office—working on the new governmental regulations for health-care benefits for full-time employees.

"This is ridiculous," she said to George, who sat across the room at his own desk. "They keep changing the benefits and cost calculations every three months. Plus, the average costs of hospitalization and medical care for a broken leg, for example, are way different from what they would cost on Nantucket. They provide far too much paperwork that hides the real costs."

"That's why I asked *you* to start on it," George told her, laughing. "Healthcare insurance is crazy. I'm glad you've taken courses at university." He swiveled in his chair. "I've been working for your father for twenty years, and it just gets more complicated. I'm so glad I've got a long vacation coming up soon."

Alarmed, Kailee asked, "What do you mean by *soon?*"

"Gary and I have booked a two-week cruise in the Mediterranean in October. First class all the way."

His words sent her into a panic. "George, you can't leave! I can't do this alone!"

"Sure you can," George replied calmly. "We'll get everything organized during the next few months. You're a smart woman."

"Thanks for your trust in me," Kailee said, adding under her breath, "I guess."

She would be in charge of the office for two weeks? She was honored and terrified. She set to work on the maze of regulations and numbers. Any other time, she would have tackled this job with vigor and zest. These days, she wanted to stay in bed all day. With a bucket next to the bed.

She had to talk to Ross.

But she wanted to talk to Heather first. Heather already knew Kailee was pregnant, plus, from what Ross had told her, Heather had managed the whole baby plus work with ease. How had she done it?

Had life for young women changed at all since Heather and Kailee's mother had been young women? Most businesses and corporations hired young women and gave them maternity leave, but what happened after the leave was up? Ross had told her that Heather had carried him to work in a laundry basket, which was an adorable image, but where had she kept the baby wipes, clean diapers, and clean clothes? Kailee wanted to nurse her babies. *Everyone* said nursing was the best thing for a baby. It gave the baby immunities he or she wouldn't get otherwise. Plus, the love. The mother got the exhaustion.

Kailee had questioned Maggie about life with newborns, but told her friend that she was planning someday to have a baby, when she and Ross were married and ready.

"Ready?" Maggie laughed. "Ha! You'll never be ready. You can't imagine the clutter and anxiety you're surrounded with, no, not surrounded, *filled* with. Is she asleep? Can I take a nap yet? Why is her poop yellow? She's sleeping too long! Where are the clean diapers? Why doesn't she stop crying? I don't think the person who painted all those calm Madonnas adoring their baby ever met a new mother."

"Wow," Kailee agreed. "That's intense."

Maggie went on forever, giving Kailee the details of the new bagginess of her body, arguing with her husband about who would get up in the night, how her shoulders and feet ached, and a thousand other things.

And yet, a *baby*.

That night, Kailee bought grilled steak tips and potato salad from Bartlett's and had dinner waiting in Ross's apartment when he came home. She was going to let him kick back for a while, have a dinner she knew was delicious, and then she would tell him she was pregnant.

"How was your day?" she asked when they were finished with their meal.

Ross leaned back and stretched. "It was great. Kailee, it's so great I can't believe my luck. Your father is wonderful, and the foreman, Dean, is cool. I'm learning stuff I never knew, not just construction stuff, but how to manage a crew and negotiate with subcontractors. You know, several other people have contacted Bob about having compounds built out on Pocomo. I mean, these guys are the real deal. Billions made from technology. Heads of corporations who want a family house and pool with a pool house and three guesthouses plus a house for their chauffeur and house-keeper, and a fountain in the middle of the courtyard—"

Kailee interrupted. "A fountain? Who needs a fountain? I assume they're facing the harbor. And they want a pool? Olympic size, I'm sure. Why do they need a *fountain?* That seems so unnecessary."

"I'm not the one to ask. The house we're working on now out at Miacomet has a dock for a yacht and a sailboat, plus an Iguana, an amphibious boat that goes from the water right up the shore so people don't need dinghies. They cost seven hundred thousand dollars."

"What does Dad say about this?" Kailee asked. "This isn't Nantucket, these huge houses, all this display, this showing off."

"Kailee," Ross shot back, "this absolutely *is* Nantucket. Your father is building these houses, and if we're lucky, I'll keep working for him and you'll keep working with George and someday we'll have a house of our own, maybe when we're thirty."

Kailee stared down at her plate. She'd forced herself to eat a bit of steak because protein was always necessary, but swallowing made her nauseous, although not at the very end of the day. Ross hadn't even noticed how little she ate.

Ross paused, waiting for her to speak. "Kailee, are you okay?"

"I'm fine," Kailee managed to say. "Ross, I think I'm just tired. I mean, I love working with George, and I've wanted to do this all my life, but George can be nitpicky and demanding. He wants everything done the way he's always done it, and he won't take my suggestions. Plus, he and his husband are going on a two-week cruise in October and I don't think I'll be capable of handling all the books by myself. I'm worried about my mother, and I can't even imagine how to plan a wedding. I'm just . . . I'm just . . . tired." She burst into tears.

"Honey, I'm sorry. Look, why not lie down on the bed, and no, I don't mean to make love."

Kailee gagged. Simply the thought of bouncing around on the bed made her want to hurl.

Ross said, "I'll clean the kitchen. I think the Red Sox are on tonight. You rest. We've got plenty of time to figure it all out."

No, Kailee thought, *we don't.* But she thanked him and went into his bedroom. She curled up on his bed and was asleep when her head hit the pillow.

It was bridge night again. Heather had made delicious lemon cookies for the group, hoping they'd be so grateful they wouldn't pummel her with questions about the Essexes.

Bridge was at Donna Skatel's house that Wednesday, a tall, narrow house on Pine Street. The house had a historic plaque on it, stating that it had been built for Captain Benjamin Black in 1840, and its front steps met the brick sidewalk, so there was no room for a garden, but the glossy black front door had a whale door knocker and a wreath of summer flowers around it. Inside, it looked as if nothing had changed since the first owner. Antiques crowded the hall and front room. The living room couches were both Victorian fainting settees that looked extremely uncomfortable. Fortunately, Donna had set up two card tables in the room with folding chairs for the bridge players.

The card players had a routine they followed for pairing up. Names were written on a piece of paper and dropped into a roomy purse. Four women drew one name, and whoever that was would be their partner for the evening.

Heather got Donna for a bridge partner. She prayed Donna wouldn't ask about Evelyn Essex or talk about anything other than cards, really. Donna had no way of knowing that Heather had read her email to Evelyn. *Or did she? How could she?*

For a while, the games went along easily, especially because Donna and Heather had been dealt beautiful hands. They took the first set, and Heather hoped that would keep Donna happy. While they were playing another round, the women chatted about their weekend, and the upcoming church fair, and their visiting guests.

It was when Heather became the declarer and Donna the dummy that Donna began to talk, which was only natural, Heather supposed, because Donna's hand was on the table and it was up to Heather to play to win.

"Can't stop thinking," Donna said softly, "about this poor little island and how it's being overrun by billionaires. I'm especially concerned about the condition of the harbor water. All the pesticides and fertilizers going into the harbor, killing fish and seaweed."

"We have rules about that," Miribelle reminded her, placing a jack on the table and taking a trick.

"True, but who enforces the rules?" Donna asked, outrage in her voice. "I'm going to petition the board of selectmen to appoint a state-approved inspector whose duty is to check out the new building sites and impose fines on the contractors who violate the rules."

Heather didn't react. She was glad she had the bridge game to distract her.

Lana said, "The contractors aren't responsible for the grounds. The landscapers are."

"Ah!" Donna pounced. "But who hires and inspects the landscapers? The people who're having their little palaces built here don't want to bother with landscapers. The *contractor* chooses the landscaper and is responsible for checking their work. I know. I've been looking into this."

"The town would have to hire someone qualified to regulate the different landscapers," Linda said. "Another cost to the taxpayers."

"*I* will set up a fund to pay the inspector," Donna said triumphantly. "I'll be willing to meet the salary and other costs for the first year, but everyone on this island knows how important a clean harbor is to us personally, and as a resort community."

Linda said, "I'd be willing to contribute. I'll write you a check right now."

"Hold off on that," Donna said. "It's possible that the fines we gather from contractors who don't make their landscapers adhere to the rules would more than make up for the cost of the salary."

Miribelle intervened. "Have you talked to the Land Council's Waterkeeper?"

"That person is only an advocate," Donna said. "We need an inspector and enforcer."

"Goodness," Lana said. "That sounds so . . . Russian."

"You're right." Donna sighed dramatically. "We're here to play bridge. I'm only sharing my thoughts with you all, and I need you to keep this under your hats until I've completed looking into this, both on the local and the state levels."

Heather played a card and took the last trick, smiling pleasantly, as if she didn't realize that Donna's idea was aimed at Bob Essex and his company. Actually, she could understand why Donna would want such a person on the island. New homes were being built daily, and anyone driving down Eel Point Road or Lincoln

Street up on the cliff could see clearly that the natural wild grasses and flowers of the island had been killed and replaced by unnaturally perfect lawns.

"Well played!" Miribelle told Heather.

"Yes," Donna said. "Good job. I hope you won't tell anyone about my proposal just yet."

Heather gave Donna an innocent smile. "Of course not!"

The rest of the afternoon passed pleasantly. Heather drank enough iced tea to float a kayak, and flattered Donna about her beautiful house. Finally, the group broke up. Heather tried not to run to her car, and once she was inside, she sat with her head against the headrest and forced herself to deep breathe.

What had happened in there? Should she mention Donna's plan to Evelyn?

No, she decided. Evelyn had a heart problem. And Heather didn't have to deal with it, at least not urgently. Right now, she wanted to deal with a cold vodka tonic and the most twisty, dark, mystery novel she had in the house.

In mid-July, the heat and humidity intensified, lying over the island like a wet quilt. Heather woke early for her walk on the beach, and by seven-thirty, when she left, people were already arriving with their beach umbrellas and coolers, making little nests at the edge of the ocean. At home, Heather took a shower and dressed for work at Miles's office. She returned to her house for lunch and to let Sugar out for a while. At one, she drove to Evelyn's house to help her with her correspondence. She was rather proud of herself. She had two real jobs!

Today, she found Evelyn downstairs, fully dressed in tennis shorts and a lavender T-shirt, settled on a living room sofa, piles of papers next to her on the coffee table.

"I couldn't stand staying in my bed another minute," Evelyn said. "When all this is over, I'm having the room redecorated."

Heather settled on the sofa across from Evelyn. "When all what is over?"

"This heart business, of course. I'm not getting as many responses to my emails about ENF and I'm sure it's because I haven't been able to attend any of the parties and galas and lectures. It's ridiculous, just sitting around! I hate it!"

Heather joked, "Calm down, Evelyn, or you'll have another heart event and I'll have to give you CPR."

"What?" Evelyn looked at Heather, appalled. "That would be awful!"

"It's not like I'd enjoy it, either," Heather said dryly, and then a wonderful thing happened. Both women burst out laughing, together, laughing so hard Heather's stomach hurt.

"I'll be good, I'll be good, I promise," Evelyn said, and laughed even more.

When they settled down, they went through the day's email. Evelyn, with Heather working on Evelyn's laptop, made large donations to several groups, with sincere apologies because she would not be able to attend. They took a break while Heather made glasses of iced tea for them both—peach-flavored tea, with no caffeine.

"I'm worried about Kailee," Evelyn said. "She doesn't seem able to concentrate this summer. She's *odd* lately. She hardly eats anything." Evelyn looked at Heather. "Do you think she's doing the 'stick your hand down your throat' thing? She's losing weight, I can tell, even if I'm not there to eat meals with her."

Heather leaned back in the couch, pretending to think. "What does Gravity say?"

"She agrees with me. Unless Kailee's taking all her meals out, she's not eating. Kailee's not touching what Gravity cooks."

"I imagine she's eating with Ross. And I think they go out to eat with friends. I wouldn't worry. It's summer. Everyone's busy." Heather tried to sound reassuring, but her conscience was troubling her. Evelyn was Kailee's *mother*. Why hadn't Kailee talked with her? The next time she saw Kailee, she'd urge her to confide in Evelyn.

"Ross is coming over tonight to install two window air conditioners," Heather said, changing the subject. "I don't mind the heat, but the humidity makes me droop. Plus, I can't be bothered to make a decent meal for myself. I've been living on takeout."

"We should take a break," Evelyn suggested. "Let's finish the next two letters, and then I think I'd better rest. Just thinking about Kailee makes me nervous."

"She'll be fine," Heather said, because that was what one said. And she did believe it.

That evening, Ross arrived with two air conditioners in the back of his truck. It didn't take him long to install them, one in Heather's bedroom, one in the far living room window.

"Thanks, darling," Heather said. "Do you have time for a drink?"

"Do you have beer?"

"Heineken," Heather replied, smiling.

"I absolutely have time." Ross threw himself down on the sofa. He was deeply tanned, and in several places, he was scratched or cut.

"Would you like some Neosporin for those cuts?" Heather asked, handing him a beer.

"No, Mom, don't bother. They're not deep." Ross took a long swig of beer. "How are you doing? I know you're helping Evelyn with her committee work."

"I think we're both doing fine. We're getting to know each other. She's a high-powered woman and genuinely concerned about the island, and I'm glad she's taking the medication she was prescribed, because it calms her down a bit."

"How are *you* doing?" Ross persisted.

Heather smiled. "I'm fine, and you're sweet to ask. I think this island is the most beautiful place on earth. I dream of living here, year-round. I like the peace, and the pace."

"It's not peaceful now," Ross said. "The island is more crowded than it's ever been. Maybe as many as one hundred thousand people were here for the Fourth of July. You should try to stay in

September and October. That's supposed to be the best time." He paused. "Do you miss Dad?"

"Truthfully, Ross, I don't. We weren't really *with* each other the past few years. I don't mean in the same location, I mean mentally, spiritually. I felt guilty for leaving him. I'm so relieved that he's found Nova—whenever he found her—and has a new life. I hope you don't feel left out, I mean with your father."

"I'm good." He turned serious. "Listen. I want to talk to you about something."

Oh, no, Heather thought. She sat across from him, looking innocent, or trying to.

"It's Kailee. I'm worried about her. She's always cranky and exhausted."

Heather tried to sound thoughtful and wise. "I suppose the first year of working after being in university, I mean, *really* working, is stressful. Plus, I'm sure she's worried about her mother. Evelyn's heart is still giving her trouble, and Kailee must be aware of that, but she's helpless to do anything." *Plus, she's pregnant,* Heather wanted to say. But didn't.

"It's more than that, Mom. She's closing off from me, I can feel it. I don't know what to do."

Heather said, very quietly, "Ross, you have to talk to her. I think . . . I think you have to ask her what's going on."

"What's going on?" Ross echoed. "What do you mean, what's going on? Mom, what do you know? Tell me!"

Heather said, "It's not mine to tell."

Ross stared at his mother for one long moment. He stood up, started to speak, sat down. "Mom. Is Kailee pregnant?"

Heather said, "Go home, Ross."

twenty

On weekdays, Gravity always made delicious dinners that she left in the refrigerator when she went home at the end of the day. Kailee microwaved a plate of shepherd's pie and took a tray up to her mother. She stayed and chatted with Evelyn for a while. Her father came home, fixed himself a Scotch, and came up to his wife's room.

"How's our patient?" he asked, kissing his wife on the forehead.

"I'm absolutely bored out of my mind," Evelyn told him.

"We're seeing the doctor tomorrow," Bob reminded her. "We'll see if she lets you get back to normal."

Kailee heard Ross's truck enter the driveway. "Dad, there's a fab shepherd's pie Gravity made on the counter. Just give it a minute in the microwave and you'll have your dinner. And you can make Mom eat hers. I'm going to see Ross."

As she went down the stairs, Kailee hoped Ross had eaten at

his mother's. She knew he was delivering air conditioners there, and installing them for Heather. Surely, she'd give him dinner in return. She loved her father, she did, but she knew the moment he came in the room that he'd ask her to fix his dinner and bring it up to him, and she was in such a cranky, uncontrollable mood these days that she didn't want to wait on him hand and foot. Taking care of her mother was enough. Her father was a grown-up. He could fend for himself, but every morning he still expected Kailee to have a cup of hot coffee waiting for him. Kailee was going absolutely crazy! She loved her parents, she loved Ross, but everyone was driving her mad.

She stomped up the stairs to the garage apartment and opened the door. She thought she'd find Ross in the shower after his long day, but to her surprise, he was standing in the living room looking like thunder.

"What's wrong?" she asked.

"Are you pregnant?" Ross demanded.

"*What?*" She'd never seen Ross look so angry. Still, he had no right to act like this.

"I asked if you are pregnant," Ross said, lowering his voice but keeping the tension.

"Oh my God. Your mother told you. I knew I couldn't trust her."

"Stop it, Kailee. Answer me, please. Yes or no?"

Kailee burst into tears. "I don't know what to do!"

Ross looked terrified. "You're pregnant."

"But I don't have to be," Kailee told him. "I know we weren't planning on having kids until we were thirty."

Ross walked to Kailee and took her in his arms, cradling her head against his chest. "It's okay. Come on, let's sit down."

They sat on the sofa, side by side, Kailee sniffing back her tears. Ross kept his arm around her, and she was grateful for that.

"Your mom shouldn't have told you," Kailee said resentfully. "*I* wanted to tell you. She only found out first because when she brought over her meatloaf, I barfed. Oh, God, it was awful."

"You've been vomiting a lot, haven't you?" Ross asked, his voice gentle.

"I thought I'd covered it up."

"The bathroom smells like you've been pouring Listerine in the toilet."

Kailee smiled. "I have."

Ross took a deep breath, his body so close to hers, so twinned with hers, she could feel him inhale and exhale.

"When did you know?" Ross asked.

"Just after the Fourth of July." Kailee took a big shuddering breath. "I tried to tell you, but . . . it didn't seem to be the right time."

Ross counted on his fingers. "So, if we have the baby, it will be in March."

Kailee stared at his face. "You said 'we.' If we have the baby."

"Kailee, of course. It's a decision we both have to make. Together. I'm sorry you felt it was all on you. Did you talk to your mom?"

"No. I didn't want to give her anything else to worry about."

"She might be happy about it. But you and I have to decide if we're going to have this baby."

This baby. "It's not a baby yet, Ross. It's, like, a cluster of cells."

Ross stood up. "I'm going to get a seltzer. Would you like one?"

"No, thanks." Her emotions were all over the place. She was shocked that Ross was so calm, and furious that Heather had told him, and worried about telling her parents, and freaking *terrified* of making a decision one way or the other. But she wasn't crying right now. Or throwing up. That was something.

Ross stood in the galley kitchen, sipping his seltzer, thinking. At least she thought he was thinking. Maybe he was wondering when he could watch the Red Sox.

Ross said, "If we have a baby, we don't want to live in the garage apartment, right?"

"I suppose." She was still stunned at Ross's reaction. "We could always find a place to rent," Kailee said.

Ross nodded. "I've been talking with some of the guys. They've bought land and in their spare time, they're building their own houses. They help each other out, like with the plumbing or electric stuff. We could do that." Ross stood up and began to pace. "We could borrow money from your parents and buy a piece of land, and over the winter, I could build a house." His face brightened. "*I could build a house, Kailee.* It wouldn't have to be big. Not at first. Mom might give us, I don't know, money for a wedding present to help us pay for part of it."

"Ross, what are you saying? Do you want to have this baby? It would ruin our plans. Well, maybe not yours, but mine. I couldn't take care of a baby and work with George, and I really couldn't take care of a baby and help my mother."

"Couldn't you have, what do they call it, maternity leave?"

"Ross, this all seems easy for you, but it's different for women. I'd be the one sacrificing her career, staying home with a baby. I couldn't work *and* take care of an infant."

"Well, my mom did it," Ross said.

Kailee picked up a book from the coffee table and threw it at Ross. It hit him on the thigh.

"I am so sick of your mother! First, she tells you a *secret* that's not *hers* to tell, and now you're holding her up as St. Mama, capable of working full-time and taking care of a baby full-time!"

"I never said she was a saint," Ross argued. "But she did take care of me and do the books at the hardware store until I started walking."

"You want me to carry our baby in a laundry basket and nurse it in front of George?"

"I didn't mean that, Kailee. I just mean I think we could figure it out."

Kailee rose, folding her arms as if she was trying to keep herself together. "I can't do this. I feel sick. I'm going home." She went to the door to the steps.

"Yeah, Kailee, you do that. You go *home,*" Ross called after her.

———

Damn Heather! Kailee thought as she raced down the stairs from the garage apartment. *How could she? How could Ross's mother tell Ross the most important, sacred secret of all?*

She hesitated by the back door to the house. She was sane enough to know she shouldn't face her parents in this deranged, furious, terrified state. She'd give her poor mother another heart attack. And this was all Heather's fault!

She went quietly into the house, found her purse, and left the house without slamming the door. She ran to her Jeep. She got in and started the engine. She drove to Heather's cottage, shaking with anger all the way.

Heather's car was in the stupid little dirt driveway. Kailee slammed her car door and hurried up the path. She knocked on the door so hard it hurt her knuckles, which made her cry and curse even more.

Heather opened the door. She was dressed in shorts and a sleeveless shirt and she looked absolutely too damn calm. "Kailee. Come in. Honey, are you okay?"

Kailee stepped inside, and the moment Heather shut the door, she glowered at Ross's mother.

"How could you? How could you tell Ross I'm pregnant? It is *my* news to give him, not yours! Now he's upset because I didn't tell him and I'm furious and it's *all your fault!*"

"Oh, Kailee," Heather said, and her voice was so sympathetic that Kailee wanted to kick her. "Come sit down. I'll get you some water."

"I don't want water! I want you to stop talking about my life. It's *my* life!"

Heather nodded. "Kailee, I understand why you're angry. But I didn't tell Ross you're pregnant. Please. Come in and have some ice water. Let's talk."

Kailee said, "Talk? I don't want to ever talk to you. I want you to *go away!*"

Heather's face crumpled at Kailee's words. Kailee thought *Heather* was going to cry, and that was *so* not fair!

Kailee couldn't stand it. She didn't come here to be nice to Heather. But she realized through the noxious swirl of her thoughts that Heather could hardly go away right now. This was Heather's home. It was Kailee who had to leave. She'd said what she needed to say.

Kailee left the cottage, slamming the door behind her, hurrying to her car as if demons were following her. She drove down the Milestone road and that took forever because eighty thousand summer people were on the island and everyone was driving everywhere. She wanted to yell "Go away!" to them all. What had happened to her sweet island? People were driving Range Rovers and huge black cars that looked like they came from the Secret Service.

When she finally got on to lower Orange, the car in front of her stopped to allow a car from West Creek Road to turn into the congested line of traffic, and the driver waved thanks to the driver of the car in front of her, and Kailee burst into tears. People were nice. Or could be. What was wrong with her? She'd never been such an insane roaring bitch before. Why were her moods so intense?

Finally, she parked in her parents' driveway and went into the house through the kitchen door.

Her father was standing in the hall, looking grave.

"Kailee, we'd like you to come upstairs and talk with us," her father said.

"Oh, um, I, I need to get Ross," Kailee stuttered.

"Ross is with Evelyn," her father told her.

Kailee cried, "What? I don't believe this!"

"Please, Kailee," her father said.

He left her side and went up the stairs.

Kailee stood frozen, frightened, and angry. Angry at everyone. But she pulled it together and grimly climbed the stairs.

Her mother was sitting up in bed. Her face was pale. Ross leaned against the wall, arms crossed over his chest. *His* face was pale.

"Hi, Mom," Kailee said softly. She went to her mother's side, sat on the edge of the bed, and held her hand. "How do you feel?"

"Curious and worried," Evelyn said. "The question is, how are *you*?"

"Ross told you," Kailee said.

Her father said, "I saw you run out to your car, crying. You didn't answer your cell. So I called Ross and asked him to come over here."

Kailee looked over at Ross, who stared stonily into the distance.

Kailee sank onto the end of the bed, hugging herself, trying to compose herself.

"Okay. Mom, Dad, I'm pregnant. Not very pregnant, and Ross and I haven't talked about what we're going to do, and I'm sorry I didn't tell you before, and I'm really sorry that Heather found out first, but that was only because I vomited in front of her."

From across the room, Ross asked, calmly but firmly, "Where did you go just now?"

Kailee hesitated before admitting, "I went out to confront your mother." She glanced at him then turned back to her mother. "I told her I was furious with her for telling Ross, that it is *my* news to share. And it *is!* And I'm sorry, but I got mad and told her she should leave. Then I got in the car and came home." Her tears started again. "This is all wrong. It's my news, not Heather's."

"I'll call Mom," Ross said. "I'll ask her to stay away for a few days."

"You can't do that," Evelyn said. "She's helping me with ENF."

Kailee exchanged worried glances with her father.

Bob went to his wife and bent over her. "Let's not try to solve everything right now. Ross and Kailee need some time on their own, to talk, and you need to rest."

Evelyn nodded. "Bobby, I can't breathe right. I'm getting dizzy."

"Okay," her husband said, as calmly as if he were discussing what groceries to buy, "let's get you lying down. I'll join you. I could take some weight off my feet."

Kailee stood up, alarmed. "Mommy?"

Her father said, "Ross, would you take Kailee to your apartment, please?"

Kailee leaned around her father to look at her mother. "Mom, are you okay?"

Her mother was leaning against her pillows, eyes closed, panting lightly.

Ross took Kailee's hand. "Kailee. Let's go. We all need to settle down."

Kailee had no choice but to go with Ross, whose hand was tightly clamped on hers. They went down the stairs, through the hall, through the kitchen, and out the back door.

"It's hot," Ross said, as if it were any normal day. "Let's get up in my apartment and cool off."

Kailee went with him, sick with worry about her mother.

After Kailee came bursting into her house, Heather sat on the sofa, trying to compose herself. She was shaking. Miles was coming to her house for dinner at seven-thirty. Should she cancel? No, she wanted to see him. She'd better get ready.

She'd planned the menu to include only dishes she could prepare ahead, so she could focus on Miles. Drinks, a bowl of olives, a wedge of cheese to start. Lasagna, salad, and garlic bread with red wine. A bowl of grapes for dessert. She worried that if they ate garlic bread, they'd be disinclined to kiss each other with their garlic breath, then she decided that might be a good thing. She wasn't ready for a lover in her life, and tonight, especially, she needed a good friend.

As she moved through the kitchen, heating the lasagna in the oven, combining olive oil and balsamic vinegar for the salad, she reminded herself of the mood swings she'd had when she was pregnant with Ross. She reminded herself that Kailee was right; Kailee should have been the one to tell Ross. But Heather hadn't actually spoken those words, and no one was focusing on the main point: *Kailee was pregnant!* Heather didn't even know what to *think* about that, what to *feel.* Happy? Elated? Sad? Worried?

What could Heather do to help?

She could stay away from her son and Kailee.

But she wouldn't leave. She felt connected to this island. Every morning as she walked on the beach, she knew she was exactly where she should be. Each day the light on the water was different, and the wind could be gentle or pushy, making her laugh. Something elemental, unnamable, as tender and compelling as light, swirled itself around her, claiming her.

She wasn't going to leave the island. At least not yet.

Heather quickly showered and pulled on white capris, a blue summer blouse, and flip-flops. She put on only a touch of lipstick and blush.

Miles arrived at seven-thirty, dressed casually as she'd suggested, in chinos and a red rugby shirt. He really was a handsome man, Heather thought when she opened the door to his knock. He kissed her cheek and presented her with a bottle of good red wine and a bouquet of flowers.

"Thank you," Heather said. For a moment she simply looked up at him, wanting to kiss his cheek in welcome—wanting to do more than that, really—but shyly saying, "Come in. This is it, my summer home. Look around if you'd like, while I put these gorgeous flowers in water."

Miles followed her into the kitchen. "Something smells good."

"Lasagna," Heather told him. "A winter meal, but it's too humid to eat out tonight." She glanced at him. "You're sunburned."

"True. I was out on the water today. That's why I couldn't come until now. I had my last sail with Emma before she goes back to Boston to join her friends playing some gigs."

Heather held up a bottle of vodka in one hand and a bottle of tonic in the other. Miles nodded, so she set to work making their drinks, slicing a lime and squeezing it into the glasses.

"There," she said. "Now we won't get scurvy."

She led him to the living room and she settled on the couch and let Miles have the sagging wing chair. God, he was handsome.

She held up her drink. "Cheers," she said, and they clinked and drank.

"Emma's such a talented musician," Heather said. "When she plays at church, I'm enthralled. Do you worry about her? I mean, when I think of a gig, I think of . . ."

Miles finished, "Bars with half-drunk, testosterone-mad males paying attention to how pretty she is?"

Heather laughed. "I suppose that's exactly what I mean. A different venue than church, for sure."

"We've talked about this. I'm fairly confident that she can take care of herself, and the gigs will be mostly weddings and anniversaries."

They relaxed as they enjoyed their drinks. Heather changed the subject of their conversation to their own adolescences, and they told stories of the most stupid or wicked or drunken thing they'd done. They both laughed so much that Heather almost didn't hear the buzzer on the stove reminding her the lasagna was ready. She led him to the table, which she'd set with the cottage's simple pottery, and poured glasses of the red wine Miles had brought, and set the salad bowl in the center of the table, and cut lasagna into perfect rectangles, and, finally, put a basket of buttered garlic bread on the table.

"This smells wonderful," Miles said.

While they ate, they talked lazily about restaurants on Nantucket, and restaurants in town, and memories of Emma or Ross doing inappropriate things at restaurants when they were children, and by the time they finished the meal, they were laughing again. Heather was glad Miles was so easy to talk with, and she found out bits and pieces of his ex-wife and their married life without having to pry, and she knew Miles was learning about her.

Heather wanted to tell Miles about her son's current situation, and about Kailee being so angry with her, but she didn't want to bring down their good time, so she pushed that subject to the back of her mind. Miles helped her clear the dishes and poured more good wine as Heather set the grapes on the table.

When they were seated again, idly picking and chewing the grapes, which were so deliciously wet and cool after the lasagna, Miles said, "Miribelle tells me you're a star at bridge."

"It's nice that she thinks so," Heather said. "Actually, I'm terrified of some of those women. They take bridge so seriously. You'd think we were working coordinates for a spaceship to Mars."

Miles laughed. "Miribelle says that Donna Skatel dislikes the Essexes."

"That's true. I can't imagine why. Also, she's started working on a way to hire some kind of enforcer to check all the properties for forbidden fertilizers and pesticides. She wants to give the contractors huge fines. She seems obsessed with it."

"Let me tell you why. In high school, Bob Essex and Donna were a couple. We all thought they would marry, but in college, Bob and Evelyn started seeing each other, and by the first summer home, Bob had broken off with Donna and he and Evelyn were together. Typical teenage breakup, and Donna married Evan, who's a good guy, and a fine lawyer, but Donna has held a grudge against Bob and Evelyn for years. Her bark is worse than her bite, but I'm sorry she's barking at you."

"I'd know what to do if I were back in Concord," Heather said. "I know everyone there. But here, of course, I'm an outsider. Not even a summer person. I've rented this cottage for only three months, and half my time is already over."

"That's too bad," Miles said. "I wish you would stay longer. Not just because I'd like to keep seeing you, but because the off-seasons are beautiful, too."

"I'd like to stay longer," Heather said. "But honestly, and please don't repeat this, I don't think Kailee is happy with me around. She thinks I'm too dependent on Ross."

"Is that true?" Miles asked.

"Not at all. I do love Ross, but I'm here because my friend

Christine found out about this funny little cottage and I needed a change after leaving Wall. It happened very quickly. I thought Ross was going to work for Wall, so being near him wasn't part of the equation for me." She sensed tears gathering. "I didn't intend to love it here, but I do. I mean, I'd live here even if Ross and Kailee lived somewhere else. I've never spent much time near the ocean. Now I walk on one of the beaches every day, and it seems that I inhale energy, and happiness, and connection. I'm reading Sylvia Earle's book *Blue Hope* and I've got a shark tracker on my iPhone, and I adore the town, and the people I've met."

Miles said, "I hope you do stay. I'd like that a lot. And I heard that you're helping Evelyn Essex with her nature foundation."

Heather smiled. "Yes, I am. Well, I have been, in the afternoons after my mornings working for you. It's not permanent or like a job, but you know she's had trouble with her heart, and she's supposed to rest, but she's not a person who enjoys resting."

"Does Kailee think you're helping her mother in order to be close to Ross?"

"I don't know, and frankly, I'm tired of talking about Kailee." Heather stood up. "Let's go outside. It will be cooler now."

At her words, Sugar opened her eyes and yawned.

Miles joked, "I'm glad you have a watchdog to protect you."

Heather refreshed their drinks. They went out to the patio, and it was cooler, and the night sky was full of stars. They stood looking up into the heavens.

"Honeysuckle," Heather said. She let her head fall back as she inhaled. "Wild honeysuckle everywhere."

"Wild honeysuckle," Miles echoed. He took her drink from her and put it on the table with his. He came close to Heather, sensed her readiness, and took her in his arms. He kissed her lightly, and then with a passion that was the warmth of the sun, and the wildness of the ocean, and the sweetness of the air. As if everything good was right here.

She'd never been kissed like this before.

"You're trembling," Miles said. "Let's sit down."

He pulled the two plastic patio chairs close together, side by side, and they sat holding hands.

"I feel like I'm very slowly drifting to earth from a cloud," Heather said. She knew she was flushed, but she couldn't stop it. Her body was dazed . . . awakened.

"Slow is good," Miles said. "I like to do things slowly."

"I need to tell you," Heather began, not sure how to say it or whether this was the right or completely wrong time to say it, and finally blurting, "I need to tell you, Miles, that I've only been with one man. Wall. I'm not very . . . accomplished or skilled . . ." She couldn't finish the sentence.

Miles said, "Well, personally, I find you quite excellent in kissing. But I understand. And I'm more than ready to be with you any way at all, and I'm also old enough to appreciate how nice it is to take things slowly."

"That sounds perfect," Heather told him.

They sat for a while, talking idly about the summer, the beaches, the sky. Then, Miles stood up, and for a moment Heather wanted to clutch him, begging him not to go.

"We've got the church fair tomorrow," Miles said. "We both had better get our beauty sleep. It's going to be a busy day."

Heather walked him to the door. They stood just outside the house. The glow of the outside light seemed harsh to Heather and she walked Miles to his car, grateful for the shadows.

"Thanks for dinner," Miles said. He kissed her forehead. "See you tomorrow."

"Yes," Heather said. "Tomorrow."

twenty-one

Kailee and Ross left Evelyn and Bob in their bedroom and walked across the drive to the steps to the garage apartment.

Kailee stopped, took Ross's hand, and looked back at the house. "My parents have such a good marriage."

"We will, too," Ross promised. "Let's go upstairs."

Kailee sank into a chair and watched Ross move around the galley kitchen. He took a beer and a jug of apple juice from the refrigerator, poured the drinks into glasses, and handed one to her.

"Thanks," Kailee said.

Ross grinned. "I never knew until this summer how much you pout."

"I don't pout!" Kailee said, realizing that she was sitting with her mouth crumpled. She imagined how she must look. She grinned back. "I was pouting just then, wasn't I?"

"You're smiling now," Ross told her. "Much better."

"I'm not sure I'm ready for adulthood," Kailee admitted.

"You'd better be," Ross said.

Kailee looked down at her hands. "I was kind of awful to your mother. I should apologize."

"Let's talk about us, first," Ross said. "Don't you think? About the three of us."

"The three of us?" Kailee asked. Then she got it, and she put her face in her hands and moaned.

Ross said, "It doesn't have to be the three of us now. We can wait to start a family. We can stick to our plan."

"But nothing is going as planned," Kailee pointed out. "We didn't plan for my mother to have a heart attack, and we didn't plan for your mother moving to the island."

Ross said very quietly, "No, and we didn't plan for my parents to get divorced. We didn't plan for my father to get involved with Nova. We didn't plan for my mother to be on the island, alone."

"Your mother is hardly alone," Kailee argued. "She's made friends here. And she's helping my mother—how did that even happen?"

"Well, Kailee, I think they like each other. I think my mother is smart and capable, and it's true she's made friends here, and one of them is your mother. But I don't think we should talk about our mothers," Ross said. "I think we should talk about you and me and what we're going to do."

Kailee looked up. "I know. You're right. Oh, Ross, I never meant for this to happen. What *should* we do?"

"I don't know. Let's give ourselves some time to think. It's not like a nuclear bomb. Plus, it's *your* body. How do you feel about your body changing, growing a human being that will change our lives?" Ross reached over and took her hands. "Kailee, our parents are our past. This baby could be our future. I'm with you every step of the way."

"Are you, though?" Kailee asked quietly, searchingly. "If we . . . have a baby, I'll be the one doing all the changing diapers and getting up at night. I won't be able to work. You'll keep working, and you'll be more important to the business than I will."

"It wouldn't have to be that way," Ross said.

Kailee scoffed. "Right, *you're* going to nurse the baby."

Ross grinned. "True, I don't have that equipment, but I could give our baby a bottle. Every week I could take a couple of days off work, and you could go into the office, and I could take care of our baby."

"You say that now . . ."

"I mean it, Kailee. Trust me."

"You keep saying *our* baby."

"True, but our baby is, at the moment, probably like a little kernel of corn inside you. I mean, I'm not educated in the whole pregnancy thing, but I don't have to be attached to it if you don't want to do all this now. It's your decision, Kailee."

Kailee looked at Ross's face, his handsome, loving face.

"I'm so tired," she said. "Let's talk about this tomorrow. I need to sleep."

They went into the bedroom, peeled off their clothes, turned back the covers, and slid into bed together. They spooned, Kailee turned toward the window, Ross close to her, his chest against her back, his arm around her waist. They slept.

Saturday morning, Heather had to park five blocks away and walk to the church fair. It didn't officially open until nine, but a crowd was already lined up at the table where tickets were sold. The street had been shut off with cones, and a policeman stood at each end, waving cars to other streets while men and women set up children's booths and rides.

Heather had been given an official-looking label that she stuck on her sundress. She smiled and went up the driveway to the used-book sale. Long folding tables had been set up and more men were carrying the boxes of books out while Miribelle and others distributed the books to their section.

Miribelle called, "Oh, good, you're here! Unload the mystery section on that table over there, and tape this label to the front of the table. Remember, hardbacks two dollars, paperbacks fifty cents. Your batch will sell like hotcakes."

Heather went behind her table and began to unload the books and stack them, spine up, grouped by author. She moved quickly. The excitement in the air was contagious. The crowd buying tickets was eager to come in and find treasures, and when Heather caught sight of the costume jewelry table, she almost abandoned her books to rush to the table, glittering with fake diamonds and pearls.

"Good morning," a man said.

Heather looked up. "Miles!" She was pleased to see him, but tried not to appear as attracted as she was to him, not now, while dozens of people were around.

"Cort and I are setting up a sun shelter over this section," Miles said.

"Thank heavens," Miribelle chimed in. "Right now, we've got the fresh air of morning, but in an hour, we'll feel like we're lost in the Sahara."

Heather continued lifting and organizing the books, terribly aware of Miles, who wore khaki shorts and a blue striped shirt with the sleeves rolled up to his elbows. When he came near, a slight enticing scent of soap and shaving cream drifted her away. She almost sniffed at it like a dog sensing a bone.

Stop it, she told herself. *Behave. You're on church property!*

She hadn't completely unloaded the books when the fair was declared open and the crowd rushed in. Miribelle handed her an apron with pockets stocked with quarters, half dollars, and one-dollar bills. People swarmed around the book tables, some of them almost salivating with excitement.

These are my people, Heather thought, hoping the complete set of mysteries by Deborah Crombie wouldn't sell. But of course, it did.

The morning passed quickly. The temperature rose. Children wandered through the fair holding ice cream cones that dripped down their chins and their shirts. The table of homemade pies and cakes sold out before noon. Across the lot, the verger and other men set up a hot dog and hamburger stand, the delicious aroma tantalizing people to flock toward it.

Heather was hungry, but she couldn't leave her post. Many books had been sold, but many were left. One of the workers brought Miribelle and Heather folding chairs, and Heather realized she'd been standing for three hours. It felt heavenly to sit down.

Miles appeared, holding a large paper cup filled with iced tea. "I thought you might like this."

Heather stood up and leaned across the books to take the cup. "Thank you, Miles. This is the answer to a maiden's prayers."

"Actually," Miles said in a low voice, "I think *I'm* the answer to a maiden's prayers."

Heather blushed. The tone of his voice made her shiver, and his words sent her body's thermometer straight up to two hundred degrees. What he was implying gave her a delicious feeling of conspiracy and guilt. "Is it proper to talk about, um, sex, during a church fair?" she asked, whispering the word *sex*.

"Heather, could you speak louder, please? I didn't hear what you said." Miles's eyes were full of mischief.

A young girl with glasses approached Heather. "Where are the science fiction books?"

Heather was glad to be pulled out of her lusty bubble. *Could a bubble be lusty?* she wondered. *Surely the lust would heat the bubble up and make it pop.*

She was losing her mind.

And she liked it.

"They're right over here," Heather said, setting her paper cup on the table near her chair. She wanted to pour it right down her shirt, but held on to her dignity. "Thank you for the drink, Miles," she said, as primly as a woman from a book by Barbara Pym.

"You're welcome." Miles smiled and vanished into the crowd.

Heather let the sci-fi fan take her time inspecting the books.

She sat down and took a long, refreshing drink of her tea. The young woman bought a complete set of Neil Gaiman's books, and an older gentleman bought an outdated book about history, a tome so heavy Miribelle and Heather had thought it would never sell.

By early afternoon, the crowds had thinned out. Children screamed with glee from the kiddie booths in the street, but few people approached the book table, which was looking very much picked over.

"Miribelle," Heather said, "could I slip out for a moment?" She didn't need to say why.

"Of course," Miribelle said.

Heather went down the stairs into the large open room where coffee hour was held, used the bathroom and washed her hands, splashing water on her neck to cool it down. She wandered back up the stairs, feeling tired and ready to go home. As she passed by the costume jewelry table, she stopped to browse.

"You've done well," Heather told Annie Martin.

"Yes, the early birds nabbed the best things," Annie said.

"What is—" Heather's gaze was arrested by the sight of a beautiful ring, a ruby surrounded by diamonds. "This ring," she asked Annie, "where did it come from?"

"I don't really know," Annie replied. "You know how people have been coming by the church office to drop off things for the fair."

Heather picked up the ring. She turned it this way and that. She studied the inscription on the inside.

She burst into tears.

"What's wrong?" Annie asked.

"This is my grandmother's ring. See, the inscription here on the band?" She leaned over to show Annie, but she couldn't let go of it for Annie to touch, to take back.

"My goodness," Annie said. "That's miraculous. When did your grandmother visit Nantucket?"

Heather laughed while she was still crying. "My grandmother

didn't . . ." She was too elated, surprised, *amazed,* to put another sentence together. "I want to buy it."

"Nonsense, honey, you take it. You shouldn't have to pay a penny for it," Annie said.

Heather broke out in goosebumps as she slid the ring onto her finger.

"This isn't costume jewelry," Heather said. "It was lost in the sand, and it found its way here. This is, this is, this is a *miracle.* I want to join this church. I want to live on this island. I want to be a grandmother. I want to help take care of nature."

"Well, that's lovely," Annie said. "Why don't I walk you over to your chair in the shade and you can drink something cool and refreshing." Annie made a *get over here* motion with her hand to Miribelle.

"Everything is connected," Heather said through her tears. "Everything lost somehow is found."

Miribelle came to Heather's side. "Heather, come sit down."

Miribelle took Heather's arm and gently pulled her away from the table toward their shaded book tables.

"I think you might be a bit overheated," Miribelle said.

Heather looked down at the ring on her finger. "Miribelle, this was my grandmother's ring."

"Of course it was," Miribelle said kindly.

For the next hour, Heather sat in the shade with a cup of ice water in her hand. She dipped a tissue into the water and dabbed it on the back of her neck. Her tears dried up and she got her breathing back to a steady rhythm.

But how had this happened? How *had* the ring made its way here, from being lost in the sand? Heather sat imagining a family tossing their blanket onto the beach, setting up their home base for the day, and a child fussing because something was sticking into his leg, and the exasperated mother pulling the blanket back and finding the ring. The mother must have seen the inscription, and known that it meant something to someone, and pushed it in her change purse so it wouldn't get lost again. Later, when the mother was dropping off books for the book sale, she would have passed the costume jewelry table and remembered the ring in her change purse. It wasn't hers. She had three children and no time for fancy jewelry, so she dropped the ring into the box of donated trinkets and went on her way.

That was one way it could have happened, Heather thought. She hoped that was the way it had happened. She would never know. She stopped crying and calmed herself, but her heart was full.

She joined Miribelle at the book table. The heat of the day beat down harshly on the fair, and the crowd was thinning out. Miribelle and Heather gathered together all the books that were left. They would be donated to the library for their book sale.

"Now you should go home and lie down," Miribelle told Heather. "The fair lasts only another hour."

"Thank you, I will," Heather said. "This was so much fun, Miribelle. I hope I can do it again. Also, someday I want you to join me for lunch so I can explain why I was so overwhelmed to find my grandmother's ring."

"I'd love to have lunch with you for any reason at all," Miribelle said.

Sunday, Heather slept late. Miles called and asked her to join him for a sail. "Bring Sugar," he said. "And wear a bikini."

Heather laughed. "Like I possess a bikini."

She'd bought new bathing suits for her summer on the island. They were both two-piece, and not bikinis, but pretty revealing, anyway. She was surprised at how pale her abdomen was. But she liked her reflection in the mirror. She didn't look like a model, but she most definitely looked feminine. She packed sunblock, bottles of water, a tin of cookies she'd made, and a bag of treats for Sugar, wondering if dogs got motion-sick. She slapped on a scalloper's cap with a long bill, slipped a light linen shirt over her suit, slid her feet into flip-flops, and put her small bag with her keys in her beach bag.

She left her cell at home, plugged into the charger. She wanted a day free of drama.

Miles was waiting for her at the yacht club dock. When Sugar saw him, she yipped and pulled at the leash. Miles wore Nantucket red board shorts, a white T-shirt, a scalloper's cap, and sunglasses.

He kissed her cheek lightly and helped her into the boat. Sugar eagerly jumped in without hesitation.

"It's a great day for a sail," Miles told her as he steered the boat out of the inner harbor. "I thought we'd go over to Great Point."

"Sounds lovely." Heather slipped off her shirt and settled on the cushions, resting her head against the boat's stern, letting the sun beat down on her face and shoulders. She didn't speak, and Miles didn't, either. He seemed perfectly content, adjusting the sails, positioning the rudder.

The water made gentle splashing sounds as they went along, and the curved walls of the boat held her as if she were rocking in a cradle. The warmth of the sun was strong and steady. Heather's body seemed to melt and all her worries disappeared. Sugar investigated every inch of the boat and barked at other boats when they passed, but after a while she found a patch of shade, curled up, and slept.

Heather slept.

When she woke, she discovered Miles had anchored in view of the tall, white, stony Great Point lighthouse. They were at the farthest end of the island, all sand and rosa rugosa bushes and seals. Lots of seals. Maybe hundreds of seals. Miles had furled the sails and dropped the anchor.

"Nice nap?" Miles asked.

"I haven't been so relaxed in ages," Heather said. "I hope I didn't snore."

Miles laughed. "Want to take a dip?"

"Sure," she said, stretching, wondering what her body would look like when she climbed out of the water with her suit plastered to every lump of cellulite in her body. But a cooling dip sounded wonderful.

She stepped up on the edge of the boat, wondering if her bathing suit covered her butt completely, raised her arms above her head, bent forward, and dove.

The water parted for her, changing from turquoise to deep blue to black as she knifed her way down. She'd never been so deep before—she was used to swimming pools. For a moment, she was exhilarated, transformed into another creature of the sea. But quickly her lungs burned and she turned and swam to the surface, gulping in the air.

Miles was treading water near her. "You're a swimmer," he remarked.

Heather laughed. "Not at all. In fact, I'll show you my favorite position, the one I taught Ross when he was first learning. We called it the jelly roll." She took a deep breath, curled herself into a ball with her arms around her knees and her face in the water and bobbed. "I would compete with Ross to see who could hold their breath the longest. It's a very relaxing move."

"I prefer floating," Miles said, stretching out full length on his back, letting the ocean support him.

Together they swam around the boat, and dove down into the water, which grew colder the farther down they went, and treaded water while they caught their breath. Finally, they swam to the small ladder on the side of the boat and climbed out, water pouring from their suits. The sun dazzled. Heather found her sunglasses and put them on. Miles wrapped a large towel around her shoulders.

"I like swimming with you," he said.

Heather knew her hair stuck out like porcupine spines all over her head, and her eyelashes were pearled with water so she had to blink several times to see properly. Here she was at her rawest self. No makeup. No flattering dress. Water drizzling down from her nose. Her teeth were chattering from the water's chill.

"I like swimming with you," she replied.

Miles kissed her on the end of her nose. "Let's eat," he said.

She was grateful he didn't try to kiss more than her nose. She was still slightly shaky from her deep-water swim.

They sat on the edge of the boat, drinking sparkling water and munching on the sandwiches Miles had picked up from Something Natural and the lemon cookies Heather had made. Sugar woke up, stared at their food until Miles gave her part of a sandwich, which she carried to a shady spot to enjoy.

"Why does food taste so amazing after a swim?" Heather asked.

"Everything feels better after a swim," Miles said, grinning.

After they ate, they slowly sailed back to the harbor. She was amazed to find that it was almost six o'clock in the evening. Other sailors were docking, too, tying up to buoys and getting a ride to shore on the launch.

Back onshore, Miles walked Heather and Sugar to her car.

"Want to go out to dinner?" he asked.

"Thank you, but what I really want is to go home, take a hot shower, put on my robe, and curl up with a book." She hadn't combed her hair or put on lipstick and she knew her nose was bright red in spite of the sunblock. It was wonderful to know she could look like this and still feel strongly how Miles was attracted to her.

"Another time," he said.

"Yes. And thank you for a perfect day."

Miles smiled and kissed her. On the mouth. It was not a simple peck. It was a warm, confident promise. She was surprised and pleased that he would kiss her like that in the parking lot where other people could see. In the passenger seat, Sugar wagged her tail like a helicopter taking off.

When she sat in her car and drove home, she couldn't stop smiling.

The next day, Evelyn invited Heather for a special tour of the island, to places tourists seldom saw. She told Heather she'd pick her up in her Mercedes SUV, and she'd bring lunch. Heather filled a bottle with water and ice and put it in her tote. She double-checked to be sure she had her phone, in case Evelyn had a bad turn. Bob knew that his wife was going out. Still, it was a responsibility.

"We're going to the moors," Evelyn said, once Heather had buckled in. "The Nantucket Conservation Foundation has bought over three thousand acres of open land, much of it in the middle of the island, where the landscape is slightly rolling, and covered in low bushes, brush, and grasses. At a glance, this area seems boring, compared to the drama of the shores. But if you stop to look closely you'll see an amazing variety of vegetation. Blueberries, beach plum. Dozens of small flowers. Heather. Wood lilies."

As she talked, Evelyn turned off the winding Polpis road onto a dirt road that led into the heart of the island. Hawks, swallows, and gulls flew overhead. Ungraded paths fanned away into the rolling hills of green.

"We'll get out here and walk," Evelyn said, pulling into a sandy area. She lifted a small basket and carried it with her as they strolled along the winding paths. "I'm taking you to lunch at my favorite spot. Well, one of my favorite spots."

Heather was glad she'd worn a straw hat to keep the burning sun away from her face. As they walked, Evelyn pointed out bushes and flowers and trails made by deer.

"You sound as if you know every rock and wildflower," Heather said.

"Oh, I do. Remember, I grew up on the island. I came here as a girl with my parents. In high school, I came out with friends to drink beer, and sometimes smoke pot. We thought we were wild. We wanted to be bad. But really, we ended up going home and sleeping in our comfortable beds."

They walked down a steep hill, turned left and walked some more, then turned left again.

"Here!" Evelyn said triumphantly.

A grassy path between leafy trees led to a perfect circle of blue water. In the middle of the pond was a small green island.

"An island on an island," Heather said.

Evelyn smiled. "True. They call this a poot pond, formed from retreating glaciers, although the Wampanoag believed this is where whales came up for air when they were swimming under the island. Most islanders refer to it as the Doughnut Pond. I thought we'd have lunch here. The trees shade the area, and once we're settled, we'll see dragonflies and maybe an egret."

Heather helped Evelyn spread out the blanket. Evelyn set out sandwiches and apples for their lunch, but for a long while they sat, legs crossed, watching the pond.

"This is beautiful," Heather said. "It's so quiet."

"I know. I love to think of this quiet, hidden spot in the midst of our crowded, congested island."

"Kailee must love it here."

"I'm not so sure. Maybe when she's older she'll appreciate the silent beauty of the moors, but now she's young. She likes the expensive restaurants, the glamour."

"What about Bob?"

"He's all about the ocean. Deepwater fishing. When he can, he goes off with his buddies to fish for sea bass." Evelyn's voice slowed, as if she were talking in a dream. "I like the wild land. That's why I started ENF. Every day that I live, saving this island's natural beauty means more to me."

"I think I understand," Heather said.

Evelyn cocked her head, looking at Heather. "Do you?"

Heather took a moment to phrase her answer. "I can't feel as strongly about it as you do, but I've come to feel very . . . *connected* . . . to my funny little cottage. And to the trees, bushes, grasses, around it. I feel safe in my cottage, and in the evenings, I like to sit on the small back patio and listen to the birds call and watch the sky change colors. It calms me. It lets me be me, not Wall's ex-wife or Ross's mother, although Ross is my heart."

Evelyn was quiet. After a while, she said, "When I come here, I believe that it's okay to die. That I'll be buried here, and I want my ashes put in one of those biodegradable tree pots." Very calmly, she continued, "This is where we all go, you know. Back into nature."

Heather hesitated, slightly alarmed. "You're awfully young to be thinking about where you'll be buried."

Evelyn smiled. "I've been thinking about this ever since I was a child and learned that people—and pets—could die."

Heather thought quickly: What's the opposite of death? "Evelyn, you only have one child, just like I do. That's unusual these days, isn't it?"

Evelyn reached out and plucked a long blade of grass. She ran her fingers up and down the slightly indented middle as she talked. "Bob and I wanted more kids. But it didn't happen. I was heartbroken for a while, especially as all my friends had absolute tribes of kids. It worked out all right, though. Kailee is such a perfect girl, and Bob and I have always been madly in love with each other. Anyone else is unnecessary."

"You're fortunate," Heather said. "Wall and I were more like friends, associates, in our marriage. It mattered a lot to Wall that he have a son, and we had Ross, and after that . . . for us, marriage was more about accomplishing than enjoying. We did accomplish a lot, building up Wall's business. Ross was an easy baby, and we had friends who hadn't slept for a year because of their babies' colic."

A fat bee buzzed near them, before speeding away toward a small cluster of purple flowers.

"I'm glad Kailee is marrying Ross," Evelyn said, staring out into the blue waters of the pond.

"I am, too," Heather replied, although in her heart she wasn't so certain.

"Kailee can be dramatic. And she's spoiled, I know that. But she's intelligent and hardworking, and she has a kind heart."

Heather was quiet. She sensed that Evelyn had more to say.

"I don't think I've been a very . . . cozy . . . mother to her. I suppose mothering isn't high on my list of talents. But I'm aware that friction exists between you and Kailee."

"Oh, not really—" Heather began.

Evelyn cut her off. "Kailee's been different since she met Ross. She's happier. I think she has a large heart. She's accustomed to being the center of attention, but she's changing. She's learning. I can tell. If I can't be around, someone else will have to help her. I hope you will help her."

Heather started to reassure Evelyn that she wasn't going to die any time soon, but she knew that wasn't what Evelyn needed to hear. "Of course, Evelyn. I'll be there to help Kailee."

Evelyn turned her head and met Heather's eyes. Evelyn smiled, and in that moment, with the sun shining on her face, she was very beautiful, and, it seemed to Heather, very much at peace.

"Thank you," Evelyn said. She put her hand over Heather's.

"Thank *you*," Heather answered. She was afraid she was going to cry, and she knew Evelyn would hate that. She glanced at the pond. "Look."

A slender white bird flew down to the little island and stalked on its long legs, peering down at the vegetation.

"Great white heron," Evelyn whispered. "This is his world."

Heather was silent, and for a while they sat together quietly, letting the sights, sounds, and sweet fresh air of this small realm envelope them. Iridescent blue dragonflies flew past, one landing on Heather's knee. It was like an angel from another universe. Heather didn't even breathe until it flew away. On the other side of the island, frogs splashed. Above them, the generous green leaves of the trees shaded them from the sun.

Heather whispered, "It's perfect here."

Evelyn nodded her head. "It's my favorite place."

Finally, they packed up the lunch box and walked back to Evelyn's SUV. Now the afternoon sun was seriously hot. Evelyn tuned the radio to a classical music station, as if to prevent conversation. Heather leaned back in her seat and rested. She could sense Evelyn returning to her more aloof, private self.

Before long, they were at Heather's cottage. She thanked Evelyn and did not invite her in. She could tell Evelyn was tired, and

Heather wanted to get out of the sun. But Sugar threw herself into such fits of joy at her return that Heather obligingly stayed outdoors, throwing a rather soggy tennis ball for the dog to chase and bring back. Finally, Sugar tired. Heather ushered her dog into the house and they both lay down on her bed for an afternoon nap.

twenty-two

Kailee was lying on the sofa in Ross's apartment, sleeping, when Ross came home from work.

"Hey," Ross said, bending over to kiss her forehead. "I brought dinner. Fish and chips from Sayle's."

Kailee sat up slowly, coming out of her dream. "I love fish and chips. Thank you. Do you want to shower before we eat?"

"Let's eat now, while it's all still warm." Ross set the paper bag on the table.

Kailee put out plates, a beer for Ross, a glass of water for her. "I don't know how you managed to work in this heat and humidity."

Ross held his arms out like a weightlifter and made muscles in his upper arms. "I'm a man, lady."

She kissed his mouth quickly. "I'm your lady, man."

They sat and ate. Ross devoured his food. Kailee ate more slowly. "Want my tartar sauce?"

"I'll trade my coleslaw for your tartar sauce." Ross handed over his small paper cup and took Kailee's in exchange. "How was your day?"

"Excellent," Kailee said. "I merged two files on the HR folders, and George thought I'd made a miracle. He's beginning to appreciate me, I think. What did you do?"

"Carried shingles. Pounded nails. Drank as much water as I could find." He paused. "Hey, you're eating."

"I wasn't nauseous today, Ross. I mean, a little, but not the yellow and purple swirl I was drowning in. I have a little more energy."

"And?"

"And it's made me feel more . . . hopeful. Like, things are possible."

Ross folded his arms over his chest. "What things would that be?"

"What would you like them to be?" Kailee smiled coyly. "All right, I'll just say it. Now I'm thinking I could have this baby and still work. My mom and your mom could babysit a lot. You could have a couple of days or whatever to take care of him. Or her. We could stay here for a year or so while we figure out the house situation. I mean, the baby wouldn't walk for a year, so we wouldn't have to worry about the stairs, and there's room in the bedroom for a crib and changing table. We could—" Kailee stopped talking, trying to figure out Ross's reaction. "What do you think?"

Ross cleared his throat. When he spoke, he blushed. "I . . . I have heard . . . that if you have a baby when you're young, it doesn't hurt as much."

"Oh, Ross." Kailee rose from her chair. She went to her future husband, and sat on his lap. "I think that's the sweetest thing anyone has said to me."

She leaned against his chest. He held her tight and kissed the top of her head.

"We're playing in the major leagues now, baby," Ross said.

Later that week, Kailee sat in Dr. Farrow's office, trying not to cry. She hadn't asked Ross to join her when she went to the lab to have her blood drawn for tests, but she'd asked him to come for the first doctor's visit, and where was he? Probably working. Probably he'd forgotten all about it, or maybe, because she had told him that he wouldn't be needed for the first visit, he'd decided not to come. It had been eight weeks since her last period, so she could be in her first trimester, even though her belly was flat. The nausea and vomiting had eased off, but she still felt like a total nutcase, manic, then exhausted, ecstatic, then depressed. One good thing: The sex she had with Ross now was amazing.

And there he was.

Ross walked into the waiting area with a big smile on his face. He was wearing cargo pants and a collarless and dirt-spotted tee. His hair still had small bits of sawdust in it, and the tanned skin on his face was marked with white where the sunglasses covered his eyes. He was the most beautiful thing she'd ever seen.

"Ross, hi!" She wanted to jump up and kiss him, but other people were in the room, so she simply stretched out her hand and pulled him toward her.

He sat in the chair next to her. "So what's going on?"

"I'm waiting to see the doctor. I think I'm next in line."

"Miss Essex?" The nurse smiled from a door, ushering her in. It was Bellemy Davis, who had been two years ahead of Kailee in high school. Bellemy had been a troublemaker and a clown, and it was just weird that she was now a nurse, capable of saving someone's life.

"Could Ross come in with me?"

"Of course," Bellemy said.

"Thank you, Miss Davis," Kailee said, and took Ross's hand.

They followed Bellemy into an inner room with a computer and an examination bed. Bellemy gestured for her to sit on the end of the bed. She fastened a blood pressure cuff around Kailee's left arm.

"How's it going?" Bellemy asked, as she pumped up the cuff.

"I guess I'll know in thirty minutes," Kailee answered. "How's it going with you?"

"The truth? Christian wants to get married and I am *so* not ready. I've got years more dancing at the Box to do. And you know how Christian and I were in high school and college. Off-again, on-again, off-again, on-again. He's driving me crazy." She let the air out of the cuff, checked the numbers. "You're fine. And who's this gentleman with you?"

"Ross Willette. I met him at UMass."

"He's working for your dad, right?"

"I am," Ross said.

Kailee had to laugh. She hadn't talked with Bellemy for five or six years, yet Bellemy knew who Ross was and where he worked.

The door opened and Dr. Farrow came into the room. Unofficially, Dr. Farrow was Maya Reis Farrow, born on the island to parents who'd been born on the island. Short, stocky, with her long black hair scooped up into a knot on the back of her head, she exuded an air of authority, and a bit of an air of *Don't mess with me or I'll slap you silly,* which she'd inherited from her mother.

"Kailee! Good to see you again." Dr. Farrow pulled the computer around and checked Kailee's chart. "So we ran a qualitative HCG blood test and yes, you are officially pregnant. I'm sure you knew that anyway. Your blood pressure is good. Cholesterol good. You are a very healthy woman, Kailee. Come back in a month and we'll do an ultrasound so you can see the baby. I've prescribed prenatal vitamins for you. Anything else?"

"So I'm two months pregnant?" Kailee asked.

"You are. See you in a month." Dr. Farrow left the room.

Bellemy smiled and patted Kailee on the shoulder. "She's a busy woman." She winked at Ross. "Good luck."

Bellemy opened the door to the waiting room. Ross took Kailee's hand.

They waited until they were in the parking lot to kiss.

"Let's go tell my mom," Kailee said.

———

They found her mother in the living room, wearing a caftan, with her laptop propped on a pillow. Ross's mother was sitting in a chair, facing Evelyn, a laptop on her lap.

Evelyn smiled up at them. "Hi, guys. What's up?"

Kailee looked at Ross. "You do it."

Ross said, "No. You should do it."

Kailee announced, "We're officially pregnant! We've been to Dr. Farrow's office and all is good. The baby is due in early April."

Her mother's face flushed with emotion. Tears filled her eyes. "Oh, I'm so glad," Evelyn said. "I can't tell you how happy I am to hear this."

"Congratulations," Heather said. She was beaming.

"I'm going to eat like a horse," Kailee told them. "I'm going to lose my waist anyway. I might as well enjoy it. Plus, I've lost weight the past two months."

"How are you going to celebrate?" Evelyn asked.

"Well, it can't be champagne, so it will have to be ice cream." Kailee turned to Ross. "Want a hot fudge sundae for lunch?"

Ross said, "I really should get back to work."

"Let him go," Evelyn said. "You stay here and we'll have ice cream. We have a wedding to plan."

Kailee put her hands to her mouth to hold back a squeal. "Go work, Ross! I've got some serious girl talk to do."

"Have fun," Ross said, waving as he left.

Kailee dug her phone from her purse and opened it to the calendar. She was so excited she could scarcely remember what month they were in right now.

That evening, the exact moment Ross walked into his apartment, his cell rang.

Kailee was napping on his sofa, still dressed in her work clothes. When she saw him, she gave him a sleepy smile and sat up.

"Hey, Mom," Ross said. He sat down next to Kailee and kissed her cheek. "Right now? Well, sure. Yeah, Kailee's right here. Okay, we'll be there."

"What's going on?" Kailee asked.

"Mom wants us to come to her house for a drink now."

"Damn," Kailee said.

"Kailee . . ." Ross blew out a long sigh.

Kailee yawned and ran her hands through her hair. "You're right, and I'm being a brat. Let's go now." She stood, shaking the wrinkles out of her clothes. "Wait. I've got to pee."

The roads going out of town were less congested than usual. People had gone home for the day, although the UPS and USPS trucks were still rolling. The heat was slowly diminishing, but Kailee was grateful for the air-conditioning in Ross's truck.

They headed down Milestone Road, turned left, bumped over the dirt road, and stopped in front of the small hedged kingdom— *queendom? Why wasn't that a word?* Kailee wondered—of Heather's summer cottage. Kailee took Ross's hand as they walked up the path.

Heather flung open the front door. "Hello, you two!" She wore a loose summer dress in turquoise, Kailee's favorite color, and her hair was held up in a loose, very short, ponytail. Sugar squeezed past her and raced up to greet Kailee and Ross, licking their legs in greeting.

"Sugar, stop that," Heather said.

"It's okay," Kailee told her. "Actually, it feels good."

Heather ushered them into the long living room. The air conditioner was chugging away, and the air was cool and dry.

"Sit," Heather said, flourishing her hands at the sofa. "I am going to amaze you."

Kailee sat next to Ross.

Heather started to pour the champagne, but Ross asked, "Mom, can I have just a beer for now? And maybe ice water for Kailee?"

Kailee had never loved him more than that moment, when he diplomatically prevented his mother from offering champagne to her. It was foolish, but it made Kailee feel that Ross was on her side, that they really were a couple, that he would help with the pregnancy.

"Sure." Heather seemed surprised, but not upset. She walked

to the kitchen, and brought back a bottle of beer and a glass of ice water.

"Now," Heather said, returning to her chair facing the sofa. "Hold on to your seats."

Kailee listened to Heather babble on about the church fair. It was so boring she could feel another yawn coming on.

"—at the costume jewelry table at the end of the day, I found this." Heather reached into her pocket and brought out a small, slightly worn, ring box. *"Look."*

Heather opened the box and set it on the coffee table.

Kailee glanced at it dutifully. Then she gasped and leaned forward until her nose almost touched the box.

"Mom," Ross asked, "is that your ring? The one you gave me and we lost on the beach?"

"It is." Heather glowed with happiness. "Go on. Pick it up. It's yours."

Ross picked up the ring, and how tiny it looked in his large, scarred hands. He turned it around and around, reading the inscription.

Kailee couldn't breathe. She was paralyzed with amazement. How had that ring been found?

"Go on, Ross. Put it on her finger."

Ross took Kailee's left hand in his and slid the ring onto her ring finger.

"It's too big," Kailee said. She held her hand up. "Look. It will fall off."

"You need to take it to a jeweler and have it sized," Heather said.

Kailee stared at Heather, as if seeing her clearly for the first time, instead of through the wary gaze of jealousy that had darkened Kailee's sight until now. "Why would you give me this ring when I'd already lost it once?"

Smiling at Kailee, Heather said, "I think it's kind of a sign, Kailee. You and Ross are meant to be together. I mean, if the ocean didn't take it, it's like the world wanted you to have it."

"Wow, Mom, you're the best." Ross rose, leaned over, and hugged his mother.

Kailee sat stunned. Heather had seen Kailee at her worst— well, not her *very* worst—and still, she'd given Kailee the heirloom ring.

"Heather," Kailee said softly, "when the time comes, we'll pass it along to our child."

Heather smiled. "That's lovely. How do you feel?"

"I've been so *nauseated,*" Kailee complained, adding, "as you know."

"Try eating a saltine cracker when you first wake up," Heather said. "The nausea usually passes by the third month."

"It's getting better now," Kailee told Heather. "But the mood swings are tricky. I never know if I'm really angry or just preggers crazy. Maybe my fingers will get fat." Kailee held out her hand, flashing the ring. "Then I won't have to get the ring sized."

"That might happen," Heather agreed. "You should have them put a ring guard on, and wear it until you start plumping up. After the baby is born, you can wear it again."

"It's so beautiful." Kailee gazed down at the deep ruby stone, the sparkling diamonds.

"Wait till you see your baby's face," Heather told her. "Then you'll know what beautiful is."

twenty-three

Monday morning, Kailee was at the office at eight o'clock exactly.

Of course, George was there already.

"Good morning, Kailee," George said. "Don't sit down. We're going to the bank. You need to sign the bank signature card."

"Can't I do it digitally?" Kailee asked.

"Sure, but they'll also need other guarantees of your identity. It's easier and quicker this way. Besides, you need to get to know the bankers."

"Seriously, George? I think I know the bankers."

"Seriously, Kailee? I don't think they know you as one of the CFOs of your father's company. Also, it always helps to keep in touch with bankers personally."

"Okay," Kailee said. "You're right. Let's go." She paused. "Should we get Ross to go with us?"

"Not yet," George said. "You know a lot more about this business than he does."

Kailee couldn't help it. Knowing this made her a tiny bit happy.

Since she was a child, the banks in town had changed, multiplied, divided, and opened up out-of-town branches. George drove—Kailee asked him to, because he had a Porsche—and they went to the Cape Cod 5 branch on Pleasant Street. Grace Milosc welcomed them into her office. They chatted awhile, and finally Kailee put her signature on the official piece of paper, they shook hands, agreed it was hotter this summer than last summer, and George drove her back to the office.

"I feel I should celebrate now," Kailee said. "Toss candy, or wear a sash."

George laughed. "You can endorse the back of big fat checks."

"I want to tell Mom." Kailee took her phone from her bag and called her mother. "How are you?"

"I'm fine," Evelyn told her. "Don't worry. And Heather is here to help me with ENF."

"I'll be home for lunch," Kailee said. "Want me to bring you something from Espresso to Go?"

"Thanks, darling, but you don't need to do that. Heather has brought me the most delicious-looking salad."

"Okay. I wanted to tell you I've been to the bank to sign the bank signature card. I'm going wild with the checks!"

"I'm not surprised," her mother said. "Have fun."

Back in the office, Kailee couldn't concentrate on the numbers running past her on her computer. She wanted to tell George she was pregnant. She wanted to phone Maggie and Dan to tell them. Maggie would *scream*. She opened a file about lumber orders, but she really wanted to search for everything about babies and pregnancy. When would she feel the baby move inside her? Should she order some sundresses without waists for the rest of the summer? Was it still blue for a boy and pink for a girl? They would have an ultrasound at their next session with the doctor, and then they would hear the baby's heartbeat. Did they want to know the baby's sex?

Would Maggie and Dan throw her a baby shower?

Life was wonderful, Kailee decided. She forced herself to focus on work.

At five o'clock, Kailee and George left the office, locking the door behind them.

"What are you doing?" George asked. "I'm meeting Gary at Cisco Beach and getting a good long swim in."

"Ross will keep working until sunset, I think," Kailee told him. "I'll check on Mom and maybe watch mindless TV with her to keep her resting."

"Good thing to do," George said. "Give her my best."

When Kailee pulled into the driveway of her parents' house, she was disconcerted to see Heather's car parked at the curb. Why would she stay so late?

She walked into the house. Immediately she heard laughter coming from the living room. She found her mother and Ross's mother drinking what looked like G and T's and falling about laughing.

"Mom. Should you be drinking?" Kailee demanded.

Her mother looked startled. "I didn't hear you come in. When did you get home?"

"Just now," Kailee answered.

"Thank heavens," Evelyn said, shooting a cryptic glance at Heather.

The two older women howled with laughter.

Kailee did a U-turn out of the room.

"Kailee," Evelyn called. "Come back. Have a drink with us."

Kailee hesitated. "I'll get myself something."

In the kitchen, she filled a glass with ice and sparkling water. A lime was open on the cutting block, so she added a twist.

Back in the living room, Kailee sat on the sofa near her mother.

"How was work?" Evelyn asked.

"Great! How was your day?"

"Wonderful," Evelyn said. "The most marvelous news. Miles Hunter has agreed to join the board of the ENF, and he's donated a nice fat chunk of money." Evelyn smiled roguishly. "And who knows. He might donate more." Again, she exchanged a glance with Heather.

"I'm going up to my room," Kailee told them. "I've got to change clothes. Then I'll see what Gravity made for dinner. Heather, are you staying?"

"No, thanks," Heather said. "I'll just finish this drink."

Kailee went to her room, taking her time changing into a pair of shorts and a sleeveless top. She had her phone in her hand to call Ross to see if he'd join them for dinner when she heard Heather's voice.

"Kailee! Come quick. Please. It's your mother!"

Kailee flew down the stairs and into the living room. Her mother was bent double, her face squeezed with pain.

"Mom?"

"Can't breathe," Evelyn gasped. "Chest hurts."

"I'm calling nine-one-one," Kailee said.

The service answered immediately and promised to send an ambulance right away.

Heather was sitting next to Kailee's mother, her hand resting lightly on Evelyn's back.

"You're okay, Evelyn," she was saying. "Help is coming. It's okay."

Her mother *wasn't* okay, Kailee thought. Evelyn's lips were blue and her fingertips were like ice.

"Mom." Kailee knelt beside her mother. "I'm here, Mom. You'll be okay."

Heather rose swiftly. "Kailee, you sit here with your mother. Try to calm her. I'll get her an aspirin. Do you keep it down here or in the bathroom?"

"An *aspirin?*" Had Heather lost her mind? Did she think an *aspirin* would help her mother's heart attack?

Heather asked, "Where are your mother's medications?"

"I don't know— Yes! There's a bottle up on her bedside table! I'll get it."

Kailee raced up the stairs and into her parents' room. At first, she couldn't find them, until she looked behind a pile of books and saw a bottle with a prescription label. She grabbed it and hurried back down the stairs.

"Here," Kailee said. "It's nitroglycerin. It says to put a pill under your tongue."

She knelt next to her mother. Evelyn had vomited onto the rug. She was almost unconscious. Her eyes were closed, squeezed shut, her face turning gray.

"Mom. I'm going to open your mouth and put a pill under your tongue," Kailee said.

Very quietly, Heather said, "I'll help. I'll hold her head steady."

With Heather holding her mother's head, Kailee managed to pull Evelyn's jaw down far enough that she could reach in and slip the pill beneath her mother's tongue.

At the same time, people were knocking on the front door.

Heather said, "I'll get it." She left the room.

Several people with EMT shirts came into the room.

"I'll need to lie her down," a woman said.

Kailee stepped away. Her mother was unconscious now. Her face was white. When the EMT gently put her on her back, the pill Kailee had given her dribbled out of her mouth.

Then everything happened quickly. A stretcher was brought in. Her mother was put on it and strapped in. The EMTs rolled the stretcher out the door, down the drive, and into the ambulance.

"Can I go with her?" Kailee asked. "I'm her daughter."

The woman EMT said, "Okay. Get in."

Heather said, "Kailee, I'll call your father."

"Thanks," Kailee said. She reached out and caught her mother's limp hand in hers. Looking out the ambulance doors, she saw Heather standing there, her face flooded with tears. "Call Ross for me, too, would you?" she asked Heather.

Heather watched the ambulance drive off. The hospital was only a few minutes' drive away, but she knew the EMTs would be giving Evelyn oxygen and beginning whatever needed to be done. She saw a woman peering out of her window across the street. Next door, a young man came out and yelled, "What's going on?"

Evelyn would not like her condition, whatever it was, to be gossiped about. Without answering, Heather returned to the house, pulling the door shut behind her. She went into the living room, sat on the sofa, and forced herself to take a few deep breaths. This wasn't the time for her to fall apart, even though she couldn't stop trembling.

She had to call Bob. She took her cell from her pocket. She nearly shrieked when she realized she didn't have Bob's cell number.

"Stop it," she told herself sternly. She found Ross's number and called him. For a moment she worried that he wouldn't answer, but finally she heard his voice.

"Ross, Evelyn's mother has had a heart attack. They've taken her to the hospital and—"

"Slow down, Mom. Do you mean Kailee's mother has had a heart attack?"

"That's what I said. Kailee went in the ambulance with her. I need to call Bob, but I don't have his number."

"I'll call Bob. We'll both go to the hospital. Mom, are you okay?"

"It was frightening, Ross. Poor Kailee is terrified. I'm fine. I'll stay here for a while."

"Thanks. I'll tell Bob and we'll go to the hospital now."

Her son's voice disappeared. Heather sat holding her phone, feeling painfully alone. She didn't want to go to the hospital. She was not family. Was she a friend? She hoped so, but if she was, it was only for a matter of weeks. Was there a close friend, someone Heather should notify? She didn't think there was. Evelyn knew hundreds of people, but Heather had never heard Evelyn refer to any one woman as a close friend. Not a friend like Christine was to Heather.

The housekeeper! *Gravity*. What a lovely, important-sounding name. In the kitchen, by the landline, she found Gravity's phone number. She called Gravity and left a message on her voicemail.

What could she do? What *should* she do? It didn't seem right to sit here while Evelyn was in the hospital, but it didn't seem right to leave, either.

Was it *her* fault that Evelyn had another heart attack? They'd drunk only one gin and tonic, but still . . . Heather searched the internet and read that alcoholism can lead to heart problems, but Evelyn was far from an alcoholic. She was more like a workaholic. An alcoholic beverage could have an anti-coagulating effect, Heather read, and that would help prevent blood clots. She searched for stress-related heart attacks and realized how complicated it all was. How she couldn't find all the answers on the internet.

Itching to do something, Heather gathered the three glasses, carried them out to the kitchen, and put them in the dishwasher. She put the remaining bit of lime into a small Tupperware container. She washed the knife and the cutting board and stacked them in the dish drainer. She returned to the living room. She cleaned up the small pool of vomit. Evelyn's papers were scattered on the coffee table and floor. Heather picked them up, shuffled them into a tidy rectangle, and set them in the flowered box labeled ENF SOIREE. She carried the box back to the conservatory and set it on Evelyn's desk.

The conservatory was crowded with tall plants in pots, low plants in Chinese jars. Should she water them? Maybe they shouldn't be watered every day. Gravity had gone for the day, and Heather didn't want to ask her about the plants. Right now, they were insignificant, although Heather decided that when Evelyn was ready to have visitors, Heather would find the most beautiful orchid she could and bring it to her.

She returned to the living room. Sat down. Looked at her cell. Only thirty minutes had passed. Maybe she should make some kind of casserole so that when Bob and Kailee returned, they would have a warm meal waiting. But no. It would feel like an intrusion, presumptuous, to use Evelyn's kitchen.

She looked at her phone. No calls, no messages, no texts. How did people get through the waiting? Television was always a good way to pass the time, but that seemed frivolous and just *wrong,* as if Heather didn't consider Evelyn's health important. God, how weird everything was!

Undoubtedly much weirder for Evelyn.

When her phone buzzed, alerting her to a text, she jumped, startled.

Mom, Ross had written, *Kailee's mother is in ICU. She had a massive heart attack. The doctor told us we wouldn't know anything for a while. I don't know when we'll be home.*

Heather texted: *Thank you for giving me an update. I'll say prayers for Evelyn. I'm still at her house but I think I'll go home now. Okay?*

Ross texted: *K.*

"Oh, for God's sake!" Heather said aloud. Could her son not be bothered to type in the entire four-letter word? Would the coming generations be communicating in single capital letters? Already punctuation seemed headed for extinction.

"All right," Heather said aloud. "Let's go home."

She scanned the coffee table, now cleared of glasses and papers. Everything was in place. Except Evelyn. Evelyn should be here.

She knew she should leave, but an invisible force, almost like an instinct, kept her there, as if she hadn't done enough, as if there was something she needed to understand.

There were times in life, she thought, reasonable, expected times, for things to happen. A girl knew things were different, *she* was different, when she got her first period. A woman could fall in love and marry at almost any time, but when she discovered she was pregnant, she stepped onto a new path. When she gave birth. Again, when she hit menopause. When her parents died. When her children became adults. When she died.

These phases of life were a physical law, like, well, like gravity. And healthy, active, first-world-wealthy women like Evelyn lived to be at least ninety, maybe one hundred. Women like Evelyn did not die at, what, forty-seven?

Heather closed her eyes and replayed the few moments when Evelyn's face changed.

Evelyn's face had registered *shock*. *Pain*. *Terror*.

For a good minute, Heather had stayed with Evelyn, wanting her simple human presence to keep Evelyn from feeling so alone, while at the same time wanting to run from the room to scream for Kailee to come. She'd called out to Kailee. Kailee had rushed into the room, and Heather's panic had calmed, a bit. Kailee would know what to do with Evelyn. All Heather could do was to keep her hand on Evelyn's back, letting Evelyn's body know that someone was there to help.

What more could Heather have done? Should she have tried CPR? She didn't even know how to do CPR. Should she have laid Evelyn full-out on the pillow, or tried to push her head between her legs? The head between her legs was for dizziness, wasn't it?

Why did Evelyn have a heart attack right then? What had they been discussing? What words had passed between them? They hadn't been fighting, and Heather hadn't told her some terrible secret.

How does a person roll back time? How does a person make things right? How does a human heart attack itself, and why?

Her phone buzzed. She snatched it up without looking at the caller ID and was amazed to hear Miles's voice.

He sounded cheerful. "Hey, Heather, what are you doing this evening?"

"Miles, Evelyn had another heart attack," Heather told him. "I was with her when it happened. I'm still at the Essexes' house. I don't know what to do."

"I'm coming over. I'll take you home. We can get your car later."

"I didn't know what to do," Heather repeated in a desperate whisper.

"I'll be right there," Miles said. "You're okay. You're okay."

She had the strangest reaction to his words. An enormous sense of relief flowed through her body. She was not alone.

twenty-four

Nantucket Cottage Hospital had been completely renovated, transformed by a ninety-million-dollar shot in the arm. It served the island community well, except in certain cases.

Kailee sat with Ross in the waiting area. Her mother had been whisked into secret serious rooms by doctors and nurses swathed in white, their faces covered with masks.

Kailee's father paced up and down the hall. He and Ross had come directly from the house they were framing, so they were in work clothes, with sunburns on their noses and wood chips caught in their hair. Ross sat with his arm around Kailee. Together they watched Bob walk, his fists clenched as if ready for a fight.

But it was Kailee's mother who was fighting, Kailee knew. What had happened to her mother was not just another painful heart attack. It had been a blow, like lightning striking a tree, splitting it into two, an ax slamming into wood, cleaving it right through the core. It had been the hand of a giant from fairy tales reaching down to grasp her mother's heart and squeeze until it was limp.

She was terrified that her mother was going to die.

She was past crying now. She was only waiting, and waiting, caught between fear and hope.

A doctor strode out of a door and summoned her father. They talked, and the doctor disappeared. Her father faced Kailee and moved toward her, and he looked terrified.

Bob Essex spoke as if reciting a text from the physician. "She's had a massive heart attack. They're medevacing her to Mass General in Boston where they'll do a kind of open-heart surgery called a coronary artery bypass graft to replace a clogged artery. They probably won't have to open her chest. They will only need to make a small incision. The surgery will take three to six hours. She'll be in the ICU for about five days. I'm going up with her. They'll take only one family member, Kailee. You go home. Ross will wait with you. I'll let you know everything as soon as I learn it."

"Oh, Dad, I'm so frightened for her," Kailee said.

Her father took Kailee in his arms and held his daughter tight. He said to Ross, "Take care of her."

Ross nodded. "I will, sir."

Her father moved Kailee into Ross's arms, went back down the hallway, and through a door.

"Do you hear that?" Ross asked her.

Kailee was trembling, letting her tears fall on his shirt. She could barely hear anything except her frantic heart. "What?"

"The helicopter blades whirring. The medevac is here."

They ran through the hospital and outside to watch the blue sky. For a while, there was only blue, and then the helicopter was moving over their heads, a dark giant dragonfly, headed toward the helipad at Mass General. It moved slowly, determinedly, out of sight, carrying her mother and father.

Ross asked, "We should go home."

Kailee nodded. Her fear had frozen her fingertips, and her

mind was numb. She sat quietly while Ross drove them back to Pleasant Street. He held her hand as they walked up the path and into the beautiful house.

The first thing they saw was a note on the front hall table.

Dear Kailee and Ross, I've gone home. Miles picked me up. Please call anytime. XO Heather/Mom

The house felt enormous and empty.

Kailee leaned against Ross. "What can we do while we're waiting?"

Ross said, "My mom always cleaned the house when she was worried."

"Our house is clean right now," Kailee told him, adding, "Gravity keeps it that way."

"What would your mom want us to do?" Ross asked.

"Seriously? She'd want us to work on ENF."

"Well, let's do it. At least we can open her mail and see if any contributions came in."

"Okay. Wait. I'm not so sure. I mean your mom was working on this. She probably has a system."

"Want to call my mom?"

Kailee hesitated. Her mind was foggy, filled with thoughts that darted across her mind, vanishing before she could settle on one. She managed to say, "Yes, I mean, she was here when Mom, when Mom had the heart attack."

"She'd want to know how your mother is," Ross said. "Do you want to call her or should I?"

Kailee wrung her hands. She let out a hysterical yelp. "Look at me, I'm wringing my hands! This is too hard, Ross. I feel that every time I tell someone, it will make it truer."

Ross led Kailee to the living room sofa and eased her down. He sat next to her. "I get it. We can wait."

"That's all we can do, is wait!" Kailee looked helplessly at her own cellphone, and as if responding to her fear, the phone vibrated and buzzed. The caller ID was Maggie. "I don't want to talk with her," she told Ross. "I don't want to talk to anyone."

"Here's what we'll do," Ross said. "Call your father on my phone. Or text him. Tell him to call this number when he has some news. Then turn off your cell."

Kailee nodded. "Good idea." She took Ross's phone and started to hit the numbers. She hesitated. "Wait, Ross. It's like . . . if I don't talk to someone, I feel like I'm giving myself some kind of relief and I shouldn't, I should let my mother have all the relief. Like we have the same emergency help bank account, and if I draw out some, less will be there for her."

"You know that's not logical, right?" Ross asked.

"What's not *logical* is that my forty-seven-year-old mother had a massive heart attack!" Kailee cried.

She jumped from the sofa and began to pace around the room. "What can I do?" she asked, over and over again.

Ross's cell buzzed. "Hi, Mom."

Kailee stood still, waiting to hear what Heather had called about, although she knew her father wouldn't call Heather with the news before he called Kailee.

Ross said, "She's had a massive heart attack. She's been med-evaced to Mass General. Bob said she was going into surgery for a coronary artery bypass graft, and he'd call us when he knew anything more."

Kailee opened her phone and googled *coronary artery bypass graft.*

"Yes, we'll call you. Mom? I love you."

Kailee stared at her fiancé. "She hasn't heard anything?"

"No. She went home after the EMTs came and everyone went to the hospital."

Kailee clutched her arms, as if trying to keep herself from falling.

"You told your mother you love her. I don't know when I've told my mom that. Oh, it's so terrible, I don't think I've told her I love her for weeks, maybe months! Ross, let's go up to Boston now. Let's go to the airport and get on the first plane to Boston and get a cab to MGH and find my father and wait with him, and I can tell him I love him, and when Mom comes out of surgery, I can tell her I love her."

Ross looked reluctant. "I'm not sure . . . Listen, Kailee. Why don't you call Gravity before we do anything else."

Kailee yelled, "Are you trying to keep me from being with my mother?"

"Of course not, Kailee." Ross walked over and held Kailee, steadying her. "I just think Gravity should know."

"You're right. Of course, you're right. May I use your phone?" Immediately, she corrected herself. "No, I'll use mine. She knows my number."

Gravity answered in a low, calming voice. "Kailee, I know. Heather called and left a message. Would you like me to come over and wait with you?"

"No, Gravity, that's sweet of you to offer, but Ross is here. I wanted to be sure you knew. We won't know her condition for a while, and then when we do know, we'll call people."

"Drink some lemonade. Or plain water. Not iced tea. You don't need caffeine. No liquor, either. It will hit you too hard. How is Ross?"

"He is a rock." Kailee managed a watery smile at Ross. "Gravity, I'm frightened."

"Yes. I am, too. We must pray."

"I will. I will pray." She ended the call. "Ross, I'm going into the other room to pray."

Before he could answer, a loud knock sounded on the door.

Kailee's fingers went numb. She couldn't breathe.

Ross hurried to open the door.

Dan, with all his strong beauty, said, "Where's Kailee?" He pushed past Ross and hurried into the house.

He went to Kailee and put his hands on her arms. "I just heard. I know you don't want me here, but trust me, it's better to have lots of people around to soak up the nervous energy. It won't be fun, but it will make time pass faster while you wait."

For a moment, Kailee stopped thinking of her mother while she registered the reality of her gorgeous friend standing there.

"Ross," she said, "this is Dan."

"I figured," Ross said. "Hi, Dan."

"Hi, Ross," Dan answered, flashing him a quick smile. "Sorry about barging in, but Kailee has saved my life several times."

He focused on Kailee's face. "Now, we're going out to your backyard to walk very fast up and down, until we're breathless. Trust me. Your heart needs this, and it will use up time. Ross can wait by the phone."

"How did you know about my mother?" Kailee asked.

"Kailee, everyone on the island knows. This is Nantucket. Maybe someone at the construction site, or a nurse at the hospital put the word out. Whatever, it is happening right now, and we have to move through it. Come on."

"I've got the phone," Ross said.

Kailee allowed Dan to hold her hand and walk her up and down and up and down the long garden. And it helped. Her heart slowed, and her mind rested, for a moment. There were birds, and sunshine, and flowers with their fragrance, and garden chairs. She could almost see her family sitting there in the early spring, grateful for the warmth.

She took a long, deep breath. By the time Dan led her back inside, she was physically exhausted and glad to sit on the sofa. She was eager for the news, but not panicked. She was aware of Dan talking with Ross, and that was helpful, too. Somehow, they soaked up some of the fear. They made the afternoon seem more normal. Dan left, and Ross tried to get Kailee to eat a piece of buttered toast, but it made her gag.

It was eight in the evening when Kailee's father called.

"Daddy!" she cried. "How's Mom?"

Her father didn't answer immediately, and his silence frightened her. She tried to delay the blow by talking. "Is she still in the OR? Where are you? Have you had something to eat? At least to drink, I don't mean alcohol, I mean water, you shouldn't let yourself get dehydrated—"

"Kailee." Her father's voice told her everything.

"She's okay, right? She's okay?"

"Kailee, we've lost her." Her father's voice was husky, as if he'd been crying.

Kailee crumpled to her knees. "*No*."

"She died on the operating table. Her heart seized again. She didn't recover. They worked on her for ten minutes, but she didn't make it."

"No, Daddy. No."

"Give the phone to Ross, please," her father said.

Ross took the phone.

"It's not true," Kailee whispered. "It's a mistake. I need to go up there."

Ross said, "I will, sir. Goodbye."

Ross came to her side and lifted her to her feet. He settled her on the sofa and sat next to her, keeping his arm around her shoulders.

"Ross," Kailee cried, "it can't be true. It can't be."

"I'm sorry," Ross said.

Kailee crumpled against him and howled.

Kailee lost track of time. Nothing made sense. Ross wanted her to go to his apartment and lie down, but she couldn't move from the sofa.

"It can't be true," she told Ross. "My mother is the strongest woman on the island. She would never let herself leave my father. She would never leave me."

Ross sat next to her on the sofa with his arm around her.

"My mother wants to see our wedding. She wants to see her grandchild. She wants to work for the island. She just would not leave now. They have it wrong. At the hospital. They've made a mistake. There are many women named Evelyn. Ross, I can't believe it."

Ross said, "I know, Kailee. I know."

"How can I go on, Ross?" Kailee asked. "How do I enjoy the taste of food? Or sex? Or walking on the beach? It will feel like a betrayal of my mother."

Ross didn't answer, but kept his arm around her. It was almost three in the morning when Kailee slid down on the sofa and fell asleep with her head in Ross's lap.

She woke with a start. The windows were full of sunlight. Ross's head was against the sofa cushions as he slept. Several phones were ringing. Her cell. Ross's cell. The house landline.

She sat up. Her clothes were wrinkled, her face stiff with dried tears. She ached.

She heard Gravity in the kitchen. She rose without waking Ross and hurried to Gravity.

"Gravity. They're saying my mother died."

"Yes, I know, Kailee. Your father is flying home this afternoon. Here, now, drink this."

It was a relief to have someone tell her what to do. Kailee took the glass of orange juice and drank it.

"Thank you, Gravity." When she handed the glass back to Gravity, she saw that she, too, had been crying. "I don't know what to do."

"Go take a shower and put on clean clothes. I'll answer the house phone. I'll take juice to Ross and wake him. We'll get through this, child."

I'm not a child, Kailee thought, but gratitude swelled in her heart for Gravity calling her "child." Right now, she needed that sense of being taken care of.

The day went forward after that. Kailee showered and dressed. Ross went to his apartment to shower and change clothes. When he returned, he told Kailee that her father had asked him to tell the construction crew to take the next three days off, because of Evelyn's death.

In the afternoon, friends came over, knocking on the front door, entering with a plate of shortbread or sweet rolls or a bowl of hard candies, which Maggie said would help, because everyone's mouth was dry from crying. Other childhood friends stopped by, and her parents' friends arrived. The women hugged Kailee and told her what a wonderful woman her mother had been and how proud she was of Kailee. The men grouped together, talking in low voices.

Kailee allowed herself to become wooden, capable of nodding her head like a puppet, while inside she was hollow.

Her father returned. Kailee went to him and hugged him, but she could tell he was exhausted beyond words, beyond feelings, just as she was.

A doctor gave her a pill to take at night so that she would sleep. She showered, she dressed, she sat on her bed staring at the wall. She wept. She held a pillow to her mouth and screamed.

The funeral took place four days later. It was a beautiful summer day.

The church was packed, because Evelyn had been a true islander, even in discord, belonging to them.

The reception was held at the Jared Coffin House, an elegant brick mansion at the end of Centre Street. Flowers bloomed on each table and mantel in massively gorgeous arrangements. The liquor flowed like the ocean during flood tide. The mourners were respectfully somber, until they'd enjoyed a drink or two, and then they smiled and softly laughed.

Heather passed among them, a stranger to most of them, hearing the women discuss Evelyn, how beautiful she'd been, how devoted to the island, how fortunate it was Kailee had Ross by her side . . . and now poor Bob would be alone.

Every now and then, Ross would cut through the crowd to find his mother, to ask how she was. She was fine, of course, she was fine.

When the crowd thinned out, Heather discreetly took her leave. She was aware that her presence was no consolation to Kailee. Her presence was little consolation to herself at this moment. Without Evelyn, Heather's work on ENF was ended. She knew she was too exhausted to read. She stopped at Marine Home Center and bought herself a flat-screen television. She paid the deliveryman to bring it to the cottage and set it up on the card table she pulled in front of the fireplace, facing the couch. It made the room look awkward, no feng shui here. But Heather sank down on her sofa, put her feet up on the coffee table, and watched endless episodes of British mysteries and instructional videos on painting or cooking, which provided a soft, gentle blur for her mind.

She slept on the sofa all night, the television on mute, its tableaux providing a kind of ghostly accompaniment.

In the morning, she showered. She was drinking coffee when her phone rang.

"Heather, it's Christine. How are you?"

"I'm stunned," Heather said. "So many changes in such a short period of time. This year has been—"

Christine interrupted. "I've got more possible changes in store for you. The owner of the cottage wants to sell it. Now. The asking price is ridiculously low, because he wants it done and over."

"Christine, I can't afford a house on Nantucket," Heather said. Sugar was at her feet, waving her butt hard, so she opened the door, let her out, and watched her run to the bushes at the end of the yard.

"I know what you're getting for selling your Concord house," Christine said. "I think you can do this. If you want to. I mean, you seem to be quite at home on that island, but you might find the winters hard to tolerate."

Christine named a price so low that Heather was shocked.

It seemed like a direct message from Fate. She could do it. She could buy this small, funky cottage outright. It would need many renovations and improvements, and it was isolated, and so completely different from her beautiful expansive Victorian mansion in Concord. Not a touch of gingerbread anywhere.

"I'll do it," Heather said, her voice shaking. "Christine, now *my* heart is racing. But I want this. And I can do this. Will you help me with the legal bits?"

She could hear the smile in Christine's voice. "Absolutely."

———

A week passed after Evelyn's death. After Kailee's mother's death.

One day, Kailee woke to the thought that she had to have *some* of her mother's traits within her. And her mother would get on with things even during grief. Why hadn't Kailee realized this before? Her mother was in her. Her mother was with her.

Kailee ached, but she tried to do what was necessary. She worried about her father. He had gone through the necessary tasks like a sleepwalker. He'd made it through the funeral stoically, without weeping, nodding robotically to the mourners who expressed their condolences. The rest of the time, he stayed in his home office, with the door shut. When Kailee knocked and entered, she'd find him sitting there, head resting on the back of his leather desk chair, staring into space like a man lost in the world and too exhausted to go on. He didn't emerge for meals, or to watch baseball or the news on television. He didn't go outside.

The owner of the house Essex Construction was building called every day from New York, wanting a progress report. He had no idea who Evelyn Essex had been, plus he didn't care. Also, the crew needed to work, and Kailee, speaking for her father, told them to go ahead.

Gravity came regularly, preparing meals they could microwave anytime, dealing with the flowers that were sent even though the family had requested that in lieu of flowers, a donation to ENF would be appreciated. She managed to persuade Bob to drink some water and eat some eggs and toast every morning, but she left him alone for the rest of the day.

"He'll be okay, darling," Gravity told Kailee. "We all grieve in our own way. He needs to be alone."

Kailee needed to be with Ross. She wept in his arms for hours, remembering all the mean things she'd said to her mother when she was a teenager and all the wonderful times she'd spent with her mother when she was a child.

"I don't know how to go on," Kailee said. "I don't know how any of us will go on."

"We'll find a way," Ross promised. He was with Kailee every

moment of the day and night, listening to her long meandering remembrances, reassuring her, reminding her that he loved her.

"You're so lucky you have your mother," Kailee cried one afternoon.

Ross said, "I'm so lucky I have you."

Kailee wept harder, grateful and happy and sad and in love and in grief all at the same time.

Ten days after her mother died, her father appeared in the kitchen where Kailee and Ross sat eating dinner.

Kailee jumped up. "Hi, Dad. Want some fish and chips?"

Her father shook his head. "No. Thanks. We're going to see Sheldon Armstrong tomorrow. We have to hear the reading of the will."

"Mom made a will?" Kailee asked. "When she was so young?"

"I have a will, too," her father said. "We both made wills when you were born."

It didn't seem right to wear a sleeveless summer dress to the lawyer's office for the reading of the will. Kailee had black silk trousers and a navy-blue silk sweater. That would have to do. At the last minute, she put on the string of pearls her grandmother had given her years ago.

She walked down the stairs slowly. She found her father sitting in the living room, wearing a dark gray suit, a navy-blue tie, and his wing-tip shoes. He was handsome, but he'd lost weight, so his face was lined and his clothes loose around him. He did not seem to notice Kailee's presence.

Kailee sat across from him, leaned toward him, and put her hand on his knee.

"Dad."

Bob looked up.

Kailee said, "It's time to go."

Bob rose. "Yes. Let's go."

When she walked into the lawyer's office with her father, she realized once again how small their family was. Her mother's parents had died a few years ago. Evelyn's brother, Jim, had died in Afghanistan. Kailee's aunt Kimberly, her husband, Ron, and their children lived on the Pacific coast. Kimberly had moved across the country years ago and never returned, not even for a brief visit.

Sheldon Armstrong, Esq., rose from behind his desk when his secretary showed them in. He was a tall, lean, handsome man who often played golf with Kailee's father. Today he wore a three-piece suit and tie. Kailee was glad the air-conditioning was on for his sake as well as hers.

"Bob," Sheldon said, extending his hand. "Kailee. This is a sad time."

They shook hands. Kailee and her father sat in the chairs facing Sheldon's desk. Sheldon was going to read her mother's will and Kailee's stomach cramped at the thought. She had taken a mild anti-anxiety pill the doctor prescribed, but anxiety was not her problem. Grief was her problem and there was no pill for that.

"You might not know that last month, after her first heart attack, Evelyn came to visit me to talk about her will. She gave me a letter she wanted me to read to you first."

"Last month?" Bob queried. "That's odd. She didn't tell me she'd been to see you."

"Evelyn made a slight change in her will. I'll read it now."

Sheldon put on wire-rimmed glasses and sat up straight as he read the letter.

"My darling Kailee and Bob,

I love you both so very much, and I love Ross, as well. I'm proud to be part of Essex Construction, and I hope Kailee and Ross will join Bob to keep it going strong.

But I am a Nantucket native, and I love this island, too, with a fierce and lasting love. When I was a girl, I roamed every possible inch of Nantucket. I swam off every beach, I hiked through every cranberry bog, moor, forest, meadow, and dune. I knew every street and road and house.

How things have changed. I'm aware of the weakening of my heart. It does not frighten me. I know I have been privileged to live on such an unusual spot on the earth, here in the vast mysterious ocean. The ocean and this island are not only for human beings. This island belongs to itself. It is also a living creature.

I won't elaborate. You both know how much I hoped to curtail the encroachment on nature by buildings and billionaires. That's why I created the Essex Nature Foundation. And that is why I am asking Heather Willette to be the director. To that end, I have set aside a special trust to provide a salary for her work and her business and publicity necessities. I've included in the letter to her an outline of how I think the foundation should work.

I hope I'll live many years into the future. I hope I'll be able to help ENF grow. But my heart, so full of love for both of you and for this island, lives within my body, and it is signaling me that it is very tired.

I'm not afraid of dying. I'm grateful to have had my life. I hope you will have lives as happy as mine has been.

Love,
Your wife, Evelyn
Your mother, Evelyn"

Kailee sat frozen. Stunned. She'd had no idea that her mother had been aware of her weakening heart. She couldn't understand why she hadn't spoken to her father or her about it. Her mother could have had open-heart surgery, a heart transplant, or they all could have found a way to calm her mother's life.

"How could Mom do this?" she whispered, torn between anger and a crushing sense of failure.

Kailee's father said, "Kailee, we will have more than enough money to live on, and you have money from your grandmother's trust that will come to you when you are twenty-five. I'm glad your mother wants ENF to continue, and I'm glad she considers Heather suitable for the job."

It was as if her father had slapped her. "Dad, I didn't mean *money!* I meant *why* didn't she tell us about her heart? Why did she keep it a secret when we could have helped her? She didn't have to die!" Kailee realized she'd raised her voice almost to a scream, and she hated herself for that, for not being composed in front of the lawyer, for being thought of as the kind of daughter who would be concerned about how much money she was getting. "I'm sorry," she said in a softer voice. "But I don't understand why she didn't tell us."

Sheldon Armstrong waited a few beats, then said, "Would you like Laura to bring you a glass of water?"

"No, thank you," Kailee said.

"Kailee," the lawyer said, "your mother left me with a sealed letter for you, and one for you, Bob. Also, she told me, in confidence, that if she had to live as an invalid, she wouldn't want to live. Your mother was an active woman, I know." He cleared his throat. "Now. For the rest of the will."

Kailee sat listening to Sheldon Armstrong drone on and on while she forced herself to take deep breaths. To appear serene.

And as she did, she sensed her mother's presence, like the sigh of a wave, or the faint call of a mourning dove, or the whisper of the sand as it slipped through her fingers.

The knowledge of her mother's love was all around her, as if Kailee were the island and her mother the ocean. She understood why her mother had named Heather to head ENF instead of Kailee, because Kailee had always wanted to work for her father, to run the business.

She wished her mother could have lived long enough to see her grandchild born, but maybe, somehow, after all, she would know.

The lawyer's phone buzzed, breaking into her thoughts.

"Yes," Sheldon Armstrong said. "Send him in."

Who would barge in on a private reading of a will, Kailee wondered, surprised.

Ross came into the room. He wore a jacket and tie and his good shoes. He was nervous.

To Kailee's surprise, her father rose and shook Ross's hand. "Thank you for coming."

"Of course," Ross said. He flashed a look at Kailee that told her Ross had no idea why he was invited to this meeting.

Kailee's father indicated that Ross should sit in the chair next to Kailee's. He adjusted his own chair so that he was facing them.

"So." Bob put his hands on his knees and leaned forward. For a moment, he stalled, dipping his head down to hide his face. He recovered, sat straight, and said, "I've been thinking a lot over the past week. I've made some decisions. I'm going to continue as president of Essex Construction. You, Kailee, are now my VP in charge of accounts and technology, and you, Ross, are my VP in charge of construction. I have spoken with both George March and Dean about these plans."

Kailee was speechless, but Ross nodded and said, "Understood."

"Also," Bob continued, and his voice was choked with emotion, "the first task that you have, Kailee, is to join USGBC. U.S. Green Building Council. Their mission is to advance green building for a more stable environment. This organization is exactly what I think Evelyn would want us to join."

"This sounds like such a good idea, Dad." Kailee tried to hold back tears.

Bob held up his hand. "There's more. Kailee, I want you to work with Heather in distributing Evelyn's plants. Not only the ones in her conservatory, but all the plants in her garden. I'm hoping we all can buy a plot of land and move the plants there. Make a garden." He choked up, cleared his throat, continued. "A garden in your mother's name, free for anyone to visit."

Kailee said, "What a wonderful idea." She reached for Ross's hand, and he took it, he held her cold hand in his large, warm, reliable hand. She was weeping, quietly, and she had never loved her father more.

twenty-five

After Evelyn's death, Heather decided to keep to herself. She took Sugar on long walks on the beach, she read and watched TV, although she was watching more television than ever before because it required so little effort. She knew Ross was very much occupied with helping Kailee and Bob, so she didn't tell him about the opportunity she had to buy the cottage.

She wanted to buy the cottage. It suited her. It *matched* her in some way. It was simple rather than complicated, obviously plain and practical rather than designed and ornamented, enclosed by the unruly forest rather than showing off its beautiful gingerbread curlicues. It was her refuge.

But she worried that Kailee would be unhappy with Heather living permanently on-island. She understood the ambivalence the young woman had about her because Wall's parents had been difficult, demanding. In her later life, Wall's mother, Estelle, had developed debilitating arthritis, and while Wall was in his store and Ross at high school and later college, Heather had been the one who helped Estelle with her many chores and errands. Estelle always said, "Thank you," but in such a tone of voice it was clear that she meant, *You are fortunate to be serving me, you lowly peasant.*

Heather's own parents had been obsessed with traveling. Their means of connection after Heather married was a succession of postcards from various countries, even after everyone used iPhones and email. Heather suspected they communicated that way so that Heather couldn't track them down to ask them for something. They had been good parents, loving parents, but when Heather married Wall—who her parents liked—their interest in Heather and their support of her stopped, as if Heather's warranty had run out.

Heather understood. She'd never been baby-crazy. If she had been, she would have tried harder to have another child, or she would have adopted, or helped in a day care center. The older she got, the more privacy she needed. The older she got, the more she valued sitting on the porch, watching the light change as the sun moved.

Maybe she was turning into a lizard.

Nine days after the funeral, she was surprised by a call from Bob Essex, asking her to join them at the Pleasant Street house to discuss some matters that might be of interest to her.

By then, it was the last week of July. The island was still congested with Range Rovers, Mercedes SUVs, the Wave town bus, UPS, USPS, FedEx, and Cape Cod Express, not to mention what seemed like several thousand people biking blithely, carelessly, around the town, darting in front of cars as if the cars were invisible, and pedestrians were still around, too, looking down at their phones as they strolled in front of traffic, as if they considered themselves something beautiful for everyone else to see, rather like Heather's former mother-in-law.

So, yes, many of the islanders were bitter, and Heather found herself siding with them. She made it a point to stop to let cars out from Marine Home Center or Fairgrounds Road. When she was in town, she politely gave people directions to the Whaling Museum or Straight Wharf to buy toys at Christina's Toys or the library or the post office. From some irrational sense of honoring Evelyn and her family, she didn't see Miles for a few days. Of course, she attended the funeral and showed up to pay her respects at the reception, but after that, she stayed home.

She agreed to be there at five o'clock Saturday evening. They chose that time, she assumed, so they could ease the conversation with cocktails.

How do you dress for a meeting, if it was a meeting, or a quiet social drink? Heather wore her navy silk dress and small pearl earrings. Some lipstick, some blush, not the full window dressing of eyeliner and mascara.

When she arrived in front of the Essexes' house, her son came out to greet her. He stood on the lawn and hugged her tightly.

"Hi, Mom."

Surprised by his affection, she returned the hug. "How are you? How's Kailee?"

Ross kept his arm around her shoulders as they went up the walk and into the house.

"We're all kind of unhinged. No, that sounds like we're crazy. We're *unmoored*."

Ross led Heather into the living room. Kailee and Bob were seated on the chintz sofa. Bob rose and gave her a brief semblance of a hug. Kailee smiled. Heather sat in one of the armchairs. Ross took the other.

Bob cleared his throat. "How are you, Heather?" Immediately, he overrode his words. "No, wait, that's not what we asked you here to talk about. What would you like to drink? I'm having a strong Scotch myself."

"Heavens," Heather said. "This sounds ominous." Immediately she wished she could take her words back, for what could be worse than Evelyn's death?

Bob handed her a Scotch in a cut-glass tumbler and settled back in his chair.

Bob said, "Ross, would you give Heather the envelope, please?"

Heather curved her nails into the palms of her hands to keep herself from giggling nervously. The envelope? It sounded like a game show. What would be behind door number three?

Ross handed her a manila envelope, fat with papers. She pulled them out and read a few lines. The first page was on creamy stationery, written in a flowing, confident hand by Evelyn herself. Heather scanned it. She flipped through the other papers, all tidy and legal.

She looked up at Bob. "Excuse me, Bob, but I don't understand what this is all about."

Kailee spoke up. "Dad and I have read it. Mom wants you to be the director of ENF. She wrote that into her will, and also in a letter to us. She's supplied money for a salary and health benefits and a pension."

"We'll find a good house for you to rent year-round and the salary will pay the rent and insurance, everything," Bob said.

"Mom, it would be so cool to have you on the island," Ross told her.

"Well, wow. That's a lot of information." Heather stared down at the sheaf of papers in her hand.

Bob said, "The legal document is something you can read at your leisure, and sign. Basically, agreeing to the terms of working as head of ENF."

"I don't know what to say." Heather turned slightly to face Kailee. "Do *you* want me to take this on? Why aren't *you* heading ENF?"

Kailee leaned forward, speaking earnestly. "This is what my mother wants. Wanted. She knew I always intended to work with my father and eventually run Essex Construction. She didn't consider ENF the best use of my time and skills. Damn, that sounds kind of like I'm insulting you, and I don't mean it that way."

Bob cut in. "Heather, it's complicated. We grew up here, Evelyn and I, and we have many friends, but my surprising financial success in the past few years made many of our friends turn away.

People thought ENF was Evelyn's way of making amends to the community and the island, and in a way, it was, but more than that, it was what Evelyn sincerely wanted to do."

"But there were so many people at the reception," Heather pointed out.

"That was for her as an islander," Bob said. "And friends of Kailee's and mine."

Ross added, "You see, Mom, you're new here, without history or baggage. You don't flash your money around—"

Heather laughed, breaking the tension in the room. "I don't have money to flash."

"Plus," Ross continued, "you made friends fast."

"You did the right things," Kailee agreed. "You met the right people without even trying."

Heather was offended. "I did not come here to meet the right people! I didn't come here to meet any people at all. A friend offered me the opportunity to rent a cottage here while my divorce went through—"

Bob interrupted. "Kailee didn't mean to insult you. We know you're not a social climber. What she was trying to say is that people *like* you. Because of Ross, you are, um, *affiliated* here. Maybe because of us, mostly because of you. It would be up to you to choose directors for the board. To decide how best to make ENF successful. Kailee and I have great faith in you. We think Evelyn did the absolutely right thing in choosing you to direct this new organization. If you read her letter thoroughly, you'll see that it's not about all of us. It's about Evelyn and her love for the island."

Heather sat quietly, staring down at the papers in her lap. "I need some time to read all this and to think about it."

"Of course," Bob agreed.

Heather felt like she'd been struck by a comet made of flowers. In her heart, she loved this idea. She'd spent enough time with Evelyn to be sure she knew what Evelyn wanted and was certain she could bring it about. There was also the matter of Kailee and Ross having a baby. She was going to be a grandmother! Heather wanted to make herself very popular with Kailee. She wanted to babysit that baby every moment she could. Could she babysit the baby and also run ENF?

One step at a time, she told herself. *One step at a time.*

Looking up, she asked Bob, "Could we change the subject for a moment? I'd like to ask how you and Kailee are doing, how you are bearing up, after . . ." She couldn't bring herself to say the words *Evelyn's death.*

"People have been kind," Bob said. "Gravity has quietly taken over running the house." He smiled slightly. "It helps that Evelyn left personal letters to each of us, just as she did to you. She encourages us to go on."

"Encourages? You mean she *orders* us to carry on," Kailee said.

"Actually," Ross said, glancing at Kailee, "while Bob remains president of the company, he's made Kailee a vice president in charge of accounts and technology. And I'm VP of construction."

"It would be so helpful for all of us if you took on ENF." Kailee reached over and put her hand on Heather's. An offering. A bridge. A warmth. "Please."

Heather said, "I'm very interested, but I still need to think about this. Running a foundation is no easy effort." She gave Kailee's hand a slight squeeze. An acceptance. A warmth. A beginning.

Ross changed the subject. "Mom, Kailee and I are planning to have a winter wedding. Maybe in December, and then a trip to somewhere warm to lie in the sun."

"What about your father's wedding?" Heather asked.

Ross shook his head. "I'm not going to be his best man. I'm not going to the wedding. I called him and told them that. And you know what? He seemed fine with it. 'No worries,' he said. Can you believe my father said, 'No worries'?"

"He sounds like a new man," Heather said. "I'm glad for him. It's about time he had no worries."

"So," Kailee asked, "will you think seriously about taking over ENF?"

"I'll read these papers and let you know."

Bob answered. "Good." He cleared his throat. "I want to thank you for the time you spent with Evelyn."

Heather smiled. "I'm glad I had time with her." She rose and walked toward the door. Turning to say goodbye, she seemed to see Evelyn there in the living room, very pale, but very happy. Heather shook her head sharply, and the vision was gone. "Goodbye," she said. "I'll talk to you tomorrow."

When she returned to her cottage, Heather changed into a caftan of swirly blues, made herself a tuna fish sandwich, and poured a giant glass of iced water. She sat at the kitchen table, staring into space. Emotions and realities swirled in her mind like strains of music she couldn't quite hear. The ENF responsibility. Kailee, pregnant with Heather's grandchild! Her son, Ross, obviously in love with Kailee and happy with his work.

And she was going to own a cottage on Nantucket! She'd already talked with her lawyer and Christine's neighbor's nephew. She'd sent a check for the deposit, and early in September she would complete the transaction. She would own this cottage.

She felt like a child at Christmas.

A knock came at the door.

"What next?" she asked the air.

Who would come here without calling? Had she ordered anything through UPS? She was wearing a caftan and sandals. Whoever it was would have to take her as she was.

She opened the door.

Wall stood there before her, neatly dressed in khakis and a dark blue cotton button-down shirt. She remembered buying that shirt for him. He had a tan, and he looked good. Oddly, he also looked like a stranger.

He *was* a stranger now, just as she was to him. After all their years together, they had lost the bonds that held them and transformed, like caterpillars emerging from their cocoons as butterflies, into very different creatures. This happened often in the natural world, with creatures and insects. Why didn't humans expect this to happen in their world?

"Hello, Heather. Could I speak with you?"

She paused before letting him enter. This was *her* home, her island, and he had no right to be here. Now she realized how hard it had been for Kailee to accept Heather's presence on the island.

"I'm actually working now," Heather said. "I wish you had called first."

Wall grinned. "You're working in your robe?"

She almost shut the door in his face. For years she'd worked in this very caftan while working for Safeguard Nature on her computer, so this wasn't anything new to Wall. Heather couldn't figure out if he meant to insult her or not.

Wall realized this. "Sorry, wait, no offense intended, Heather. I'm kind of nervous. I want to talk with you, seriously."

Heather said, "Go around back. I have a small patio. I'll bring you a glass of water. I'll let Sugar out while we talk."

Wall grinned. "Multitasking as always."

Heather shut the door in his face. "Come, Sugar," she called, and her dog trotted up next to her. She filled two glasses with ice water and went outside.

Wall was sitting in one of the plastic chairs. She set the glasses on the table and took her own chair, as far away from him as she could be at a round table. Sugar sat loyally at her feet.

She realized that Wall wasn't wearing cowboy boots.

"Thanks," Wall said. He drank some water, set the glass down, and folded his hands on the table.

"Heather—" His voice broke as he said her name. "Heather, I miss you. I want you to come back. I don't like living without you. Heather, you are the love of my life. I'm sorry I didn't realize it before now."

Heather made a scoffing noise. "I'm sure Nova isn't thrilled about that."

"Nova and I have split." Wall's lips thinned into a tight line. "She wasn't pregnant, after all. She was just . . . trying to reel me in."

Heather blinked. Pity bit at her, and no sense of triumph. She wanted him to be happy.

She wanted him to be happy somewhere else.

"Oh, Wall, I'm sorry to hear that. But I'm sure there are a lot of women who would enjoy being your partner. I'm simply not one of them. I like being on my own." *There,* she thought, *that was gentle enough. It's me, not you.*

Wall's face darkened. "I'm going to tell Ross that I asked you to get back together with me."

"You do that, and I'll tell him, too," Heather said pleasantly.

Wall shook his head, a sign of frustration. "I didn't mean to sound like I was threatening you. I really miss you, Heather. I know we've worked hard all our lives. We deserve a vacation. I've been studying all kinds of luxurious cruises and hotels. We could spend a week in Paris, a week in London. We could find a new, different house to live in now that our house has sold, and we could build an office in it for you, for your save the earth business or whatever—"

Heather held up her hands. "Wall. No. It is not going to happen. Ever. I've changed. You have changed, too." She fought off her natural instinct to console him, to remind him that he was handsome, and smart, and attractive. But he would interpret her kindness as an invitation. She'd spent so many years of her life complimenting this man. She couldn't, not anymore.

She said, "I'm sorry, Wall. I know you'll find someone who will truly love you. I'm just not that person."

She picked up her glass of water, drank it down, stood up, and walked to her door. "Sugar, come," she called. Her dog raced up to her, ready for a treat.

"You're going to walk off?" Wall asked. He was angry now. Heather could see his forehead reddening. "Can't we discuss this some more?"

"There's nothing to discuss," Heather said. She went inside and shut the door.

twenty-six

The second week of August on Nantucket was viciously hot and humid. The skies lowered themselves over the island like a damp gray tarp. Workmen at the Essex Construction site sweated through their T-shirts. Tools slipped from their hands. Tempers flared over the slightest problem. Their hard hats kept the heat in, simmering on their heads like overturned kettles. Bob Essex was pulled between having the job done on time and preventing his men from having heatstroke. He finally ordered them to stop work from one through four, during the worst of the heat.

Kailee and George were insulated by air-conditioning, but they were tired and cranky, as if the humidity filtered in through the tiniest crack in the door. Kailee was suffering less from nausea, but in exchange, her exhaustion made her slow-witted and limp. She wanted to sleep all the time.

Heather wore shorts and a tank top, showering twice a day after taking Sugar out for a brief walk—the poor dog was so exhausted by the heat she slumped around outside like Eeyore. Inside, the dog lay comatose. Heather drank iced coffee. She stayed inside her cottage where the air conditioners, clunking and roaring, kept the rooms pleasant enough. She missed her early morning walks, but even at five or six in the morning, the air was like steam heat, the ocean as warm as a bath.

She enjoyed long, leisurely phone conversations with Christine and Ross and Miribelle and Miles. She declined invitations to several parties. Because of the heat, of course, but also because she was trying to decide what to do. Should she take on Evelyn Essex's foundation? She might be criticized by the citizens of the island who would think it was presumptuous and wrong for an off-islander to run an island foundation. She'd read the folders Bob had given her. She knew she could do the job. She would have to visit several spots on the island to become knowledgeable about them. She'd have to ask islanders to join the board. She knew Miles and Miribelle would help, but she remembered how Donna Skatel had been at bridge night, and she wondered if she had an enemy before she even started.

By Friday, when she was eating peanut butter on crackers for lunch, she knew she had to go out to the grocery store. She called Sugar to go with her. She'd take her for a walk up and down Main Street, her favorite sniffing spot, and leave her in the car with the windows down while she raced through Stop & Shop.

In spite of the heat, or maybe because of it, town was busy. Girls in sweet summer dresses whispered to one another, giggling, while lean, sophisticated women wearing size 2 Lilly Pulitzer dresses considered thirty-thousand-dollar necklaces in the windows of jewelers' shops. Heather left Sugar tied to the railing in the shade of the library steps and hurried through the library, exchanging old books for new.

Back in her car, she drove to the out-of-town Stop & Shop.

"I'll hurry," she promised Sugar. She rolled all the windows down so her dog would have fresh air. "Stay in the car."

She raced through the store, filling her woven bag with fruit, fresh bread, and a variety of gourmet cheeses. She was dashing out the door when someone took her arm.

"I thought that was you," Donna Skatel said. "How are you? It's a shame bridge has broken up for the month, but everyone has houseguests."

"I'm good, Donna, thanks, how are you?" Heather speed-talked, worried about her dog in the car.

"It's so sad about Evelyn, isn't it?" Donna was all wistfully sorrowful.

"Yes, I know. But I have to—"

"My husband and I are going to make a substantial donation to ENF in Evelyn's honor." Donna's eyes gleamed with triumph.

Heather blinked with shock. "Wow, Donna, that's wonderful!"

"I'd love to talk with you about it sometime. I was hoping I could be on the board. I know I could be helpful raising funds."

Heather stammered, "Oh, I—"

"I know you're taking over ENF. Evelyn willed it to you. I suppose you'll be sending out some sort of introductory note about yourself and the foundation's goals."

Heather pulled herself together. "Yes, I'm reading Evelyn's files now. I had no idea that it was common knowledge that—"

"Sweetie, *everything* that happens here is common knowledge," Donna said, with a twinkle in her eye. She waved her fingers at Heather and swept out the door.

Heather hurried to the car. It was hot inside. Sugar was sleeping in the backseat, not panting, so the dog was okay. She started the engine and the air-conditioning and sat there a moment, catching her breath.

Donna Skatel was formidable, Heather thought. And so, of course, had been Evelyn. It would be a challenge, running ENF, and Heather smiled.

She liked that.

In her parents' kitchen, Kailee heated up one of the lasagnas the kind people of the town had given them. She set the kitchen table and poured two glasses of ice water. She knew that Ross would want a cold beer pulled right from the refrigerator.

Ross came in through the kitchen door, kissed Kailee absent-mindedly on the cheek, took out a beer, and said, "Something smells good."

"You must mean me," Kailee joked.

Ross grinned at Kailee, his irresistibly sexy, *you're my girl* grin, and Kailee nearly swooned.

"I've got to tell Dad dinner's ready."

Kailee found her father in his home office, sitting at his desk, gazing into space.

"Dinner's ready, Dad," she said.

He nodded and stood up, moving slowly.

But when he sat at the table with Kailee and Ross, her father actually ate. He didn't touch the salad, but he'd always hated salad.

When they finished, Kailee stacked the plates on the counter, took out two pints of ice cream, set them and bowls and spoons on the table, and sat down again. "Who wants ice cream?"

Her father surprised her when he spoke. "Kailee. Ross. I need to talk to you and it might as well be now."

"Okaaaaay," Kailee said warily.

"I'm going to put this house on the market. It's too big for one person. Plus, the conservatory and the garden are all your mom's idea. I can't tell a rose from a radish. I want to sell this place, use the money to buy a smaller place of my own, and give you enough money for a decent down payment on a house you two would like. And I'd like to do it soon. The truth is, it's hard living here. It makes me miss Evelyn even more. Anyway, that's what I'm going to do."

"You don't have to give us money, Bob," Ross said.

Kailee's father laughed. "Ross, I was always going to give you money for a starter place. I also was planning to pay for a five-star wedding for you two, but now with Evelyn gone . . ." Bob paused. He looked at Kailee. "Do you still want a big wedding?"

Kailee turned her spoon over and over, trying to form the right words. "Things are different without Mom. Now that I'm pregnant, I considered moving the date forward, but a big wedding seems wrong, somehow."

Kailee's father said, "Evelyn would like you to have a big wedding. At least, a biggish one."

Ross put his hand on Kailee's. "What about a wedding on New Year's Day? That gives us time to plan it."

Kailee nodded. "But it can't be crazy expensive if we're going to buy a house."

Ross agreed. "Sure. It can be a small ceremony with a reception at the Brant Point Grill."

Tears came to Kailee's eyes. "I won't be able to wear a fabulous wedding gown."

Her father chuckled. "Sweetheart, anything you wear will be fabulous on you."

"Thanks, Dad." Emotions flooded Kailee. So much was happening, so soon. "But Mom won't be there to see the ceremony."

"Kailee." Her father spoke her name seriously, quietly commanding her attention. "You know your mother. She'll see your ceremony, even if we don't see her."

After her visit to the grocery store, Heather lay on her bed with the clunking air conditioner blowing on her and fell asleep. When she woke, she made herself a glass of sweet iced tea and sat at her dining room table to work. She knew her computer and the flash drive had all the ENF's information on it, but she liked dealing with hard copies. Her mind worked better when she read files on real paper.

Sugar suddenly raced to the door, yipping with eagerness. What a good dog Sugar was, her little alarm system.

Heather opened the door. Miles stood there, holding a bag of ice in one hand and a bottle of sparkling rosé in the other. His face was sunburned and so was . . . she blushed when she looked at his strong, tanned arms and hands.

"Is it too early for a drink?" he asked, smiling.

Heather opened the door wide. "Not at all," she told him. "Come in."

"I'd like to talk with you about something," Miles told her. He was giving off an energy, a vibe, that made her skin tingle.

Why did his words make her heart flicker like a flutter of butterflies? She took the ice from him and put it in the freezer. "I had no idea it was after five. I've been working on Evelyn's ENF papers."

Miles was cracking open the ice tray from her freezer compartment, filling tall glasses with ice, and pouring the sparkling wine over it.

"I've got olives and nuts here." Heather busied around, filling two bowls. "That will provide sufficient salt." *Sufficient* salt? Who says that? Maybe chemists? This man affected her as no one else ever had. She was dazed and dazzled, like someone in a 1950s movie. "I mean, we sweat so much in the summer, we need salt. I found that out on the internet, of course."

She set the bowls on the coffee table, sat on the sofa and looked expectantly at Miles.

He sat on the sofa next to her, and handed Heather her drink.

"Cheers," he said, touching his glass to hers. "If you're wondering, no, we didn't have a date. I dropped in on you on the spur of the moment."

"Spur of the moment." She tried to hide her desire to kiss him by talking, which really was babbling, the best she could do. "I wonder where that saying came from. I suppose because we use spurs on horses. I don't mean *we* do, but don't cowboys?" She took a gulp of her drink.

Miles said. "Okay, here's the deal. You told me you're considering buying this cottage."

"I *am* buying it," Heather told him. "Now that I have a job and a salary. I'm sorry I can't work for you anymore."

"That's all right. Abby will be back." Miles took a deep breath. "Heather, what I want to say is—I like you a lot. I think you like me. I wish . . . I wish I knew what words to use. I don't know how to ask you to be my serious girlfriend."

Amazed, Heather laughed. "*Serious* girlfriend? Could I laugh occasionally?" She saw that he was blushing, and he was adorable. "Miles, I think I've been your serious girlfriend for weeks."

Miles grinned. "I mean, I want to tell my daughter about you and me. I'd like to take you to dinner with my friends. Maybe take trips together, to see theater in New York. And . . . you would spend the night with me at my house. I'd spend the night with you here. And I wouldn't see anyone else, and you wouldn't see anyone else."

Heather stopped laughing. She gently touched the side of his face with her hand. "Miles, whatever we call it, I want it, too."

Miles reached for her, and she went willingly into his arms.

During the hot days of August, Kailee kept herself busy with work at the construction company. George had already taken care of all the necessary permits for the house they were building, and Ross worked with the foreman as the crew lifted, hammered, and tiled. At night, she and Ross ate one of Gravity's delicious meals in the dining room with her father. Bob Essex *was* eating, to Kailee's relief, even though he always left the table before they did. He went into the den to stare at the television. Kailee and Ross cleared the table and tidied the kitchen and went to Kailee's childhood bedroom to watch television. Ross left for his apartment around nine, because they both had to get up early for work, and Kailee stayed in her bedroom, because she thought it might comfort her father to have someone else in the house.

She missed her mother. Every moment of the day was a decided act of stepping into a world with half of it missing. She often cried herself to sleep at night, when her father and Ross couldn't hear.

One morning, she went down to the kitchen to find a note waiting for her.

I'm having breakfast with the Romeos, then going sportfishing with Jason Goode. Probably I'll eat with Goodes. See you tomorrow.

Kailee stared at the note. She knew that Romeos stood for *Retired Old Men Eating Out.* Or, the men joked, *Rowdy Old Men.* Even *Randy Old Men.*

She knew that Jason Goode was one of her father's oldest friends.

She knew that today was all hers.

Kailee hurried across the drive and up the steps to Ross's apartment. She flew in the door, locked it behind her, raced into Ross's bedroom and crawled into bed with him. He was sleeping on his back, snoring slightly, one arm over his head.

"Hey," he murmured, "what are you doing here?"

"I bet you can figure it out," Kailee told him. She put her hand on his strong shoulder and bent down to kiss him.

He pulled her to him.

Afterward, lying close and cozily together, Kailee told Ross about her father's note.

"I'm so glad for him," she said. "That he can go out with friends and have a life."

"I'm so glad for *us*," Ross told her. His head was propped on his elbow and he was staring down at her. Gently, he moved a strand of her hair from her face. "I'm so glad," he said, "that we can have *this* life." He put his hand on her belly.

Kailee burrowed her face into his chest, and realized that she had brought this much happiness to her mother.

Heather had brought a picnic snack of cheese, crusty bread, and grapes, along with deviled eggs, plums, and chocolate. Miles brought champagne and sparkling water. They'd left Sugar napping on the sofa and Ross had agreed to come spend the night with her. They'd sailed out of the harbor into the calm waters of the sound. They'd eaten, and now they were lying on the bow of the boat, watching the stars come out.

"Hey," Miles said.

"Hey," Heather answered.

Miles raised up on his elbow, smiled down at Heather, and kissed her very slowly, very gently. She turned toward him without breaking their kiss, and the boat rocked slightly. She put her hand on the back of his neck. He ran his hand down her cheek, along her neck, and down her arm. Heather shivered.

Miles drew back. "Cold?"

"No," Heather said. She knew what he wanted to do, what she wanted to do, and she was eager, but lying on the bow of a boat rocking gently in deep water made her cautious.

"Want to go below?" Miles asked. "I have a bed there."

"Yes." Her heart was beating in her throat.

While she got to her feet, she was clumsy, because the bow of a boat wasn't as stable as a floor, and for a second, she thought she might fall overboard. Miles took her arm to steady her.

"Don't want to lose you now," he said, smiling.

"You won't want to lose me later," Heather replied brazenly, and she was glad it was dark so that he couldn't see her face.

Had she really said that? How could she have even *thought* those words? She was hardly an expert at lovemaking. She couldn't remember when she'd last made love with Wall. And Wall had been her first and only.

Miles stepped down into the cabin and reached out to support Heather as she came, ungracefully, down to join him. The champagne bottle and her picnic basket rested calmly against the seats, and two flutes lay on their sides, empty.

"I've got you," Miles said.

Heather paused, suddenly aware that she had to go backward down a short ladder, which meant that the tops of her thighs and probably the bottom of her bottom would be the first sight Miles would see as he watched her descend.

I can't do this! she thought, but when she stepped onto the floor of the cabin, Miles put his arms around her from the back, and held her, and kissed the back of her neck and her shoulders, his arms warm and secure around her waist. He pressed the front of his body all along the back of her body, and Heather knew that he was aroused, and so was she, and she knew she couldn't *not* do this.

He held her hand and led her into a triangular space covered with a thick white mattress. Pillows, covered with white cases, plump and inviting, lay at the far end. Heather slipped her feet from her shoes.

"I'm afraid there is no graceful way to lie down," Miles told her. "You just have to crawl in and on."

Heather almost joked, *You're the one who has to crawl in and on,* but she refrained, mostly because her mouth was dry from nervousness.

Once they were on the mattress, Miles knelt and peeled his rugby shirt up over his head and off. His arms were ropy with muscles, his chest hair pale brown. He slipped off his board shorts, and Heather could see how white his skin was where it hadn't turned a dark summer tan.

Heather wasn't wearing a bra, and as she pulled her tank top off, she thought how she was not a young girl, and she had nursed her baby, and anyway, she was in her forties, so Miles had to be prepared for a less than perfect body.

"You're beautiful," Miles said, his voice husky. He reached for her, and together they yanked down her shorts and panties and were naked together.

It was so warm, so hot, so smooth, so *centering.* Nothing else in the world existed. Heather stopped thinking and surrendered to sensation.

When they were through, Heather lay on her back with her hair wet from sweat. Miles opened some portholes she hadn't noticed before, and she wondered if he'd kept them closed so their noises wouldn't sweep out over the water.

She said, "I can't move."

Miles chuckled. He went away, returning with a bottle of icy cold water. Heather drank it greedily; it was the best water she'd ever tasted in her life.

"Thank you," she said. "I mean for the water." She laughed. "Well, for everything."

Miles said, "Let's sleep."

"Out here?" Heather was rolling the cold bottle over her chest and down her arms.

"I sleep out here often," Miles told her, adding, "and not with women."

"But I'm a woman," Heather said, wondering if she were drunk, or in a dream.

"You certainly are," Miles said. "You are *the* woman. That's why I want you to sleep with me."

A slight breeze drifted into the cabin. She was cooler. She was very tired. She lay down. Miles lifted the water bottle away from her and set it in a holder in a ledge. He lay down next to her and pulled over them both a sheet so light it seemed made of stars.

It was the last day of August. The slant of the sun changed, less glare, more gold. The humidity dropped, and the evenings were cool. In the late afternoon, Kailee and Heather stood on a green rise of land on the west end of the island near Madaket. From here, they could see a blue smudge of ocean to one side and a blue gleam of Nantucket Sound on the other. The plot of land was only two acres, but it was level and slightly protected by wild shrubs and grasses.

"This is the perfect place," Kailee said. "Don't you think so?"

"I do," Heather agreed. "I've researched various plans for public gardens and made my own sketch. Nothing set in granite. Just a talking point."

Kailee took Heather's iPad and studied it. "This is where you want the shed built?"

"Yes, close to the parking lot, so that it will be simpler to tie in to Wannacomet's water line in Madaket. Also, we'll store garden supplies there. And the water meter and faucet so that no one plays around with it. But the shed can be cute, with window boxes on two walls for flowers, and annuals planted in a border around the shed."

Kailee smiled. "You've drawn in a quarterboard over the door to the shed. 'Evelyn's Garden.'"

"Yes. When the garden opens next spring, we can have small brochures printed with a note about the garden and the various flowers. About Evelyn, too, of course."

"What is this?" Kailee pointed to a small plot designated "Children's Garden."

"I think you'll like this," Heather answered. "It will have flowers and grasses that children like to smell and touch. Lamb's ears are soft and fuzzy. Roses smell sweet and we can plant some varieties that don't have prickers. Mint and herbs, of course, and honeysuckle. Lavender. Hens and chickens are always fun to see."

"I'm not sure my mother had all those in her garden," Kailee murmured.

"She had most of them." Heather reached over and tapped the iPad. "Here's a loose sketch of your mother's garden and the plants she had."

"Wow. Such a variety. I had no idea."

"I think your mother would like a children's garden for her grandchild, don't you?"

Tears glistened in Kailee's eyes. "That's a lovely idea. Of course, she would. And her grandchild would be able to know what his or her grandmother was like. Thank you, Heather."

The two women wandered over the future public garden, discussing how to improve the soil over the winter, what month was the best time for transplanting, where shade trees should be planted and what flowers grew well in shade.

"You've left this spot, here at the back, blank," Kailee said.

"Yes. We can always change it, but I thought it might be nice to keep it natural, sandy and weedy and rocky. Exactly as it is now. It will be only a small piece of earth, but it will be a visual memory of the real island that Evelyn loved."

Kailee asked, "Are you sure you can do all this and the rest of the foundation work, too?"

The two women began walking back to the small sandy parking space by the road. "I'm sure. I have to research what plants can be transplanted when and where, but your mother's foundation has sufficient funds to pay for landscapers to improve the soil. It's sandy, which means it needs organic materials added. Compost. Manure. And seaweed."

"Dad hasn't put the house on the market yet. He's talking to realtors, and so are Ross and I." Kailee glanced at Heather. "I hear you've bought your little cottage."

"I have, yes."

"My father doesn't want the sale to become a circus. He wants to get rid of a lot of the furniture and general *stuff*. Ross and I will take a few things, and Dad will take a lot of the furniture for his new place. You should go through the house, see if there's something you'd like."

"Seriously? You would be okay if I took some furniture? I love my cottage, but it could use a few rugs and fireplace tools, but I wouldn't want to upset you by having them in my house."

"It would be wonderful if you took whatever you want," Kailee said. "My mom obviously liked you a lot. And she didn't like a lot of people."

"Maybe she just didn't have time to get to know me," Heather joked.

They had arrived in separate cars, and now they lingered, with so much more to say.

"Have you found a house you and Ross like?" Heather asked.

"We're deciding between two different ones." Kailee leaned against her car. "The one we like best is off Surfside Road, near the schools and the bike path to the beach. You know, we'd thought we'd build our perfect house, but now that we've got the Kid on the way, we don't have time for that kind of project."

"Does it have a backyard?" Heather asked.

"Yes! Already a small patio, and a lawn perfect for a swing set and a tree at the back where Ross can build a tree house."

"It all sounds like heaven," Heather told her.

"It would be heaven if my mother were alive," Kailee said. "But at least we'll have this garden. Thank you for that."

"Thank you for that," Heather said, pointing to Kailee's belly.

Kailee laughed. "Want to feel? I'm bulging out a little bit now."

Heather crossed the short distance between them and gently

put her hand on Kailee's belly. "Nice and firm. Lovely." She bent down and whispered, "Hello, baby."

When she stood up, she saw tears streaking down Kailee's face.

"Oh, honey," Heather said. She took Kailee in her arms and hugged her as the young woman wept on her shoulder. This was what she could give, because no words would suffice.

"Sorry," Kailee apologized, pulling away and taking a tissue from her pocket. "I'm so emotional these days."

"You have a lot to be emotional about, plus you've got all sorts of rampaging hormones inside."

"Sometimes . . ." Kailee paused, not sure if she should share this. She hadn't told Ross this. But she thought Heather would understand. "Sometimes I think Mom is near me, not visible, not a ghost, but a . . . warmth."

" 'There are more things on heaven and earth, Horatio, than are dreamt of in your philosophy,' " Heather quoted. "I'm sure your mother is near you, and I'm sure she is happy."

Kailee nodded, sniffing. "Thanks, Heather. I should get back."

"Yes, me, too." Heather went around her old Volvo and got in, waiting until Kailee had settled in her car and buckled up and left the parking lot. " 'I think this is the beginning of a beautiful friendship,' " she said, quoting from *Casablanca*.

She laughed at herself, sitting in her car talking to herself. She started her car, did a three-point turn, and drove home.

It was Heather who loved Kailee first, and as time went by, Kailee loved her back.

About the Author

NANCY THAYER is the *New York Times* bestselling author of more than thirty novels, including *All the Days of Summer, Summer Love, Family Reunion, Girls of Summer, Let It Snow, Surfside Sisters, A Nantucket Wedding, Secrets in Summer, The Island House, The Guest Cottage, An Island Christmas, Nantucket Sisters,* and *Island Girls.* Born in Kansas, Thayer has for nearly forty years been a resident of Nantucket, where she currently lives with her husband, Charley, and a precocious rescue cat named Callie.

nancythayer.com
Facebook.com/NancyThayerBooks
Instagram: @nancythayerbooks

About the Type

This book was set in Garamond, a typeface originally designed by the Parisian type cutter Claude Garamond (c. 1500–61). This version of Garamond was modeled on a 1592 specimen sheet from the Egenolff-Berner foundry, which was produced from types assumed to have been brought to Frankfurt by the punch cutter Jacques Sabon (c. 1520–80).

Claude Garamond's distinguished romans and italics first appeared in *Opera Ciceronis* in 1543–44. The Garamond types are clear, open, and elegant.

CEN c^2